I0634444

# FIRST DRIVE

## A SEPH VERMILLION WESTERN ADVENTURE

## DAVID FITZ-GERALD

DAVID FITZ-GERALD

First Drive: A Seph Vermillion Western Adventure

Copyright © 2024 by David Fitz-Gerald

All rights reserved.

No portion of this book may be reproduced in any form without written permission from the publisher or author, except as permitted by U.S. copyright law.

Cover design by White Rabbit Arts

Edited by Lindsay Fitzgerald

ISBN: 979-8-9898896-5-5

# CONTENTS

# FOREWORD

The inspiration for *First Drive* came while attending high school baseball games and observing the interactions of the players over the course of a season. Rather than call each other by their names, every player went by a nickname instead, or simply, *kid*, kind of like Billy the Kid.

On television and in movies, cowboys are often played by middle-aged actors, but most or many cattle drives were staffed by much younger men. A notable exception is the 1971 movie, *The Cowboys*, starring John Wayne, which featured children plucked from a one room schoolhouse. In *First Drive*, the characters are young men who at least claim to be adults.

The hero of this story is Joseph "Seph" Vermillion, who knows little about the world beyond the farm where he was raised. He wants to leave the plow behind, dreams of a beautiful young woman who lives only in his imagination, and would like to see towering mountain peaks someday.

Seph doesn't know that he's destined to be a hero. He isn't sure whether he will fit in, and he doesn't know that he needs to find a place where he belongs.

*First Drive* is a coming of age story. It is told without profanity, but utilizes euphemisms. At times, this is a violent story. At the end of the trail, when the cowboys visit the painted ladies, what happens behind closed doors is modestly depicted, but not ignored.

Young men riding for the brand in the 1800s inhabited a very different world. Maybe what they want and need hasn't changed as much as we might think. Perhaps there's little difference between team spirit and riding for the brand.

But, when the day was done, there was no escaping the trail without traveling that last mile.

# CHAPTER 1

The sharp crack of gunfire sliced through the air, jolting Seph Vermillion from a daydream. He sat up tall in the saddle. The skin on his forearms prickled. A familiar punch detonated in his gut. That blast in his belly signaled danger.

His ear twitched, and he blinked rapidly.

The first shot was followed by several more, each one closer than the first.

Seph glanced down at the buttstock of his rifle. His father called the Hawken *Uncle Yves*, but Seph never knew his grandfather's brother—or why his father had named it after his long-departed uncle. He considered drawing the gun from its scabbard.

His heart thundered in his chest. He glanced at his partner, Slaw. The look on his friend's face mirrored his own sense of dread.

They had hoped to avoid trouble on their journey to San Antonio.

The sound of pounding hooves on the trail behind them grew to a rumbling thunder. With an urgent nod, Slaw signaled a detour off the trail.

Seph dug his heels into the side of his claybank dun, a fast horse named Sheriff, and dropped the lead rope on his pack mule. Immediately, Seph was on the heels of his partner's horse, a dapple-gray called Win, short for Winter.

Dirt chunked from Win's hooves, pelting Seph. Seph hunched over Sheriff's neck and squinted, hoping to keep the gravel from stinging his eyes.

As they raced across rugged terrain, Seph spared a glance over his shoulder. Dread coiled in his belly at the sight of three familiar figures in hot pursuit. The approaching riders hooted, hollered, and howled.

These weren't random bandits. Seph knew these skunks all too well. He couldn't count the times they had raided the Vermillion family farm. They'd gallop into the barnyard, help themselves to whatever they wanted and ride away, heckling and cajoling. Seph was always left to deal with the aftermath.

But this time was different. Seph was no longer a helpless victim. *Never again*, Seph told himself. He gritted his teeth, urging Sheriff onward. Determination flowed through his limbs, and Sheriff lengthened his strides.

He was thrilled to own a horse that loved to run.

With another quick glance over his shoulder, Seph saw the riders skid to a stop. The trio's leader pointed in their direction. They were too far away for Seph to see their expressions or hear their laughter, but he knew their ways so well that he could imagine their mocking voices. During their frequent raids, they always blustered after robbing his family and ransacking the barnyard. This time, though, Seph wouldn't be making repairs.

A surge of defiance coursed through him. It occupied the same space in his stomach as fear, yet it felt different. He wasn't just fleeing danger. He was riding off into his future.

On the trail, the outlaws' horses danced, eager to race off in pursuit.

Coyote smashed his hat tighter onto his head and asked, "What now, boss?"

Chaw stretched his arms wide and echoed, "Yeah, Swoop. Whatcha wanna do?" He chortled, scratched his backside, and added, "Can we chase 'em some more?"

Swoop chuckled, rubbing his jaw. "That would be fun," he said. He glanced briefly at his buddies. "Let's continue on. We ain't been to town in a while, and I got a powerful thirst." Harassing travelers was enjoyable, but he was ready for a couple nights of carousing in the big city. Coyote and Chaw swiftly agreed with Swoop's decision, as if they had a say in the matter.

As Swoop reined his horse back onto the trail, he looked to the north and thought about the hard working farm boy. The lad had kept the trio well-fed through the years. It wasn't like the kid to leave the homestead. Also, Swoop couldn't remember ever seeing Seph with a partner.

Something had changed.

Swoop didn't want anything to change. Robbing small farms was easy, and Seph Vermillion's farm was Swoop's favorite target.

Miles to the north of the trail, Seph and Slaw slowed their sweaty horses to a walk.

With a disgusted sneer, Slaw turned to Seph and said, "How do ya like that?"

Seph grumbled back, "It's those same men I told you about. The ones that always robbed us, stole our food, and blasted holes in the outhouse."

They looked back in the direction they had just traveled and watched Melba, Seph's loaded-down mule, as she trotted toward them. She was quite a distance away, which gave their horses a chance to rest after their mile-eating gallop.

Seph slumped in his saddle and thought of his prized possession, stowed away in a saddlebag. For a moment, he forgot where he was and that his pal was nearby.

The brightly colored cigar box once held his life's savings, but now it was empty. After burying Ma and trading the family farm to Slaw's father for a horse, Seph couldn't bear to part with the box. He had owned it since he was twelve years old. He didn't need to lift the lid to see the beautiful woman inside—the image was singed into his brain. Gazing at her picture was a guilty pleasure. His blood boiled and he felt short of breath. *If only she were real.*

Slaw interrupted his thoughts. "We ain't got time to waste, Joseph Vermillion."

Disoriented, Seph looked at Slaw, blinking rapidly. Slaw was the only friend he had growing up, though they hadn't known each other well. Farm chores kept both boys busy, and months often passed between their visits. Close friendships were a luxury nobody could afford when there was always work to be done.

Seph laughed. Slaw's formal use of his full name made him sound like his own mother, Loretta Ballard. Rarely did Seph joke, but he shot back, "Don't get smart with me, Townsend Ballard."

Nobody called Slaw *Towns* or *Townsend*, except for his mother. His messy hair resembled shredded cabbage, and he smelled so bad that bathing couldn't wash away the foul odor. The nickname *Slaw* clung to him, though he didn't seem to mind.

Seph always did his best to position himself upwind of Slaw.

Rather than returning directly to the trail, Slaw suggested they ride west instead of south and intersect the trail ahead. "Might save us a couple of miles." Slaw looked at the sun's position, and Seph could tell that he was worried.

They were in a hurry to reach San Antonio.

After Ma died and Seph traded the farm, Slaw's mother insisted that Seph move in with the Ballards. After a couple of days, Slaw showed Seph a bulletin. Though Seph had only seen it once, he committed it to memory, and Slaw knew every word by heart. It advertised:

*Now hiring. Ride the trail to Abilene. Depart as cowboys, return as cattle-men. Apply at The Prickly Pear Saloon, San Antonio, on April 25, 1868. The Deatherage Longhorn Cattle Ranch—Pierce and Glenn Deatherage, proprietors.*

Shortly after midnight the night before, they had left the Ballard farm. Slaw reassured Seph, "We're both eighteen, so we ain't runaways. We're men now, off to seek our fortunes." Slaw hadn't told anyone about his plans, nor had he left a note. As they led the mule and rode their horses quietly up the road, Slaw's young sister, Margaret, caught them sneaking away. The girl who went by the nickname Grit promised not to tell but demanded that Slaw write to her when they got where they were going.

When Melba caught up to them, Seph gathered the lead rope and followed Slaw. The mule brayed in protest but gave in.

Slaw liked to talk and was rarely quiet. Seph wished his partner would quit yapping.

After years of having nobody to talk to except Ma, Seph wasn't accustomed to nonstop conversation. Seph thought most people talked too fast. Maybe he listened too slowly, but there was only so much chatter he could take before he had to stop and think. It was difficult to separate the mindless banter from the important stuff, and Seph sometimes struggled to figure out what people meant by what they said.

As they triangulated their way back to the road, Seph thought about the outlaws. He'd been sure that after trading the farm, he would never have to worry about that trio again. Seeing them on the trail was disturbing. As sure as he knew who they were, Seph was certain they knew who he was. Would he ever be free of them?

Slaw's voice broke his thoughts. "Ain't you heard a word I said?"

Seph had forgotten that Slaw was still talking. He shook his head, shrugged, and apologized. "Sorry, Slaw. My mind wandered away."

"Bah! You jasper. Your mind is always drifting away somewhere. I asked how many miles you think we've gone. What do ya figure?"

Seph was good at keeping counts and tabulating numbers in his head, but judging distances was another matter. They had set out after midnight but were delayed by Grit. With a frown, Seph guessed, "Maybe thirty miles." He knew Slaw wouldn't like that answer and added, "Who knows?"

Slaw commenced a rant. "We can't be late. What if we miss our chance? We've just got to get there in time." He looked behind him again.

Seph knew that Slaw was worried his father would follow and drag him back to the farm. But Seph was sure that Grit would keep their secret.

Seemingly exasperated, Slaw urged, "We'll have to ride nonstop. What if Pa comes after us?"

Seph was more concerned about the outlaws. Still, he asked, "Think he will?"

"No telling what he'll do." Slaw spit. "I've spent my whole life trying to guess what that man will do or think, only to be surprised when he gets all fired up about something that never crossed my mind. No siree, I ain't never going back. He can kiss my...." Slaw hesitated, then defiantly cursed.

With a glance over his shoulder at Melba, Seph thought about the endless hours he spent trying to coax a living from the soil. Then, as he turned his head back toward Slaw, his chin jutted forward and he proclaimed, "Me neither. I said my farewell to Poesta Creek, and I don't ever want to see it again."

Despite his words, Seph's eyes filled with tears. It pained him to think of the wretched coffin he'd built for Ma and how they dropped it as they lowered her into her grave. She deserved to rest in peace rather than have her body all crumpled up at one end of the casket. He hated that he'd been forced to use bullet-pocked boards from the outhouse to bury her. At least her grave was in a picturesque spot a short distance from a shady tree and the tranquil Poesta Creek.

Slaw's question shook Seph from thoughts about his mother's burial. "Do you think we'll get away scot-free?"

More often than not, Seph thought of the best outcome as most likely. "Sure," he grumbled, knowing that he didn't sound as confident as he would have liked.

Seph didn't like the way Slaw thought about their departure. They hadn't done anything wrong. Lots of folks set off on their own when they were full-grown.

He hung his head at the thought of his brothers and sisters. Ma had wanted Seph to promise he'd seek them out after she passed. Seph would've done anything for Ma, but he couldn't bring himself to give his word. He barely remembered his siblings—they had left home so long ago. They never returned for a visit. They never sent a letter. He'd cared for Ma for years while she withered away in her sickbed. Now it was time to do something for himself.

Though he felt bad about denying Ma's final request, he always came back to the same conclusion: *Hang the siblings. They should have helped take care of Ma. Who cares about them anyway?*

Slaw chirped. "Can you believe we're gonna be cowboys? Think of it, Seph."

"Whoa, buddy. Don't get ahead of yourself. First we have to get there. It's a long way to San Antonio. Then we have to be hired. What if they want men with experience? We might have to find other work."

"Pfft. Like what? I don't want to do anything else."

"I dunno. But we might have to find something else until we find an outfit that'll hire us."

They spent several hours discussing various jobs they could apply for in the event that the Deatherage Longhorn Cattle Ranch didn't hire them, and Slaw dismissed each potential occupation. Finally, Seph stopped making suggestions, and even Slaw became tired of talking.

After dark, Seph kept catching himself nodding off. Once, he slumped over his horse's neck and his arms draped over Sheriff's withers. He awoke with the horse's mane in his face. The knobby saddle horn dug into his stomach, but somehow he had fallen asleep without sliding off. Finally, Seph insisted on stopping for a couple of hours, and Slaw gave in.

When Slaw awoke well after dawn, he was furious. "We were only supposed to stop for a couple of hours." He stomped his foot and fumed. "How could you let us sleep so long?"

Seph shot back, "You're as much to blame as me."

In a snit, Slaw saddled Win and said to Seph, "I'm not talking to you."

Seph wanted to laugh. As he loaded saddlebags onto Melba's back, he wondered how long his chatty pal would manage to keep quiet. As the quiet hours passed, Seph felt more and more at peace with the world. When he realized that he felt more like himself than he had in ages, he resolved not to think about Ma for a while.

At dusk, the night before the Deatherage Longhorn Cattle Ranch interviews, they came upon a campfire beside the trail. As they drew closer, the orange glow showed that someone had a blazing fire going. Seph could hear a boisterous conversation.

Slaw wanted to stop and talk for a minute. "Maybe they can tell us how much farther we gotta go."

Seph wasn't so sure. "They sound like trouble to me." Their banter reminded him of the way the outlaws had spoken to him after a raid. "What if we ride wide around them instead?"

"Then we'll never know how much farther we gotta go." Without waiting for agreement, Slaw called out. "Hello the camp. Can we ride in?"

A tall man who looked like he made a living from the back of a horse called back, "Ride ahead."

On the way in, Slaw announced, "I'm Townsend Ballard."

The man seemed amused. "Townsend Ballard? That's a whole lotta name, right there."

"You can call me Slaw. Everyone else does."

"And who is everyone? That kid there? Who are you?"

"I'm Seph."

The stranger echoed, "Seph?" He blew the "ph" sound from his lips as if trying to ignite a fire from an ember. "Something wrong with the way you talk?"

"It's short for Joseph," Seph answered, plain as day.

"Is that a fact?"

Slaw interrupted, "Do you know how far it is to San Antonio?"

"Ain't you polite enough to hear our names before you commence to interrogating?"

"Of course. Sorry, friend."

"Friend?" The man by the fire chuckled. "How quaint." He paused, then continued. "Parents named me Griffin." He made a face at Seph, stressing the "ffs" in the middle of his name. "But everybody calls me *Stoke*." He said his nickname like he was introducing a legend.

Slaw asked, "What do they call you that for?"

The question seemed to delight Stoke, and his friends slouching around the fire laughed. They knew what was coming. Stoke boasted, "I am *The Ignitor*. If you need a fire, I can whip one up out of nothing in a matter of seconds. Are you familiar with locomotives?"

"Never seen one," Slaw replied, "but I heard of 'em."

"They're powered by steam. It takes a lot of power to move them along." Stoke's cadence slowed. "Do you boys know about *the ladies*?"

Slaw took Stoke's bait. "The ladies?"

Stoke boasted, "When it comes to doing a bit of business with the ladies, my ignitor powers the locomotive." He made a chugging sound with his cheeks and gyrated his body like he was doing the sort of business he had suggested. Finally, his hips stilled.

Pounding his chest with a fist, he added, "I got an inferno raging in me, so they call me Stoke." He glanced at Seph. "If you play with fire, you'll get burned."

Seph didn't know much about people, but it seemed like Stoke went out of his way to be intimidating. He had never met anyone so boastful.

"Good to meet you, Stoke," Slaw said, glancing at the trail ahead. "So, do you know how far it is to San Antonio?"

"You ain't met the gang yet." Stoke feigned politeness. "Let me introduce Mr. Sheridan Hockstep and Mr. Houston Spire." His friends chuckled. "But they won't answer if you call 'em by those names. Best stick with Thumbs and Dredge."

Slaw asked, "Thumbs?"

The man by the fire lifted his fists and pointed his thumbs up toward the sky, shaking his digits in the air. They were thick as war clubs. There was no denying the nickname suited him.

Seph figured that it was his turn to ask a question, so he tossed in, "And Dredge?"

Stoke sounded like he was making an excuse for bad behavior. "He can't help himself." He let the next sentence drag out. "Just keeps dredging up the past. Sometimes he gets to complaining so bad, I gotta let Thumbs pound him so we can get a moment of peace around here." Stoke scratched his chest. "So, why are you in such a hurry to get to San Antonio?"

Slaw told Stoke about the advertisement, and Stoke seemed interested. "Well, it just so happens me and the boys are looking to ride for a new outfit. After our last drive, the boss retired—a rich man. Guess he moved back east." Stoke turned to his buddies. "The Deatherage Longhorn Cattle Ranch. Sounds like just the place for *us*, don't it?"

Turning back to Slaw, Stoke said, "The Prickly Pear Saloon, you say?" He smirked. "It's not my favorite place, but I have had me a time or two there." He raised his brows, hinting at past pleasures. "San Antonio's nine miles from here. Climb down and rest your bones. In the morning, we'll all ride in together."

When Slaw's boots hit the ground, Stoke pinched his nose. To Slaw, he said, "You get bombed by a polecat?"

"No sir."

Stoke jerked a thumb toward Rosillo Creek. "Better wash up good. Can't even get a job as a cow hand smelling like skunk piss."

Seph dismounted.

Stoke sneered up at him. "Well, get a load of this. Do you get lost easy?"

Seph blinked. "What do you mean?"

Shaking his head, Stoke said, "How can you see anything with your head up there in the clouds?" His tone was thick with disgust. Stoke stood up as straight as he could, as if he was used to being the tallest man in any crowd and didn't appreciate being dwarfed, particularly by a wet-behind-the-ears plowboy. In a voice meant only for Seph, Stoke threatened, "Don't cross me, boy."

Seph stood with a blank expression, wondering why the man asked them to stay if he didn't want them around. He considered mounting his horse, but then Stoke tipped a shoulder toward the campfire.

Without responding, Seph led his horse toward the picket line. Stoke repeated his warning, "Don't you ever cross me." The words echoed in Seph's head long after he heard them.

# Chapter 2

As Seph untied his bedroll, he whispered to Slaw, "I got a bad feeling about that Stoke fellow." He turned his head to look at his partner and waited for a response.

Slaw frowned. "Alright, Seph. Let's sleep lightly and keep an eye out. My grandpa always said, *A man's got to trust his gizzard. When you have a bad feeling about something, it's wise to heed the warning.*"

"What's a gizzard?" Seph asked.

Slaw shrugged and rubbed his belly. "It's kind of like a plum pit. It sits in your stomach. Think of it as a second brain."

As Seph tried to fall asleep, he thought about what Slaw had said. He was glad that Slaw didn't dismiss his concern about Stoke.

He thought about Slaw's grandpa's advice. Those were words to remember. *A man's got to trust his gizzard.* It sounded silly and yet it made sense.

Seph had an uneasy feeling about the trio nearby. Were they really cowboys? Maybe they were highwaymen, like the bandits he knew far too well. Was the world full of such characters? Seph tried to sleep lightly, and eventually drifted off to sleep despite his worries.

In the morning, when Seph climbed from the ground, Slaw had just returned from washing up. Slaw shook his wet head and griped, "That creek is mighty cold." As he buttoned his shirt, water dripped from his messy hair. His shoulders were so wet, it looked like he had washed his shirt while he bathed.

Seph stepped aside as Slaw approached the campfire, placing a comfortable distance between himself and his friend. Despite the dip in Rosillo Creek, Seph didn't think that Slaw smelled any better than usual.

Dredge finished making coffee while Thumbs packed supplies. Stoke leaned against a nearby tree and poked holes in a piece of leather with the tip of a sharp knife.

When Dredge was satisfied that the coffee was ready, he filled three cups and handed them to his fellow travelers. Then he turned toward Seph and Slaw. "Coffee?" He held the pot while Seph and Slaw scrambled to fetch their cups.

Thick coffee poured from the spout. Seph tried to remember whether he had tasted the stuff before. Maybe when Pa was around, they had coffee in the house.

He thanked Dredge, lifted the cup, and inhaled the aroma. It seemed vaguely familiar.

Perhaps Loretta Ballard made coffee in her kitchen, and that was where he had encountered the scent. He blew on the surface and sent a puff of steam into the cool morning air.

He took a hesitant sip. Almost as quickly, he turned his head and fought the urge to spit it out. He looked back at Slaw, who managed to swallow a sip but Slaw's expression revealed his distaste.

Stoke stepped forward. "Drink up. It'll put hair on your chests. Might even make men outta ya." He puffed his chest out and proclaimed, "The ladies like hairy chests—I can assure you."

Seph thought drinking the foul liquid would make hair grow on his tongue and the insides of his cheek rather than on his chest. He pinched his nose, brought the cup to his lips, and gulped the coffee down. When he was finished, his throat burned. He should have let it cool first.

"Delicious, ain't it?" Stoke chuckled. "Dredge makes a *mean* cup of coffee."

With a shudder, Seph agreed. "That's for sure."

When nobody was looking, Slaw dumped his coffee on the ground and stowed his cup.

Minutes later, Stoke led the gang of five riders, followed by Thumbs. Seph was glad to ride at the back of the line, occasionally listening as Slaw and Dredge conversed. He was glad that his partner had somebody else to talk to. Sometimes, Seph preferred talking to animals. His new pal, Sheriff, was an attentive listener.

As the miles passed, Seph saw more and more houses. It amazed him to see so many people, and he wondered how they managed to feed themselves on ever-shrinking parcels of land.

They rode into town on Alameda Street and passed a small sign that said St. Joseph's Church, but there was no church. They could, however, see the foundation of what would be an immense structure when it was completed.

After turning onto Bonham Street, they rode up two blocks and turned again onto Crockett Street. Seph slowly shook his head at the sight of a block full of buildings with no spaces in between them. He felt crowded in just looking at them. A block beyond, Crockett Street opened into the Alamo Plaza.

Directly ahead, Seph saw crowds of people at the market house and loads of wagons delivering goods there. It amazed him to see so much activity in such a small space.

He turned his head to the right and spied the Alamo's facade. He couldn't believe his eyes. He didn't know much about notorious buildings or other landmarks, but he had heard about the famous mission where over thirty years earlier, General Santa Anna overpowered a stubborn group of frontiersmen who had been determined to win Texas' independence. Pa had fought in that war. Seph hoped that he'd have a chance to get a closer look at the place.

Finally, the five men arrived at their destination. The Prickly Pear Saloon was not an impressive-looking place, at least not from the outside. Dull green letters and faded paintings of cacti on a false front of graying wooden planks welcomed thirsty patrons. The warped boards were pocked with bullet holes and looked like they needed to be replaced. Somebody had painted the word *saloon* over what had once read *cantina*.

Seph was apprehensive about entering the building. He had never been inside a saloon or a cantina before. He was more comfortable outside than indoors, and immediately after ducking his head to enter, he glanced around, taking in the layout.

There was a long, crude bench of a bar along the right side of the room, with a big mirror that made the place seem much larger than it was. On the wall opposite the bar and mirror was an enormous mural and Seph gasped when he saw it. Blinking rapidly, he turned to face it and took a couple of steps back, crashing into Slaw. He gulped and looked quickly at his friend before turning back toward the painted wall.

Nothing could have surprised Seph more than to see a painting of the woman from inside his cigar box—larger than life. It wasn't somebody else. He would recognize *her* anywhere. She was completely naked, from head to toe, but the fleshy pads of a curvaceous prickly pear cactus provided modest cover. Seph felt as if she were looking directly at him. His legs wobbled and his head felt dizzy.

Slaw punched a fist into Seph's shoulder. "Quit gawking." Then he chuckled. "Get a hold of yourself."

Seph turned away from the painting. He tried to think about something else, but he could still see the woman behind the cactus in the mirror.

Hazy smoke billowed near the ceiling. Even through gray clouds, it was impossible for Seph to ignore the dark-haired beauty.

The Prickly Pear was mostly empty, but a couple of tables were occupied by men that looked like they wanted to be left alone. Seph kept glancing over his shoulder at the woman behind the cactus and wondered how the other men managed to overlook her presence.

In a back corner of the room, two men sat behind a triangular table. The man on the left was clean-shaven. The man on the right had a thick beard. They didn't look much alike, though they both had brown hair. One had a touch of gray among his whiskers, and the other had large patches of gray peppering his temples.

The Prickly Pear Saloon's five new arrivals sat nearby and waited to be noticed or acknowledged by the men doing the hiring for the Deatherage Longhorn Cattle Ranch.

Seph propped his elbows on a table, held his hands beside his eyes, and tried to forget the presence of the woman of his dreams on the saloon's wall. After listening for a while, he was surprised to realize that he could overhear the ranchers as they interviewed a fella that didn't take up much space in the chair across from them.

The man on the left drawled, "Afternoon, son. Name's Pierce Deatherage, and this here's my half-brother, Glenn. Folks call him Dusty."

Pierce and Glenn Deatherage's father had a freight business that ran from San Antonio, Texas to Springfield, Illinois by way of Sedalia, Missouri. The half brothers served opposing sides during the war, and when their father died, they discovered that their father kept two families—one at each end of the route. The freight company was sold. The net proceeds were divided in two, with half to each widow. Pierce and Glenn didn't have much in common, but they discovered that they enjoyed each other's company. One thing they did have in common was that both men were single. They got to know each other even better when they were hired by the same outfit. After riding the trail from San Antonio to Sedalia together in '66 and '67, Pierce and Glenn decided to pool their savings and start their own ranch.

Dusty nodded at the youngster following his brother's introduction.

In a squeaky voice, the kid replied, "My name is Thomas Orpington, sir. Heard you were hiring, and I'm in need of a job."

At noon, the cavernous saloon was quiet. The scratch of pencil lead on rough paper could be heard beyond the first row of tables. The older man made notes of the boy's responses.

Dusty said, "You heard right. We've got a spread thirty miles southeast of here. We're putting together a cattle drive to Abilene. Is that the kind of work you're looking for?"

"Yes, sir."

Pierce looked up from his paper and asked, "What do folks call you? Thomas, Tommy, Tom, or something like that?"

"Torp, sir. Folks call me Torp. *T* from Thomas and *Orp* from Orpington."

The brothers took turns firing questions at the lad.

"Can you ride?"

"Yes, sir. Been riding all my life."

"Can you rope?"

"Yes, sir. Not the best, but I've been practicing."

"Can you load and fire a gun?"

"Yes, sir."

"What kind?"

"Rifle, sir. Winchester."

"How old are you?"

"Eighteen, sir."

Both men sat quietly, looking at the would-be cowboy as if waiting for a more honest answer, but none was forthcoming. After a while, Pierce wrote down Torp's response, but Seph could tell the man didn't believe Torp.

"Where are your parents?"

"They're dead, sir. It's just me now."

"Any experience with cattle, Torp?"

"Um. Um. Er." It was clear he didn't want to admit he had none. Finally, he confessed, "No, sir."

"Can you sign your name?"

"I can make my mark, sir."

Pierce frowned and turned a piece of paper toward the kid. After the youth scratched an *X* by his name on a roster, the ranchers shook Torp's hand and congratulated him. "Be ready to ride at three."

Gleefully, Torp chirped, "Yes, sir." His already high voice sounded higher still.

With that, young Thomas Orpington was gainfully employed. After thanking the ranchers, he turned away from the hot seat, and Seph was struck by just how young the kid looked. Perhaps he could pass for sixteen, but more likely, the kid was way younger.

Dusty turned to Pierce and asked, "How many is that?"

His brother answered, "Ten."

"Isn't that enough?"

Pierce frowned. "It should be. Depends on how big a herd we put together. But none of these *men* have any real experience." The way he said *men* made it clear that he didn't think it was a fitting term for the fellows they'd hired that day. "You'd think we could find a top hand in San Antonio."

Before Dusty could finish saying, "It's late in the season," Stoke interrupted them.

"I'm a top hand," he declared, thumping his chest with a fist. "I'll teach them kids a thing or two—for top hand pay, of course."

Dusty looked at the seasoned cowboy and the four seated nearby. Speaking to his brother, he said, "Surely we don't need all of them."

Pierce thought for a minute, then shrugged. "Let's meet them and decide what to do."

Stoke assured the brothers there wasn't anything he couldn't ride, mentioned he'd been on three previous drives, and boasted that he could hit any target that he could see. They readily agreed to pay him top hand wages—twice what the others would earn—fifty dollars rather than twenty-five per month.

Stepping away from the Deatherage brothers, Stoke tipped his head back, looked down his nose at the remaining four, and sauntered to the opposite end of the saloon. He walked with a swagger, like he'd been in the saddle all day.

Thumbs was up next, followed by Dredge, who took the hot seat after him. Unlike with Torp and Stoke, Dusty didn't give them immediate offers. Instead, he told them to sit and wait to hear if they'd be needed.

Next, they interviewed Slaw. Seph got more and more nervous as Slaw answered questions. He noticed Pierce sniffling and wiggling his nose. Did Slaw smell *that* bad?

When they sent Slaw back to his seat, Seph felt a knot of discomfort. He felt it under his arms, his back slicked with sweat, and beads appeared on his forehead. His throat was dry, and his belly churned. All he could think of was, what would he do if he didn't get the job?

When Seph stood, Pierce and Dusty exchanged a glance before looking back at him.

Seph wondered, *Do they think I'm dim-witted?* The thought had been stuck in his brain ever since Slaw's father had called him that.

Blinking rapidly, Seph stepped toward the empty chair. He had almost forgotten the painting on the wall, but he suddenly remembered and glanced at it. Determined not to let her presence rattle him, he took a deep breath, tipped his head forward, and reminded himself that his future depended on this interview. Then, he tripped over his toe. A quick grab at the back of the chair prevented a fall, but he already felt like he'd made a bad impression. "Pardon me," he whispered.

Hoping to make the brothers' work easier, he blurted out all the information he thought they needed. *Talk slowly*, he told himself, *but not too slowly.* "I'm Joseph Vermillion, but folks call me Seph. I'm eighteen. I have a horse, saddle, mule, and a rifle. Ma just died, and Pa didn't return from the war, so I'm alone now. There's lots I don't know, but I work hard."

Dusty asked, "How tall are you?"

Seph gulped and stammered. "Uh...." The brothers waited and Seph added, "I'm sorry, don't reckon I know how tall I am."

Dusty stroked his beard. "Clumsy?"

"Gosh. Not usually, I don't suppose." The more Seph thought about it, the more uncertain he became. Had he lied? Sometimes long legs and arms were a blessing, but occasionally, they tripped him up.

Pierce motioned with his hand and Seph stood to take a seat beside Slaw to wait for the ranchers' decision.

The applicants could hear the bosses deliberate. They made no attempt to speak confidentially. Pierce said, "How can we choose between them?"

Dusty replied, "It ain't that hard to pick. What difference does it make if we pick one versus another? Beeves are worth more than cowboys. Cowboys are all pretty much the same anyway. But how many do we need?"

Pierce said, "The more we hire, the more cattle we can move. And, since most of them are tenderfoots, we can afford to bring more along."

Dusty waved his hand dismissively. "I don't think we need any more. We've got enough already."

Pierce frowned. "Some of the ones we hired might not make it very far. We might need extras."

"You keep the books. Can we afford it?"

"If we find enough mavericks, we can. They'll have to earn their keep by picking up enough scrubs to cover their cut."

Dusty shrugged. "I don't think we need 'em."

Pierce countered, "Let's at least hire the two that have experience."

Dusty tugged his beard and said, "If you insist. More mouths for Dunk to feed." He looked around The Prickly Pear Saloon as if he were looking for the cook. Dusty continued, "We'll have to bring more food. After a long day on the trail, growing boys turn into hungry men."

Before he knew what he was doing, Seph shot to his feet and hurried toward Dusty and Pierce. "Hire me and Slaw," he begged. "We'll work for half wages. If we're no good, you don't have to pay us at all."

Seph was so nervous he thought he might keel over. What if the ranchers got mad at him for being too pushy? He'd heard of people getting shot in saloons. What if they started throwing punches? Would he hit them back?

He heard a voice in the back of his head. It told him not to be timid. He remembered his mother's final words, urging him to be tenacious. Seph opened his mouth and another sentence spilled out. "I'm loyal. Nobody is going to work harder for you than me, and I don't eat much."

Seph let his words hang in the air like the cloud of smoke in the rafters. In a clear, confident voice, he said, "Sign me up, sir. What do ya say?"

# CHAPTER 3

DUSTY TIPPED HIS HEAD back as if weighing Seph's offer. His beard jutted toward Seph, and for a moment, Seph wondered what the rancher was thinking. The ramrod let out a sigh and tapped his forehead with a fist. Finally, Dusty spoke, his voice gruff but clear. "Looks like this kid means business. Ain't no harm in hiring someone who's willing to work for half wages, right?"

Pierce nodded, his decision made. "You've got yourself a deal, men. After hearin' ya talk, I don't know how we could get on without you." Pierce turned to Slaw and motioned him forward with a flick of his finger.

Slaw wrote his name on the roster first. Then, Seph flashed a grin as he neatly signed his name at the bottom of the page. The thought crossed his mind, *I'm the last cowboy hired. How about that for a claim to fame. The bottom of the barrel.* Despite being the tallest kid, he felt like the runt of the litter, but at least he had talked his way into getting a job.

When they were done and the ranchers were out of earshot, Slaw said, "What did you go and do that for? Why should we get half as much as everybody else?"

Seph winced. "Gosh, I'm sorry, Slaw. I shouldn't have done that to you without asking. I didn't plan to say those things, they just slipped out. I panicked. What if I didn't say them? What would we do then? They weren't going to hire us. They had decided not to. Besides, you said a man should trust his gut."

Slaw exhaled, his body slumping. "Maybe you're right. I just figured, at the last minute, they'd change their minds and hire us on anyway."

Most adobe structures had an earthy patina and blended into their surroundings, but the Deatherage Longhorn Cattle Ranch's walls shone. The ranch house, barn, bunkhouse, smithy, and outhouse had a uniform look, as if they were built all at once. The mud-colored structures gleamed in the late-afternoon sunlight.

The new arrivals rode in, single file, behind Pierce and Dusty.

Seph was the last rider in line and the last to tie his horse to the hitching post. The rest of the crew had been relaxing and greeted the Deatherage brothers as they stepped onto the veranda.

Seven cowboys played cards at a long table with matching benches. The covered portico had benches flanking the bunkhouse door. On one bench, a guy sharpened his knife on a stone; on the other, a dark-skinned fellow held a harmonica near his lips, like he was just about to play.

The front entrance to the veranda was crowded, so Seph made his way around to the right. He was glad to have plenty of shoulder room. From the side, he was able to see everybody.

Dusty raised his voice. "Listen up, men." He clapped his hands, with a closed fist pounding into his open palm. Then he turned toward his brother.

When the cowhands quieted, Pierce said, "Me and my brother wanna welcome y'all. We're mighty glad you signed on with our outfit. Make yourself at home."

Dusty rolled his eyes. His louder voice took over. "What my brother meant to say is, you're here to do a job. Expect to work like dogs. You'll start before dawn and work until dusk. Then, you'll take turns standing night watch. We're a new outfit, so there ain't a lot of rules yet. But if I tell you what to do, snap to it. The only things on your mind should be: how do I get it done, and how fast can I do it?" He rubbed his hands together. "Now, let's make some introductions."

With a sneer, he continued. "We don't want your life story. We ain't got time for that. Just tell us what we should call you, and why you're called that. My brother's memory ain't too good, so make it short." Dusty grunted and jabbed a finger toward the faro dealer.

"They call me Chops," the man said, setting a deck of cards down. "Probably 'cause of these." He patted the massive sideburns that looked like pork chops nailed to his cheeks. Chops had a rough complexion.

Dusty's finger pointed to the right of Chops and the next cowhand spoke. "I'm from back east. We got thick forests. Always been at home in the woods, and my last name is Woodruff, so I go by Woodsy."

The next kid spoke up, "My old man's last name is Blaisdale. You can call me Blaze." He looked across the crowd and saw people staring. He added, "My father was a gambler. My mother is Lipan Apache." He waited a moment and then spat, "Any questions?"

Several cowboys shook their heads. Dusty said, "Nope. No questions."

The next cowhand said, "I wish people would call me JJ or Strawberry, but everybody calls me Wobble. Because I *used to be* clumsy." The kid's emphasis on *used to be* made it sound like wishful thinking.

A deep-voiced black man patted his chest and spoke slowly. "Granny Matilda always said I could sing a room to sleep. Folks say critters take to music, so I reckon I found my calling—working a cattle drive. I'm Lullaby, and that's my brother, Yodel." He gestured toward the man on the bench holding the harmonica.

A wrangler with a Mexican accent spoke next. "My mother complained that I was always stealing buttons from her sewing basket. But it was not just buttons. Small, shiny things please me." He pulled a handful of lustrous pebbles from his pocket. "Mama calls me Trinket."

The next fella chuckled. "These guys are sick of hearing about my sweet Mama, our family dog, and the girl I left behind. So, they took to calling me Conjure. It's because I'm always *conjuring* up scenes, and I figure it sounds better than my real name." Seph tried to imagine what name could be so bad that a guy would prefer to be called Conjure.

Dusty pointed at the man with the harmonica. "We already met Yodel." The cowboy nodded. Dusty pointed to the man with the knife.

With a frown, the man tipped his hat forward. "Mama had twelve kids before me. She said I was her puker. I go by Zeke, but everybody calls me Hork. So, don't try to feed me nothing nasty."

The crowd chuckled, and Dusty shook his head. "Mama, Mama, Mama... your mamas ain't going with us to Abilene. Don't let me be hearing about your mamas all the time."

Dusty turned toward the new arrivals. Stoke began telling a boastful story, but Dusty cut him off. Thumbs and Dredge introduced themselves quickly, as did Torp. Slaw removed his hat, ran his open fingers through his hair, and complained that it looked like shredded cabbage.

When it was Seph's turn to introduce himself, he simply said, "I'm Seph, short for Joseph." He thought about the time Slaw's sister, who was sweet on him, called him Stilts but decided not to mention it.

Dusty cleared his throat and said, "Thanks for being *short*, Seph."

The crowd guffawed. Seph was easily the tallest member of the outfit.

Dusty continued, "I thought that was going to take all day." He brushed a cloud of dirt from his thighs and said, "I guess you know why I'm called Dusty. A dirty cowboy is a hard-working cowboy. A clean cowboy is a lazy one." Turning toward his brother, he added, "Pierce don't know you call him Squat."

Pierce looked confused. Dusty explained, "He's always squatting, studying the world, perched on his ankles. He's a squatter." Shaking his head, Dusty asked, "Got any advice for the boys, Squat?"

Pierce scratched his head, then said, "How about this: Don't fall in love with your horses, the painted ladies, and for God's sake, don't fall in love with each other." Then, he warned about the many perils ahead.

After Squat finished, Dusty waved his arm, and a broad-shouldered man stepped from the shadows. Dusty's voice softened. "Meet the most important man in our outfit."

The cowboys squirmed, looking around to see who Dusty meant.

The man stood confidently, his gaze sweeping the crowd. Seph guessed him to be in his mid-to-late twenties.

Dusty said, "Christopher Moon has many skills. He's strong as an ox, a heck of a blacksmith, and an excellent scout. We served together in the war. I never met a better horseman or soldier, but that's not the best thing about him. Just thinking about his biscuits makes my mouth water. On most cattle drives, the hands call their cook Old Lady. Maybe you don't want to call our heroic soldier that." Dusty raised an eyebrow and rubbed his chin. "It takes a lot to make him angry, but he throws a mean punch when he gets riled. Anyway, most folks call him Dunk."

Torp tossed out a question. "Dunk? Why do they call him that?" Torp liked to ask lots of questions.

Dusty chuckled. "Well, he's a dunker. If you ever see him eating, you'll notice that everything gets dunked in something."

Dunk smirked. His lips shifted between his cheeks. With one hand he held an imaginary coffee cup, and his other hand dipped a make-believe donut. To Dusty, he said, "I don't mind being called Ol' Lady. It'll make me think of my own Mama. They say I take after her. So, I'll consider it a compliment. Fact is, she taught me how to cook on the way to Or'gon."

Torp blinked fast. "Organ?"

Dunk corrected him, as if he were talking to a little brother. "Oregon. The Oregon Trail. Sorry, Torp. Sometimes, I leave parts of words out. You'll have to f'give me." Seph thought he saw a twinkle in the soldier's eye and decided that he liked the man. He didn't need to taste Dunk's cooking.

Dusty added, "Maybe you signed on for the pay, but Dunk's vittles will keep you around. One biscuit, and you'll be hooked."

With that, Dusty wrapped up his welcome speech. "Well, tenderfoots, enjoy your last day off. Work begins tomorrow. It may be Sunday, but there ain't no day of rest on a ranch." After a brief pause, he continued. "Better get a good night's sleep tonight. I can see it's gonna be a challenge, turning you buckaroos into ace cowpunchers."

Seph glanced around, matching faces to names. He hadn't met many people, so his skull wasn't overcrowded with too many names. Keeping track of things in his head was a strength, and he quickly realized that he had the nicknames and faces properly paired.

To further cement them in his head, he ran through the roster: Chops, Woodsy, Blaze, Wobble, Lullaby, Yodel, Trinket, Conjure, Hork, Stoke, Thumbs, Dredge, Torp, Slaw, and himself. Fifteen cowpokes. Dusty,

Squat, and Dunk—it was hard to imagine using such nicknames for the bosses.

The seated wranglers resumed their faro game, wagering on the next card flip.

Stoke, Thumbs, and Dredge wandered into the bunkhouse, followed by Slaw and Torp.

Seph stopped to shake hands with Hork and Yodel.

Hork set his knife on the bench when Seph extended his arm. As Hork stood, he let off and passed a noisy flutter of gas. It was loud enough to pause the nearby card game. Hork said, "Dang me. Them beans! I swear."

Seph reached a hand to the other man and said, "Yodel?"

Passing the harmonica from his right hand to the left, Yodel slowly gripped Seph's hand. "That's right. Sounds silly, don't it?" His voice was deep, but not as deep as his brother's.

Seph shrugged. "I like it. Can't wait to hear you play."

"Much obliged." Yodel sat back on the bench and looked down toward his shoulder.

Ducking his head, Seph made his way inside the crowded bunkhouse. Hats, blankets, and saddle bags were everywhere.

Stoke brushed past him, saying, "Smells like an outhouse in here." It was clear he was suggesting that Seph's presence had stunk up the place.

Seph ignored the insult. He told himself that Stoke just had a miserable way with people. The truth was, The place smelled fresh and new.

There were two rows of eight, stacked bunks, and a narrow hallway in between them. After searching for a bunk, he began to worry. Was there a place for him? He should have claimed a spot sooner. Now, he had last pick. He was the last cowboy to sign on and got last dibs. A short set of bunks by the front door was all that remained, and the top bunk was already claimed.

He set his possessions down, crouched, and entered the narrow opening. With his back on the lumpy mattress and his head against the wall, he stretched his feet beyond the end of his bed. If someone swung the door open in a hurry, they'd trip over his legs. He pulled them in and tented his knees. As the tallest cowboy, it wasn't fair that he got stuck in the smallest bunk.

He considered asking someone to trade with him. Instead, he clamped his jaws together, determined to take what comes and make the most of it.

The next day was spent riding, roping, and branding. Dusty, Squat, and Dunk put the crew through a series of chores designed to see what the boys knew and what they needed to learn.

Seph thought he did a passable job performing every task assigned, except for roping. He particularly enjoyed riding. Many hours in the saddle only made him appreciate Sheriff more.

Every time he pressed the Deatherage brand onto a longhorn's hide, he felt proud.

They called it the Dagger D, Angry R to represent death and rage. Most brands were simple, but the Deatherage brand was unique. It featured a backward D and a forward R joined by a shared vertical line, shaped like a dagger. The tail of the R extended sharply, resembling a lightning bolt.

That brand made a fierce statement. And it would be hard for rustlers to counterfeit or alter.

But roping was Seph's weakness. Forming the loop and swinging the rope worked well for him, but when he tossed the lasso, it always flew too far.

Late in the afternoon, Seph realized that Slaw had barely spoken to him all day. Slaw had partnered up with his bunkmate, Conjure.

Meanwhile, the kid from the bunk above his own had stuck to Seph's side all day. Torp reminded Seph of Slaw's little brother, Columbus. That child liked to pretend he was invisible, just so he could trip people. Seph bit his cheek and told himself Torp wasn't like Columbus.

That evening, Seph overheard a conversation between Dusty and Squat. He had been standing in the shade, leaning against a column outside the bunkhouse. Before he knew it, he was hearing things he wasn't sure he should be overhearing.

Dusty said, "A man makes his own choices. He chose to be here."

Squat replied, "These aren't men. They're nothing but a bunch of over-grown children. Some of them ain't even full-grown yet."

As if citing a well-known fact, the ramrod said, "Hard work turns boys into men. Let's see how the kid works out."

Seph felt a wave of apprehension in his gut. Were they talking about firing somebody?

Dusty continued. "Remember, he said he's eighteen."

"Really, Dusty? They all did. How many lies do you think those boys told us to get a job?"

The younger brother grumbled. "Who cares how old they are anyhow, as long as they work hard?" He frowned and added, "I didn't wanna hire that one in the first place, but now that he's here, let's see how it works out. We can always send him back if he cain't cut it."

Seph was the last one hired on. He remembered begging the ranchers to take him and Slaw. Were they sorry now? Seph thought he had been doing okay—perhaps not the best at anything, but good enough. If only he could master the lariat.

Squat groaned. "I'm sorry, Dusty. I shouldn't have done it, but that kid don't have anyone. Where would we send him back to?"

Seph raised a hand and covered his mouth. Now, he was convinced they were talking about him.

After dinner, exhausted cowpokes slumped at the table and on the benches. Dunk set a kettle of coffee on the table and told them that all cowpunchers drink coffee. Seph had gotten to the point where he could tolerate the taste and even enjoyed the little jolt that came with it.

Torp, however, couldn't get past the bitterness. Seph tried to convince the kid that it might do him good if he could try to stomach it.

Stoke was passing by and chimed in. "The kid don't like coffee? We can't have that." He shook his head, tsking. "Can't be a cowboy if he don't drink coffee. What if we sweeten it up with some sugar?" Stoke moved like a tempest. "And how about some milk. Children drink lots of milk. Good for the bones. Maybe that'll help."

Seph wished that Stoke would help Torp without making him out to be a baby. He watched as Stoke spooned sugar into the cup and stirred the coffee recklessly. A little bit spilled over the edge as Stoke slammed the cup onto the table in front of Torp. "Now, be a good little boy and drink up."

Torp hesitated, and Stoke barked. "I said drink it."

Torp flinched and picked up the cup.

Stoke planted his hands on the table and leaned forward. "Hurry up. I ain't got all night. Drink it down." Then, he stepped around, just behind the kid.

Torp took a big mouthful of coffee, then spit it out just as fast.

Stoke slapped Torp's back as he coughed. Then, Stoke bent at the waist, slapped his knees, and howled with laughter.

Torp's nose crinkled, and his cheeks twisted. He tried to scrape the taste from his tongue with his front teeth. Tears came to his eyes as Thumbs and Dredge joined in on the merriment.

Dredge said, "Stoke, did you put salt in that boy's coffee instead of sugar?"

Thumbs added, "Don't you know any better 'n 'at, Stoke?"

Stoke stopped howling long enough to chime in, "Sometimes I get confused." He crossed his eyes and wobbled his head in an exaggerated fashion.

Seph stood slowly. He stomped his feet and pounded the table with a big fist. Leaning toward Stoke, he shook a finger at him. "From now on, if you feel the need, prank me. Not Torp."

Stoke jumped at Seph, grabbing his shirt. "Don't tell me what to do."

# CHAPTER 4

SEPH STOOD, FROZEN IN place. He didn't apologize or reclaim his words.

Stoke's eyes bulged, and Seph figured the man was waiting for the faintest reason to start swinging his fists. A thick vein pulsed near Stoke's temple as he hissed, "You mind yourself, boy. I told you before, don't cross me."

Seph told himself not to flinch. Stoke's grip tightened, and the fabric of Seph's shirt bunched into a wad at his chest. Seph swallowed hard, his mind racing, anticipating Stoke's attack. He knew he'd have to defend himself, though it was hard to imagine how.

"Don't *ever* cross me," Stoke growled again.

Several slow seconds ticked by, and Seph could feel the heat of Stoke's breath on his chin. Inhaling slowly, he recalled how he felt when bandits raided his family's farm—not fear, exactly, but the sense of being intruded upon. He hated the feeling. Maybe he'd rather have a busted lip, ripped brow, or a black eye. Then, if he felt like a victim, he'd have something to show for it. He braced himself. When Stoke commenced to brawling, he must be ready.

But, before Stoke could unleash the anger boiling inside him, Thumbs and Dredge cornered him.

Thumbs said, "Simmer down, Stoke."

Dredge warned, "Boss nearby."

With a sneer, Stoke warned, "You got a lesson coming to ya, kid. Mind your manners, or I'll break you."

Stoke finally released Seph's shirt as Thumbs and Dredge eased him away, chuckling as they departed.

Seph stood—still frozen. His shoulders slowly lowered and his body sagged. It was over. For now. But, Seph thought, *The worst is yet to come.* One day, Stoke was going to pound him. He would need to face the man. But, what did he know about fistfights or self-defense?

Behind him, there was a loud crash. He jumped, twisting around fast.

Dunk was brushing bits of bark from his arms and chest after dropping a load of firewood into a bin beside the hearth. He nodded toward the stump where he split the wood and said, "Wanna help me bring in the rest?"

Seph nodded and followed Dunk from the veranda. As they walked, Dunk glanced at Seph and said, "Looks like you've got your hands full." There was no way of mistaking the question, though it was worded as a statement.

Crossing his hands behind his back, Seph confirmed, "I reckon so. Don't know why, but Stoke don't seem to like me much."

Dunk dipped his chin and said, "Ain't your fault. His kind just has to be the *most*."

"The most? Most what?"

Dunk set a hand on Seph's shoulder. "Everything, really. He can't stand another man besting him at anything. But there's one thing he can't deny—you're taller. Betcha anything, that's what irks him. So you can either cower in a corner or prepare yourself. Did I overhear him saying he'd break you?"

Seph's head dropped, and he turned away. "Yeah. That's what he said. He said other stuff too." He raised his hands and splayed his fingers before clenching them into fists.

"You got strong, work-hardened hands, kid." Dunk pinched his chin thoughtfully, then added, "But you've never used them in a fight, have you?"

Seph shook his head, frowning. Crossing his wrists behind his back, he finally muttered, "Never learned how. Fact is, I hardly ever saw *anybody* on the farm. Friend or foe. Just weren't nobody to quarrel with."

"Ah," Dunk nodded. "Farming can be lonely. No brothers? No neighbors?"

Seph bit his cheek and told Dunk about his older, long-gone siblings. He explained that Slaw lived a good distance away, growing up. Then, Seph's eyes lit up. "You were a soldier. Could you teach me how to fight?"

"Nope."

Seph was crestfallen. He rarely asked anyone for help, preferring to rely upon himself. Maybe he had misjudged Dunk.

"I can show you how to throw a fist. I can tell you ways to make yourself stronger. But there's no way to teach a guy how to fight." Dunk jabbed fists at an imaginary opponent. "We can practice, but it ain't a fight until it's real. When you're standing there and somebody wants to rip your face off, that's when you learn how to fight. The bad news is, at first, you have to learn by losing. The good news is, you look tough enough to take the knocks." Dunk held out his hands and said, "Here, do this."

Seph copied him and was surprised when Dunk loaded chunks of firewood into his arms. Dunk nodded approvingly as Seph held the load without complaint. "How many pieces of wood is that?"

"Twenty."

"Ah, a counter. That's good. A good cattleman is always counting." Dunk instructed him to lift the wood up and forward, then down and back. "Feel that? Makes your arms stronger."

Seph nodded and didn't complain about the heavy load.

Dunk said, "That's good." He thought for a moment. "Hmm. Tomorrow, let's you and me ride out and see if we can find some critters."

Seph said, "Yes, sir. I'd like that."

Dunk told Seph to take the firewood to the portico and walked off toward the ranch house. After Dunk was gone, Seph made several more trips until the bin was full.

In the morning, after Dunk served breakfast, Dusty sent the crew off in pairs to search for mavericks. "If you see a brand, don't touch it, unless it's ours. Whichever pair brings in the most critters gets tomorrow off." The cowhands hooted and hollered, but only two of them would win a day of leisure. Just the chance of having a day off was worth celebrating, and the crew behaved like they had just reached the end of the trail.

When the boss announced that Seph would partner with Dunk, Seph looked at the cook, who winked back confidentially. Seph hoped that Dunk hadn't told the ramrod why he requested the assignment.

Dunk shouted, "Who's cooking if me and Seph win?" He held his hand to his chest as he laughed, and the rest of the crew groaned. Clearly, nobody wanted Dunk and Seph to bring in the most beeves.

After a couple of hours in the saddle, they dismounted. Seph followed as Dunk led his horse to the river, and they tied their horses in the branches of a scrubby shrub.

Seph followed Dunk into a ring of sunshine.

Dunk turned to face Seph and said, "Now, mind you. I'm more experienced with firearms, but here's what I know about fistfighting. Don' just swing your arms like a wild animal."

Seph nodded.

"First thing you gotta know is where to place a punch. The jaw's a good spot—sends a message. Aim here." Dunk pointed to the jawline. "Hit hard, but hit clean."

Seph mimicked the motion, throwing a few practice punches at the imaginary target. Dunk nodded approvingly.

"Now, about that fist. Close your hand tight, thumb outside the fingers. Bend your thumb across the knuckles of your first two fingers, like this." Dunk demonstrated with his hand, then repositioned Seph's fingers when he formed a fist. "Ease up a mite. Don't strangle your fingers," he advised.

Seph adjusted his grip, heeding Dunk's advice.

"Good, good. Now, taking a punch is as important as throwing one. Keep your chin down, shoulders up. Don't be afraid to dance a bit. Move your feet. And when that punch comes, roll with it. Less damage that way."

Dunk threw a light jab at Seph, who followed Dunk's advice and shifted his weight, avoiding the full impact of Dunk's playful blow.

"Now, there are different punches you can throw." Dunk continued, demonstrating a jab, a hook, and an uppercut. "Each has its purpose."

He then gestured for Seph to throw a punch at his belly. As Seph lunged forward, Dunk deftly sidestepped the attack, leaving Seph off balance. With a quick shove, Dunk sent Seph sprawling to the ground.

"Don't be predictable. Keep 'em guessing."

Seph sprung to his feet.

"Even when it seems like you're beat, find a way to turn the tables. Victory often comes to those who refuse to stay down."

Dunk showed Seph several moves and explained how he could work them into a fight. "Sometimes, you can lessen the force of a blow by stepping into it. Other times, you can use your forearm to block a punch, then follow up with a quick counterpunch. Use your long arms to your advantage. Deflect the force of the other guy's movement and turn it against him."

Dunk told Seph to throw some punches at him and demonstrated various feints that could be used for misdirection. "It gets 'em off balance, and that's when you follow through with a strong punch or a quick move. Like I said, keep 'em guessing." He demonstrated each move and watched as Seph copied each one.

"Remember, Seph," Dunk said, clapping him on the shoulder. "It ain't magic. It takes practice and quick thinking. On the frontier, you need every advantage you can get."

As midmorning gave way to midday, Dunk left Seph with advice about how he could strengthen the muscles that he would rely on in a fight. "Volunteer for every task, from chopping wood to carrying water. It'll make you stronger. Even when you're resting, think about how you can flex your muscles. It'll make you more powerful. If you find yourself in a fight, picture victory. Tell yourself that you will win. Keep your emotions in check. Don't let anger cloud your judgment. And if you lose, which you probably will, rely on your inner strength. Sometimes, a valiant concession is as good as winning."

Dunk looked skyward, as if checking the sun's position, and said, "Now, let's see if we can flush any critters from the brush. Let's split up. You go that way, and I'll go down there."

Seph watched as Dunk rode toward the southeast. Seph mounted up and went the opposite way. He untied the lariat from his saddle and nudged Sheriff forward.

The sun burned hot on his shoulders as the temperature climbed. It was warmer than normal for a mid-spring afternoon, and after two hours of weaving through dense thickets, Seph stopped to wet his lips with a small sip of water from his canteen. As he corked it, he thought he saw movement between two large shrubs near the river.

Leaning forward and peering from the shadow of his hat brim, he spied the expansive horns of a stout bull. Marveling at the marbled coloring of the critter's coat, he felt a jolt of excitement in his gut. Blinking fast, he wondered whether he could rope the rascal.

Seph thought of Lullaby's claims about singing to longhorns in a low voice. He looked around, saw nobody, and decided to give it a try. His heart pounded, but he tried to keep calm and sang in as low a voice as he could.

Seph worried that he might lose the creature. He couldn't get close enough to throw a rope, but slowly nudging the bull seemed to be working, so he persisted.

When Sheriff and Seph got too close, the bull twisted its neck and snorted angrily. As they drew closer to the ranch, Seph worried that the animal would bolt back toward the mesquite, but instead, the bull seemed curious and picked up his pace.

Patience and persistence paid off, Seph thought. He had managed just the right balance between nudging and holding back. He didn't even need to try to rope the bull. Now that they were close to the ranch, he wondered whether to continue along or try to rope it.

Seph could see the top of the Deatherage buildings from his saddle and wondered whether the other teams had returned or were still scouring mesquite thickets? He hoped somebody would notice his approach and help him coax the bull into captivity.

He couldn't help being proud of the animal. Maybe he'd seen others as large, but this bull seemed perfectly formed, with broad, symmetrical horns. It wasn't like the scrawny mavericks he had seen—underweight with bulging ribs. He tipped his head and admired the colors that rippled across its coat in waves of black, brown, red, and a color that reminded Seph of oxidized iron. A name popped into his head, and Seph decided to call the longhorn *Skillet*.

Seph was so intent on the task of bringing Skillet in that he didn't hear Dunk ride up on his flank.

In a hushed voice, the seasoned frontiersman said, "I like that critter. Whenever you see him, remind yourself: you did that. Nice work, kid."

With a flush of pride, Seph realized that he had hoped to impress the bosses. He thought of the conversation he had overheard. Hopefully, Dusty and Squat would feel the same way about Skillet as Dunk did.

Dunk reined his horse to follow the bull, mirroring Seph's distance on the other side. As they began their final approach, a couple of cowboys noticed and galloped toward them.

Skillet tossed his head and snorted. He skidded to a halt and crouched defensively.

Seph looked at Dunk, who swung his arms wide, high in the air, trying to halt the oncoming riders.

With a grunt, Skillet pivoted and charged toward Sheriff.

Seph dug his heels into Sheriff's belly and reined hard toward Dunk, hoping to avoid a collision with the angry bull. "Hi-yah!"

At the last moment, Skillet twisted his neck. The bull's long horn ripped into Seph's leg, lifting him from his saddle and flinging him over the maverick's back.

The sensation of soaring through the air froze in Seph's mind. It felt like he hung in the air for minutes rather than seconds.

When he crashed into the ground, shoulder first, he felt the impact—and then he felt nothing.

Cowhands spilled from the portico and rushed to saddle their horses. Soon, they caught up to those who had enraged the maverick and helped pursue the renegade bull.

Torp ran to fetch a bucket of water as Dunk scooped Seph from the ground.

The kid was unconscious, but Dunk spoke to him anyway. "Big as you are, you're light as a feather."

Seph didn't answer and Dunk thought of all the times he'd carried men from the battlefield. Few of them had survived. He tried to reassure the kid, "You'll be alright. We'll get you fixed up, lickety-split. You'll see."

Seph's long legs dangled over the edge of Dunk's arm. The cook tried to get a look at the kid's injury from the corner of his eye as he shuffled quickly toward the bunkhouse. He couldn't get a good look at it as he went but hoped that Seph hadn't broken any bones or suffered any unseen injuries. He had seen the kid hit the ground hard, bounce, and roll.

Dunk thought of the time when he broke an arm along the Oregon Trail when he was trampled by oxen in the Sweetwater River. He figured it was a good thing Seph was young. It was amazing what trauma youth could overcome. Dunk had seen that during the war as well.

When Dunk reached the portico, he carefully placed Seph on the long table. He straightened the kid's limbs and examined his injured leg. The sharp horn shredded Seph's chaps, ripped his trousers, and left a wide gash on the outside of his left leg.

Dunk lightly slapped Seph's face, but the kid didn't regain consciousness.

The blade of Dunk's knife slashed through the fabric and revealed the full extent of Seph's wound. It ran from mid-shin to mid-thigh, and though it was wide, it wasn't deep. Dunk was certain that Seph would find it painful, but if that were his only injury, the kid should consider himself lucky.

Dunk didn't notice Torp's arrival. The kid hastily unloaded the bucket onto Seph's face, but Dunk figured that most of the water splashed back onto him. With a chuckle, he shooed Torp away and told him to bring back another bucketful of water—only this time, he shouldn't drown the patient.

Seph gasped for air and sat up, rubbing his eyes. "What happened? Where am I?"

Miraculously, Seph's trousers and chaps were the only casualties of the day. With his back curved, he jackknifed his body and looked intently at the gash on his leg. "Aw, Skillet," he gasped.

Dunk said, "Skillet?"

"Yeah. What happened to him?"

"Him?"

"Yeah, the critter. You know, that maverick I found. Skillet."

Dunk chortled, "Oh, so he has a name, eh? Yeah, he got spooked and hooked you pretty good."

Slaw appeared, breathlessly beside Seph, interrupting. "What happened?"

As Seph told the story of finding the brindled bull, cowboys crowded around. When he was done, he looked about and asked, "Who won the day off?"

The musical cowboys, Lullaby and Yodel, answered in unison. "We did."

Lullaby said, "We brought in seven scrubby longhorns."

Yodel said, "Lullaby sang 'em to sleep."

Modestly, Lullaby shrugged.

Dusty proudly said, "It was a good day. All together, you picked up twenty head." He patted Seph's shoulder and added, "And that's a strong bull you brought in, cowboy."

Stoke sneered. "That's a big one, I'll grant you. But he's the ugliest thing I ever saw."

Seph glanced at Stoke. He didn't say anything, but he thought about that longhorn. It didn't matter what anybody said. That maverick was majestic. Looking at his leg, it was hard to think kind thoughts about wild cattle, but it wasn't the bull's fault. The guys who galloped toward them spooked it. What else could Skillet do?

Stoke turned toward Dunk, feigned a retch, and said, "Why did you set the louse on our dinner table?"

Dunk twisted his face and attempted a humorous response. "Ain't had time to cook nothing better, but it looks like he'll survive, so we'll have to find something else for supper."

Seph placed his hands on the table beneath him and slid his legs to the bench. "I better get offa here before somebody skewers me."

Slaw and Torp offered to help, but Seph insisted he would be fine. He shuffled through the open doorway into the bunkhouse and retrieved his spare trousers.

Dunk met him at the doorway, placing a wad of soap into Seph's hand. "It's going to sting, but wash that leg good. Then dress it with this." Dunk handed Seph a bundle of scraped lint bandaging.

Seph shuffled off toward the San Antonio River. His leg throbbed, but he didn't complain. The truth was, his shoulder hurt more than the leg.

The cold water dulled his pain and he remained submerged as long as he could. His legs were almost numb when he stepped from the river, shivering and dripping wet. He thought, *Why bother with the dressing?* Dunk told him to dress the wound, so Seph decided to use the bandaging anyhow.

By the time he finished, his leg was no longer numb and began to throb again. With clenched teeth, Seph pulled his pants on, closed his eyes, and counted the seconds until the pain caused by the movement of the pant legs dragging along the bandages subsided.

Then he noticed that his boots weren't where he left them. They stood a short distance away and he shuffled toward them. He looked into them and saw that they were filled with pasty sludge. Quicksand!

*Who would do such a thing?*

He should consider himself lucky. At least they'd left his clothes.

# CHAPTER 5

AFTER A MONTH OF combing mesquite thickets and picking mavericks from the countryside like ticks off a hound's fur, the Deatherage outfit was ready to head north with a herd of three thousand fidgety beeves, a remuda of sixty saddle horses, and a crew of over-eager, fiddle-footed cowhands.

Seph couldn't wait to depart.

The journey's first milestone was the Guadalupe River, almost fifty miles up the trail. Dunk told the boys at first light on the day of departure that the river was probably a four-day's ride to the north.

The Guadalupe was merely the first of the major crossings. Dunk named off the waterways like a parent teaching a child how to recite the months of the year: Guadalupe, Colorado, Brazos, Trinity, Red, Washita, Canadian, North Fork, Cimarron, Salt Fork, Bluff Creek, Arkansas, and Smoky Hill. There were plenty of other rivers, creeks, and estuaries, but Dunk claimed that those thirteen were the most noteworthy. After crossing the Smoky Hill River, the end of the trail would be near.

The next ninety days and 800 miles were critical for the future fortunes of the new outfit on its first drive.

Leaving seemed to take forever. Seph sat tall in the saddle, eager to get moving. He ground his teeth impatiently, watching the herd slowly stretch and narrow into a thin line. After a while, his posture slumped and his mind wandered. Three thousand steers might as well have been three million.

He thought about the long days spent with Torp and Slaw, rounding up mavericks. Seph wasn't good at roping, Slaw wasn't much of a rider, and Torp didn't have much of any kind of skill, but usually they managed to wrangle at least a couple of beeves every day. The rest of the teams were far more successful, and the other cow punchers constantly made sure to remind Seph, Slaw, and Torp of their shortcomings. Perhaps, Seph thought, he and his buddies would do better on the trail.

After branding hundreds of critters, Seph had gotten used to the smells of singeing hair and burning hides, but castrating bulls was another matter. It was a necessary part of ranching, yet Seph cringed every time he made the incision.

Squat and Dusty decided to leave Skillet intact, much to Stoke's chagrin. The top hand thought that the bull should be butchered. Seph liked the thought of a herd of brindled longhorns that resembled Skillet, which he had come to think of as *his* bull, though he knew the longhorn was ranch property.

Nearly two hours had passed since the Deatherage outfit's first drive commenced. Instead of riding point, the trail boss, Squat, left before anybody else. He had appointed himself scout. Dunk was the next to depart, driving the bright green, freshly-painted chuckwagon.

Assigned to ride *point*, the top hand, Stoke, led the procession with his companions Thumbs and Dredge, nudging a feisty red cow that Stoke believed the others would follow. Beyond them, the cowboys rode at intervals so that each could sometimes see the rider ahead and behind them. The first pair, Lullaby and Yodel, rode in the *swing* position; Conjure and Trinket, Blaze and Woodsy, and Wobble and Hork rode *flank*.

Seph, Slaw, and Torp had the unenviable job of riding *drag*. That meant breathing the maximum amount of dust at the end of the column. They also had to contend with the most contrary beasts—the ones least given to follow a leader. Seph thought that instead of assigning feral mavericks to the least experienced wranglers, the responsibility should have been given to the veteran cowboys. Why not let the hands making top pay do the hardest work?

Chops had been appointed wrangler. He rode with the remuda and dealt horses to the cowpunchers whenever they needed a fresh mount. Seph felt a twinge of envy when Chops was placed in charge of the horses. He would have liked that assignment himself. Even so, it made him chuckle to think of the faro dealer passing out horses like he dealt cards.

Seph shifted his weight in the saddle and looked into the distance. Somewhere, far to the north, the top hand and his cronies rode point. How long had it been since he had watched Stoke lead the procession, followed by Thumbs and Dredge? The feisty red cow that they nudged forward first looked like a good choice. The long column of critters seemed to prove it.

Now, all of their hard work had led to this moment—leaving. Seph ran a hand along his thigh. His wound had healed.

For a week, his leg had throbbed whenever he sat in the saddle, but he gritted his teeth and endured the pain without complaint. When no one was looking, he'd bend his arm and rub his shoulder, which had mostly healed as well.

Though a month had passed, Seph still rankled at the thought of his boots. He wriggled his toes, and tried to think of something else. He never found out who filled them with quicksand, not that it mattered. It took forever to clean them. For the better part of two days, he hobbled around, barefoot, waiting for them to dry. Even now, he could still catch a putrid whiff when he took them off. They smelled like fermented excrement, and knowing how bad it was, he made an extra effort to stand as far away from people as he could.

Finally, with Torp to his left, and Slaw to his right, the last of the braying cattle reluctantly followed those that had gone before.

Seph clucked his tongue against his cheek, waved his hat, and nudged Booger, a wild-eyed albino steer, forward. It was time to think about the trail ahead rather than the month gone by.

All he wanted was to impress the ranchers. Next year, instead of working for half pay, Seph meant to draw full wages.

It wasn't just about the money. He couldn't figure out why he cared, but he did.

At the end of the first day, after supper, Slaw elbowed Seph and said, "We did it. We got hired and now we're on a cattle drive. I told you we could do it. Not only that, we didn't lose a single critter today. Not bad for tenderfoots, wouldn't you say?"

Seph nodded and thought about Slaw's family. He hated to think that he had almost talked himself into remaining behind with them. Looking westward, admiring the sunset, he felt free and was glad to leave farming behind.

Slaw added, "It's all I ever want to do, Seph."

Instead of playing cards, the others lazed about, chatting, and Seph listened in.

Wobble lamented, "I miss Ma." He didn't seem to care what the other cow-boys thought, but the collective groan echoed his sentiment. Seph glanced at Torp, who was sitting beside him. Ever so quietly, the kid whimpered, and Seph wondered how long it had been since he had lost his parents.

Woodsy pined for his mother's thick pancakes and heavy maple syrup. He always accused Dunk of watering down the syrup to make it last, and the cook never denied the accusations. Woodsy frequently grumbled, "The farther west you go, the thinner it gets."

It occurred to Seph to remind Woodsy that they would ride north, not west. The truth was, he too had noticed the watery syrup.

Hork groaned, clutching his growling belly. "Durn beans. Get me every time." He turned toward Woodsy and said, "We shoulda brought your Ma instead of Dunk. Then we'd have pancakes all the time instead of beans." He hacked a wad of phlegm and spat. "Beans, beans, beans. All the stinking time. I swear!"

As tough as they pretended to be, thoughts of friends, family, and home-cooked meals made the cowpokes whine like children. Neither Wobble, Woodsy, nor Hork had celebrated their eighteenth birthdays yet, but they had miles of hard work ahead. They needed to be men, not boys.

Lamenting the lives they left behind was interrupted by Dusty's announcement. "Wobble, Woodsy, and Hork, you've got first watch tonight. Trinket, Blaze, and Conjure, you're on the graveyard shift. Keep 'em calm—the first couple of days are the hardest. Critters ain't trail broke yet."

Seph would have liked to stand watch that evening. He wasn't tired, but he knew his turn would come. The days would get more taxing, and he needed to rest when he could.

As he stretched out on his back and gazed at the stars, he heard the sniffling sound of stifled sobs. He'd heard Torp's cries before and had tried to talk to him when they were alone, but Torp always refused to acknowledge it.

Finally, that night, the kid was ready to talk. Torp was born in Goliad, a quiet town along the San Antonio River. His parents were hard-working homesteaders, and he was an only child.

When he was twelve, his mother, Nora, was killed by a stranger on her way home from church. The drifter had struck her with a thick staff and rifled through her pockets, but she wasn't carrying anything of value.

That's when Torp's father, Theo, started drinking and never stopped. One year after Nora's death, Theo drank even more than usual. At first, it seemed he had vanished, but two days later, Torp found him half-submerged in the river. From the dent in his father's head, Torp was sure that his father had slipped on a rock and cracked his skull.

Torp labored for two days to bury his father near the river. Then he packed a few belongings and set out for San Antonio, some ninety miles away. The penniless found odd jobs—hauling crates, sweeping floors, and begging for work. He slept in alleys, abandoned buildings, and beneath porches.

He had tried to join half a dozen cattle drives before finally convincing Dusty and Squat to hire him. Six months after burying his father, Torp signed on with the Deatherage brothers.

Torp whispered, "I'm happy to be here." With a sniffle he added, "I just can't help being sad sometimes." His voice cracked but he didn't sob.

Seph wished he could find a way to comfort Torp, but what could he say?

The first day on the trail taught Seph and his partners that it was best to wait on foot for the herd to get moving. They were used to hard work and had spent plenty of time in the saddle, but weren't accustomed to riding all day. Soaking in the hot water of Cibolo Creek's sulfur springs provided some relief but came with the unpleasant smell of rotten eggs.

The second day was even harder. The stragglers were determined to remain behind rather than follow the herd, and they challenged Seph, Slaw, and Torp at every turn. At times, Seph felt like he had traveled more miles riding left and right than moving forward.

After following Cibolo Creek all day, they crossed it late in the afternoon and then bedded down the herd. Driving cattle was mostly lonely work.

After supper, the cowboys gathered briefly around the campfire, eager for company, but too tired to stay awake for long.

Seph stood and listened for a while. Everybody seemed to have something to say, but he didn't like listening to complaints.

Torp griped. "I'm sore all over."

Slaw said, "I'm tired, I'll grant you. But it's a good tired."

Blaze shook his head. "Boss won't cut me no slack. Dusty's always telling me what to do. Don't like it one bit."

Slaw shrugged, "Dusty's fine. You want bossy, try working for my old man. Shoot, I'd work a thousand days in a row rather than go back to the farm."

Seph rubbed his shoulder and thought, *Slaw's right. Even without a bossy father, I ain't going back to the plow.*

Conjure's voice sounded distant, as if his mind was somewhere far off. "You boys can have the rotten egg rivers and stinking beeves. Heck, I'd sell you all for a slice of Mama's honey cake."

Nobody said a word.

Conjure stretched his body on the ground, lying on his belly, elbows in the dirt, propping his chin in his hands as he gazed into the crackling fire. "I shouldn't have left home. Who's gonna take care of Bonnie? Poor dog. Nobody else ever paid her no mind." He sniffed and tipped his head forward.

Seph wondered if Conjure was crying. It seemed like family dogs were on everybody's mind as, one after another, the guys lamented leaving their pets behind.

Seph had heard enough. He never had a dog. *Maybe someday*, he thought. He stretched out on his back, crossed his legs at his ankles, and rested his head on his saddle. He was content to let the others wallow in their misery.

Living outdoors suited him. Seph was glad to be on the cattle drive, even at half pay. He wouldn't have admitted it to anybody else, but he would have gone along for nothing but meals, if it had come to that.

As the fourth day on the trail began, Seph remembered it was the day they expected to reach the Guadalupe River—their first major milestone. Most of the beeves had fallen into a rhythm, as if they had already forgotten there was ever a time when they weren't on the move.

At the tail end of the drive, the cowboys riding drag had a different experience. The troublesome stragglers persisted, ever hopeful that they would find an opportunity to escape. Some were lazy, others ornery, and a few were downright mean. Seph was constantly on guard, but that didn't stop the dangerous albino steer they called Booger from trying to hook him every chance it got.

They made good progress through the morning, but clouds gathered in the early afternoon. By mid-afternoon, a gentle mist descended, turning into a steady rain. The beeves bellowed as the temperature dropped and the wind picked up, making the waterlogged cowboys shiver.

It was nearly dark when Dusty galloped toward the back of the line. Seph watched as the boss spoke with Slaw. Seph wondered what the ramrod had to say. As Dusty turned his horse toward Seph, Booger made a break for it. Seph kicked his horse forward, heading the maverick off.

Seph liked to count things—whether they were worth counting or not. He hadn't tallied the number of times Booger had tried to escape, but he decided to start keeping track tomorrow.

Once Booger was nudged back in line, Dusty rode up beside Seph. "Good riding, kid," he said with a nod. "That one's a handful."

Seph's spirits soared. He thought back to the conversation he'd overheard a while ago and felt relieved. "Thank you, sir," he replied.

A gust of wind sent a spray of wet sand into Seph's face, and he shut his eyes until it subsided.

Dusty continued, "We're pushing the herd across the river."

Seph hesitated, wanting to ask, *Now? In the middle of this storm?* But he kept quiet and tilted his head.

"If we don't cross now, we might get stuck on the wrong side of the Guadalupe. Keep your distance. These doggies ain't gonna like it, but they're crossing today if it kills 'em." Dusty glanced toward Torp, and Seph detected a note of concern in his voice. "Watch out for Torp, and don't let him get down river from the herd."

It suddenly dawned on Seph that when the bosses talked about a kid with nowhere to go, they were talking about Torp, not him. The realization hit hard. Of course, they'd been worried about the scrawny orphan. He blinked rapidly, trying to catch up with his thoughts. "Yes sir," he answered.

Dusty nodded and said, "Actually, I'll tell the kid to hang back. I don't want him crossing until the last critter's halfway across."

Seph watched as Dusty rode over to Torp, instructing him to stay back. Seph felt a pang of sympathy for his friend, hoping it wouldn't bruise his pride too much.

Minutes later, the cattle slowed and the riverbank emerged from the fog. Seph reined his horse left and then right, keeping the beeves in line. They hesitated at the water's edge, but it was up to the cowboys to make sure they entered the raging river. Seph didn't know what the Guadalupe looked like in good weather, but he was pretty sure that it was much deeper and faster-moving now.

He glanced over at Slaw, who was prodding cattle into the current. Then Seph looked and saw Torp waiting on the riverbank, just as Dusty had ordered. Though it was the right call, Seph felt bad for the kid.

As the cattle crossed, Seph's nerves tightened. The water was rising, and it was hard to tell if the dimming light came from the late hour or the thick clouds. He didn't want to think about what would happen if they didn't get the herd across before nightfall.

By the time the last of the cattle reached the far bank, Seph and Slaw were riding through the river, pushing the final stragglers. Seph could hear Slaw shouting over the roar of the water. "Lovely weather we're having, ain't it!" Slaw's laughter carried over the storm. It was clear he was enjoying himself.

Seph shook his head, frowning. Slaw always seemed to find humor in the worst situations.

Suddenly, Booger jackknifed and spun toward Slaw.

Slaw dug his spurs into his horse, trying to cut off the ghostly beast.

The wild-eyed albino snorted, shaking his head menacingly. Booger wasn't backing down. With a powerful pivot, the steer charged straight at Slaw.

Seph yelled, "Get outta there, Slaw!"

Slaw's horse shrieked, a terrifying sound that made Seph shudder. The panicked horse bucked and reared, pawing the air with its front hooves. Somehow, Slaw clung to the saddle horn.

When the horse's hooves hit the ground, it twisted away from the steer just in time, tearing off at a gallop like a stick of dynamite had exploded behind it.

Seph watched in horror as Slaw flipped from the saddle, his right boot caught in the stirrup.

The light was fading fast. Seph slapped a hand over his mouth in shock. He couldn't tell exactly what had happened, but the horse wasn't slowing down.

Slaw's body bounced along beside the frantic dappled gray.

Seph dug his spurs into Sheriff's side and raced after his friend, his heart pounding.

He tried not to think the worst, but a sick feeling wrenched his gut.

# CHAPTER 6

"I DON'T KNOW WHAT else to do for him," Dunk said to Dusty and Squat. The camp cook rubbed his eyes and yawned. "I thought last night would never end." He frowned and looked down at Slaw, who lay on his back beneath a heavy wool blanket.

Lousy weather had continued overnight. It took half of the crew to erect a tarp beside the chuckwagon. Shortly before dawn, the wind died down and heavy rain gave way to a foggy drizzle.

Seph stood just beyond the canvas covering. He hadn't slept either. He tipped his head back, letting the gathered moisture cascade from the brim of his hat to the ground behind him. Then, he stretched his sore neck, rotating his head from side to side as his mind wandered.

Last night, Dunk had suggested a fire might offer some comfort. "We need to keep Slaw as warm as we can and it's impossible to see a thing."

It had been a challenge to build a fire during the blustery storm. Fortunately, Dunk kept a well-stocked tinderbox in the chuckwagon. The brittle makings were as dry as ancient parchment. Even so, the fire kept dying out. It took over an hour before Seph could maintain a steady blaze. Once the small fire was lit, Seph spent half the night stumbling in the darkness, collecting wood along the flooded river.

For most of the night, Slaw's mouth hung open, a steady stream of drool oozed from the corner. His chest rose and fell, but other than that, it was hard to tell that his friend was still alive.

It was well after midnight when Slaw began to groan. His eyes fluttered open, wildly. His head thrashed from side to side, but the rest of his body stayed limp. Seph and Dunk rushed to his side.

Dunk said to Seph, "We must make Slaw as comf'table as we can." He pulled a small glass bottle from his pocket, showing it to Seph. "A quarter teaspoon of this should do."

Seph squinted, reading the label in the dim light. *Dr. Dabney DeGroat's Tincture of Opium.*

Dunk pulled the cork and carefully measured out a small amount of the amber liquid. "Tip his head back for me."

Seph took a deep breath. The stuff smelled like a witch's brew of whiskey, tea, dirt, and pie, though imagining a sorceress taxed the limits of his imagination. It seemed to take forever before the medicine took effect. Then, all at once, Slaw went limp again, his mouth hanging slack.

Dunk placed a hand on Seph's shoulder. "Laudanum is the only thing I know to help him." Then Dunk said the words that echoed in Seph's mind all night. "Don't get your hopes up. It don't look good." With that, Dunk stood and busied himself among the chuckwagon's contents.

Seph remained on his knees. He looked down at his friend's chest as if willing him to keep breathing. He pressed his hands together, tenting them in prayer, and closed his eyes as the tip of his nose touched his fingers. He didn't know what to ask the Lord, but hoped that even vague prayers might help.

Standing in the drizzle at dawn, Seph realized that he was praying again. *Oh, please God, help Slaw.*

His attention returned to the men nearby.

Dunk said, "Reminds me of the war."

Dusty grumbled, nodding in agreement.

Squat said, "I'll ride into town and fetch a sawbones."

Dusty frowned at his brother. "Doubt it'll help."

"What can it hurt? New Braunfels is just a couple of miles away." Without further discussion, Squat called out, "Chops! Get me my horse."

As his brother dashed off, Dusty grumbled under his breath. "May as well try." He turned to Dunk. "Why didn't he mention there was a nearby town sooner?"

Dunk shook his head, rubbing his eyes. "I don't 'spect it would've made a diff'rence. Sometimes you just can't win for losing."

Seph glanced at Slaw just as his partner's bloodshot eyes popped open. They darted around, searching. Seph grimaced, feeling as if a giant hand were squeezing his heart. Squat's departure had left more room under the tarp, and Seph rushed forward to Slaw's side as Dusty stepped back.

"There you are, Seph. I thought you'd never come."

"Shoot, Slaw. I been here with you all night."

"Oh." He was quiet for a moment. "I'm sorry. I didn't know. I ain't myself no more."

Seph could see the pain etched on his friend's face.

Slaw lifted his head slightly, glanced down the length of his body, then let it fall back.

Dunk returned to his knees across from Seph. "I don't know how many bones you got broken. Squat's gone to find a doctor."

"I heard," Slaw grunted.

"It hurts, don't it?" Dunk asked gently.

Slaw's face twisted in pain, but he didn't say anything.

Seph asked, "Can you move?"

Slaw's expression strained, as though he was trying to move, but his body failed him.

"Be still, Slaw. Let's wait for the doctor." Dunk said, his voice soothing.

"I can't move." Slaw blinked slowly, a tear sliding from the corner of his eye. "I'm never going to move again." His lip trembled. "We gotta face the facts." He turned his head, locking eyes with Seph. "You made my dreams come true. I never coulda done it on my own. I always wanted to be a cowboy. If you didn't partner up with me, it never would have happened."

Seph sniffled, a lump forming in his throat. He hated letting his emotions show in front of others, but he couldn't stop it.

Slaw interrupted his thoughts, "Snap to it. I got a few more things to say."

Seph let out a shaky laugh, his friend's sharp tone both familiar and heart-breaking. Tears welled up, but he didn't sob. He just nodded.

"Tell my family it was worth it. And I want you to have Win." Slaw paused, catching his breath before continuing. "Don't forget what I told you, Seph. When you get that funny feeling, trust it. Your soul knows things your thick head never will. And don't worry about what your Mama said. The rest of your life belongs to you. It's not your job to find your brothers and sisters. Live large. Take me with you. When you see a brilliant sunset, think of me so I can see it too. And don't bother with no coffin. Just pitch me in a hole by the river."

Slaw's voice faded. When his strength gave out, his lips kept moving, but he had said all he needed to say.

Seph saw Slaw's chest sag. He wiped his eyes with his sleeve, turning his head away from Dunk. "Slaw never complained," Seph said softly. "He talked way too much, but he never complained."

Dunk nodded. "We should be proud of him, Seph. He'll always be a part of the Dagger D, Angry R. He was a good cowboy, loyal friend, and we were lucky to know him."

After a quiet moment, Dunk added, "I've heard too many men say their last words. Slaw's were beautiful, Seph. Don't forget 'em. Life is short. Whether it's a brilliant sunset or a scattering of stars, soak up the beauty you find along the way."

As Seph turned back toward Dunk, he saw tears in the veteran cowboy's eyes as he tugged the blanket over Slaw's head.

Most folks in town were having breakfast and drinking coffee, but Swoop didn't care what time it was. For him, anytime would do.

Nothing made Swoop happier than spending the day drinking. And when he was drinking, he liked to complain. He especially liked to complain about work, but he also liked to complain about Germans.

He always sat with his back to the wall, his busy eyes noting every detail within his field of vision. Whenever he wasn't talking, he ran his tongue across his teeth.

In his younger days, he had been known to pound shots of whiskey and chug tankards of beer as fast as he could. Eventually, he grew tired of working hard through the week just to spend all his pay on one night's entertainment he couldn't remember the next day. Instead of sweating away as an apprentice to picky old Sattlermeister Steinmetz, Swoop decided to free himself from the saddle-making trade.

Over the next eleven years, he perfected the art of drifting from place to place. He was always on the lookout for easy marks and discovered that it wasn't hard to make a living by *taking* what he wanted. All it required was picking the right targets and striking when they couldn't fight back. The war had only made things easier. With the men away, their families were easy prey. Swoop, Coyote, and Chaw followed a route, visiting the same places over and over. But, as the war dragged on, the farms they plundered grew poorer. They figured it was time to up the stakes if they wanted to keep living large.

Now in his mid-thirties, Swoop drank slowly but steadily, always thinking about his next easy score. He had his eye on Alaric Merkens, the hard-working German proprietor of the inn. Swoop, Coyote, and Chaw were the only customers. Maybe things would liven up in the afternoon or evening, but Swoop couldn't resist needling the man. "You're making me nervous. You been cleaning that same glass for ten minutes."

The innkeeper sighed, his voice heavy with resignation. "You are right, of course. But what am I to do? We have no customers. Nobody got money. All I do is clean the same tings. But nothing ever get dirty. Soon, I tink we go out of business."

Instead of griping about hard-working German people, Swoop launched into his favorite rant. "Imagine standing over a blazing forge all day, sweat dripping down your brow, your hands singed by the searing heat. The air's thick with the stench of burning leather and hot metal. The heat presses down on you. Every breath is a struggle. Nothing is ever good enough for that wretched Sattlermeister. You have to shape the leather just so. Every stitch must be perfect. Every cut clean. It's like being trapped in a furnace."

Swoop began to pant, his eyes wide with the memory. "There's no escape." He looked at his hands as if they were still calloused and swollen. "Five years I spent, hammering, stitching, bending over a workbench till my back ached like the devil. And the leather—don't get me started on the leather—it's tough as nails, like wrestling a mule. But old Steinmetz was never satisfied. Nothing was ever good enough. He was lucky I didn't send him to the underworld when I left."

With a sigh, Swoop slumped in his chair. Just talking about the work he once did made him tired. He took a swig from his tankard and glanced out the window.

A rider on a fast horse galloped past the inn. Curious, Swoop rose from his seat and moved to the window just in time to see a tall young man dismount from a claybank dun in front of the doctor's office. When the young man turned his head, Swoop's spirits lifted. "Well, get a load of this. It's the kid. What in the tarnation is he doing *here*?"

Coyote followed Swoop to the window. "What luck!" He turned to Chaw, who hadn't bothered to leave his stool. "It's our favorite meal ticket."

Swoop watched the kid race into the doctor's office. A few minutes later, he emerged with a man who looked to be in his early forties. As they mounted up, Swoop ran his tongue across his teeth. "Nice looking horses." He glanced at Coyote, a greedy grin spreading across his partner's face.

Rubbing his chest with his knuckles, Swoop muttered, "Patience, knuckleheads. We must be patient."

Squat and Seph returned to the cow camp at a slow lope, the journey slowed by the swollen river they had to cross again. Fording on horseback was much easier without a herd of bellowing beeves, but Seph's mind was consumed by grief. Not long ago, he'd buried his mother. Now he had to bury his pal.

After dismounting, Seph walked beside Squat to the chuckwagon. He said nothing as Dunk recounted Slaw's final minutes to the trail boss.

Seph glanced at his friend's body. While he was in New Braunfels, Dunk had wrapped Slaw in a heavy wool blanket and tied it with rope at the knees.

Squat rubbed his chin. "The kid have any last wishes?"

Dunk nodded toward Seph. "He left his horse and gear to his buddy. That's about it. Good kid. Died a cowboy, just like he wanted." Dunk turned to Seph. "Want his boots?"

Seph shook his head fiercely. "No. He's gonna need 'em where he's goin'." He pictured a well-heeled cowboy surrounded by gleaming angels.

Squat asked, "Got a cup of coffee for me, Old Lady?"

True to his habit, Dunk turned his palm outward and rested it on his hip, as he did whenever somebody called him that. Meanwhile, Seph reached for a shovel. Dunk nodded at him while pouring the trail boss's coffee.

As Seph left camp, he frowned at the flooded river. It was late afternoon and the weather had finally improved. He was still soaked from fording the river and the hot sun felt pleasant on his shoulders as he searched for a good spot to bury Slaw.

He couldn't help thinking of his mother's grave. She had died only a month and thirteen days ago. He shuddered at the thought of his poor mother, buried in a casket made from bullet-riddled planks torn from the family's outhouse. He groaned, remembering the wolves and vultures that he had to chase away from her coffin before burying her.

He looked into the sky, as if appealing to the heavens for help, and shook his head.

Slaw had helped him bury Ma, but at the last minute, he dropped his end of the casket. Instead of climbing into the grave to rearrange her limbs, so that she could rest in peace, they hastily piled dirt over the coffin and hurried away.

It was hard to think of Ma now without feeling guilty. He should have taken the time to reposition her, but he couldn't bear to see her corpse again.

There weren't any hills, and Seph knew water would flood Slaw's grave if he dug too close to the river. Finally, he spotted a slope about a mile from camp that rose twenty feet above the waterway. He flipped the shovel so that the spade rested on his shoulder and marched like a soldier toward the incline.

The dirt felt heavy at first. He jumped on the blade, stomping its rounded edge into the soil. His thoughts drifted to his childhood, spent behind a mule and pushing a plow. Farming made him strong, taught him how to work hard, fed his family—and supported a trio of outlaws.

Thinking about the raiders always sparked anger. The last time they hit the family farm was right before Ma died. They'd grown reckless, calling each other by name, not caring that he could hear every word.

After having been robbed at least twice a year, he promised himself that he would not let them catch him without a rifle in his hand. Yet here he was, busting sod again, and he'd left his rifle back at camp.

Their names shuffled through his mind: Swoop, Coyote, and Chaw. It wasn't their fault Ma had died after the last raid, but it burned him to think of them helping themselves. If they had to rob the place, why wreck the barnyard too? He shut his eyes, recalling them toppling the chicken coop, busting the pigsty, and shooting up the outhouse.

What made him the maddest was when they waltzed into the house, helping themselves to food while Ma lay helpless in her sickbed. He couldn't protect her, and it gnawed at him knowing one of them held the cigar box with his girl's picture on the lid. They took his life savings and left him penniless.

He was lucky that Slaw's parents, Nells and Loretta Ballard, had taken him in. But how did he repay their kindness? By running off with Slaw in the middle of the night. Now their son was dead. How could he have let this happen?

The sun's warmth was no longer a comfort. He yanked off his shirt and tossed it aside, attacking the ground with a fury. Dirt flew over his shoulder in a frenzy. His mind went blank as his limbs moved fast and faster. It felt good to strain his muscles. Thunder surged through him as he drove the shovel ever deeper.

It was as if time stood still. What might have taken someone else all day seemed to take Seph no time at all.

A loud voice from behind startled Seph. He turned quickly, dropping the shovel. Blinking fast, as if he had just awakened from a nightmare, he leaped from the depths of Slaw's grave.

"Woah, boy. Ease up, Seph."

"Lullaby!" Seph leaped from the grave, blinking rapidly. "What're you doin' here?"

"We thought we'd help out. Take turns." Lullaby peered into the hole. "Wah! I almost can't see bottom. If I hadn't seen it myself, I wouldn't believe it. It's like..." Lullaby trailed off, whispering, "magic."

Seph took a deep breath as a breeze cooled his skin, gooseflesh prickling his arms. "You're exaggerating, friend."

Lullaby raised both eyebrows. "Exaggerating, huh. Sure, pal." The drover jumped into the grave, pitched out the shovel, and struggled to climb back up. As he emerged, he said, "Let's set a spell, Seph."

As they sat cross-legged, watching the rest of the crew approach, Lullaby said, "It's tough to bury a buddy. What was his given name?"

"Townsend Ballard," Seph replied.

"A fine name for a good man. He's with God now. Take comfort in that," Lullaby said, his tone reassuring.

"Would you mind saying a few words over his grave? Maybe recite some scripture. His family would appreciate it. So would I," Seph added.

Lullaby nodded, his voice rumbling deep. "I'd be honored. I'll say a prayer or two."

While the others gathered near the freshly-dug grave, Stoke ducked behind the chuckwagon. He glanced left and right, making sure he was alone. Reaching for the grease bucket hanging from the back of the wagon, he pulled the dipper through the hole on top and smeared a gooey gob on the seat of Seph Vermillion's saddle.

He chuckled to himself, imagining what might happen next. The kid could use the saddle as a pillow and end up getting foul-smelling grease all over his face. Most cowboys cradled their heads on their saddles while they slept.

Maybe he would be too tired to fetch his saddle after staying up the previous night. How foolish would the kid look, hopping into the saddle only to slip right off the other side?

Either way, it'd be a good laugh.

Too bad Stoke wouldn't be there to see it. Most likely, by the time the tenderfoot climbed into the saddle, Stoke would be way up the trail, riding point.

# CHAPTER 7

SEPH LIFTED HIS HEAD well after sunrise, sat up, and rubbed his eyes. It wasn't like him to sleep so long.

He remembered thinking about what to write in a letter to Slaw's family as he rested his head on the ground and gazed up at the stars. It was an empty feeling. A couple of mournful words came to mind, but he couldn't imagine scratching them onto a sheet of paper.

As he climbed to his feet, he imagined Slaw's family going about their day as if nothing were wrong, unaware that Slaw was dead. Seph shoved his hat onto his head and tipped the brim forward, covering his eyes. They needed to know.

He scratched the back of his neck and yawned. The idea of writing that letter to Slaw's family filled him with dread. Waiting wouldn't make it easier, but now he needed to get ready to move. Letter writing would have to wait.

His stomach growled and he looked over to where the chuckwagon had been. Knowing he'd missed breakfast made his gizzard feel like it was grinding against his spine. With a frown, he thought about the many meals he had missed growing up, with mostly empty shelves in the larder. He told himself he wasn't hungry and walked toward the herd.

Torp ran toward Seph, swinging his arms and shouting. When he caught up, he said, "There you are." Speaking rapidly while trying to catch his breath, Torp gasped, "Hurry up, lazy bones. I got your horse. It's time to go."

Seph made quick work of stepping into his boots and tossing his saddle onto his shoulder. But not quick enough to suit his partner.

"C'mon." Torp pointed urgently. There was a gap between the dutiful cattle that followed the procession and the stragglers that wouldn't move unless somebody forced them forward. Torp whined, "We'll spend all morning trying to catch up."

Seph frowned as he tossed his saddle on Win's back. When Torp said that he had his horse, Seph was expecting to ride Sheriff. He wasn't sure if he was ready to ride Slaw's mount.

His fallen friend wanted him to have his horse, but Seph didn't feel right about riding Win. It was too soon for his taste, but the remuda would have left shortly after the chuckwagon. There was no choice in the matter. Seph flopped the stirrup over the saddle and hastened to tie the cinch strap to the rigging dee.

Seph glanced at Torp and watched the kid mount up. Torp grabbed the saddle horn, jumped, and hoisted himself into the saddle with his arms, since his foot couldn't reach the stirrup from the ground. "Why does Chops always make me ride such tall horses?" Torp complained.

With a shrug, Seph flipped the fender and stirrup from the seat of his saddle into place. He thought about Torp and wondered when the kid would hit a growth spurt. Then he fixed his gaze on the beeves as he put his left boot in the stirrup. Torp would have an easier time of it if he were taller. Seph swung his leg over Win's rump. Instead of landing comfortably in the saddle, he overshot the seat. *What went wrong?* Instead of landing in the saddle, Seph slid over the edge and crashed onto the ground.

At first, Seph didn't notice that his partner was peeling with laughter and giddily slapping his thighs. He hurried to his feet, rubbing his sore shoulder. *That's never happened before.*

Seph made his way back to Win's left side, his brow furrowing as he glanced at the seat of the saddle. Earlier, he had been distracted, but now he noticed the shine and smelled the pungent grease slicked from horn to cantle.

He turned to face his partner and leaned forward. "You knew about this?"

Torp's laughter subsided, but he couldn't stop himself entirely. He said, "What?"

"My saddle," he growled, his voice booming. It wasn't common for Seph to raise his voice. "Somebody greased my saddle. And you're in on it?"

"What? Me? No." Torp turned his head to the side, then back again. "Gosh! Heck." He paused for a second before adding, "No, Seph."

Seph didn't believe Torp. Shaking his head in disappointment, he asked, "Why didn't you warn me?"

Torp answered seriously, his laughter completely gone. "I didn't know. I swear, Seph."

Seph said accusingly, "I would have warned you."

"But I didn't know. You gotta believe me."

"Alright, alright." Seph wasn't entirely sure he believed Torp, but there wasn't time to dwell on it. He turned his head, trying to figure out what to do next. Then he squatted, scooped a large handful of sandy dirt between his palms, and rubbed the trail dust over the seat of his saddle. Looking down, he noticed that his pant legs were also smeared with grease.

"Ugh. Bleh," he groaned.

Torp glanced at the beeves and warned, "We better get a move on, Seph. Booger's pushing them in the wrong direction."

Seph hastily sat on the ground and rubbed his thighs with dirt. Moving quickly, he remounted Win, making sure to stay in the saddle.

It took half the morning to round up Booger and the stragglers. They goaded the ornery critters forward, pushing them hard. It was tough to keep them moving fast enough to catch up.

Moving the stragglers was easier when there were three of them, but now there was just Seph and Torp riding drag. The kid did his best, but Seph felt like he was constantly looking Torp's way to make sure Torp was safe. It had been easier when Slaw rode to the right. It was as if Booger and the others knew that coverage was weaker on the left side. Torp struggled to keep them from breaking on the left, and sometimes Seph had to ride over to help.

The thought crossed Seph's mind, *It's bad enough having to ride drag and eating dust all day. Now, I gotta do the work of three guys.* He knocked his chin with a fist and felt guilty for letting such complaints cross his mind. Instead, he tried to figure out how he could help Torp become a better drover.

The first night out of New Braunfels, they bedded down the herd beside a small trickle of a creek. Late on the second day, they crossed the San Marcos River. They were lucky to find another barely flowing waterway on the third night, and a somewhat larger creek on the fourth.

On the fifth day, the cowboys were promised an easy ride. Squat had scouted ahead and told them that the Colorado River was just a couple of miles away. After crossing, they would stop for the night, and the cowboys could loaf about while the herd grazed.

First, Seph stood in line for breakfast. After a plate of corn mush, a thick hunk of bacon, and a swig of coffee, he queued up for a horse. He frowned when Chops dealt him a nasty brown mare named Hortense. The distinctive white blaze practically glowed in the dark. Some of the others were harder to identify, but Hortense was unforgettable.

Most of the barely broken horses liked to start the day with a bucking fit, but Hortense seemed to wait until a guy got comfortable in the saddle. Then she'd leap from the ground, twist violently to one side or the other, and if that didn't send a rider flying, she'd plant her hind legs firmly on the ground, rear up, and paw at the air. The first time Seph rode Hortense, it was all he could do to keep from being thrown.

After an hour on the trail, Seph saw Dusty approaching. It was rare to see the boss during the day. He generally rode near the front of the herd. Seph thought back to the day Dusty rode back with instructions for crossing the Guadalupe River—the day that Slaw died. He checked the skies. The weather didn't look threatening and the boss didn't appear hurried or worried.

"Howdy," Dusty said as he pulled up beside Seph and Hortense, who angrily threw her head in Dusty's direction. "Tough draw today," Dusty chuckled.

Seph nodded. "Yes, sir."

Dusty shook his head and frowned at Seph. "Better you than me." After a quiet moment, he pointed at a wide cow with a white body and a brown neck and head. "See that one?"

"I do. Ain't seen her before, but I see her now."

"Most critters take the same place in line every day. This one usually marches near the front, not far from the lead bull. You know, that brindled bull you brought in."

"Skillet?"

"Yeah. Skillet? Don't reckon I knew he had a name. Hmm." After a brief silence, Dusty continued. "Anyway, that wide cow probably won't make it to the river before dropping a calf. Here's what I need you to do: let Torp push the herd by himself. You stay with that cow. Shoot the calf after the cord snaps off. Drive the cow slowly back to the herd when she's ready."

Seph nodded dutifully.

Dusty looked at the rifle in Seph's scabbard and asked, "Rather use a pistol?"

Seph shrugged slightly and said, "Yes sir."

Dusty handed Seph one of his guns. "Don't forget to return that," he said with a grin.

Seph said, "I will." As the boss rode away, Seph rode over to tell Torp what the boss had said.

Torp blurted, "Okay. Alright. Gosh, Seph, I wouldn't want to have to do that."

Seph shrugged. "It don't worry me, Torp. I've butchered pigs and chickens. I guess you get used to doing what you've gotta do."

Seph carelessly dropped a rein and Hortense bolted forward. He reached for the saddle horn with his left hand and took the reins back into his right. Hortense skidded to a stop and started bucking. Instead of just twisting, she spun continuously. After completing several revolutions, she suddenly reversed direction and spun some more. Seph had anticipated her movements until she leaped into the air and corkscrewed to the left. Seph had leaned in the opposite direction, expecting her to twist to the right. He tipped further and further from the saddle and knew he was going down.

His last thought was about the position of his boots in the stirrups. He was still thinking about Slaw's foot getting caught and his body being dragged as he soared through the air. He felt like he was floating. He thought of Slaw, Ma, and the girl in the cigar box. Maybe it lasted only a fraction of a second, but it seemed much longer. He tried to curl into a ball and brace himself for impact.

Seph smacked into the dirt, sat up quickly, and gasped for air. It felt like he was drowning, even though he was on dry land. Desperation gripped him as he tried to suck air into his lungs. Each time he tried to inhale, he failed. Panicking, he gulped and gasped until finally, his lungs allowed him to take in air.

Torp appeared beside him, reached for his elbow, and squeezed. "It's okay, Seph. You just got the wind knocked out of you. It's happened to me a couple of times. Don't worry, you'll be okay in a minute."

Finally, after puffing a couple of breaths, Seph realized the kid was trying to comfort him. "Phew! I'm okay. Thanks, pard."

Seph made his way to his feet and Torp said, "I'll get your horse."

Seph looked over his shoulder and saw Hortense. Her head hung low, and her body pitched like a dog about to vomit. Seph never saw a horse do anything like it. She appeared to be watching him—laughing at him, even. He rubbed his temples. Did his head hit the ground when he was thrown? Then he felt a twinge in his shoulder—it was always that same shoulder. This time, he was afraid it might be broken.

Hortense didn't notice Torp. If she had, she might not have been caught.

Instead of mounting up, Seph led the mare a hundred feet forward. The cow was down and wouldn't get up again until the calf came. Seph waved at Torp as the kid rode away, nudging the stragglers toward the Colorado River. When Torp disappeared from sight at the tail end of the cattle drive, Seph watched the pregnant cow for a couple of minutes.

The white cow with the brown head and neck looked strange to him. He didn't feel like witnessing the miracle of new life that day. He wandered away and left the longhorn to its labor. He wasn't looking forward to shooting the calf after it took its first breaths, but it had to be done. There was no way to care for newborn calves on a cattle drive, and the boss's orders were clear. When he was alone, facing the western prairie, his thoughts returned to the still unwritten letter he dreaded having to send.

When the calf was born, Seph found it much more difficult than he had imagined to pull the trigger. He couldn't convince himself it was just a hog or a chicken. This calf had long, fluttering lashes, and its eyes shone. Seph took a few steps back, gritted his teeth, reminded himself that he was a man, and pulled the trigger.

Seph's limbs sagged when the calf dropped dead. Then he jumped as the skittish mare behind him bolted northward. He had neglected to tie Hortense securely, leaving her ground-tied, and the startling shot sent the skittish mare running.

He looked at the cow, still on the ground, and the cow looked back at him. *Cows are dumb.* How many times had he heard that? As he turned his back on the longhorn and began walking north, the image of the calf appeared in his mind. He couldn't blink it away.

Cowboys hated to walk, especially when they could ride, but Seph tried not to dwell on the fact that he was afoot. The long walk gave him time to think. In his mind, he arranged words and phrases, formed sentences, and resolved to finally write that letter to the Ballard family on Poesta Creek.

When he reached the wide Colorado River, he saw Hortense scaling the opposite bank. In the distance, he thought he saw a smudge of dust in the sky and figured the herd was there. Of course, the mare was on her way back to the remuda.

Not wanting to slog across the prairie in soggy clothes and wet boots, he stripped down and wrapped them in a bundle. He entered the cold water and waded as far as he could. If only he had secured that mare. It was challenging to swim on his side, but he managed to keep his right arm, boots, and clothes above water.

When he reached the opposite bank, he untied his bundle and waited for his skin to dry. He felt awkward and exposed, yet at the same time, he fantasized about being alone in an alpine wilderness and experienced a sense of freedom—until he heard a man laughing behind him.

"Hands in the air, farm boy."

Seph squeezed his eyes shut tightly. He recognized that voice, and the taunting laughter was unmistakable. In a flash, the feeling of liberation quickly shifted to a sense of being trapped. Seph thought of the rifle in its scabbard on Hortense's back, then remembered Dusty's pistol. The gun was nearby, tucked in his boot.

The man spoke again. "Get a load of this, boys."

Coyote said, "What's that kid doing here?"

Chaw added, "Ain't no point in robbing him today. Could steal his hat, but he ain't got nothing else."

Coyote said, "Looks like he's missed a few meals. What's the plan, Swoop?"

Seph started to turn his head to look at the outlaws, but didn't turn his body.

Swoop answered, "I always thought we'd ask the kid to join us someday, but he kept us so well fed it was better to leave him on the farm where he was. What happened, Seph?"

A wave of panic surged through Seph's gut. These men knew his name. How was that possible? A few seconds ticked by and he found himself at a loss for words.

Swoop growled. "What happened, brat?"

Seph gulped and blurted, "Ma died." He considered adding that he sold the farm. He opened his mouth to say the words but swallowed hard instead.

Then Swoop asked about the property.

"Gave it to the neighbor."

"That wasn't very smart, but you always were dim-witted. At least you work hard. Want to join up with us?"

That was the last thing Seph ever expected to hear. He repeated the question back to Swoop. "Do I want to join you? No way. I got a job already." As the words left his mouth, he worried that the outlaw might shoot him.

Swoop laughed recklessly. "Too good for us, are you? You should've never left the farm. It's alright. Stick to your cattle drive. Find your little horsey. Drive them moo cows through Injun country. Take good care of them critters for us."

Seph looked ahead, then turned his head back to glance at the outlaws over his shoulder again. "For us?"

Swoop spoke in a mocking tone. "Do I have to spell it out for you, child? You know how this works. You do all the work, and when you're done, we'll take over. *Comprende?*" The outlaw stepped forward and pressed the muzzle of a pistol into Seph's back, just beneath his left shoulder blade. "Can you keep a secret, Seph?"

Seph didn't answer.

Swoop's voice dropped to a near whisper. The threat was unmistakable. "If you tell the others, we'll kill them all. If you keep our secret, some of them will survive. The choice is yours, farm boy."

# CHAPTER 8

AFTER HORTENSE RETURNED RIDERLESS, Squat and Torp saddled up to search for Seph. They were just about to depart when Seph walked into camp.

Chops stood nearby, and Dusty stepped over cautiously. Without looking away from the brim of his overflowing tin cup of coffee, the ramrod asked, "What happened?"

Seph quickly explained and ended with an apology. "I should've tied that mare securely before shooting the calf. I'm sorry I had to leave the cow. I'll grab a horse and ride back for her." He knew that he should tell Dusty about the outlaws' threat, but he couldn't bring himself to do it. Not yet. But soon, he would have to tell them.

Chops asked, "How far back?"

Seph thought for a moment and answered, "Maybe three miles."

Chops chided, "Want me to get Hortense for you?"

Seph looked at the waddy, furrowed his brow and replied, "That mare's had enough of me for one day. What else you got?"

The wrangler chuckled and turned away. "I'll see what I can come up with." There were plenty of horses traveling with the Deatherage outfit. Few were fully broke, except for the cowboys' own horses.

Squat dismounted and said, "I'll let you boys bring that critter in."

Dusty added, "Best get a move on. After all, cows are money."

While the herd grazed through the afternoon and the cowboys loafed around, Seph and Torp returned for the white cow with the brown head. Seph was glad to have Torp along. It didn't take two cowboys to push one slow-moving critter along the trail, but it made the job easier.

Torp tried to strike up conversation along the way, but Seph didn't have much to say. Eventually, Torp gave up and rode quietly beside him.

Seph thought less and less about the dead calf. Instead, he couldn't stop thinking about the muzzle of Swoop's revolver pressed into his back. Hours later, he could still feel the cold metal poking into him, inches from his heart. The familiar feelings of being robbed, vandalized, and violated overwhelmed him. He thought he had left all that behind when he traded the farm to Nells Ballard.

As they rode, Seph constantly scanned the horizon, looking for trouble. He couldn't see Swoop, Coyote, and Chaw, but he knew they were out there. When Swoop had asked him to join them, Seph was shocked. There was no denying that the trio frightened him. He was powerless to fight them, but nothing they could have said would have convinced him to agree. He remembered thinking that he would have refused, even if they threatened to fill him with bullets—and even if they carried out that threat. *If only I could hunt those scoundrels down and rid the world of them.*

It was easy to think brave thoughts when riding a quiet trail. Why had the outlaws told him their plans? Wouldn't it have been better if they just surprised him instead of revealing their intentions? Did they really think he would keep their secret? What if he didn't? Squat, Dusty, Dunk, and Stoke had served in the war. Many of the cowboys had experience with guns. There were only three outlaws, after all. The numbers were on Deatherage's side. Seph knew telling the bosses was the right thing to do, but he needed to think through the problem from every angle before deciding for certain.

A fleeting thought niggled at Seph's mind. *What if it's* me *they're after?* The outlaws knew his name. They made it sound like it was his job to feed them, and they sounded perturbed about losing their so-called *meal ticket.* Seph glanced at Torp and considered riding away alone. Maybe, if he disappeared, the rest of the outfit could make it safely to Abilene.

Having fretted the whole way, Seph concluded that he could decide later what to do about the outlaws and telling the bosses. There was a valuable critter that needed saving first.

After hiding behind a large shrub and eluding them for an hour and a half, the obedient cow finally marched dutifully north, though she often bellowed as if calling out for her lost calf. Seph frowned every time she sounded off.

Seph and Torp were lucky that Dunk had set supper aside for them. They sat on the ground, hunched over tin plates, shoveling beans into their mouths well after dark. It was fortunate that neither of them had night watch, but morning came fast the next day.

Before dawn, Stoke cussed at Skillet, and the bull trotted to the front of the column, pointing north. Seph and Torp chatted with Dunk, who told the boys, "The next milestone is a hundred miles away."

Torp said, "The Brazos is next on the list, right?"

"That's right." Dunk looked at Seph and added, "There's a small city there, called Waco. You could post a letter if you wanted to."

Seph frowned. "How many days away is that?"

Dunk tapped his chin and looked at the sky before answering slowly, "Eight days, I'd say."

To Seph, that sounded like plenty of time to write a letter. Waiting made it harder, not easier. Instead of fretting, he should just sit down and put the facts to paper. There was nothing a man could say to make such hard news easy to take, even if he had a way with words. Seph considered talking with Dunk about the outlaws' threat but decided to tackle that problem when his letter was finished.

That night, after a fourteen-mile day, Seph sat by the campfire with a pencil and paper as the sun set. It had taken him half an hour to neatly print, "Dear Mr. and Mrs. Ballard, We rode to San Antonio and got a job driving cattle north." He paused to think about whether he should tell them about the Deatherage Longhorn Cattle Ranch or get straight to the bad news. Unable to decide, he set the paper aside as the rest of the men gathered around the fire.

Dusty, Thumbs, and Dredge took first watch. Squat was snoring beneath a blanket, and Dunk was busy tidying up the chuckwagon. Most of the cowboys sat cross-legged, slumped beside the fire. Stoke, however, paced around the fire circle. "How can you just sit there after being in the saddle all day?"

Nobody answered him.

He reversed his direction. "I may as well be talking to my horse."

The boys remained quiet.

"I swear. This is the dullest crew I've ever seen." He paced around the circle and stopped behind Seph. Jabbing a fistful of knuckles into that tender spot on the shoulder, Stoke challenged. "What are you afraid of, Nanny Joe Jo?"

Seph turned and sneered at Stoke but didn't answer.

"Your shadow? The wind? Something going to happen to your baby?"

Torp looked at Seph then looked back at Stoke. "What baby?"

The cowboys laughed but Torp looked confused.

Seph said, "Never mind about that, Torp."

Stoke laughed and stepped around the circle, stopping behind Lullaby. "What do you think God looks like? Me? You? Somebody else?"

In a low voice, the man answered the question with a question, "How should I know?"

"You talk to him all the time. I figure maybe you know him real good."

Lullaby said, "I talk to Him every chance I get. I tell Him everything, share my prayers with Him, and ask His forgiveness when I sin. But I don't know what He looks like."

"What if he appeared before you? Would you know it was him?"

"I expect so."

"How do you know I'm not God?"

"If God appeared before me, I would not look directly at Him. I would tip my head forward."

"How would you know it was him?"

"I have faith that I would know."

"How do you know I'm not God?"

"I have faith that you are not."

Stoke laughed and turned away. He didn't stop pacing when he asked his next question. "Anybody ever kill a man?"

The guys answered in a chorus. "No."

Stoke continued his orbit. "You really are a bunch of tenderfoots. Ain't you."

Woodsy boasted, "Someday I'm gonna shoot lots of men. I practice with my guns every chance I get. Maybe I'll become a lawman or a gunslinger, but there's lots of men need killing. That'll be *my* job. That's why I came west."

Stoke nodded, appearing to be impressed. "It's good to know that we got one good man to protect us if outlaws swoop down upon us. Maybe you can teach these other children how to use a gun, Twig."

Stoke stopped behind Wobble. "Got any whiskey on you?"

The gangly cowboy answered, "No. Why?"

"You look like a drinker. Always stumbling around. Ever been drunk?"

"No, sir."

"How old are you anyway? How old are you *really*?"

"Sixteen."

"Just a baby." Stoke changed direction again and stopped behind Torp. "What about you, Tommy?" Stoke asked in a mocking tone, "What's your true age?"

Torp didn't answer until Stoke nudged him forcefully in the small of the back with the side of his boot. In a quiet voice, Torp answered, "Fourteen."

In a loud voice, Stoke said, "What's that, sonny? I didn't hear you."

In a louder voice, Torp said, "Fourteen."

Stoke moved on, tsking and said, "Don't worry, Tommy. Old Lady and Nanny Joe Jo will take care of you."

Seph considered getting up and wandering away. Stoke's attempts at sparking an *interesting* conversation annoyed him. It seemed to him that the cowboy was trying to rile up a crowd and spark a controversy. Maybe even start a fight.

Stoke said, "Who is afraid of ghosts?"

Conjure answered, "I am."

"What about the shadows?"

"That too. All of that stuff—spirits, ghouls, demons." He shuddered at the thought. "I wish the sun never set." He turned his head and he looked off into the darkness. "Nothing good ever happens at night."

Stoke laughed. "Is that a fact?" He walked briskly around the fire and answered his own question. "No, Conjure. That is *not* true. When we get to Abilene, you'll see for yourself. A lot of good stuff happens at night. Anybody ever been with a woman?"

Several cowboys groaned. Chops, the pimply-skinned wrangler piped in, "I did. Last year."

Seph turned his head and listened closely.

"It happened in St. Louis. First, I got lucky playing faro. Three calico queens pushed and shoved each other. I couldn't believe what was happening. The biggest one dragged me upstairs. She squeezed my arms, told me I was strong, and when *it* happened, she couldn't stop squealing. When it was over, she said I was the best there ever was. She took half my winnings and told me to come back again real soon. Don't know why I left St. Louis."

When Chops was done, Stoke laughed at him. "Maybe you should go back to St. Louis." Shaking his head, he added, "Best there ever was, huh? Whores always say that." He took a few more steps around the ring and said, "Anybody else been with a woman?"

Conjure, the cowpoke who feared ghosts said, "I almost did."

Stoke encouraged him. "Almost? Really. How do you *almost* did?"

Conjure was always keen on telling stories about home. The way he went on about his mother, the family dog, Bonnie, his brothers and sisters, and the girl next door made most of the fellas long for the things they left behind.

Seph listened to Conjure talk about a wholesome girl named Mary and thought about the beautiful woman on the inside lid of his cigar box.

Conjure wasn't in any hurry to finish his story. "It was late one afternoon. I stopped by for a visit and hoped I might steal a kiss on the porch when it was time to leave. But there was nobody home, except for Mary. Sweet, pretty Mary. The family went to visit aunts, uncles, and cousins, but Mary told them she didn't feel like visiting." Conjure looked up from staring at the embers and smiled.

He drew a wistful sigh and continued, "Turns out, Mary *did* feel like visiting. With me, that is. I couldn't believe my luck, stopping by when I did. I don't remember what we talked about, but when she asked me if I wanted to kiss her, I admitted that I did. It wasn't like our usual, Saturday evening kisses. This kiss didn't stop. My head spun. I lost my mind. All of a sudden, she had her hands down my pants. When she touched me, I thought I would explode. When my trousers hit the floor, the front door flung open and her pa ran me out of the house. Then he run me out of town and told me never to come back. When I get paid, I'm going back to steal my Mary away. I reckon that counts for an *almost*." Conjure gently tapped his hand over his heart. "My darling Mary."

Hork spoiled Conjure's tender moment with a rapid fire string of questions. "How does it work with them whores, Stoke? What do you say? How much do you pay them? Where do you go? What do you... do? Do you pay them first or after? How do you know when it's over and done? And then what, do you just leave?"

Seph was glad somebody asked. He wouldn't have admitted it, but he was curious too.

Stoke rubbed his hands together as if he were trying to warm his palms. The top hand finally seemed to be enjoying a conversation. "Well, let's see," he began. "Do you all know the basics?" Most of the guys nodded, but Torp did not.

Tentatively, Torp inquired. "Can you keep your clothes on?"

Stoke frowned and shook his head. He began, "You got a tallywag. She's got a tulip." Several jaws dropped when Stoke explained in great detail how doing a bit of business with a calico queen worked. When he described the coupling's combustible conclusion, several of the guys gasped and Torp covered his face.

Wobble's voice cracked. "What if it doesn't work? What if I get scared and chicken out? Do I still gotta pay?"

Stoke answered. "If it doesn't work you gotta pay double. If you chicken out you have to pay triple. So make sure you've got enough coin on you, just in case."

Seph wondered whether everything Stoke was saying was true. Would the man make up stuff that wasn't true?

Conjure repeated his unanswered questions.

Stoke took them one at a time. "What do you say? Well, with whores it's the opposite. Whatever you say is backwards. Instead of telling her she's pretty, you gotta say she looks like a witch or a troll. If she asks you if you like it, you say no—you hate it. Get it?"

Conjure gasped, "Gosh. Why?"

"It's kind of like a game, you see. I don't know why, that's just how it's played. It's probably been that way since the beginning of time." Stoke went on to warn the boys about what could happen in rare cases. He described potentially grisly outcomes in elaborate detail and concluded, "It almost never happens, but I thought you should know—just in case. I say, it's worth the risk."

Torp covered his ears and began to wheeze.

Dunk stepped forward as Stoke's lecture concluded. "I reckon I've heard everything now. All you boys better head off to bed. Remember this: never call a cowboy a liar but don't believe everything he tells you either. If it sounds crazy, beware. If he tells too many tall tales, don't believe *anything* he says. If you spend all night thinking about the whores in Abilene, you'll never get any sleep. Tomorrow will be a long day."

In the morning, several cowboys had questions for Dunk. Seph decided to wait until later to make inquiries. Others may have lost sleep thinking about the fancy girls at the end of the trail, but Seph was still stuck on the task of writing a letter to Slaw's family. That, and what to do about the outlaws' threats.

Late that afternoon, Seph walked to the edge of Brushy Creek, flipped an empty wooden bucket, and sat on the bottom of the pail. He read out loud what he wrote the night before. "Dear Mr. and Mrs. Ballard, We rode to San Antonio and got a job driving cattle north." He checked the spelling in his head and added another sentence. "We signed on with the Deatherage Longhorn Cattle Ranch."

The next night, beside the San Gabriel River, Seph added, "Towns worked hard to help round up mavericks."

On the fourth night, seated beside the bank of a large pond, Seph wrote, "I don't know how else to tell you this. Tragically, Towns was killed at the Guadalupe River." It seemed unnatural to use his given name rather than Slaw.

At Salado Creek, Seph penciled, "A disagreeable steer charged his horse, Towns got throwed, and his foot got caught in the stirrup."

Along the Leon River, Seph labored to come up with the next sentence. He finally committed to saying, "I'm real sorry we rode off the way we did."

All the way to Cow Creek, Seph thought about how to put down what he wanted to write next. The page was a little more than halfway full of words. Whatever needed saying, he'd best come up with it soon. Beside Cow Creek, Seph printed, "There's nothing Towns liked better or wanted more than being a cowboy. He said it was his dream come true."

Finally, the next evening, they reached the Brazos River. Seph had planned to post the letter in Waco. To leave room for a signature at the bottom of the page, Seph gripped the pencil tightly and wrote his letters smaller. "Towns left his horse and gear to me but I don't feel right keeping them. I'll bring them by as soon as I can."

When the letter was finished, he looked at the page. He thought it looked like it was written by a child and considered asking somebody to copy it over for him. It said everything it needed to say, but he couldn't think of what to put before his signature. He didn't like the sound of your servant, sincerely yours, or your friend.

Seph said a brief prayer, glanced toward the heavens, and folded the piece of paper. It wouldn't be done until he wrote his name at the bottom and even then, it still had to be delivered to a postmaster. It would have to wait. Seph had night watch from dark to midnight.

Seph rode clockwise around the herd. Thumbs and Dredge rode in the opposite direction. Their paths crossed near the banks of the Brazos River and Seph was well out of sight when Swoop emerged from the darkness, flanked by Coyote and Chaw. All three had their guns drawn.

In a cheerful voice, Swoop ordered, "Hands up, fellas."

Thumbs and Dredge looked at each other. They were surprised, but Swoop didn't think the experienced cowboys looked shocked.

Dredge said, "We knew somebody was out there."

Swoop instructed them to join their hands together on their heads and slide off their horses. Swoop smiled and said, "Today's your lucky day, fellas."

Thumbs grumbled, "How do you figure?"

Swoop answered, "Instead of working for short pay, you'll work for us and we'll pay you equal shares. That's one fifth for each of us."

Dredge said, "And what if we refuse?"

Swoop tilted his head and replied. "It's a free country. The choice is up to you. If you refuse, we'll slit your throats and split the take three ways. What's it gonna be, friends?"

# CHAPTER 9

SWOOP DIDN'T HAVE TO wait long for a reply.

Thumbs said, "Equal shares beats riding for short pay any day. Fact is, we've been waiting for our luck to change."

Dredge added, "Your way sounds better than what we done planned and I don't feel like getting my throat cut today. What do you want us to do?"

Swoop said, "Good, good." He paused for a moment and nodded slowly before continuing. "I can tell we're going to get along just fine. Let's get better acquainted. This here is Coyote, and that there is Chaw."

When Dredge repeated his question, Swoop tipped his hat forward and answered, "It's simple, really. Stay with the herd. Keep doing what you're doing as if nothing has changed. Find out their weaknesses and report them to us whenever you can. Meanwhile, we'll let those addlebrained cowboys do all the work, grind 'em down every chance we get, and before they reach Abilene, we'll take the beeves. Because we ain't rustlers. Rustlers take a critter here and there. No siree. We're gonna take them all."

Thumbs and Dredge looked at each other, nodded in unison, and turned back toward Swoop. Thumbs spoke for the pair. "You got yourself a deal, boss. I see why they call you Swoop. Fits you good."

In the morning as the cowboys waited in line for breakfast, Dusty announced that they would lay by. The grass was lush and plentiful. "It'll do the herd good to graze."

Stoke slapped a hand on Dredge's back and shouted, "Let's go to town." A chorus of cheers followed Stoke's suggestion.

Dusty growled, "No. Until we get to Abilene, no towns."

The men groaned.

Stoke appealed. "Cut us some slack, boss."

Dusty cursed and threatened. "If you must go to town, draw your pay. You signed on to do a job. Long as we got a herd, you'll stick with them." Thumbs and Dredge glanced at each other. Stoke sneered, and Dusty continued, "Save your carousing. Plenty of time for that when the herd is sold. Dunk can go for provisions. If Seph wants to mail a letter, he can tag along, but that's it."

Stoke cast a murderous glare at Seph but held his tongue.

Wobble blurted, "I hate cows. I really do." He stomped a foot and added, "Don't care about carousing, but it would sure be nice to get away from these brutes for a couple of hours."

With a judgmental scowl, Dusty poured himself some coffee and shook his head. "A drover that don't like cows. Better find you a new line of work after we reach the end of the trail, Wobble." Several cowboys chuckled and Seph wondered whether they agreed with Wobble or Dusty.

Finally, breakfast was ready and Dunk's line began moving. The cowhands dispersed quickly. Most of the guys made their way to the river. Seph waited until Dunk was alone and said, "I ain't ready to mail that letter yet."

Dunk turned away from the chuckwagon and said, "Sometimes words fail us. You don't need to be a poet. Just write down what needs saying. Best to not put it off too long, Seph."

With a frown, Seph looked down at his feet and ground a heel into the dirt. "I know. I'll post it in the next town, for sure. What's the next town?"

"Fort Worth is about ninety miles north. Most folks call it Cowtown."

Seph nodded and thought about a town so important it deserved two names, rather than just one.

Dunk added, "I'll definitely need to resupply by then. Think you can get that letter done by next week?"

Seph was done with the letter already. All he had to do was sign off and let it go. He rubbed his eyes and yawned. "Yeah." He didn't figure his voice sounded very reassuring. He tried to sound more confident and added, "Reckon so."

That day, temperatures soared. It was as if spring gave way to summer all at once. It was a good day to idle beside a swiftly-flowing river, but the menacing afternoon heat was just the beginning. As if it weren't hot enough, Dunk spent several hours showing Seph how to shoe horses while the other cowboys loafed around.

Overnight, the temperature remained above seventy degrees. After a day off, as they departed from the Brazos River, Dunk warned the crew, "Make sure those canteens are full. It's gonna be a hot one." If the temperature didn't top one hundred degrees that day, it came close.

The early summer heatwave persisted and one sweltering day followed another. The beeves plodded along and the cowboys quietly grumbled complaints, mostly under their breaths and pined for cooler weather. After trudging seventy-five miles in six days, they reached Deer Creek. It wasn't much of a waterway, but it was the best they'd encountered since the Brazos. Once the herd was bedded down, most of the crew made their way to the water's edge.

Seph washed his socks and wrung them out before soaking his feet in Deer Creek. The cool water felt good between his toes. He pulled his unfinished letter to the Ballard family from his vest pocket. Tomorrow they would reach the West Fork of the Trinity River and Fort Worth. After that, they would truly leave civilization behind.

It had gotten to the point where just thinking about finishing that letter made him sick to his stomach. On the other hand, that uncompleted task weighed on him. He marveled to think how heavy a single sheet of paper could be. Yet still, he couldn't think of how to end it.

As he was contemplating what words to use, Lullaby approached, cleared his throat, and asked if Seph would welcome some company. Lullaby sat beside Seph and pulled his boots off. "That looks heavenly," he said, looking toward Seph's feet. Lullaby snapped his socks off, wiggled his toes, then dipped them in the creek. "Praise the Lord! How refreshing."

After sitting a spell, Lullaby inquired, "What's that you got there?"

Seph looked quickly at Lullaby and answered. "It's that letter to Slaw's family. I just gotta finish it."

"Stuck for words?"

"Yeah."

"Let's pray for inspiration." Lullaby closed his eyes and tipped his head. After a couple of moments, he opened his eyes and turned his head. "Maybe I can help."

Seph read the letter he had written and showed Lullaby how much space was left on the page. "I don't know how to end it. I could just write my name, but I don't know."

Lullaby said, "May you find comfort in God's grace."

Seph hesitated. He understood Lullaby had a way of putting things and managed to frequently work his reverence for the Lord into conversations. Finally, Seph said, "Thanks, pal. That's kind of you to say."

When Lullaby began to chuckle, Seph looked at him. Lullaby clarified, "I meant to suggest you could close your letter with those words."

"Oh." Seph had to think quick to recapture them before forgetting. He repeated the phrase and splashed his feet in the water. "Why, that's perfect! Then what, just my name?"

"Hmm. That would do, or you could use a phrase like *Slaw's friend*."

"Yeah. That's good. How about, *Towns' partner*."

Lullaby's low voice sounded reassuring. "That should do fine, Seph. I'd say go with that."

Seph read the words out loud as he neatly printed them in the remaining space on the page. "May you find comfort in God's grace. Towns' partner, Seph." As he folded the page and returned it to his pocket, he thought about how much he had suffered over those final words.

If his friend wasn't gone before, now that the letter was done, Seph had to fully accept that his only childhood friend was dead. If it wasn't for Lullaby, he wasn't sure if he could have found the right words. He had almost reconciled himself to ending abruptly and just writing his name at the bottom of the page.

Lullaby rolled his trousers up from his ankles to his knees and moaned as he lowered his calves into the cool water. "You know, Seph, when you find yourself at a loss it might help you to appeal to God for guidance."

"You mean, say a prayer?" Seph thought about how Ma had taught him to read the Bible before dementia overtook her. It was the only book in the house. He diligently read the good book, but often didn't understand what the words meant, stuck together. "I never felt like troubling God with my worries."

"That's humble. I think God appreciates humility, but whatever burdens weigh you down, He can take it. Don't be afraid to lean on Him. Would you pray with me?"

Seph nodded. *Should he clasp his hands together like he did when he was a child, kneeling beside his bed?* He watched Lullaby from the corner of his eye to see what the cowboy did.

Lullaby tipped his head forward but did not close his eyes. He gazed at the water's surface and began to speak. "Oh Lord, we give thanks for this fine day. Show us the way so that we may never be lost. Guide us so that we may navigate the rugged terrain. Grant us the fortitude to confront the rigors of the trail. Challenge us so that we may prove our devotion to You."

Seph wondered whether Lullaby made up the words on the spot or had memorized them.

"Protect us and bless our endeavor, oh Lord. Strengthen us so that we may face adversity with Grace. Shield us from disasters such as prairie fires, floods, tornados, and stampedes. Deliver us from evil, whether in the form of spirits or the hazards posed by our fellow man."

Seph closed his eyes tightly as he considered the potential disasters Lullaby had mentioned. As the prayer went on, Seph wondered whether the cowboy should be a preacher rather than a drover.

"Watch over the herd, bless our river crossings, fill us with courage, and provide us with sustenance. *Humbly,* I beseech Thee, help me guide my fellow cowboys so that they may follow Thee, be patient with those who fail to find the right path. Forgive our sins, though they be numerous. Should disaster befall us, oh Lord, have mercy on our souls. Amen."

Though Seph had not worshiped the Lord in church, he knew to add his own, "Amen." When he inquired, Lullaby answered that the prayer was spontaneous. Seph told Lullaby, "You sure have a way with words."

As Lullaby pulled a fresh pair of socks from his pocket, Torp ran toward Deer River, throwing clothes off as he went, and splashed into the water. Sometimes, Seph forgot how much younger Torp was.

Torp sat near Seph as they ate supper. When they were finished, Torp whined, "Stoke asked me if you changed my diapers and burped me after meals. He's calling me a baby, ain't he?"

Seph wanted to lie to the kid, but couldn't do it. "Some people like to be mean, Torp. I know it is hard to overlook, but sometimes I don't think they can help it."

"But doesn't he know I work hard and help? I ain't no baby. Maybe I'm not fully-grown, but I do a man's work, don't I?"

Seph attempted to reassure Torp, but the kid didn't seem to respond as Seph hoped he would. If only he could get Stoke to leave Torp alone. He wondered what it would take.

Torp whispered, "What about the whores? All that scary stuff ain't true. It can't be. Those things Stoke said."

"I'm sure they're not true, Torp."

"But I can't stop thinking about it."

"You shouldn't have to worry about that. You don't have to visit the whores. I don't think Lullaby is going. You could stay with him. Who knows, I might not go either."

"But that's the thing, Seph. I *want* to go. I don't care if it *is* true." Torp's trembling whisper became even fainter. "It's worth the risk. It's all I think about, all day long, at least when the doggies are behaving."

Seph thought about his girl. He didn't like thinking about her when others were nearby. He'd been longing for her since he was younger than Torp. Seph reached over and shoved the kid's shoulder. "I know the feeling. Try to forget about it. It's a long way to Abilene, Torp. Plenty of time to worry about whores later." He excused himself and climbed to his feet.

The sun had set but the heat hung stubbornly in the air. A soothing breeze would have been welcome. Seph strolled away from the comfort of the campfire. Often, in the evening, he liked to spend time among the horses. He made his way to the remuda and sought out Sheriff. Though he only got to ride his horse every second or third day, he found it comforting to stroke Sheriff's soft muzzle. Even if there was plenty of green grass to graze on, Seph tried to find something to bring his horse. The way Sheriff held his head whenever Seph was around made him feel as if they were friends.

"Howdy."

Seph turned quickly. He hadn't expected to run into anybody. "Blaze!"

A grunt confirmed it. The cowboy said, "Remember what Squat said?"

"What?"

"That first day. Remember what the boss said about falling in love with a horse? You done it."

Sheriff muzzled Seph's back playfully. A defensive retort crossed his mind but he tamped it down. Instead he said, "I was already in love with this horse before that day. Besides, I think Squat was just trying to be funny."

Blaze snapped, "Why? It is not funny." After a moment, he continued in a more agreeable manner. "But *you* understand the spirit of a horse. I can tell. It is good to fall in love with a horse, not bad. But you are lucky. You own the horse." He turned and ran a hand across the back of a slate gray mustang with a black mane and tale. "This is Noomoo, Lipan Apache for Wind." Blaze ran his hand down Noomoo's neck and patted the mare's chest. "She is very fast. When I ride her, we are one. One day, I will own Noomoo. I don't care what it costs me."

Seph complimented Blaze on his choice of horse.

"Do you want to learn how to ride like Indians?"

Without thinking, Seph answered, "Sure. But what do you mean? Like, trick riding?"

Blaze nodded and said, "It would be better if you were small, but I will show you how. Can you pick up a hat on the ground while riding by?"

"No."

"Can you hang over the edge and ride invisible?"

"No."

"Can you ride without a saddle?"

"I don't know. I reckon so."

"Better know for sure. Next time we get a day off, I'll show you."

Seph thanked Blaze and admitted it would please him to learn.

After a quiet moment, Blaze said, "Did you hear that?"

"Maybe."

Blaze pointed to a spot near Deer Creek. He said, "Do you know we're being followed?"

Seph was sure that Blaze could see the frown on his face even in the darkness. "I've had a bad feeling about that."

Blaze shot back. "It is not a feeling. You can see their sign everywhere. Maybe they think they are clever but it is not hard to know they are there. Do you think the bosses know?"

Seph shrugged. "Squat's our scout. If the sign is everywhere, he must know, right?"

Blaze grumbled. "Hmm. I am not sure."

Seph replied. "We need to be sure he knows. I will tell him. One of these days, I'll tell them we're being followed." He rubbed his chin and considered Swoop's threat. Why not let Blaze tell Squat? It seemed like a good idea, but Seph dismissed it. The bosses needed to know about Swoop's threatening words. He hated to admit knowing the bandits and felt guilty about leading them to the Deatherage outfit's cattle drive.

Yet he kept putting it off.

It was a long ride from Deer Creek to the Trinity River. Most days, they traveled twelve or thirteen miles, but to reach Fort Worth in a day required a fifteen-mile trudge. After six hot, dry days, the seventh was hotter still. They had no way of measuring the temperature, but there was no doubt that it was well above a hundred degrees. Squat and Dusty spent most of the day bringing the crew fresh canteens.

Seph spent half the day wishing the wind would blow. Even the slightest of a breeze would have brought a measure of comfort. It was so hot, with the blazing sun beating on his shoulders and back, that merely riding at a slow walk caused him to sweat profusely. He thought about Deer Creek the night before and longed to soak in cold river water.

Several times during the day, a howling wind picked up, lifting dust and gravel from the trail, and mercilessly pelting the crew. The tempestuous wind seemed even hotter than the stagnant air, as if it had blown in from a furnace or forge. Even with his neckerchief securely tied over his face, it was impossible to keep the swirling sand from his mouth and nose. He squinted so hard he could barely see and he had to resist the urge to try and blink the dirt from his eyes. Doing so would only invite in more.

Seph had spent most of his days outdoors but couldn't remember a day that alternated between hot sun with no wind, and howling winds with no clouds or rain. He had heard that sometimes cowboys' minds wander away and never return. Perhaps, he thought, the weather was the cause.

At drag, Torp complained about the heat and kept removing his hat. Every time Seph saw him fanning himself with his hat, he rode over and told the kid to put his hat back on. Finally, Seph said, "That sun will burn your face and then you'll be even more miserable." He felt like he was talking to a child. He knew how sensitive Torp was about his age but was too hot to care about the kid's feelings.

For emphasis, he added, "Don't let me catch you taking that hat off again, Torp."

Squat and Dusty would have liked to cross the river at the end of the day, but knew better than to push the crew and longhorns any further. It was more than enough to reach the banks of the Trinity. As soon as camp chores were tended, everybody piled into the river, leaving Dunk to toil over supper by himself.

Instead of complaining, Dunk brought the boys' dinner plates to the river and let the hungry men soak in the cool water as they ate. Nobody said much. They were far too tired to converse, tell stories, or banter. Even Stoke seemed content to sit still quietly in the cool water.

Early in the morning, the cowboys saddled up and prepared to cross the Trinity. After that, they would take the rest of the day off and let the beeves graze. When Dunk and Seph went to town, the rest of the cowboys would take it easy.

As Seph rode up to the herd he noticed that his fellow cowboys had stopped. It was rare to see them all looking at the same thing. He glanced about to see what they were looking at. When he saw Booger, his back bent and his chest deflated. Somebody had scratched words onto Booger's side in charcoal. Seph didn't need to squint at the maverick albino. He wished it didn't, but it made him mad to see the words: "Nanny Joe Jo's Pet" on the steer's hide.

Seph didn't wonder who done it. He wanted to strangle Stoke.

# CHAPTER 10

INSTEAD, SEPH RODE FORWARD as if nothing had happened. He began nudging the herd across the river, starting with Booger.

As he worked, he thought about Stoke. He had figured that by now, the top hand would have grown tired of the mean-spirited pranks. Most of the time, the bosses ignored how Stoke treated the cowboys, especially Seph. Seph thought about a conversation he had with Chops a couple of nights earlier. The boss told Chops that men had to work things out, just as the horses did. Sometimes that meant nipping at each other's heels or delivering a powerful kick to establish their rightful place in the herd. Chops quoted Dusty, "What do I care which cowboy is top dog, long as they know I'm boss?"

Did Seph aspire to become top hand? He felt as if he had learned a lot, and did more than his share, but all he wanted was to get through that first drive, draw his half pay, and get hired on for full wages next year.

Overlooking Stoke's frequent need to put Seph in his place didn't seem to improve the situation. How long could he ignore the brute? When Seph signed on with the Dagger D, Angry R, he figured he could weather the storm. He still thought that eventually, Stoke would tire of tormenting him. Nevertheless, Seph continued training with Dunk, and practiced throwing fists at imaginary foes when he was alone.

What's more, Seph no longer dreaded the notion of a fight with Stoke.

When they reached the other side of the river, as Seph prepared to ride into town with Dusty, Torp stomped up to him, hands on his hips, and whined, "Why did you have to yell at me?"

Seph stood and remembered how he had been short with his pint-sized partner. What could he say? That he hoped to spare him the agony of a nasty sunburn?

Torp's mouth turned down at the corners, and Seph could see the hurt in his eyes.

Torp leaned forward and added, "Everybody always yells at me. Only *you* treat me like I'm not a child. Now you've gone and spoiled it."

After a moment of searching for the right words, Seph made a feeble apology. Torp turned heel and stomped off without another word.

Stoke and Torp were still on Seph's mind as he rode with Dunk from cow camp to Cowtown. It was a short two mile ride. A couple of times, Seph turned to look at the camp cook, but Seph didn't feel like talking. It seemed that Dunk had a way of knowing when Seph needed to stew in his thoughts and when he needed to confide in somebody.

Seph tried not to think about the letter in his pocket and the heartbreak his written words would cause Slaw's family. It was too late to change what had happened, and there was no more time to search for the perfect words. The ones scrawled on weathered paper would have to do. It was as if the tragedy was in the crude envelope rather than back on the banks of the Guadalupe River.

For a couple minutes, Seph was distracted by thoughts of long lost siblings. Then, the changing scenery caught his eye and focused his attention on his surroundings.

They rode into town along Weatherford Street. Dunk stopped at a tanner's shop and directed Seph to the mercantile a couple of blocks away.

Seph glanced at a string of vagrants as he rode past them, and turned onto Rusk Street.

Seph saw an emaciated man, clothed in rags, sitting on the ground in front of a dry goods store. The weathered man had his back against a stout banister supporting a hitching post. Seph avoided strangers whenever he could, but something about the man beckoned him forward. He loosened his hold on the reins and let Sheriff make his own, slow way. The claybank seemed as drawn to the seated man as his rider, or maybe Seph's favorite steed was lured by hopes of idling beside the rail.

It felt to Seph as if their paths were destined to cross. Their meeting was unavoidable but not urgent. As Sheriff's hoofs clopped quietly up the dirt street, Seph tried to guess the idler's story.

The man turned his head and looked at Seph. It was unusual for strangers to look at each other for too long. It occurred to Seph that he should look away, but he couldn't make himself do so. The stranger had long hair, a flowing beard, and the most unusual eyes Seph had ever seen. Most people had brown, blue, or green eyes, but this man's eyes were golden.

From the corner of his eye, Seph noticed that the man's left arm was missing and surmised that he had lost his limb in the war. He finally looked away from the man and said, "Howdy, friend," as he swung his leg over Sheriff's back and dismounted, casually draping the reins over the post rail.

As Seph turned away from the dun, the one-armed man said, "Always knew you'd come. I've been waiting for you."

Seph tipped his head forward and lowered his eyebrows skeptically. Did he say that to every stranger he met? He felt bad for the man, wished he could do something to help him, and yet, there was something off-putting about him. Seph didn't know what to say in response and was about to ask if he could help him to his feet when the man reached across his chest and scratched the shoulder above his missing arm.

"Dangdest thing. Arm's been gone five years, but it itches like crazy. Scratching my shoulder don't help, but what else can I do?" He reached for the hitching post's top rail, and dragged his wobbly body from the ground. Then, he reached to the ground and retrieved a tin cup. Seph noticed the rattle of coins as the man straightened his body and looked back at him.

"Where's my manners?" the man said, carefully balanced the cup on the rail. "Name's Charlie." He extended his good arm and Seph accepted it, gently at first and then matched the frail man's firm grip as it tightened. "Charlie Coppedge." Their handshake ended and the man continued, "Knew your father, son."

Seph stepped back. How could such a thing be possible? He couldn't help noticing the man spoke of his father in the past tense. In a flash, he thought about Ma and how difficult it was to make sense of anything she said in the years before she died. Maybe this old fella suffered the same way Ma did.

Seph turned his head, uncertain of what to say or do next and noticed the gleam in Charlie's golden eye. Seph's throat felt dry, but he couldn't ignore what the man said. Seph croaked, "You did?"

The old man nodded and then stroked his beard. Seph thought he looked like one of the begetters from Ma's Bible. Was he some kind of ancient prophet?

Neither man said anything. It was as if the fellow waited for Seph to say something, but Seph was aware that he had spoken last, and the old man hadn't responded to his question, other than to nod. Finally, Seph realized that the man had given his name without reciprocation. "Name's Seph, sir."

"You have the same squinty eyes."

"Sir?"

"I'd know you anywhere." The man grimaced and scratched his shoulder again. Then, he smacked his lips and said, "Buy me lunch and I'll tell you about the war."

Seph glanced at the sign on the false front of the mercantile, thought of his errands, and the heavy letter in his saddlebags that needed to be posted. He should tend to his tasks and get back to the herd. He didn't have time to entertain an old man, but he couldn't bring himself to deny Charlie's request. Frowning, Seph said, "I'd like that."

Charlie grunted and pointed a knobby finger toward a humble café across the street. A simple sign over the door said, "Stew."

Seph glanced at Sheriff and Charlie told him not to worry. "We can watch the dun from the window." Seph nodded, dipped a hand into his saddle bag, and retrieved his drawstring coin pouch.

As they made their way across the street, Seph feared the old man might not make it. He didn't figure Charlie weighed a hundred pounds and wondered when he last ate. The waitress frowned as she brought Charlie a big bowl of stew and a small loaf of bread. She confirmed, "Sure you don't want anything, cowboy?"

Seph nodded. "Yes ma'am. Not hungry." Then, he sat quietly while Charlie ate. It pleased him to hear the man. The humming sounds he made remind him of Lullaby's late-night cattle mollifying serenades.

Charlie ate slowly, relishing every bite, and slurped lustily as he spooned the last of the broth from a big spoon. When he was finished, he pushed the bowl away, sat back and looked at the young man across from him. "I got bad news for you and I'm afraid it's gonna hurt. Fact is, after all these years, it still pains me to think about it." He spun his tongue around inside of his mouth, as if making sure there were no remnants of stew left to be swallowed, all the while watching Seph. "You don't believe I knew your pa, do ya?"

Seph shrugged and said, "Half the time, I never know what to believe."

Charlie held his belly and laughed deeply. "I know what you mean." After a pause, he clarified, "Either a destitute old man just swindled you out of a free meal, or your Pa was my pal, Sébastien Vermillion."

Seph gulped and gripped the sides of the table. So it was true. Somehow, the old man knew who he was. He had the sensation of a wave of goosebumps rising on his arms and legs. Questions ricocheted in his mind and his lips bumbled for something to say.

"Quiet, son. I'm afraid there's more." The waitress took Charlie's bowl and offered to wrap the loaf in paper, for later. When she was gone, Charlie leaned forward. "You look exactly the way I imagined you would. I must have had the same dream a hundred times, only it didn't come with a hearty meal."

Charlie's head lolled forward and Seph was afraid that he had fallen asleep in the middle of their conversation. Charlie looked back up and said, "You're a fine boy. I'd have been proud to have a son like you." He wrinkled his nose, like a rabbit does, and Seph was afraid that Charlie might weep. "You probably don't remember, but I spent a night at your house between the wars."

Seph didn't say anything. He just searched for the wisdom in the old man's eyes.

"Between the Mexican War and the War Between the States, that is, but me and your pa also served together in '36."

Seph nodded, understanding, and tried to imagine his father in his mid-twenties, during Texas' revolution.

His thoughts were quickly interrupted when the old man spoke again. "Also knew your great uncle. Yves."

Seph stuttered. "Uh... uh... Uncle Yves?"

"Yes. Your father's uncle was a hero."

Seph was fascinated. He had always wondered about the man. "Really?" he gushed.

Charlie said, "Yes. Yes, it's true. Your pa talked about the man all of the time. He hailed from Louisiana—a child of the swamps and bayous—an explorer and adventurer. He performed daring reconnaissance missions during the Battle of New Orleans. In '52 he led a group of settlers to the banks of the Guadalupe. Sadly he was ambushed by a band of outlaws, but saved the settlers who named their new town in his honor."

Seph frowned. The Guadalupe—that was the river where Slaw died.

"I guess that's about the end of the story," the old man said. "After Yves Vermillion died, the settlers sent his brand new rifle to your pa."

Seph nodded and whispered, "The Hawken."

"Yes. That's right. It was a Hawken."

Seph pointed to his horse. "That rifle's in the scabbard, right out there. So that's why we call the gun Uncle Yves." Seph's head turned and his mind wandered.

The old man cleared his throat and returned to his story about the big war. "Anyway, me and your pa were positioned on Missionary Ridge. I'll never forget the deafening roar of artillery. The noise was terrifying. Clouds of smoke hung everywhere. The stench of gunpowder stung our nostrils. We held our ground, but there was no stopping them. I was standing by Sébastien when it happened. First we heard a thunderous crack and then a high-pitched whine."

Seph noticed a twitch beneath Charlie's left eye. Seph could tell what was coming. He knew it before Charlie told him, and yet it didn't feel real.

"Just as I turned my head, something blew a hole through your pa." Charlie frowned as he thumped the middle of his chest with his fingertips. "Then, I felt a searing pain in my arm. It felt like I had been stabbed with fire and ice at the same time. The sensation charged through me like a thunderbolt. I looked down at my arm and there it was, a hideous wedge of twisted metal sticking out of my arm. Another pal, Johnny, raced to my side and I looked back at your pa. There was nothing we could do for him. I'm sorry Seph."

It had been years since Seph had seen his father. When the war ended and he didn't return home, Seph was sure that he had been killed. But it was still a shock to hear for certain what had happened. A tear sailed down his cheek and in a choked up voice, Seph urged, "Please go on."

"Johnny didn't hesitate. His eyes were wide, and he said, 'We can't leave it in there. It's got to come out.' I nodded, and he started tearing at my sleeve, digging that shrapnel out of my arm. I wanted to scream. Maybe I did. There was so much noise everywhere, I guess it wouldn't have made a difference. When I looked at my arm again, I had to vomit. My flesh was all torn to hell. I couldn't stand to see my bloody, mangled arm. I don't remember anything else. Next thing I knew, Johnny was gone. I emerged from a haze in a squalid tent. Somebody must of hacked off my arm. I don't know how I got to Camp Morton or how I managed to survive. It was crowded. Filthy. And there was never enough vittles. When we got paroled in April of '65, we marched like an army of zombies back to Texas. I meant to come find you, but then I started having that dream. The one where you came to me on a horse with a fiery mane. I didn't have it in me to go no farther, so I waited. Now, you're here."

The corners of Charlie's lips turned up into a smile. "What took you so long, Seph?"

As Dunk and Seph rode slowly back down Weatherford Street, Seph was quiet. He wished that he could give the old man more than a hearty lunch and a couple of dollars. It had been hard to say goodbye to the coot, but his feelings about his father's friend at least made it easier to mail that impossible letter to the Ballard family.

He thought about Charlie and what the old man told him about his father and Uncle Yves. After all that wondering, now he knew. Charlie Coppedge confirmed that truth. Pa was dead.

Dunk asked Seph what happened.

Seph turned his head and looked at the man. He didn't want to talk about it. At least, he didn't think he did. But then he started telling Dunk about the strange encounter and couldn't stop.

When he was done, Seph looked down at his saddle horn. He thought about Slaw. His friend had a habit of talking way too much, never knowing when to stop. He glanced back at Dunk and was comforted by a nod that seemed to say, *It's alright, Seph.*

They didn't know that they were being followed.

Swoop was in a foul mood.

He sat at Lou's Two Bit Lunch Counter for hours complaining about the weak coffee. A sign in the window promised all the coffee one could drink, free with the daily special, and despite the poor quality, he was determined to get his money's worth.

Periodically, the proprietor cast an unwelcoming glance in Swoop's direction. Swoop felt like teaching the man a lesson he wouldn't forget.

Earlier that morning, when Swoop attempted to mount his horse, his stirrup broke and he crashed to the ground. His elbow collided with a rock. The pain was unbearable, and hours later, it still troubled him. He was pretty sure it wasn't broken, merely bruised, but he coped with pain like a grizzly bear manages an empty stomach. Never mind that Swoop made the saddle himself. He blamed Sattlermeister Steinmetz who insisted on top quality craftsmanship but must have overlooked imperfections when it came to Swoop's saddle.

It wasn't just the saddle and elbow that set Swoop off. He couldn't stand it when his partners fought. Today, they bickered endlessly. The way they needled each other reminded him of the way his folks argued when he was growing up.

Coyote and Chaw's patience with each other declined in proportion to their wealth and the trio was almost out of money. Swoop would have never stooped as low as Lou's Two Bit Lunch Counter unless they were practically broke.

After an early morning rant, Swoop ordered Chaw to fix the saddle and soap the tack until it was soft to the touch. Coyote was charged with the task of procuring provisions to last a month on the trail, not an easy job considering their dwindling budget.

Swoop thought about pulling a job in Fort Worth but decided against it. During their time in town, he felt the evil eye of the marshal and it seemed there was a deputy standing on the corner of every block.

Maybe they could get a few dollars rolling drunks and shaking down vagrants, but what was the point of stealing a couple of lousy coins? Soon, they'd be filthy stinking rich and rolling around in luxury.

A sneer crossed Swoop's lips as Lou topped off his coffee. He thought about how he might rob the establishment, even though he had decided against doing so. Imagining scenarios to enrich himself often improved his mood.

A bell rang when the door opened and Chaw hurried to Swoop's table. Before Chaw had a chance to say anything, Coyote busted through the doorway. Coyote raced to Swoop's side, leaned forward, and whispered, "That kid's in town with the cook and the chuckwagon."

Chaw pulled a rickety chair from a neighboring table and the three of them sat around conspiring. Swoop watched Lou as they talked. The man looked spooked. Did he think he was about to be robbed?

Through clenched teeth, Swoop said. "Follow them back to the herd, Coyote. Wait for the right moment. It's time to thin the herd. If you pick the right one, the rest might quit overnight. Just make sure you get away clean. Cover your tracks, and meet us at Red River Station. And make sure to leave the body someplace they can find it."

Chaw interrupted. "Let *me* go, Swoop. Why risk somebody hearing a gunshot?"

Swoop thought for a moment. Once he announced a plan, he hated to change his mind, but Chaw's way sounded better. Coyote was better with a gun but Chaw was the best man for hand-to-hand combat and brandished a knife better than anybody Swoop knew. Finally, Swoop said, "Have it your way, Chaw. Just make sure they don't track you outta there."

The outlaw mastermind stepped from the doorway of Lou's and watched Chaw ride slowly out of town. He had meant to tell Chaw to spare the tall kid, but forgot.

Now, it was too late.

# CHAPTER 11

THE JOURNEY FROM THE Trinity River to Red River required eight solid days of travel. Instead, Dusty moved the herd slowly and stretched the journey into nine days.

With every river crossing, they got closer to realizing their goal, but no milestone was more significant than the one they were about to reach. When they traversed the Red, they'd leave Texas behind. They'd leave the States and enter Indian territory.

An early season heatwave made the ride miserable and monotonous. One hot day followed the next, and the closer they got to the Red, the more everybody talked about laying by. Seph couldn't wait to spend a couple of hours relaxing in the river.

With six days behind them, Dusty said, "We might lay by for two days when we reach the Red." Those words repeated in Seph's head. He knew it wasn't for the benefit of the drovers, but rather to allow the beeves to graze. As eager as he was to spend a couple of days off by the river, it was unsettling to think of the dangerous, unsettled realm to the north.

Water had been scant north of the Trinity. Occasionally, they found small bodies of water that Squat called puddles. Dusty said they should consider themselves fortunate. River crossings were treacherous, but marching past puddles was easy.

The temperature climbed to eighty degrees by late morning on the seventh day. Clouds gathered and by the afternoon, there wasn't a spot of blue sky to be seen. The late-spring, early-summer heatwave had broken.

The herd moved faster, and by the end of the day they had logged sixteen miles rather than the usual twelve.

When the herd was bedded down and the chores were finished, Blaze suggested working with the horses for a while. At the remuda, Seph saddled Sheriff, while Blaze looked for Noomoo.

The gray mare was easy to catch, but Blaze clucked when he led the horse over to where Seph waited patiently. Blaze shook his head and frowned. "Just look at that, will ya, Seph? I figure she's been rolling in them puddles. There must be an inch of mud on her."

Seph offered to help brush the mustang, but Blaze waved him off. Blaze pointed to a lonely-looking tree a mile to the north. "I'll meet you out there. You can practice jumping off and leaping back on at a trot. Remember how I showed ya?" They had worked on the basic trick a few evenings that week, despite the oppressive evening heat.

Chaw spied on the cowboys' encampment from behind a solitary tree. He had been waiting for the perfect opportunity to catch somebody alone, away from camp. Since leaving Cowtown, he'd passed on a few opportunities that he considered risky.

He tried to avoid an encounter with the scout. Swoop said that he was one of the bosses. If Swoop wanted him to kill the bosses, he would have said so. Instead, he was told to slay a cowboy.

Chaw peered around the tree trunk and saw the farm boy from Poesta Creek on his claybank dun. The kid seemed to be riding directly toward him. What good fortune! He might not get a better opportunity to catch one of the cowboys off on his own, away from the rest of the crew.

The kid was riding fast and galloping purposefully toward the outlaw. Chaw drew his Bowie knife from its shoulder sheath. A surge of electricity gripped his innards. He spoke to the blade he called *Rodaja*, sometimes *Rodaja de Muerte*. An experienced dagger deserved a worthy name, and Chaw liked the Spanish words for Slice of Death. Chaw muttered, "Get ready to have a little bit of fun, *Rodaja*."

Chaw expected the horse and rider to skid to a stop upon reaching the tree. He figured the kid planned to sit with his back against the tree trunk and laze away the early evening hours, though on account of the clouds, the shade was no longer necessary.

Instead, the dun seemed to gallop faster. Chaw imagined himself reaching out, grabbing the rider, and plucking him from the saddle, but there was no way he could accomplish such a feat.

The bandit scrambled to keep himself hidden, circling the tree trunk as the horse and rider galloped three quarters of the way around the tree and continued off in another direction. Was the kid just riding for the heck of it?

Chaw still held the dagger and peered around the tree trunk. It surprised him to see the kid vault from his saddle. At first, he thought the plowboy had fallen off. He wouldn't have believed it if he hadn't seen it himself. The kid's feet hit the ground fast, and then his long legs sprung him back into the saddle. Moments later, the kid did it again, leaping to the right rather than the left. "Get a load of that," Chaw muttered to himself.

Movement to the left caught his eye. Another rider had departed from camp on a gray, Spanish mustang. He looked back to the Poesta Kid, who stopped and turned to face the approaching rider.

Chaw returned *Rodaja* to its sheath, crouched down, and scampered along a shallow swale. He would have to find another opportunity to skewer a drover.

The weather remained overcast the next day. The skies seemed to threaten rain, but it never came.

The herd traveled several extra miles and the bosses figured Red River Station couldn't be far away. Instead of riding off alone, Squat and Dusty rode north together to check the banks of the Red River and to see if other herds were waiting to cross it. They planned to overnight at Red River before returning to the herd. It was the first time they had left the cowboys alone overnight with the beeves.

After supper, Blaze and Seph rode off again. They practiced a new trick that Blaze had shown Seph the day before. The previous evening, Seph took several tumbles before finding success. After flinging himself from the saddle, he grabbed the saddle horn with his right hand, bent his right knee, and stretched his left leg along Sheriff's neck. His left arm extended backward and he rode in that position in a big circle before pulling himself back into the saddle at a lope.

Blaze clapped and Seph cheered, pumping his fists in the air. Seph had visualized the trick in his head overnight, carefully thinking of each movement and performing them exactly as Blaze had instructed.

They didn't know that Chaw watched from the cover of a thicket of shrubs.

Blaze complimented Seph's skill as he unsaddled Noomoo. "If you want, I'll show you how to ride invisible, only bareback. This time you go head forward, drape an arm over the withers, and place your ankle above the tail."

Seph watched as Blaze rode Noomoo and gracefully draped his body over the edge of the horse, before pulling himself back on board. Then he rode back to Seph. "Want me to show you again?"

After three demonstrations, Seph told Blaze that he was ready to give it a try. The first time, he failed to hook his arm over Sheriff's neck. He landed, hard on his side, on the unyielding prairie.

The second time, his ankle missed the mark above Sheriff's tail and he took a gangly tumble to the ground. He brushed himself off and denied he felt any pain.

For a couple of seconds, on his third attempt, Seph clung to Sheriff's side at a lope. His hat tumbled from his head and he felt the wind through his hair. He imagined what Sheriff looked like from the opposite side, running riderless. His thoughts came fast. Four seconds later, he lost his hold and skidded along the dirt as Sheriff loped off without him. Seph's shirt was torn along the side and he had a nasty scrape from his armpit, along his ribs, all the way to his waist, but he felt elated.

Blaze shouted. "You did it. For a couple of seconds there, you did it perfect."

They didn't see Torp riding toward them. He vaulted from the saddle before his horse came to a stop and he landed, running, and crashed into Blaze. Torp gushed, "You did it, Seph. Everybody saw. You held on and did it. You rode just like an Indian." He looked back at Blaze and questioned, "Didn't he?"

"Yup, he sure did. If he keeps practicing, maybe he can manage to do it without crashing to the ground at the end. Indians don't like to do that part."

Breathlessly, Torp changed the subject. "Guess what? Dunk made short-cake. Peach Shortcake. Hurry up. It's going fast."

Blaze appeared more excited by the news than Seph. He had a legendary sweet tooth. They quickly resaddled their horses and galloped back to camp. Torp returned their horses to the remuda as Blaze and Seph strode off toward the chuckwagon.

Dunk nodded and said, "You got here just in time. There's enough for two more, only there ain't many peaches left." He sliced two biscuits and placed them, sliced side down, on tin plates.

Seph said, "Where did you find peaches?"

"At the mercantile. The cans were dented and the grocer gave me a good deal on 'em." Dunk had earlier diced the peaches, having saved the syrup they were packed in. He spooned the last of the diced fruit onto the top of the biscuits, attempting to put the same amount on each cowhand's dessert. Then he drenched the biscuits with the syrup.

Seph's mouth watered in anticipation as he watched Dunk clip hunks of sweetener from a cone with sugar nips. He glanced at Blaze whose wide eyes followed Dunk's every movement. The cook didn't hurry. It seemed to Seph that Dunk enjoyed making them wait while he methodically ground the clumps of sugar with the mortar and pestle.

As Dunk sprinkled the sugar over the peaches, Blaze said, "I'll take all you can spare."

Seph chuckled and said, "I only need a little. Give the rest to Blaze."

Dunk made a show of sprinkling the sugar over Blaze's biscuits. It's a good thing it wasn't windy at the moment—or most of the sugar would have been carried away.

Seph made quick work of the shortcake, but Blaze hunched over his dish taking the smallest bites he could and chewing slowly, as if prolonging the sweetness as long as possible.

Dunk poured himself a cup of coffee and dipped the last biscuit. Torp said, "You didn't get any peaches?"

"Nope. There was barely enough to go around. I should have gotten two cans. But, no matter. It gladdens me to see you boys enjoy a treat."

It began to rain as Blaze scraped the last of his dessert from the plate. Then he licked it clean, making sure to capture every grain of sugar, drop of syrup, and biscuit crumb.

With the bosses gone, Dunk doubled the night watch. They'd been lucky so far, but extreme weather was known to spook a herd. They may as well have *all* been assigned watch. There was no shelter. The only dry spot was provided by the chuckwagon. Who could sleep in a wet bedroll?

The crew donned India rubber ponchos and huddled together beneath a canvas awning attached to the chuckwagon. The deluge drowned the campfire during the first hour. Space was limited and the men were forced to crowd in closely. Cowboys preferred to keep a comfortable distance apart. They grumbled but didn't voice complaints. At least they could hunker down. The other half of the crew was stuck with the herd. Seph prayed that the rain would end before midnight, when they would trade places.

Hork was the first to begin retching. His back hunched and everyone looked at him. Even with the loud patter of rain on the awning, the sound was unmistakable. Stoke gave him a shove and Hork stumbled out into the rain. Seph couldn't see where the puker went, but the sound of him emptying his stomach made Seph shudder. Wherever Hork went, he did not come back.

An hour later, Seph yawned. He wished he could stretch out and go to sleep. He shifted his weight from one leg to the other and then back again. Then he heard a familiar sound. Somebody else had whatever ailed Hork.

Stoke swore and stepped out into the night, making that sound one makes when they're trying to keep from vomiting. Half an hour later, the sickness spread. Cowboys darted out into the rainy night.

Seph thought Dunk looked nervous. He asked the cook, "What can we do?"

"Nothing, I reckon. I wish there was somethin' but there ain't. We'll just have to weather the storm."

Seph thought about Lullaby. He must be one of the men on watch. Lullaby would offer God a prayer. The words didn't come to him easy, but Seph prayed to the Lord for mercy.

When they were down to just Dunk, Blaze, and Seph, the cook moaned. "I bet it was the peaches. What if the dent in the can spoiled 'em? Aw, I shouldn't a bought 'em."

Blaze shook his head. "They weren't spoilt. They was tasty." He barely got the words out before a gaseous belch bubbled from deep in his chest. It was followed by a convulsion. Seph thought he never saw such a confused expression as he saw on Blaze's face. Blaze dashed into the night, the latest victim of food poisoning.

Seph looked at Dunk then closed his eyes. "I guess I'm next." He frowned and thought about how much he hated to puke. It didn't happen often, but when Ma died, and he left her casket briefly only to return to see vultures picking at her body between the wooden slats, he couldn't help vomiting.

Twenty minutes later, Seph gripped his belly. It began to churn something fierce. He felt like something was ripping his innards apart. He realized what was about to happen almost too late. He would rather have retched the contents of his stomach than have the trots. Even so, he endeavored to get as far from camp as possible before dropping his trousers.

A dark night was just what Chaw needed. He didn't care that it was raining. He thought he would pluck a cowboy from night watch, but hadn't expected that the guard would be doubled.

Instead, Chaw tiptoed through the rain making his way closer to the encampment. He thought, perhaps he would have an opportunity to drop a cowboy if one of the fellows stepped out to relieve himself.

He almost stumbled over the back of a man on his hands and knees and quickly stepped back when he realized the man was there. He squinted, listened carefully, and was surprised to discover that the cowhand was puking. He didn't care if he got blood on him, but vomit was another matter. Chaw stepped farther back into the darkness and waited.

Before long, Chaw was surrounded by nauseous, waterlogged cowboys. He wasn't prone to superstition but he was starting to feel spooked. The nearest cowpoke had dropped his trousers and grunted, attempting to empty his bowels while maintaining a tenuous balance.

Chaw was even less interested in being crapped on. He stepped through the rain around him. Did they have some sort of fast-spreading disease? Maybe he should get away from them as quickly as possible. He ran smack into another cowboy, who barked, "Watch where you're going, chowderhead."

Chaw plucked *Rodaja* from his shoulder holster and clamped a hand over the cowboy's face. He buried his blade in the man's back as vomit erupted between his fingers. He dropped his victim and kicked him in the belly. He rolled the man over, tried to clean the puke from his hands and feared he might barf himself. He grabbed the cowboy's ankles and dragged the corpse off to the north. He'd better not catch whatever sickness they had.

When Chaw reached his gear, he fetched his axe and chopped off the cowboy's arms at the shoulders. Then he chopped off the dead man's legs at the knees. He made quick work of scattering limbs along the most likely northbound route, then packed up and rode his horse to the east before turning north toward Red River Station. He couldn't get the sensation of the dead man's vomit gushing between his fingers out of his mind.

# CHAPTER 12

CHAW RODE NORTH THROUGH the rain. The bandit didn't like killing people, but it didn't bother him as much when he was following orders. He didn't figure this was any different from the battlefield. When a superior officer said *charge*, you didn't ask questions.

He glared at his hands. Why did that kid have to vomit on his fingers?

He couldn't count how many men he had killed, but something about that young cowpoke was different. At that moment, Chaw decided that he didn't like butchering children.

A mile to the west, Squat said to Dusty, "How far along do you figure the herd is?"

His brother shrugged. "Who knows?"

Squat postulated, "Dunk knows what he's doing. He'll get 'em moving, won't he?"

Dusty answered, "It rained pretty hard last night. The herd coulda scattered." Dusty trusted his friend completely. But he didn't want to tell his brother everything about Dunk. Since the war, Dunk had avoided serving in positions of authority. He'd had his fill of such responsibilities. In a pinch, Dusty was certain that Dunk would lead those jaspers better than Squat and Dusty could.

His opinion started to change the nearer they got to the chuckwagon. Longhorns wandered every which way. It was as if they had been abandoned. They passed a cowboy who was dry heaving beside a bush. They tried to speak to another drover who struggled to remain standing, but the cowboy meekly answered, "I ain't myself today, boss." He gripped his head and moaned.

Squat frowned and looked at his brother. "They're hungover. Heck, could be they're still drunk? Where in the blazes would they get whiskey?"

Dusty removed his hat and stirred up his hair. "It don't figure, Squat." The friend he knew would never have let the crew get drunk, especially in the middle of a raging storm, but it was hard to explain the situation as it appeared. They encountered another cowhand who was passed out, lying in the dirt, apparently oblivious to the lightly falling rain. Dusty lamented, "I shoulda stayed with the herd instead of riding off with you."

They found Torp sitting beneath the chuckwagon, elbows on his knees, head in his hands, moaning. Dusty spoke harshly. "What's going on here, Torp? Looks like a battlefield." He spat and uttered a string of swear words. "Where's Dunk?"

Torp rubbed his wrists into his eye sockets and moaned. A gassy belch accompanied his answer. "Dunk and Seph are trying to round up the herd."

Squat interrupted. "What happened, kid?"

Torp answered, "Peaches, sir. Dang peaches."

Normally, Dusty was quick to anger and Squat was more measured. Usually, Squat rode off away from the crew when he was perturbed. It was Dusty's job to keep the hands in line.

Squat turned to Dusty and said, "You hear that?" He turned back to Torp and railed, "Don't get smart with me, kid. I want to know what's going on. I don't want to hear about bloody fruit."

Torp tried to comply. He pushed himself forward with his hands and squeaked. "It's food poisoning, boss." He pitched forward and crashed into the mud just beyond the shelter provided by the chuckwagon. He rolled onto his back. "Everybody got it but Dunk. Seph has a mild case. Everybody else is wrecked."

Squat shouted back. "Food poisoning! Food poisoning? Now I've heard everything." He turned his horse away and rode toward the beeves.

Seph was luckier than most. After a couple of hours of dealing with the skitters, he began to feel better, though he was soaked to the skin and drowsy from a lack of sleep.

He made his way back to the chuckwagon and was glad to find Dunk. They brought water to each of the hands and tried to convince them to drink up. Then, they saddled up and rode off to see if they could keep the longhorns from wandering too far away from the herd until the rest of the crew recovered enough to help out.

Most of the herd remained bedded down. Those that had begun to wander away were easily nudged back toward the herd. The second time around the perimeter, they rode a wider circle.

North of the herd, Seph saw a flash of color on the ground. He didn't know what to make of it and rode closer. He glanced back toward Dunk, but the man was beyond his field of vision.

*It can't be*, Seph thought. He dismounted and stepped closer. *It looks like somebody's arm.* He leaned over and saw a hand with fingers and clapped his own hand over his mouth. He felt the sour taste of bile at the back of his throat, but didn't hork. Though he was alone, he spoke out loud. "Oh, no. I'll be...." He dropped to a squatting position and picked up the limb. He shuddered at the thought of holding a severed appendage.

Seph swallowed hard. He and Dunk didn't manage to find everybody that morning. But who was missing? Maybe the arm belonged to a stranger. Somebody they didn't know. Did it have to be one of his friends' arms? Food poisoning didn't cause people's arms to fall off. He forced himself to look at the bloody, shoulder-end of the arm. It looked like it had been sliced off with a sword.

He shouted. "Dunk! Come quick. You gotta see this." Still holding the arm, Seph climbed up into his saddle.

Dunk wasn't far away. "On my way," he shouted back.

Seph held the limb high. "It's somebody's arm, Dunk." He felt light headed and woozy. It occurred to him that he might slide from the saddle, but he managed to keep his seat as Dunk trotted closer. Seph said, "Gosh, what do you make of it?"

Dunk stretched his legs, standing as high in the stirrups as he could manage, and glanced about. "I don't know, Seph. You okay?"

"I think so."

"Let's see what else we can find. Shout out if you see anything else that don't look right." Dunk rode to the left. Seph reined his horse to the right and tried to forget that he was carrying somebody's arm.

He didn't get far. Something else caught his eye. It was not the same color as the arm. His heart lurched and he gulped again. He squinted and dismounted. There in the short grass was a boot and half of a leg. The sour taste returned to his mouth. He turned his head slightly and shouted. "Dunk, I found a leg." Then he muttered under his breath, "Or, half a leg anyway." The sick feeling in the pit of his stomach blossomed.

When Dunk rode up, he said, "Where?"

Seph bent at the waist and picked up the leg. "Looks like Woodsy's boot, don't it?"

Dunk frowned deeply and the tendons in his neck were visible. "I think you're right, Seph." Dunk looked about but didn't see anything more. "Do you want to go back to camp, Seph?"

Seph shook his head slowly. "Naw, I'm alright, Dunk." He thought of Woodsy, the kid that wanted to be a gunslinger. He had dreams of being a hero. The west needed lawmen like him. Seph shook his head at the injustice and steeled his resolve. The more he thought about it, the more sure he was that the arm and leg belonged to his fellow cowboy. "We owe it to Woodsy to find out what happened, Dunk."

They split up again. It wasn't long before Seph discovered Woodsy's body. It was hard to look at the corpse. The missing arms and legs that only went down to his knees made the scene even worse. The aspiring marshal's untouched guns remained belted to his hips. His face was dirty and hard to look at. Seph's teeth chattered and he fought the urge to cry. He tried to call out to Dunk, but words wouldn't come.

It wasn't long before Dunk rode up. He had found another arm and leg. Dunk quickly slid from his saddle and set Woodsy's missing limbs on the ground. Dunk stepped toward Seph and gripped his shoulder firmly. "Aw, I'm sorry Seph. Nobody should have to see that. Why don't you turn away?"

Seph turned angrily away from Woodsy's remains, jutted his chin forward and said, "No, Dunk. I won't." He looked back at the corpse with the hacked off limbs. "It ain't right. Who would do such a thing? We gotta find them. For Woodsy. We just gotta." Seph turned his back to Dunk. He thought about his friend, Slaw. That was a tragic accident. This was different. Woodsy was killed on purpose. Murdered. He turned back to Dunk. "We do owe him, don't we, Dunk?" At that moment, Seph realized that he would be glad to kill the man that did this to Woodsy.

Squat rode up before Dunk could answer Seph's question about seeking vengeance. Dunk said, "Man, are we glad to see you."

Squat hopped down and started shouting, "What in tarnation...." He choked on whatever words he had planned to say. His gaze locked on the dead body and he moaned, "Oh, Dunk. That's awful. What do you figure? Indians?"

Dunk tried to answer. "I don't know, Squat. Maybe. I don't think so."

Squat said, "We're only a couple of miles away from the Nations."

Dunk shook his head. "I know a fair amount of Indians. I think something else is going on here. Not sure just what." He glanced at the gathered limbs. "It's like somebody *wanted* us to find the body. They didn't try to hide it. But where are they now?"

Squat pointed at Woodsy's pistols. "Didn't even take his guns."

Dunk frowned. "Don't make no sense."

Seph returned to camp to get a shovel and rode back to Woodsy's remains. Before punching the spade into the ground, he thought of Ma. Then he thought of Slaw. How many graves must he dig?

The rain started to come down heavier. Earlier he had felt weak. He scooped a couple shovels full of mud and tossed the dirt to the side. The more he shoveled, the stronger he felt. His nerves had been frayed and his emotions had swirled within him, but chopping away at the hole in the ground helped restore his spirit. He pounded away with a fury, oblivious to the heavy downpour that soaked his clothes. He lost track of time and had no sense of its passage. It was as if he didn't occupy his body while digging the grave.

The urge to dig gave out suddenly and Seph tossed the shovel from the muddy grave. He realized he'd have to run and leap to get out of the hole, deep as it was. He turned, looked up, and saw Dunk and Lullaby standing in the rain at the foot of the grave. They helped him climb from the hole and Lullaby said, "God bless you, Seph."

Dirty, soggy, and bloody, Chaw rode into camp a short distance from Red River Station.

Swoop said, "What took you so long? We've been waiting here, broke, with nothing to do and durn little to eat. We was beginning to think you'd never get here."

"Dang, Swoop. It wasn't as easy as I thought it'd be, but I got it done."

"You didn't kill the Poesta Kid, did you?"

"No, sorry. Did you want me to?"

"No, knucklehead. That kid's our meal ticket."

"You shoulda said so. I almost had a chance at him, but got some other kid instead. Why do we gotta kill children, Swoop? I don't like it none."

"Hush. Forget about that. Now they're down a man. Hopefully that'll scare a few of them off. How far back are they, Chaw?"

"Just a couple of miles. They could ride in tonight, but I doubt it. There was something wrong. It's like they had the plague or something. Hope I don't come down with whatever it was."

Swoop said to Coyote, "Alright, let's get packed up and light outta here. Better hope we got enough provisions or we're gonna be mighty hungry the next couple of weeks."

After a somber funeral for Woodsy, the Deatherage outfit mounted up and drove the herd toward Red River Station. The exhausted crew pushed the beeves in silent misery. Though the after-effects of food poisoning had waned, the lack of sleep and the unrelenting rain tormented them throughout the afternoon.

Riding drag, Torp and Seph were the last to arrive. Before dismounting, Seph watched Booger step into the river and drink. He could still see where the charcoal letters had been scratched onto the maverick's hide, but days of rain had caused them to drip and smear. Seph dismounted with a snort. He was glad that the message was no longer readable.

Optimistically, Torp chirped, "We made it. Look at that river. We're almost halfway there, Seph."

Seph was glad to see that Torp was feeling better. And, it seemed, the kid had finally seemed to forgive him for speaking harshly. Seph didn't know what he was going to say when he began to speak, but it didn't matter.

Stoke bumped Seph's shoulder, laughing as Seph stumbled, and said to Torp, "You gotta be kidding me, squirt. Texas is the easy part. It's like we ain't even started."

Seph scowled at Stoke as Torp said, "We ain't?"

"Heck no. I thought you knew that." He shook his head, rolled his eyes, and looked to the heavens. With an outstretched arm, Stoke pointed to the north. "When we cross that river, we're gonna be in Injun Country. That's the worst part of the trail."

Chops approached, took Seph and Torp's horses, and led them off toward the remuda.

Stoke continued. "You children ain't seen nothing yet." He tipped his head back and howled, then stepped closer to Torp, ominously lowering his voice. "When you hear a wolf howl, it ain't a wolf. When you hear an owl hoot, it ain't a bird. When you hear an elk bugling, don't be fooled. Most likely, it's one Injun sending secret signals to another." His eyes bulged and he nodded slowly.

Seph was sure that Stoke was going out of his way to make his warning sound even more frightening.

Stoke bared his teeth. "And you should see the things an Indian will do to a man. One guy I knew had a friend who got his skin peeled off his body. If you ask me, anybody who makes it through Indian Country deserves to whoop it up at the end of the trail. Don't let anybody tell you different."

Seph hadn't realized that the rest of the gang had gathered around as Stoke talked about the next leg of the journey. Stoke began to pace. The rest of the crew needed a dry change of clothes, a good night's sleep, and a warm meal, but the top hand's boundless energy was proof that he had recovered from peach poisoning.

Stoke spun in a circle as if he were trying to make sure that everybody was present before speaking again. "If you survive the next twenty days, you might just get to do a little business in Abilene." He raised and lowered his eyebrows several times and laughed. "You ladies spread out and bring back anything that looks like it will burn. Search far and wide." Stoke's animated gesture almost clocked Seph in the jaw.

Seph knew that it would not be easy to start a fire and keep it going after several days of rain. As the crew radiated from the center of camp like spokes in a wagon wheel, Seph wandered off in search of tinder.

The heatwave seemed like months ago. Seph had lost count of how many days in a row it had rained. He shivered at the thought of trying to float the soggy beeves across the swollen river. It wasn't just thoughts of a dangerous fording, Seph realized that he'd been shivering most of the day.

Except for dried grass, it was hard to find anything to burn on the prairie. Sometimes, they got lucky and came across buffalo chips. The busy cross-ing at Red River Station had been picked clean by other drovers and trampled by tens of thousands of heads of cattle. If it weren't for the trees lining the banks of the river, it might have been an impossible task. As it was, Seph had to make his way almost a mile to find an armload of fodder for the fire.

As Seph returned to camp, he passed Dusty, Squat, and Dunk.

Squat was in a foul mood. He groused, "I don't care if we take a month off. I just want to get to the other side of that stinking river." Seph didn't hang around to hear what else the boss said.

The rest of the gang had returned and stood in a circle. Stoke squatted in the middle and struck a lucifer match.

Seph set his collection of branches and twigs next to the combustible materials collected by the other cowpunchers.

Stoke grumbled, "Everything is so wet, It ain't easy to start a fire. But don't you girls worry none. I told you before, I am The Ignitor. I could make fire underwater. So this is gonna be easy." He touched the match to several spots that had been carefully placed to nurture a flame. He added, "I found this old hunk a junk."

Seph leaned forward to get a look at what Stoke was talking about.

Stoke said, "That pretty lady is just what The Ignitor needs. Just watch those flames dance."

Seph gasped. His shoulders sagged and his arms dangled limply by his knees as he watched the fire burn the girl of his dreams.

In less than a minute, the box that once held his treasure was incinerated. Seph turned away from the growing campfire and stepped off alone. When he said farewell to Poesta Creek, and left his childhood home behind, he departed with few possessions. The thought flickered in his head, *What did it matter?* He could still see the beautiful woman in his head whenever he closed his eyes. But it wasn't the same. Seeing her in his head didn't stir him like looking at her picture did.

Seph wanted to wrap his hands around Stoke's neck and press his thumbs into the man's windpipe. He had never imagined doing such a thing before, but at that moment, he wanted to choke Stoke until he was gasping for breath. Seph tried to stop thinking it, but he couldn't chase his dark thoughts away. He imagined himself holding on until Stoke's body spasmed in the final throes of death before letting go. It felt like justice. An eye for an eye. It was as if Stoke had killed Woodsy and needed killing himself, rather than burning a hunk of junk.

In the dark of night along the Red River, choking Stoke seemed like a fitting punishment.

# CHAPTER 13

SEPH NEEDED TIME ALONE. After dark, he walked along the riverbanks and camped beneath a cottonwood tree.

In the morning, he was aware of being away, but wasn't yet in the mood to open his eyes. His first waking thoughts were of Stoke setting his cigar box ablaze. He had wanted to choke him, but killing the man was just in his imagination. It was a dark fantasy, but it wasn't any more real than the illustration inside the carton.

It was time to forget about childish notions and focus on things that were real. Maybe Stoke had done him a favor. He should have left that empty cigar box at Poesta Creek. It was time to move on—time to be a man. Instead of possessing a woman made of cardboard, ink, and paper, why not find a real woman?

He remembered a recurring nightmare. It was a naughty dream involving Slaw's sister, Mary Ballard. She wasn't the girl he left behind, but rather, she was the fate he knew he was lucky to avoid. Mary was an unwelcome memory. Blinking his eyes open banished her from his thoughts.

But he couldn't help thinking of his friend again. All that Slaw wanted was to ride the range and live along the trail, but now Slaw was dead and buried. For a moment, it occurred to Seph that he was living his friend's dream, but being a drover meant more to Seph than that.

Maybe being a cowboy had started as Slaw's dream. But Seph had escaped the plow, he had dodged a life as Mary Ballard's husband, and he had wrangled a job with the Deatherage outfit. He would make his home at the back end of the herd.

He thought, *It won't always be this way. Next year, I'll make full pay. Someday, I'll be a top hand. Why not ramrod or trail boss? What's to stop me?* He stretched his neck and his imagination. *Maybe one day, I'll be a cattle baron.* There were many, many obstacles. He was penniless, owned little more than a rifle, horse, and saddle, and then, there was the question about whether he was smart enough. There were lots of things he didn't know.

He yawned and told himself that he didn't care about being rich anyway. As long as he could make a living outdoors, and ride for a brand like Deatherage, what more did a man need than that? His thoughts drifted and the answers to his questions came to mind.

Somewhere in his future, he hoped to encounter tall mountains. He palmed his face and thought of his dream girl. Would he ever meet a woman like her? Would a woman like that be interested in a man like him?

Seph managed to set aside thoughts of beautiful women and towering peaks. *This* was the life for him. He had tried his best to do a good job for the Deatherage brothers, but that wasn't enough. There was much more to a cattle drive than riding drag. He resolved to learn everything there was to know. Whatever it took, he would learn it all.

He thought, *I'll volunteer for everything. When the others loaf about, I'll keep working.* He thought of all the skills that he could improve upon, which certainly included roping, shooting, and fighting. *What about cooking, horsemanship, and blacksmithing?* Seph compared himself to Stoke. *Our top hand can't do half of those things.*

Seph had always worked hard. Even before he was a teenager, he worked the fields, tended the barnyard, and took care of his ailing mother. Ma hadn't been gone that long, but it seemed like ages since Seph had left Poesta Creek.

He thought about Ma's last words. She had called him timid and told him that he must be tenacious. *I'll do just that*, he thought. Then he recalled her wish that he seek out his siblings and was glad that he had never promised her that.

Despite his denial, Seph found that it was hard to turn his back on promises, even ones he did not make. Once again, he turned his thoughts away from long-lost siblings and returned his focus on becoming tenacious. Seph didn't like Stoke, but he had to acknowledge that man was full of bluster and thoroughly tenacious.

Seph resolved, *Nothing will stand in my way. I may never be top hand, but nothing's gonna stop me from trying. I owe it to myself, and I owe it to Slaw—by golly.*

He thought of Slaw's last words: "Live large. Take me with you. When you see a brilliant sunset, think of me so I can see it too."

Seph sniffled. *Dang, those are pretty words. There won't be much time to gawk at, but I'll ride the trails for both of us, pal. Count on it.*

As Seph stood, a blanket fell to the ground. Where did that come from?

Dunk appeared beneath the cottonwood tree with a cup of coffee. Saddlebags were draped over his shoulders. Cheerfully, he said, "You missed breakfast, Seph. You must be famished."

Seph nodded gratefully, and took the coffee. "How did you find me?"

Dunk chuckled. "I didn't. Last night, Torp followed you. Then he returned to camp for your bedroll. This morning, he came back in time for breakfast. He said you needed your sleep."

"Gosh, I had no idea."

Dunk nodded. "Loyalty makes a good cowboy and a better friend. You can't find one truer than Torp."

Seph nodded agreement. "Sure enough."

As Seph took a sip of coffee, Dunk fished a hand into the saddlebags. "Have some of Mama's biscuits."

After taking a bite, Seph said, "They make my mouth water so hard my jaw hurts. Will ya teach me how to make 'em?"

Dramatically, he raised his hands into the air and said, "Good heavens, yes. That's what Mama would say, and just how she woulda said it. You have no idea how happy it would make her, to hear you praisin' 'em! But enough about Mama. Come with me, Seph." They didn't talk as they walked along the river, away from camp.

When Seph had reduced three large biscuits to a handful of crumbs, he wiped his face with a sleeve and asked, "Where we going?"

Dunk turned and opened the saddlebags. "These b'longed to Woodsy." Dunk handed Woodsy's gun belt and double holster to Seph. "You found him. You buried him. I think he woulda wanted you to have these. Wouldn't you say so?"

"Gosh, thanks Dunk." Seph strapped the belt around his waist. As he let go, it slipped and slid down his legs, landing with a thud on the ground.

Dunk laughed. "You're going to have to eat more or we'll have to make an a'justment."

Seph stepped out of the gun belt at his ankles. "Better bore a hole or two into that leather." He picked up the rig, unsnapped the straps, and held the Colt 1851 Navy revolvers in his hands. They felt like they were made to fit him, and yet it was unsettling to think of all the things those guns were made to do.

Dunk led Seph to a nearby log. He unpacked a leather pouch, powder flask, lead balls, and a tin of percussion caps. Dunk explained the difference between paper cartridges and the time savings that came with using them. He concluded, "We'll start with loose powder and lead balls. It's more 'fordable and good for practice."

Seph hesitated. He had always been mindful of the cost of ammunition. Dunk told him that the cost of practicing was nothing in comparison to the cost of being a poor shot. "Knowing you can hit where you aim could save your life, Seph. How much is that worth? Spend money on ammunition and save money on other things."

Dunk gave Seph a lesson in how to load, fire, handle, and clean the guns. He explained all of the dangers and how to prevent accidents. He warned about misfires, hang fires, and accidental shootings. When they practiced firing, Dunk was impressed with Seph's natural abilities. He patted Woodsy's Colt in Seph's hand and said, "You might want to consider exercising them wrists. Get a good sized rock. Do wrist curls and rotations while you ride. It'll keep your wrists strong."

Seph pointed at a nearby rock. "How about that one there?"

Dunk picked it up and tossed it from hand to hand. He grunted approval and then demonstrated. He curled his wrist up and down, then rotated it in a circular motion. "Start with curls like this. Do a few until your wrist feels tired, then switch to the other hand."

Seph reached for the rock and copied the movement. It worked. The muscles in his wrist and forearm flexed, and he indicated his satisfaction by grunting. "This is good, Dunk."

Dunk nodded. "You know, these exercises will also come in handy in a fistfight."

Seph was surprised to hear it, but curious. "How do you figure?"

"Strong wrists and a solid grip mean you can hit harder and control your punches better," Dunk explained.

Seph nodded. Every day it seemed easier to picture himself mixing it up with Stoke. "Makes sense."

Dunk added, "A long fight can wear you down, but if your wrists and forearms are strong, you'll have the stamina to keep going."

Seph pocketed the rock and grinned. "I can use any advantage I can get. It won't be long, Dunk. There's a fight brewing."

Dunk said, "Reckon you're right about that, Seph. Sometimes men can't help themselves. That fight's been a long time coming."

Seph almost growled when he replied. "I may never be ready, but I can hardly wait."

When they returned to camp, Torp approached Seph. With his hands on his hips, Torp said, "Are you avoiding me?"

Seph turned and looked directly at him. "No. I just been distracted lately. Thanks for covering me with that blanket last night. I'm lucky to have you looking out for me."

A radiant smile stretched across Torp's face.

Seph was glad to see it. He thought about what Torp had said the day before—about being halfway to Abilene. "Hey, Torp. Let's countdown those rivers." One at a time, Torp bent his fingers as Seph recited: "Guadalupe, Colorado, Brazos, Trinity, Red. Five down. Washita, Canadian, North Fork, Cimarron, Salt Fork, Bluff Creek, Arkansas, and Smoky Hill. Eight to go."

Torp nodded vigorously. "And who knows how many creeks there are in between." Then he whispered, "Are you afraid of them Indians Stoke was talking about?"

Seph frowned. "He's just trying to scare everybody. There's Indians up there alright, but I expect they're used to seeing longhorns and drovers march on by. That reminds me, Torp. Where is Stoke?"

Torp thought for a moment before pointing. "I last saw him near the chuckwagon."

Seph thanked Torp. He didn't get far before he heard Stoke's voice. Seph marched directly up to Stoke and said, "Don't never touch my stuff again, ya hear?"

There was a startled look on Stoke's face. "What stuff?"

"That box you burned last night was mine. I had it since I was a kid. Don't touch my stuff. I won't tell you again." Seph didn't wait for a response. He just turned and walked away.

He had no idea where he was headed. His heart pounded and his face felt like it was on fire. The emotions washing through him were unfamiliar—and hard to name. Maybe it was a strange combination of fear, rage, and a strange sort of thrill he hadn't felt before.

Seph wanted to look back and see if Stoke was following him. Instead, he forced himself not to. If Stoke was coming, then let him come.

Seph's rage didn't subside until he reached the remuda. A few minutes with Sheriff always did wonders for his soul.

The Deatherage outfit was stuck on the wrong side of Red River, waiting for the waters to recede. Finally, after five days of waiting that included a lazy Fourth of July celebration, Squat announced, "We go now."

Dusty shouted, "You heard the man. Get ready to cross."

Dunk was the first to cross with the chuckwagon.

Squat said, "If he don't make it, there's no point in the rest of us going."

Dusty and Chops readied the remuda. The horses forded next.

The crew sat high in their saddles and watched the chuckwagon inch its way across the raging river. When it bobbled, they groaned. At one point, it looked like the current would sweep the wagon away, but Dunk angled it with the prevailing current. Crossing the Oregon Trail in 1850 had made him an expert at crossing rivers.

Getting the horses across was easy. The beeves were another matter. Several leisurely days of grazing had reinvigorated the herd, and they had no interest in travel. It took hard riding and insistent nudging to move them.

Seph found it hard to think. The constant bellowing was distracting. It took hours to get the steers into the river. Once there, they were disinclined to swim across. Rather than stringing the herd in a long column as they did on the trail, all three thousand of them bunched up in the water. Seph glanced at the distant shore and saw Skillet climbing the slope of the river bank, but few steers followed.

It was hard to watch from his position. From time to time, he went out of his way to check on Torp. He thought back to when they crossed the Guadalupe. Dusty had insisted that Torp hang back and sit it out. Now, with Slaw and Woodsy gone, they didn't have the luxury of coddling anyone. Torp didn't protest taking the upriver side of the herd. It was a perilous assignment, but downriver was even riskier.

The cowboys screamed themselves hoarse, pushing those beeves across what seemed like an ocean. The front half of the herd finally emerged on the far shore, but the back half turned. Once they began swimming in circles, it was hard to stop them from milling.

The surface of the river had looked calm enough. Underneath, the currents moved faster than Seph would have thought possible. It was a challenge to keep Win's head above water.

Seph had just confirmed that Torp was still in position across the herd when a splash ahead of him caught his attention. Before realizing that a man was overboard, he spurred the dapple-gray horse forward.

A steer lost its footing. The beast had been pawing the water on the outside ring of milling steers. It wasn't far from the desperately splashing cowboy who had slipped from his saddle. He tried to remember who had the position ahead of him. Was it Wobble or Hork?

Before Seph could get to the man and attempt a rescue, the steer disappeared underwater. It had gotten caught in a swirling eddy of water, like a tornado in the middle of the river.

Seph noticed a cowboy hat floating down river and nudged Win in that direction. He almost crashed into Hork who emerged, gasping for air and clawing the water's surface.

With a swift arm, Seph threw a loop over his head, dropped it over Hork, and pulled hard. Seph's voice croaked when he screamed, "Grab the rope!"

Hork reached his arms forward.

Seph worried that Hork would slip through and be lost. He kept tugging at the rope, trying to keep it taut.

Hork thrashed and struggled against the rope and current. Then, suddenly, there was no fight at all. It was as if he had given up, letting the current draw him downstream.

Seph tugged desperately, tightening his loop as he rode through the deep water.

Straining, Seph fished Hork from the water and swiftly ferried him to the riverbank.

Still coughing up water, Hork waved Seph away. "Go on, I'll be fine. Don't worry about me."

Win tossed his head in protest when Seph forced him back into the river. Seph rode toward the milling beeves, screaming like a banshee and flailing his arms. The critters spiraled, but Seph lost track of his thoughts and had no sense of time.

In times like that, a man's instincts took over. There was no telling where they came from. The mission was to save as many steers as possible. Seph attacked the herd with ferocity and intense concentration. He never quit.

He barely noticed his thoughts or considered what to do. He just did what needed doing.

Finally, when it was over, Dusty rode up and knocked Seph in the arm with a gentle fist. "Let up, kid. It's over. There's nothing more we can do."

After an exhausting afternoon crossing the Red River, they camped another night before returning to the trail.

Before long, the spoiled herd got used to traveling again. They spent the next night at Beaver Creek and the night after that on Cow Creek. At the end of the fourth day, they were halfway between milestone rivers.

It still felt strange, leaving Texas behind.

Seph spent most of the day tightening and releasing his grip on the stone in his hand. Mostly, he thought about the herd and watched the horizon. Gripping that rock reminded him of his impossible decision.

He should have told Dusty and Squat about the outlaws weeks ago. He had considered leaving the drive. Initially, the outlaws had followed him, but now the herd was more important. Seph was caught in the middle. He hated that the Dagger D, Angry R was in peril. Even more, he hated that it was his fault. The more he thought about it, the less he believed the outlaws' claim that they'd let the cowboys live if he kept quiet.

As they made camp, Squat rode in and said, "We're being followed." He pointed to the east. Silhouetted on the horizon, five horsemen sat motionless. They weren't trying to hide the fact that they were there.

Blaze whispered over Seph's shoulder. "It's Indians. What do you think they want?"

Forty miles to the north, the outlaws lazed beside a cheerful fire on the banks of the Washita River.

Swoop said, "I'm sick of beans. We got anything good to eat?"

Coyote groaned. "Stop pestering me. Why do I gotta do all the cooking?" He grumbled. "Didn't have enough money for much more than cheap vittles, Chaw. Dang beans."

A smile crept across his face. He had remembered buying something else. "Oh, I got a treat for you."

Coyote rummaged through a sack of provisions and pulled out a dented can. "I saved a heap on these here peaches."

# CHAPTER 14

SWOOP GROANED, GRASPING HIS stomach as he leaned against a tree.

The sun was barely up and already the day was a disaster. Swoop's insides felt like they were being twisted around a hot iron, and the stench of vomit and diarrhea fouled the air. He could hear Coyote and Chaw suffering nearby. Their groans and retching added to Swoop's misery. He thought about pumping them full of lead, but talked himself out of it.

Between groans, Coyote cussed at Chaw. "This is your fault. You brought this sickness back from that cow camp."

Chaw didn't have the energy for a long argument. "Did not. It's them peaches, you idiot."

"Dang them peaches," Swoop muttered, doubling over as another wave of nausea hit him. He could barely think straight, but he was sure that Chaw was right. That fruit was tainted. Pain and sickness overwhelmed his senses. As long as he lived, he resolved he would never put peaches in his pie hole again.

The cheerful fire from the night before was now reduced to smoldering ashes.

Coyote stumbled from the bushes, slick with sweat. "We gotta move, Swoop," he said weakly. "Can't stay here. The herd will be coming this way. Who knows how soon?"

Swoop wanted to argue, but he knew Coyote was right. They couldn't afford to be caught. Not if they wanted to take the herd. He forced himself to stand. Every movement sent fresh waves of agony through his body. It was like the worst whiskey fever he ever had, multiplied tenfold.

Chaw was bent over a bush, retching violently. "Ain't never been this sick," he gasped between heaves. "Why'd you buy them dang peaches, Coyote?"

Coyote didn't answer. He was too busy trying to keep his own insides from escaping.

Swoop scanned the camp. His vision was blurry. His head throbbed. Every step felt like a monumental effort.

The camp was a mess. Bedrolls were scattered, the fire was out, and the sick smell hung heavy in the air. Swoop forced himself to move, kicking at Coyote. "Get your gear. We need to leave. Now!"

He staggered to the edge of camp, grabbed his saddle, and threw it over his horse's back. The animal snorted, indignantly. Swoop fumbled with the straps, his hands shaking. He shook his head and grumbled, "I smell so bad, I've offended my horse."

Behind him, Chaw collapsed to his knees, groaning in pain. "I ain't gonna make it, Swoop."

"Yes, you are," Swoop snapped, though he had doubts of his own. He was barely holding on, and the thought of traveling was almost too much to bear.

They finally managed to break camp. The empty can of peaches lay on the ground and the foul stench of vomit and diarrhea lingered. Swoop wondered what else they might have left behind, but didn't care enough to check.

Swoop looked at Coyote and Chaw, pale, haggard, and barely able to sit upright. "We ride slow, but we ride. We can't be here when those jaspers come."

The trio plodded off. Swoop's vision swam, but they had to keep moving. They had been careful to hide evidence of their presence on the trail, but there was no covering up their misfortune on the banks of the Washita River.

As the herd moved north on the fifth day, Seph couldn't shake the feeling of being watched.

Whenever they looked to the east, those five riders moved slowly, parallel to the herd. They kept their distance but were always there, like ghosts in the shadows. The cowboys muttered amongst themselves, casting wary glances toward the silent figures.

At one point, Blaze rode back from the flank position for a brief break and conversation with Seph and Torp. Blaze nodded to the east.

Torp squinted at the horizon. "We seen 'em. They been there all day."

Blaze nodded. "Chickasaw."

Seph wanted to ask a few questions, but several errant beeves strayed from the herd. Blaze talked to Torp for a couple of minutes as Seph rode off to maneuver the steers back in line. Before Seph could return, Blaze spurred his horse and returned to flank.

Day turned to night and the Chickasaw riders maintained their position on the horizon. On the sixth day, they were still there, mirroring the herd's movements. It was disturbing. Seph tried to focus on keeping the critters in line, but his eyes kept drifting eastward. He had tried to convince Torp that Stoke had overstated the dangers of Indian territory, but every passing hour, he worried more about what was to come.

On the seventh day, as the cowboys bedded down the herd, the Indians rode into camp. There was an air of authority about them. Their faces were stern and unreadable. As they approached, Squat and Dusty stepped forward to meet them.

Squat introduced himself and his brother. Then Squat said, "Why have you been following us? What do you want?"

Nearby, Torp, Seph, and Blaze inched forward, watched, and listened.

The Chickasaw leader spoke, his voice calm but firm. "Fifty head of cattle. Toll."

Squat's jaw tightened. "Fifty? Oh, no. That's out of the question. I'll give you one. That's fair. More than fair, I'd say."

Torp, Seph, and Blaze looked at each other and shook their heads.

The Chickasaw conferred with his men. They spoke in low tones, their expressions serious. The leader turned back to Squat. He opened and closed his right hand three times. "Fifteen."

Squat shook his head. "No. One. That is my final offer."

Blaze groaned and looked at Seph. "He ain't gonna like *that*!"

Stoke stepped up, joining Dusty and Squat. "We should give 'em Skillet." His expression looked sour as he said the bull's name. Usually, he avoided using that name. Stoke had it in for that critter since the day Seph found the brindled longhorn.

Torp shook his head and whispered to Seph and Blaze. "Ain't right. Skillet's a good bull and the others follow him."

Squat ignored Stoke but remained firm with the Chickasaw.

The negotiations were tense. After restating their positions, they remained at an impasse. Finally, the Chickasaw leader shrugged.

Squat interpreted the gesture as agreement and turned toward Seph, Torp, and Blaze.

It didn't surprise Seph to hear the boss condemn Booger. The albino longhorn was a notorious troublemaker. He was always causing problems at the tail end of the drive, and Seph blamed him for killing Slaw. Despite the trouble Booger caused, Seph had mixed emotions.

The trio mounted up and nudged the steer from the herd. Seph muttered, "Time to say goodbye, Booger." True to form, the longhorn feinted and dodged, resisting his banishment. The beast snorted, eyes wild, as if he knew his fate.

"Good riddance," Torp said, a grin spreading across his face. "I never liked that monster anyway."

Seph nodded, but there was a tightness in his chest. He'd never liked Booger either, but watching him go felt strange. He couldn't figure why.

The Chickasaw took Booger and rode off into the night. The camp settled, but an uneasy silence hung over the cowboys.

Blaze stood by the fire, muttering, "They'll be back."

Seph and Torp looked at Blaze. "Why do you say that?" Torp asked.

"The chief wasn't satisfied," Blaze replied. "The deal didn't sit good with him. One ain't enough. They'll want more."

Seph's stomach churned. Blaze's gloomy words sounded threatening. They still had a long ride ahead, and nobody wanted another encounter with the Chickasaw.

Blaze added, "Next time, there will be more than five Indians. Lots more."

As dawn broke on the eighth day north of the Red River, the cowboys prepared to move out. They edged northward and looked forward to reaching the Washita, but the threat of angry Chickasaw lingered.

The herd moved steadily throughout the morning. Dust swirled around them as they rode. The endless clatter of hooves made Seph feel as if the journey had gone on for years. His eyes kept drifting east, half expecting to see a swarm of Indian warriors.

Blaze rode back from flank, and Torp reined his mount to Seph's side. Sometimes when the herd became docile, it was possible for the three friends to visit for a couple of minutes before returning to their places.

Torp said, "They say we'll be at the Washita by nightfall. You think that's where those Chickasaw will show up again?"

Blaze answered, "That'd be my guess. We need to be ready, just in case."

Seph nodded agreement. He could feel it in his gut. His mind raced as he considered scenarios. The fear of another encounter with the Chickasaw was ever-present. Blaze's prediction of many warriors made it worse.

But they had to keep moving.

As the day wore on, the air grew cooler. Finally, they heard the distant murmur of the river. They were close now. The promise of water and rest were within reach. The beeves picked up their pace, drawn by a primal urge to drink. That uneasy feeling never left Seph.

The river was a welcome sight, but the cowboys remained vigilant. Seph's eyes scanned the eastern horizon, searching for any sign of the Chickasaw, but something nearby caught his attention.

Something smelled foul, but familiar. Too familiar. Then he saw the remains of a campfire. Beside it lay an empty, dented can of peaches, its lid still attached, and then it hit him. Whoever had camped here also suffered from food poisoning. He sneered at the discarded can and thought of the outlaws, then smiled.

The herd drank eagerly as the cowboys set up camp. Seph, Torp, and Blaze stood together talking about Indians, but nobody mentioned the abandoned campsite. They looked at the evidence. They wrinkled their noses, and they frowned, remembering the horrors of being turned inside out, but said nothing.

Lullaby stepped forward and said, "God sees our struggles, friends. He gives us strength to endure. Whatever will happen, it is in God's hands. Remember that."

Seph nodded. Blaze frowned. And Torp hung his head.

As night fell, Seph sat by the fire. He couldn't stop thinking about the unpaid toll, Squat's refusal, and Booger's grim fate.

Dusty and Squat gathered the cowboys around the fire. "We made it to the Washita," Squat began, his voice steady. "But we need to stay sharp. Those Chickasaw might not be done with us. And, who knows how many other tribes we'll encounter ahead."

The cowboys nodded.

Squat continued, "Conjure, Wobble, and Stoke will take first watch tonight. Yodel, Trinket, and Lullaby take over at midnight. We need everybody else rested and ready."

Seph took a deep breath. He thought about all of the disasters they might yet face. How could he sleep with such troubles on his mind?

As the camp settled for the night, he lay awake, listening to night sounds. The Washita River's gentle flow should have been enough to soothe away his worries, but sleep eluded him.

Blaze's words echoed in his thoughts. "They'll be back."

Seph's resolve hardened. Sleep or no sleep, he would be ready.

The herd moved across the Washita River as the sun rose. The cowboys urged the cattle forward, water splashing around them. The front half of the herd emerged on the north banks, dripping and restless.

Seph's eyes scanned the horizon from the middle of the river. Unease nagged in his gut.

Just as he looked away, a thunderous roar filled the air. From the east, a swarm of fifty Indians descended upon them. Their war cries carried above the din of the moving herd.

"Indians!" Squat shouted. He was far off, but he yelled loud enough to carry his voice.

At point, Stoke, Thumbs, and Dredge readied their rifles. Just behind them, Wobble and Hork, riding swing, looked back with wide eyes. Dunk had emerged from the river with the chuckwagon. Dusty was still in the water, urging the rest of the cowboys forward.

The Indians charged. Their horses' hooves kicked up clouds of dust. They whooped and hollered, spooking the cattle—it was a stampede in the making.

Seph's heart raced as he drew Woodsy's revolver. How was he supposed to fight Indians and keep the cattle from milling in the middle of the river? He saw the Indians in the distance, rounding up steers. As he pushed beeves from the river, he saw that they seemed to be taking only what they had demanded earlier, but the chaos of cowboys riding every which way did nothing to slow the Chickasaw.

Wobble's horse reared, pitching him to the ground. An Indian galloped past, his lance grazing Wobble's arm. Wobble howled, clutching his bleeding arm.

Seph shouted Wobble's name. Abandoning his position, he urged his horse forward, climbed the river bank, and galloped to where Wobble had fallen. He fired his revolver to scare off the attackers and prevent the herd from trampling his friend.

Jumping from his saddle, Seph extended a hand and shouted, "Get up, Wobble. Hurry! You'll be trampled."

Wobble nodded. His horse had stood dutifully by. With a hand on the saddle horn, Wobble attempted to drag himself aboard. Seph roughly shoved Wobble, almost pitching him over the other side, and grimaced at the sight of Wobble's bloody sleeve. There wasn't time to tend that wound—not yet.

Seph turned his attention back to the herd. The Indians had managed to drive fourteen steers away from the main group. Seph's stomach churned, but there was no time to think. They had to protect the rest of the beeves.

Gunshots rang out. Stoke, standing tall in his saddle, fired at the Indians. One of the Chickasaw fell from his horse, a bullet thwacked his chest.

Stoke grinned, his eyes wild. "Got him!" Stoke yelled. "That was *my* shot!"

The battle raged on until the Indians began to retreat. They had accomplished their mission. Seph's heart thundered. He glanced at the tail end of the herd and realized that he was out of place. Swiftly, he returned to the back of the herd.

Torp pointed toward a handful of slippery beeves that were breaking away. With a nod, Seph rode in pursuit of the familiar getaways. Even without Booger, the stragglers never missed an opportunity to attempt an escape.

As Seph returned the errant critters to the column, Dusty rode up, his horse lathered in sweat. "Keep moving!" he shouted. "Forget about what happened this morning. No time to dwell on it. Think of the end of the trail!" Before Seph could affirm the boss' orders, Dusty was gone.

Seph glanced back at the Washita River. After such pandemonium, it was surprising how quickly the herd fell into its routine, orderly march. It was as if nothing had happened. It was a miracle they didn't stampede. If the herd ed the loss of their brethren, it wasn't evident.

The memory of the attack lingered in Seph's mind for hours, until his thoughts drifted.

The herd moved steadily along the two day journey between the Washita River and the Canadian River. Hour by hour, the tension eased.

"We don't need to worry about the Chickasaw anymore," Blaze said, his voice confident. "They got what they wanted."

The rest of the cowboys were reassured, but Seph continued to worry. "What about the Indian Stoke shot?"

The Indian threat had distracted them. The real worry was outlaws. Seph rode alone at the back of the herd and avoided conversations. He dreaded what he needed to do. Every day that he put it off only made it worse.

How many days and miles had passed since the outlaws had approached him near the Colorado River? A month? He frowned, recalling that it was more like five weeks. He couldn't decide which was worse, that they tried to recruit him, or their threat.

The words replayed in his head. "If you tell the others, we'll kill them all. If you keep our secret, some of them will survive. The choice is yours, farm boy."

Every day and every night since, Seph had wrestled with what to do. Indecision gnawed at the edges of his gizzard. Tonight, he decided, he would tell Squat and Dusty. Whatever the consequences, he couldn't live with the secret any longer.

When they reached the banks of Canadian River, as the other cowboys settled in for the night, Seph took a deep breath and approached Squat and Dusty. His heart pounded, but he marched forward anyway. Just as he reached them, he saw Stoke. The top hand was talking animatedly. Seph was close enough to hear what he said.

Stoke blustered. "I saw him, meeting up with them outlaws. I heard every word they said. I shoulda said something sooner, but I don't like to snitch.

That Seph kid is rotten. Fire his can and send him packing. Get him outta here."

Seph's stomach dropped. He tried to speak, but Stoke continued. "Did you know he sneaks off and practices firing his guns? I'm sure he's getting ready to join up with them outlaws when they finally attack."

Seph's anger flared. He no longer dreaded fighting Stoke—he wanted to go after him *now*. Even if Stoke flattened him.

As he stood there, seething, he noticed Thumbs and Dredge, nearby, exchanging an odd look. It was quick, but something about it seemed odd. Of course, the Stoke, Thumbs, and Dredge were thick as thieves, but there was something about the look on the faces of Stoke's sidekicks that Seph couldn't understand.

Squat noticed Seph's presence. Disappointment and suspicion smoldered in his eyes. "Come 'ere boy. Is this true?"

Seph opened his mouth to explain, but the words stuck in his throat. He glanced around and saw the other cowboys watching and tightening in closer. His heart pounded as he tried to find the right words. This was his moment to clear his name. He took a deep breath and prepared to speak, but Stoke's mocking laugh cut through the silence.

"What's the matter? Got nothing to say?" Stoke taunted.

Squat's eyes narrowed as he watched the exchange, waiting for Seph to respond. Dusty stood beside Squat, arms crossed, his face unreadable but stern.

Seph clenched his fists, his resolve hardening. He was ready to say his piece and he was ready to confront Stoke. The time had come.

First he would fight Stoke, and then he would defend his honor.

# CHAPTER 15

SEPH CLENCHED HIS FISTS. "I would never betray the Dagger D, Angry R. Never."

Somehow, every man knew when a fight was brewing. It was as if they were pulled toward the conflict by an invisible, horseshoe-shaped magnet.

All of the cowboys were on their feet. Their eyes were glued to the unfolding drama, but he could barely see them. It was like he had blinders on.

Without a word of warning, Stoke lunged at Seph. Stoke's fists swung wildly, but Seph kept his cool. He repeated Dunk's advice in his head.

Seph ducked just in time, but felt the rush of air from Stoke's missed punch. Only the edge of Stoke's knuckles grazed his cheek.

The camp erupted in shouts and cheers. Seph heard them, but rather than finding the sounds distracting, Seph focused on what to do next. He also heard the scuffling sound of their boots moving in the dirt. His and Stoke's.

Seph's first punch landed squarely on Stoke's jaw. The impact sent a jolt of pain up Seph's arm, and he was glad. If his arm hurt, Stoke's jaw must hurt worse.

Stoke grunted but retaliated with a ferocious jab to Seph's ribs that winded him. Seph had to fight on while gasping for breath.

They grappled, and Seph's wind came back as they crashed to the ground in a tangle of limbs. They scrambled for control, with first one and then the other seeming to gain the upper hand in the scuffle.

Seph heard Wobble shout, "Show 'em what you're made of!"

Torp cheered, "Give him a taste of your knuckles, Seph."

For a moment, Stoke and Seph were frozen in position, both straining, but neither able to gain an advantage.

Seph heard Dusty say, "Let it be, Dunk. They need to settle this." Seph was glad that the bosses didn't intervene. *Hang the consequences.* It was time that he and Stoke settled their differences.

With a surge of energy mustered from deep within, Seph shoved Stoke hard, and they separated briefly. Long enough for them to return to their feet.

Wobble shouted, "Knock his block off!"

Seph thought about his next move and blinked. He hesitated, just a moment too long.

Stoke sprung toward Seph and delivered three quick blows. One to the chest, one to the ribs, and one to the chin.

Seph's head hit the ground hard. His vision exploded into stars. He could taste the metallic tang of blood in his mouth and sweat stung his eyes. Before he could gather his wits, Stoke's fist collided with his cheek. The impact reverberated through his skull.

Seph gritted his teeth and swung back, his knuckles scraping against Stoke's teeth.

"You're nothing but a coward," Stoke hissed, his breath hot and rancid. "You'll never be one of us."

Seph's anger flared. "Today we can't stand each other, but one day we'll be friends." What possessed him to say such a thing?

Stoke laughed. "That'll be the day."

"Mark my words." Seph scrambled backward, kicked Stoke away, and scrambled back to his feet. When Stoke charged again, Seph dodged and landed a punch of his own—to Stoke's stomach. The force sent a shockwave up Seph's sore shoulder. With a wince, he thought, *It's always that same blame shoulder.*

Stoke responded with a forceful headbutt and Seph reeled. If only he could break away for a moment, maybe he could rally again.

They broke apart, both gasping for air, their bodies battered and bruised.

The other cowboys circled tighter.

Seph didn't care how tired he was or how much his body hurt. The fight was not over.

He tried to visualize himself the victor. First, he'd have to find a new angle. But his shoulder throbbed. It was a deep and grinding pain, but he pushed through it.

Seph locked his gaze on Stoke, shutting out everything else. Stoke didn't flinch or break eye contact. Seph caught every twitch in the man's face, every bead of sweat on his brow, and the constant, spiteful gleam in his eyes. All of Seph's energy was aimed right at him. Stoke stood like an angry, impatient bull, ready to charge.

Stoke sneered, then lunged forward.

Seph sidestepped Stoke and delivered a powerful kick to his thigh.

Stoke stumbled. His balance faltered, but he quickly regained his footing. The man's face twisted in fury. They clashed once more, a whirlwind of punches and kicks, neither man yielding.

Chops shouted, "Finish it!" Seph had no idea who had spoken or which man they were rooting for. With a final burst of strength, Seph drove his fist into Stoke's jaw.

Stoke's head snapped back, and he crashed to the ground. Seph stood over him, chest heaving, his entire body trembling. Just breathing required effort.

But Stoke didn't stay down for long.

Seph glanced away and into the crowd. He had no idea what he was looking for. The pain his his shoulder flared and he took a slight step backward.

Stoke saw his chance and took it. He sprang to his feet and delivered a crushing blow to Seph's temple.

Seph's vision blurred as he staggered backward, struggling to stay on his feet.

Stoke pressed his advantage, landing blow after blow until Seph's knees buckled. With a final punch to the jaw, Stoke sent Seph sprawling to the ground.

Seph lay there, dazed and defeated, his chest heaving. His ribs hurt, his body trembled, and he gasped for breath.

Stoke stood over him, triumphant. "I'm The Ignitor," he boasted. "I'm like a locomotive. Nothing can stop me. Nothing can slow me down."

Dusty stepped forward, raising his hand. "Show's over, men. Time to hit the hay."

The cowboys began to disperse, murmuring amongst themselves.

Squat's voice cut through the noise. "Be ready to ride at first light."

Seph's legs shook as he climbed from the ground.

Squat placed a hand on his shoulder to steady him. "Stay put, Seph."

Seph nodded, wiping blood from his lip. Squat's eyes bore into him. He hadn't beaten Stoke, but he had survived. Now he must survive the bosses.

Squat said, "Tell me why I shouldn't give you the boot right now."

Gasping between every second or third word, Seph said, "I did not meet with the outlaws by choice. They tried to recruit me. When I refused, they threatened to kill everyone if I told. I kept quiet to protect the crew."

Squat's expression tightened. Dusty and Dunk stood nearby, listening intently.

Dunk stepped forward. "I b'lieve him. And, as you know, I'm a great judge of character."

Squat studied Seph for a long moment. "Is there anything else I should know?"

Seph shook his head. "No, sir. That's the truth." Then he told a quick version of the story about the outlaws raids on the Vermillion family farm. "That's everything. I swear."

Squat sighed. With a frown, he said, "Get some rest, Seph. I don't envy you. You'll be feeling them aches and pains tomorrow."

Seph nodded, grateful for the reprieve. As he limped towards his bedroll, he could feel the eyes of the other cowboys on him.

He hadn't won, but he did not concede either.

Seph groaned as he got up. Every muscle ached, and his shoulder felt like it had been cranked through a meat grinder.

As the crew waited in line for breakfast, Seph couldn't help but notice Stoke. The man had a black eye and several fresh scars. Despite his victory, Stoke didn't look much better off.

Stoke snarled at him. "Want me to clobber you again? Just say the word, Nanny Joe Jo." The words sounded tough, but the tone lacked Stoke's usual intensity.

Seph shrugged and hoped that his face didn't betray his thoughts.

Mounting a horse was agony. The strain on his shoulder made him grit his teeth, but he forced himself up into the saddle.

As he rode, he thought about Stoke. The man had ratted him out, pounded him senseless, and never missed an opportunity to prank or belittle him. Yet in the heat of that fight, he remembered telling Stoke that one day they'd be friends. *I must be out of my mind*, Seph thought.

Seph knew that if he ever found out who killed Woodsy, he wouldn't hesitate to take that man's life, but short of murder and thievery, Seph believed in redemption.

The heat grew oppressive as the day wore on. Sweat trickled down Seph's back, soaking into his shirt. Every step jostled him. It wasn't easy to think of something else when every breath brought a fresh wave of pain. *Will this day never end?* The stifling heat and barren landscape only made matters worse.

Torp rode up beside Seph. "You alright, Seph? You look like you ain't doing too good."

"I'm fine," Seph snapped. Immediately, he regretted it. "Sorry, Torp. Didn't mean to bite your head off."

Torp nodded. With a sympathetic smile, he said, "I understand. Holler if you need me." He looked like he was about to ride away, but instead he gushed, "That was really something, the way you put the fists to Stoke last night. You almost got the better of him. I couldn't believe it."

Seph grunted in acknowledgment. He wasn't sure, but he might have smiled, ever so slightly. If his face didn't hurt, he might have grinned.

When Torp rode back to his position, Seph focused on the trail ahead. The ride was a miserable slog. The humidity soaked his skin and his shirt. Determined to maintain a stoic demeanor, Seph thought the aftermath was worse than the fight itself. He tried to distract himself by thinking of ways he could have done better, and how he could have avoided the agony.

Mercifully, Squat found a bountiful meadow, and they took the next day off to graze the herd. The heat was unbearable, but nobody complained about taking a break.

The next day was hotter still. Seph's aches and pains had not subsided, but he fought not to show it. The day seemed to go on forever. All he could think about was making it through the day.

The landscape slowly began to change. Every now and then, Seph saw a small tree. Finally, he saw a ribbon of greenery ahead, proof that they were nearing the North Fork. But the promise of water and rest did little to alleviate Seph's suffering.

By the time they arrived, Seph was exhausted. He dismounted slowly, biting back a groan as his feet hit the ground.

Seph did what he could to help set up camp, then found a spot to rest. He leaned against a tree and closed his eyes. He hoped the bosses would decide to lay by again tomorrow, but wouldn't have dared to ask them. The sound of the river was soothing and he imagined it washing over him.

As night fell, Seph couldn't shake an uneasy feeling. He tried to recite the rivers in his head, but couldn't recall them.

As Seph stepped toward his bedroll, Torp reminded him that it was his turn to stand night watch. Again.

Well after dark, Seph guarded the remuda. Thumbs and Dredge watched over the beeves. The cattle were quiet, but the sound of the river filled the night.

Seph paced among the horses, moving slowly but steadily, constantly glancing into the darkness. He thought he saw something but convinced himself that it was just his imagination. A couple of minutes later, he thought he heard a noise that he couldn't explain, but the night was always full of wild, haunting sounds.

Sheriff, nickered softly—a familiar, comforting sound. Seph patted his neck and whispered, "Good boy."

His shoulder throbbed, but he told himself to ignore it.

At the far end of the herd, five men gathered in a secretive huddle. Swoop, Coyote, and Chaw met with Thumbs and Dredge.

Swoop spoke in a low, dangerous voice. "What happened after Chaw killed that kid?"

Chaw shifted uncomfortably, his hand resting on the hilt of his knife.

Thumbs said, "Ah! It's all they can think about. Especially at night." He chuckled at the thought. "Even their own shadows scare the daylights out of 'em."

Swoop replied, "Good. Any quit?"

Dredge answered. "Nope, not yet. And nobody's mentioned it either, but you can see it in their eyes—constantly peering into the darkness. Only a matter of time, if you ask me."

Swoop grunted. He was satisfied that the plan was working, only not fast enough. "We need to take out another one. If we kill one more cowboy, the rest will turn tail and head back to Texas."

Thumbs affirmed, "They're hanging by a thread already."

Swoop grinned. "We need to be smart about this. We can't just kill anyone. We gotta break their spirits."

Dredge offered, "How about the cook? That'd do it. Only, I'd miss them biscuits. Better pick somebody else."

Thumbs ran down the list of choices. "Chops, Hork, Lullaby...."

Swoop became impatient, cutting Thumbs off. "I don't care which one you pick, long as it ain't the tall kid. I'm not done with him yet."

Coyote eagerly asked, "What's the plan, Swoop? How are we gonna take the herd?"

Swoop's expression darkened. "We need to act before they reach Bluff Creek. We can't let them leave Indian country. First, we'll raid the remuda. Tonight. That should spook 'em good, slow 'em down, and leave 'em weak. If that don't scare them off, Coyote here will take down one of the cowboys at the Cimarron and another at Salt Fork."

Coyote nodded, a wicked grin spreading across his face. "That'll do it, by golly. They'll be too scared to keep going."

Swoop's gaze intensified. "Make sure the tall kid sees it all. I want him to remember who's really in charge."

The men were quiet for a minute. Finally, Thumbs broke the silence. "What do you want us to do?"

Swoop said, "Keep doing what you're doing. Anything changes in camp, tell us. We'll hit the remuda in about an hour—next time you're at this end of the herd. Make sure they blame the kid. And if by some miracle, them cowboys don't run off before Bluff Creek, be ready with your guns."

As the men dispersed, the outlaws slipped back into the shadows.

Thumbs and Dredge emerged from opposite sides of the bedded down herd. They seemed calm, but Seph felt uneasy.

Slaw's advice chimed in his head. "Trust your gut, Seph. It's rarely wrong to rely on your instincts." Something wasn't right, and Seph kept his hand close to Woodsy's revolvers.

Thumbs and Dredge waved at Seph before crossing paths and continuing their rotation, making yet another lap around the beeves. It wasn't like them to greet him like that.

The night was thick with mist. The river seemed to hiss and whisper. As time passed slowly by, Seph patrolled the remuda on foot and strained to hear any unusual sounds.

A twig snapped behind him.

Seph's heart raced. He turned, but saw nothing.

Suddenly, bedlam erupted. Horses screamed. Shadows moved fast. Seph drew his revolver and ran toward the commotion.

Torp came running from camp. "Indians!" he yelled.

Seph fired into the air, trying to scare off the attackers. The horses panicked. Someone must have cut one of the picket lines.

Seph saw Sheriff bucking, wild with fear.

"Get them under control!" Torp shouted.

Seph grabbed for Sheriff's lead rope, but the horse was too scared. He broke free and bolted into the night. Seph's heart sank to think he could lose Sheriff.

Shots rang out. Seph ducked, feeling the heat of bullets whizzing past. He saw shadows on horseback, but couldn't make out the riders' faces. Were they Indians or outlaws? He couldn't tell.

Torp dropped to the ground. Seph feared the kid was hit.

The raiders were fast. They cut the ropes and drove many horses away. Seph chased after them on foot, but tripped and fell hard. Pain shot through his leg. He struggled to get up, but the raiders were already gone, disappearing into the night with half the horses.

Panting, Seph limped back to the remuda just as Torp climbed to his feet.

The longhorns bellowed and rose to their feet as the commotion from the remuda died down. Thumbs and Dredge emerged from the darkness, shushing the herd. Dark scowls twisted their faces.

Seph's gut twisted. Sheriff was gone. It was hard to think beyond that.

"You lost half the remuda," Thumbs said, his voice cold and accusing.

Seph's head spun. "I tried to stop them," he said. "But they were too fast."

Dredge shook his head. "You were supposed to watch them, Seph. How did they get so close without you seeing?"

Seph felt a wave of guilt. "I don't know. It was all so sudden."

"It must have been Indians," Thumbs said. "Who else would do something like this?"

Seph wasn't sure. He replayed the attack in his mind—the shadows, the speed, the sounds. It didn't feel like an Indian raid, not that he would know.

"You need to explain this to Squat and Dusty," Dredge said. "They're not going to be happy."

Seph nodded, his mind whirling.

Camp was a frenzy. Startled cowboys grumbled and shouted in the dark. Wobble groaned. "What's happening?"

Seph's heart was heavy. He had failed in his watch, and now Sheriff was gone. He saw Stoke standing with Thumbs and Dredge, then they walked together toward Seph. His shoulder throbbed as he remembered that fight.

Stoke's sneer was unmistakable. "This is all your fault, Seph," Stoke said, his voice loud and accusing. "If you weren't so useless, we wouldn't have lost those horses."

Seph felt his anger flare. "They came out of nowhere."

Thumbs sneered at Seph. "That ain't good enough."

Before Seph could respond, his friends stepped in. Torp stood by his side. Lullaby placed a hand on Seph's arm. Blaze glared at Thumbs and Dredge.

With a sharp voice, Torp said, "It ain't Seph's fault. We were under attack."

Lullaby added, "It could have happened to any of us."

Blaze's eyes narrowed. "Blaming Indians seems too easy. Don't sound right to me." He glared at Thumbs, then Dredge.

Thumbs stepped forward, fists clenched. "You calling us liars, Blaze?"

Blaze met his gaze, unflinching. "Just saying it don't add up."

Fists were about to fly. Seph's shoulder throbbed and his leg hurt, but he braced himself for another fight.

Just in time, Squat and Dusty intervened. Dusty's voice boomed across the camp. "Enough!"

Squat stepped between the cowboys. "We got no time for brawling. We got a job to do. These beeves ain't gonna march themselves to Abilene."

The cowboys stepped back.

Squat turned to Seph. "You need to explain what happened."

Seph took a deep breath and recounted the raid. He kept his eyes on Squat, ignored the pain in his shoulder, and pretended not to see Thumbs and Dredge's accusing glances.

Squat listened, then turned to the rest of the cowboys. "We can't afford to wait. We need those horses back. Yodel, Trinket, come with me. We're going after them now."

Seph's heart sank. He wanted to go after Sheriff and the other horses himself. "Let me come with you," he pleaded.

Squat shook his head. "No. You stay with the herd. Riding drag is where you belong."

"But—" Seph started.

Dunk placed a hand on Seph's good shoulder. "Now's not the time to argue. You ride for the brand. Do your job. On another day, things will work out differently."

Seph nodded, his heart heavy. He was desperate to rescue Sheriff, but he had a duty to fulfill. Even if that duty was the lowliest position on the Deatherage roster.

# CHAPTER 16

SWOOP STEPPED AWAY FROM his partners to savor the moment. It was exhilarating.

After their late night raid, they'd ridden hard for several hours, and it was time for a break. Swoop stood beneath the half-moon, watching the stolen horses drink from the North Fork of the Canadian River.

The thrum of success hummed through his veins.

He smiled proudly. Watching the movement of the horses, and listening to them whinnying and snorting pleased him. He counted them again—thirty horses!

This wasn't just petty thieving. Taking an entire cattle drive was something big. It required careful planning, patient execution, and gumption. In the past, he'd been content with smaller payoffs, but now he was on his way to being rich. Getting away with the horses was a big step toward reaching that final goal. Life would never be the same.

Coyote and Chaw interrupted his thoughts.

"Look at that dun with the fiery mane," Coyote said. "Bet that one's worth a pretty penny."

Swoop chuckled. "That's the one the tall kid rides. Yeah, that's a fine horse—too good for a simple puncher like him." He turned toward Coyote and said, "This is bound to slow them cowboys down." Then he faced Chaw. "When we finish this job, we'll have everything we want."

Swoop licked his lips and ran his tongue over his teeth. His gaze swept across the herd. "No more scraping for meals. Nothing but the good stuff for us!" He could picture the demoralized drovers struggling to push the herd with half their horses gone.

He felt invincible, but it was time to move. "C'mon boys. It won't be long now. Everything's going according to plan."

A long day in the saddle followed the disastrous night. It was their first day after leaving the North Fork of the Canadian River.

The dust from the herd swirled around Seph. He tried not to think about his aches and pains. If only he could forget last night's raid on the remuda. Frequently, he squeezed the stone he carried in his pocket.

As the miles stretched on, Seph's thoughts grew darker. He replayed the tragic events of the cattle drive. The death of Slaw still haunted him. All the miles Slaw would have traveled, sunsets he would have enjoyed, and beeves he would have helped deliver to market—what a waste.

And Woodsy, poor Woodsy—hacked to pieces and left for dead. It was hard not to think of the work he would have done as a lawman, protecting people and making towns safer. How many lives might he have saved?

Losing Sheriff wasn't like losing Woodsy and Slaw, but it weighed heavy on Seph's heart. He fought against the urge to ride off alone and not look back. But it was just an urge. He knew he'd never do such a thing while there was a job to do.

If only Squat had taken him along to rescue the horses. It was his fault they were gone. He ought to have a chance to make it right. When Lullaby rode back for a brief visit, Seph told him as much.

Lullaby said, "We have to trust Squat and the others. We have our own job to do here."

Seph took a deep breath. He didn't like hearing it, but it was true. "You're right, Lullaby," he conceded. As they talked, Seph watched Torp, riding proudly and watching the herd intently.

Lullaby interrupted Seph's thoughts. "Remember, God watches over us, even in the hardest times. We all have our burdens, Seph. Keep the faith." With that, Lullaby loped forward, returning to his place along the chain of hooves, horns, and cow tails.

Seph rode on. He felt his resolve strengthening, and thought, *Just focus on keeping the beeves in line. Do your job and trust your fellow cowboys.*

After riding a couple of miles to the west, the outlaws turned north before dawn, then rode hard all day. Swoop was tired and had been looking for a good spot to rest. He crested a butte to survey the land. His eyes locked open as he spotted a lone wagon in the distance, near the Cimarron River. "Well, well. What do we have here?" he muttered.

Swoop descended the butte and rejoined his companions. "There's a wagon up ahead," he said. "Wonder what's inside."

Coyote's eyes lit up with interest. As if on cue, his stomach growled. "Let's find out."

They rode toward the wagon, leaving Chaw to watch over the horses. The sound of their approach startled a few birds into flight, but otherwise, the prairie remained eerily quiet. When they reached the wagon, Swoop and Coyote rapidly assessed the situation.

Coyote said, "Abandoned?"

Swoop shrugged.

A quartet of mules stood nearby and looked at them. Swoop wasn't accustomed to mules, but Coyote made quick work of harnessing them. Minutes later, Coyote hopped onto the bench, sparked the mules, and drove the wagon in the wrong direction.

Swoop rode along beside, holding Coyote's horse's reins.

After a couple of miles, they turned the wagon and reversed course to where Chaw waited with the stolen horses. As the wagon came to a stop, Swoop barked at Coyote, "Don't just sit there like a fool. Find out what's in that wagon."

Coyote sprung from the wagon bench and leaped into the wagon bed.

Swoop rode around the wagon and peeked into the back. His eyes widened in surprise.

Coyote backed up and almost tripped over the bench at the front of the wagon. Always one to state the obvious, he gasped, "Uh—we're not alone, boss. There's somebody in the back of this wagon."

Seph figured there were two hours until dawn. He had night watch again, and just finished riding around the herd. The critters had been restless most of the night, but had finally settled down. He stopped and listened.

Experience had taught him to be wary. He didn't want to be responsible for another costly raid. It grated on him knowing that their loss had been his fault and was determined that it would never happen again.

Seph's eyes caught movement. He glanced about, looking for his partners, Torp and Blaze. He thought, *They must be on the other side of the herd.*

He looked back toward the remuda and squinted. There it was again. A glimmer of movement—two figures creeping toward the horses. *Not again*, he thought, drawing Woodsy's Colts and nudging Win forward.

As he got closer, he couldn't believe his eyes. He recognized those sil-houettes—Conjure and Hork—what in the devil were they doing? He couldn't blink away the disbelief. *That's stealing!*

A couple of steps closer, Seph could hear their voices.

"I just gotta get outta here, Hork," Conjure whined. "I'm scared. This herd is cursed. The days are a fright and the nights are a horror." His voice quaked. "I don't wanna die."

"Me neither," Hork grunted as he saddled his favorite cowpony. "But honestly, I just need a decent meal."

Conjure tightened the cinch on his horse and grumbled, "How can you think of food at a time like this? We're surrounded by ghosts. Something bad is gonna happen, I just know it."

Hork let off. "If I eat one more plate of beans, I'll puke myself to death. I can't take it no more."

"Me neither. I gotta get home. Mama misses me. I just know it. And Bonnie, poor Bonnie. Nobody loves that mutt but me, I swear. And Mary, my sweet Mary—I shouldn't a let her daddy run me off."

"We're half-starved. I'm sick of eating dust. This ain't livin' Conjure."

Seph had heard enough. He nudged Win forward. "So that's it then? You boys just gonna up and quit on us?"

Conjure froze, his hand halfway to the saddle horn. Hork stiffened, then they both turned around.

Seph had forgotten that he held one of Woodsy's Colts in each hand.

Conjure stammered. "Don't shoot, Seph."

Hork held his hands up in the air.

Seph holstered the revolvers and dismounted. "So your plan is to ride off on horses that don't belong to you? These nags belong to the Dagger D, Angry R. Not you."

Conjure swallowed hard and stammered, "Seph, I... I can't do it no more. I'm a coward. Is that what you want me to say? We're sitting ducks out here. If the shadows don't get us, the outlaws will. Or them Chickasaws. I'm too young to die."

With a moan, Hork said, "Ugh. I didn't even think of it as stealing, Seph. I spent so long sitting on them horses, I didn't even think of it. But a fella can't be afoot out here."

Seph said, "These horses have the Deatherage brand." Seph and Slaw had been lucky enough to own a horse when they signed on, but most of the cowboys weren't as fortunate. "You can't leave now. There's still work to be done."

Conjure said, "We don't want to leave Dusty and Squat short, but we just can't go on any more."

Seph said, "What about the rest of us? I thought we were partners. Brothers. Friends. It's not just leaving the bosses. If you light out, where does that leave the rest of us?"

Hork groaned. "Aww, Seph. I never thought about that." He turned himself sideways and pointed at his belly. "I'll stay but they gotta feed me. I'm wasting away! These durn beans are killing me. I'm rotting away from the inside out. I can't think straight without a real meal."

"Alright, alright. I'll stay, Seph." Conjure looked defeated. "But I don't know what good I'll be. I'll probably just die of fright. Never mind getting shot by bandits or hacked to pieces, like Woodsy. One day, I'll just keel over."

Seph walked over and patted Conjure's shoulder. "Betcha won't." He glanced at Hork. "When we get to Abilene, you can eat anything you want. Meanwhile, we gotta stick together. See it through. You ain't quitters. I don't believe that. I bet you were just sleepwalking, and your minds wandered away taking you along."

He put his arms over their shoulders and led them back to camp. "Just take it one day at a time. Before you know it, we'll be there. You'll see."

Swoop watched as Coyote gathered wood for a campfire. Chaw busied himself picketing the horses. Swoop was just about to spread out on the ground and relax when a sound reached his ears. It was the unmistakable sound of a crying baby.

The outlaw climbed into the stolen wagon and looked at the furious infant. With a frown, he muttered, "What are you doing here? I told Coyote to leave you behind."

He thought that they should just put the baby girl out of her misery rather than letting her suffer and die. As he climbed aboard, Swoop decided to take care of that task himself.

When he picked up the child, she began to coo. Swoop cradled her in his left arm. As he gently rocked the baby, he noticed a tiny spoon next to a jar that looked like it contained a gloppy mixture of ground corn and oatmeal.

Rolling his eyes, Swoop dipped the spoon in the jar and fed the cooing bundle a spoonful of mush. It smelled foul and looked disgusting, but the baby made a satisfied humming sound. Swoop shook slowly from side to side and muttered, "It's a cruel world, Baby Doll. I ain't sure we're doing you any favors, keeping you on."

Swoop knew the baby was full when she pushed food back out of her mouth with her tiny tongue. "Alright, alright then. Hold your horses." He looked about, found a rag, and wiped the baby's face.

Stepping from the back of the wagon, carrying the contented infant in his arms, he remembered holding another baby. It was long ago, before he was apprenticed to the saddle maker. He must have been sixteen, maybe seventeen years old at the time. His father had yelled at him just for holding his baby brother.

"What am I gonna do with you, Baby Doll?"

The second day out of North Fork was no better than the first.

Squat, Yodel, and Trinket had returned empty-handed. But every time they came back for a meal or a break, Seph felt more discouraged. How could they have lost the trail of thirty horses?

It was hard to keep the faith when everything seemed impossible. If only Squat would let him go along. He was sure that he could find the horses, though he wasn't an experienced tracker.

Before they hit the hay, Lullaby said, "Let us pray." He tipped his head forward and said, "Oh Lord, please watch over those with troubled hearts tonight. Never let us forget, there's always hope. Keep us safe in Your care and guide us through these dark times."

The friends dispersed and Seph sought the comfort of his bedroll. Lullaby's prayer lingered in Seph's mind. A sliver of hope was better than no hope, he thought as he drifted off into a fitful sleep. Somehow, they had to make it to Abilene.

The next day was long and arduous, but when the day was done, they had finally reached the Cimarron River.

There was something about the sound of that river's name that pleased Seph's ear. He thought it would be a glorious sight to behold. But dark thoughts distracted him. The memories of Slaw and Woodsy were haunting. He couldn't stop seeing their dead faces in his head. And he pined for Sheriff.

He rubbed his eyes and worried about Conjure and Hork. What if they snuck off again? Should he tell Dusty and Dunk what had happened?

What if they didn't sneak off, only to be killed by outlaws or Indians? Then it would be his fault for making them stay. He told himself that he had to think about something else.

Dusk was approaching. Seph stood to get some wood for the fire.

A rustling sound caught his attention. *Not again!* He looked to the side and saw somebody stumbling into camp.

What was a woman doing in the middle of nowhere? Her clothes were tattered and her hair was wild. She looked around frantically.

Seph turned to face her directly.

"Wills! Is that you, Wills?" she called out, desperately.

Seph took a couple of cautious steps toward her. "Ma'am, are you alright?" he gently asked.

The woman's eyes locked onto his. "Wills, thank God I've found you!" she cried, rushing toward him. She threw her arms around him, crushing him within her surprisingly strong embrace. "I've been looking *everywhere* for you." Her fingers dug into his back. "Our baby! Where's our baby?"

Seph was taken aback. Confusion clouded his mind. "Ma'am, I think you've got me confused with someone else. My name is Seph, not Wills."

The woman's face dropped. Her eyes welled with tears. "No, you're Wills." Exasperated, she continued. "I should know my own husband. Please, you have to help me find our baby."

Gawking cowboys gathered around, inching forward to get a better look.

Dunk and Dusty stepped forward.

"Who is this?" Dusty asked gruffly, his eyes fixed on the woman. "What the dickens is going on here?"

Seph shook his head. His heart pounded. "I don't know. She thinks I'm someone named Wills and that I can help her find her baby."

The woman clung to Seph. Her fists gripped the fabric of his shirt. Her desperation was heart-wrenching. "Please, Wills, don't leave me. Not again. I need you. Lily needs you too. Don't ever leave us again."

Dusty looked at Seph. "You're married?" With a sneer, he said, "And you left this woman? I don't cotton to abandoning a woman or a baby." Dusty shook his head.

In a high voice, Seph protested, "I never saw this woman before in my life, boss. I ain't married. I swear." Even so, he tilted his head and looked into her face. He was unaccustomed to being so close to a woman, let alone having one cling to him. Softly, he pleaded, "Do tell us, ma'am, what is your name?"

"Oh Wills, I declare. What am I going to do with you?" She pressed her forehead firmly against his chest.

Seph looked over her head at the gang surrounding them. Finally, not knowing what else to do or say, Seph said, "Tell the folks your name." He hesitated and added, "Darling."

The woman turned, leaned against Seph, and said, "Pardon our manners. It's been a dreadfully long trip. I'm Bonita, this is my husband, Wills Tanner, and our baby, Lily is in the wagon over there." She pointed toward the chuckwagon, and the cowboys turned their heads to look, as if expecting to see a baby among Dunk's provisions. Before they could look back at Bonita, she crumpled in a heap at Seph's feet.

Dunk stepped in. "Give me a hand, Seph."

Ignoring his aches and pains, Seph scooped up the tiny woman and set her near Dunk's cook fire. Bonita came to, but looked even more disoriented as he gently set her down.

Dunk said, "You look like you need a good meal, ma'am. Er, Mrs. Tanner. First, you'd better have something to drink," he urged.

She touched her chapped and parched lips. It was plain to see the desperation in her eyes. She wore a simple dress with a shawl. Her bonnet barely clung to her head, twisted to the side. Her dress was torn in several places. Mud caked about the hem, and thick dust clung to her body. Though she was dressed like a married woman, she didn't look to be any older than twenty.

She took a small sip of water, blinked, and quickly took a second sip. Then, she gulped down the rest of the tumbler of water.

Dunk said, "How about having a bit to eat?" He handed her a plate of beans.

She ate hungrily. After a couple of bites, she looked into one cowboy's face after another. If it bothered her to have them watching as she ate, it didn't show. She scraped the last few beans from the plate and passed it back to Dunk.

"Oh dear," she gasped. Her hands covered her cheeks and tears welled up in her eyes. "It just came back to me." She squeezed her eyes shut. "Wills and I were headed to California. Our baby girl was born along the way. We got homesick and decided to return to Dayton. Dayton, Ohio. We shouldn't have set off on our own. Wills tried to talk me out of it. He said it was foolish to ride off alone like that, but I was so homesick."

Her voice trembled. "Wills rode off to hunt for food. We waited and waited. I don't know how many days we waited, but he never came back. Then, tragedy struck. I went to the river to fetch some water, and when I came back, strangers had stolen our wagon. They took everything." She looked at Seph and added, "I... I shouldn't have left our baby alone in the wagon."

Seph didn't know what to do or say.

Mrs. Tanner paused and said, "You're not Wills." There was a sad expression on her face. "I suppose there's some resemblance, but you're definitely not my husband."

Seph stuttered. "Y-y-yes, ma'am."

She looked away from Seph and into the curious eyes surrounding her. "Please call me Bonita, if you don't mind." She looked down at her hands and continued. "For two days I wandered, not knowing which way was which, until I finally stumbled upon your camp."

The woman seemed like she was done speaking. Dusty said, "Pardon me and the men, ma'am. Miss Bonita." He pointed to the northwest, the direction from which she had approached. "You came from that direction?"

She looked worried as she answered. "I don't know where I've been. I have a terrible sense of direction, sir."

Dunk handed Bonita more water. As she drank, Dunk asked, "Would you rather have some coffee?"

Bonita shifted her lips, coating them with moisture, but they still looked painfully chapped. Then she said, "I'd prefer to have some more beans, if you can spare them."

Hork scoffed. "That's all we got around here, ma'am."

As she ate, Dusty introduced the men. "We got a few men out..." he paused and decided not to burden the woman, "scouting." When he finished introducing the crew, he said, "You already met Seph. He's the one that looks like your husband, I reckon."

Seph nodded and tipped his hat as if he had just met the woman.

With a sigh, Dusty added, "The guys better hit the hay. We've gotta move in the morning, you see." Seph remained behind as the others peeled away.

Dunk added, "I'll set you up under the wagon. You should be comfortable there. On the way north, we'll see if we can find your family. I'm sorry for what you've had to endure, Bonita."

Seph took a step back, but continued to watch Dunk and Bonita. He was relieved that she no longer claimed to be his wife, but he felt bad for her. Stoke stood beside him, but everyone else had stepped away. Neither man said a word.

As the woman settled in beneath the chuckwagon, Dunk said, "Holler if you need anything, alright?"

She said, "You're too kind, Mr. Dunk."

Just then, a shot rang out.

The camp exploded into pandemonium. Cowboys scrambled from their bedrolls and darted in every direction.

A man stumbled into camp, wobbled unsteadily, and dropped to the ground. It was impossible to see who had been hit.

Seph rushed forward to help, and Stoke was right beside him.

# CHAPTER 17

IT WAS WOBBLE. HE had night watch and somebody had shot him.

First thing in the morning, Seph checked on him. When he saw Dunk kneeling beside the kid, he worried. Had he worsened overnight?

The kid's face was pale, but his eyes were open. The bullet wound wasn't life-threatening. Wobble was lucky to be missing only a small chunk of flesh from his arm. Dunk had patched him up quickly before bed, but now, he lay on his bedroll, groaning.

Dusty joined them. In a gruff, but gentle voice, he said, "You'll be alright, son. Just take it easy."

Wobble shook his head. His limbs trembled, and his voice cracked as he said, "I don't want to be Wobble anymore. I'm going back to being Jerry Strawberry and I'm going back to St. Louis where I belong. I shoulda never left there. It'd suit me fine if I never leave St. Louis again."

Dusty sighed. He wasn't surprised by the boy's decision. He reached into his pocket and pulled out a few dollars, pressing them into Wobble's hand.

"Take this. It's not much, but it'll help. Sorry I can't pay you full wages. Remember, the deal was you only get paid at the end of the trail."

Dunk tried to talk Wobble out of a foolish decision. "It's dangerous out there alone. Won't you change your mind and stick around until we reach Abilene?"

Wobble shook his head. "I ain't staying. I don't care what happens to me. I want outta here now."

Dunk tried one more time. "I really hate to see you go."

The disheartened cowboy climbed from his bedroll. "You can't make me stay, can you?"

Dusty shook his head and walked away.

Dunk answered, "No. Nobody can make a man do what he don't want to do, but please don't do this to yourself."

Wobble shook his head but didn't say another word. As Chops brought his horse, Dunk gathered a small bundle of food. Torp rolled his bedroll for him. Before Wobble left, Dunk said, "I wish I could send you off with more. It's gonna be a long ride, Jerry."

Wobble nodded. He'd had enough of talking, but he looked each man in the face before riding out. Then, with a wave, he was gone. Seph thought he looked grateful and sad at the same time.

Lullaby bowed his head and prayed. "Lord, please watch out over our friend as he makes his way home. Grant him safe passage back to St. Louis and comfort his troubled heart. Amen."

The cowboys echoed, "Amen," as Jerry placed a hand over the bandaged spot on his arm and rode away slowly to the northeast. Seph watched the horse and rider fade into the distance.

As the camp stirred, Bonita Tanner joined Dunk by the cook fire. Her hands moved deftly. She prepared breakfast as if she had been along from the beginning of the drive.

Dunk stepped back and nodded at her. He said, "Thank you, Bonita. It's good to have an extra pair of hands around here."

Bonita smiled, though Seph detected a hint of worry on her face. She said, "I'm eager to pack up and go. I must find my baby and my..." She looked away, unable to finish her sentence.

In his head, Seph finished her sentence. *Wills.*

The cattle drive hastily prepared to leave the sandy banks of the Cimarron River. The horizon still hadn't yet swallowed the slow-moving, injured cowboy who had called it quits. Despite his friend's request, Seph refused to think of him as Jerry Strawberry. He didn't understand Wobble's decision to leave. It was foolhardy and selfish, but the boss said he could go.

As the herd began to move, Seph noticed another odd glance exchanged between Thumbs and Dredge. His skin prickled, and a cold shiver ran down his spine.

There was something sinister about the look they shared—something that promised trouble ahead.

As they traveled throughout the day, Seph thought about a lot of things.

It irked him that Wobble had left. It didn't make any sense to him. There was work to do, and they didn't have far to go. Besides, it was dangerous for a lone rider on the open plains. The landscape had grown arid and inhospitable, particularly in the direction Wobble went. It would take a whole lot of good luck and some of Lullaby's prayers to get that kid safely home. Cowardice he could understand, but the selfishness was beyond his comprehension. How could Wobble leave them short a man?

Riding up the trail, Seph also thought about Thumbs and Dredge. His instincts screamed that they were up to no good. And something told him that more trouble was just around the corner. He was glad when the riders at point began bedding down the herd.

When the last of the beeves caught up with the front of the herd, Seph dismounted. He rubbed his shoulder but didn't think about the ache. After turning his horse over to Chops, he made his way to Dunk's wagon.

In a low voice that he was sure would not be overheard, Seph said, "I need to talk to you about Thumbs and Dredge. Something ain't right."

Dunk's expression mirrored the concern that Seph felt in his gut. The cook said, "We'll talk later t'night. For now, let's get the camp set up, the cattle settled, and dinner served."

Seph nodded, but the sense of unease clung to him. He busied himself gathering buffalo chips and brittle twigs for Dunk's fire. He and Dunk didn't get a chance to talk that night, but Seph resolved to remain wary and alert. It was hard to be ready for anything. All a guy could do was try to keep his wits about him—and do his job.

After a day of rest and two more worrisome days along the trail, they had one more day of riding before they were due to reach the Salt Fork of the Arkansas River. It was almost possible to imagine leaving Indian country, but Seph knew they still had to face the outlaws. The gnawing feeling kept niggling its way into the core of his gut.

He realized that instead of gathering wood, he was pacing. He thought of Stoke, who never stood still for long. Pacing was in Stoke's nature, not Seph's. He shook his head and thought about whether he was becoming more like the top hand than he'd like to admit.

Seph glanced at the chuckwagon and noticed that Bonita was wearing Dunk's apron. He watched as she rolled up her sleeves. A floury cloud enveloped her as she worked.

He turned toward the wagon and took a couple of steps toward it. He was surprised to see Stoke, walking quickly, carrying a bucket. Clumsily, Seph tripped over the toe of his boot, but righted himself rather than falling. Torp scampered from the banks of the tiny creek with another pail of water.

Bonita put her hands on her hips and called out, "How many buckets of water do you cowboys think I need?"

Seph grinned as he slowed to a standstill beside the chuckwagon. He watched Bonita return to her work. He felt a pang of something he couldn't quite place and struggled to identify—perhaps it was sympathy, admiration, and maybe even a touch of protectiveness.

He thought of Ma, when she was young. Before she got sick.

Seph opened his mouth to speak, and tried to sound casual. "Could you teach me how to make biscuits?"

Nearby, Dunk looked at Seph strangely. Long before Bonita stumbled into camp, Dunk had taught Seph how to make them. Seph shrugged and Dunk shook his head.

Before Bonita could answer, Stoke stepped forward, his usual swagger replaced with a rare, sheepish grin. "Can you learn me how to make them biscuits too?"

Seph's mind wandered. He still felt wary whenever Stoke was near. It was as if they were competing for the woman's attention, though both of them knew she was married and had a baby somewhere.

Bonita smiled and continued her preparations. "I'll need some more flour, a pinch of salt, another bowl, and just a little bit of water from the bucket. If one of you gentlemen could fetch those, we'll get started."

Seph hurried to comply. Stoke, not wanting to be outdone, quickly followed.

Bonita clucked her tongue against the roof of her mouth and admonished them. "You must wash your hands before cooking."

Bonita's presence seemed to bring out a strange mix of camaraderie and rivalry among the hands. When Seph glanced at the crowd of onlookers, he was certain that he saw a jealous look plastered on their faces.

As they worked, Bonita spoke fondly of her family. "Wills always loved my biscuits. Said they reminded him of home." She went on to repeat her story about leaving and returning to her hometown.

The cowboys exchanged uneasy glances every time she mentioned Wills, but no one dared voice the grim thoughts that surely crossed their minds.

Seph felt a growing sense of dread. He couldn't shake the feeling that something terrible had happened to Wills and little Lily. What if Bonita never learned their fate?

Bonita's cheerful chatter filled the camp. "Dayton is a lovely place. Full of greenery and kind folks. Cheerful gardens. I can't wait to get back there." She made it sound so welcoming, Seph thought he might have to plan to visit Dayton himself someday.

Torp asked, "What else do you like to cook, Bonita?"

"Oh, I can make a mean pot of stew and the best cornbread you've ever tasted," she replied with a laugh. "What about you, Torp? Ever been to Ohio?"

Seph was impressed by how quickly she had learned everybody's names.

Torp shook his head, his eyes wide with interest. "Never. This is the first time I ever left Texas. What's it like?"

"It's beautiful, Bonita said wistfully. "Full of rolling hills and friendly people. It's downright homey."

As the biscuits baked in the Dutch oven, Seph found a moment to speak with Lullaby. "What do you make of all this?" he asked quietly, nodding toward Bonita.

Lullaby's brown eyes were kind but serious. "She's been through a lot, Seph. It's not our place to judge, but to help when we can. Let's pray for her and her family."

The reverent cowboy bowed his head. "Lord, please watch over Bonita and guide her steps. Grant her the strength to face whatever comes and bring her peace. Amen."

Seph found comfort in Lullaby's words, but uncertainty still gnawed at him. And, whenever he got that feeling in the pit of his stomach, he remembered Slaw's words of warning. *Trust your gut.*

The sudden arrival of horses in camp surprised everybody. Seph and Lullaby made their way to the chuckwagon as Yodel, Trinket, and Squat dismounted. They looked tired and unhappy.

Yodel nodded, solemnly in his brother's direction. Lullaby was the talkative one. Yodel rarely said a thing.

Squat shook his head, dusted himself off, and said, "We lost the trail."

Dusty's eyes narrowed. "How can you lose a trail when you're following thirty horses?"

Squat's face hardened. "The river is wide. The ground is rocky. Wind's always blowing. Tracks disappeared."

Dusty stepped forward. "You should've found another way. There's three of you. If you can't track 'em, *that* kid can." Dusty gestured toward Trinket. "We need those horses, Squat. You know these cow ponies can't go all day."

Squat's temper flared. "You don't need to tell me that. You think you could do a better job as trail boss? Be my guest. We're doing our best, Dusty."

"That ain't gonna cut it, man. You gotta do better 'n that."

The two squared off, their voices rising as their argument went on. The rest of the camp fell silent, watching and listening to the brothers' spat unfold.

Bonita looked on, her eyes wide with concern, while the cowboys exchanged uneasy glances. They were unaccustomed to seeing the Deatherage brothers argue. The more they squabbled, the less sense they made.

When Bonita reached her arms forward with a cup of coffee for each of them, the argument came to an abrupt stop.

Squat stared at her for a long moment, his mouth hanging open. "Well, I never... who are you, and what are you doing *here*? Ma'am."

She answered briefly, and Squat grunted in response. He yammered a half-hearted welcome before frowning at his brother.

Dusty and Squat turned away from each other and walked in opposite directions.

Yodel, Trinket, and Squat saddled up early the next morning, and departed camp, determined to find the horse thieves. Wobble's quitting the drive, arguing with Dusty, and stolen horses weighed heavy on Squat's mind and fueled his determination.

They had tried to look in other directions. This time, Squat decided to ride due west.

The day stretched on as they followed faint trails and subtle signs left by the outlaws days earlier.

The land was rough and rocky. After witnessing the dustup between Squat and Dusty, Trinket didn't hesitate to point out traces of a large band of horses when he found them along the trail. His sharp eyes missed nothing, and Squat was pleased with Trinket's tracking skills.

At one point, Trinket dismounted, picked up a rock, and pointed to a scratch. He tipped his head back, revealing the face that normally was hidden in the shade of his sombrero. "This was left by a horse's hoof, boss."

Mostly, Trinket was able to read tracks without dismounting.

As the day neared its end, Yodel spotted something in the distance. He raised a hand, signaling to Squat. He pointed and whispered, "There they are."

In the fading light, if they strained the limits of their eyesight, they could see three men, a wagon, and a herd of horses moving slowly north. Squat's heart quickened with anticipation. "No fire tonight," he said firmly. "We don't want them to spot us. We'll have a cold dinner and hit the bedrolls early. Tomorrow, we'll get 'em."

The three men ate in silence. After supper, Squat settled into his bedroll. He had stated the plan, but it lacked detail. It was easy to say, but just how would they get the job done?

Late in the afternoon on the fourth travel day after leaving the Cimarron, the Deatherage outfit reached and crossed the Salt Fork of the Arkansas River. Like most river crossings, it was a popular place for bedding down a herd.

There was evidence of many previous campfires. Whoever had been there last left behind a good bunch of firewood, but Seph figured they'd need more. As he was dragging a large branch back to camp, he noticed Dusty standing, looking off into the distance.

The man barely moved. He stood, still as a statue, his hands gripping his lower back. Only his head moved. Seph figured Dusty was scanning the horizon for signs of trouble.

Then it struck him: Dusty was worried.

When dawn broke, Yodel, Trinket, and Squat were already on the move. They followed the outlaws' trail with painstaking care, keeping a safe distance to avoid detection.

From what Squat could tell, the outlaws seemed unaware of their pursuit.

As the day wore on, the terrain grew more challenging. Squat signaled for a halt, and they made a camp in a small copse of trees, hidden from view.

Swoop settled in the shade with his back against a tree and looked off toward the south.

Instead of napping in his arms, the baby had fallen asleep on his chest. He used both hands to keep her secure and prevent her from slipping.

A flicker of movement caught Swoop's eye. The reflection of the setting sun hitting a metallic object confirmed that somebody was out there.

He couldn't say how he knew, but he did. Maybe some of those drovers had followed them, tracked them here, and were fixing to reclaim their stolen horses.

Swoop made a tsking sound with the tip of his tongue against his upper teeth and the baby yawned in her sleep.

In a low voice, he said, "Looks like Uncle Chaw's got a job to do tonight, Baby Doll."

"We'll surround them at first light," Squat whispered, his voice barely audible.

He rubbed his chin. "Trinket, you'll take the left flank. Yodel, you take the right. I'll approach from the front. We need to be swift and silent. Meanwhile, keep low to the ground. Move as little as possible."

Squat lifted a canteen. He took a mouthful of water, swirled it around, and swallowed before corking the vessel. He muttered, "Save as much water as you can. Just in case."

They split the night into thirds. Trinket took the first watch, Yodel the second, and Squat assigned himself the last shift.

The night passed slowly. Every rustle of grass and whisper of wind foretold danger.

Squat was dead tired when Yodel shook his foot. He had to stand to keep from falling back asleep.

The sky began to lighten, hinting at the approach of dawn. Squat stretched, weary but increasingly alert. His eyes scanned the darkness.

Squat was surprised when a strong hand clamped over his mouth. His heart pounded as he felt the cold tip of a knife blade pressing beneath his chin.

"Make a sound, and you're dead," a harsh voice whispered in his ear. "*Rodaja* is itching to have a little fun today."

Squat tried to stand on his tiptoes to get away from the poking end of the blade. He didn't bother to try to make sense of what the man was saying, but he knew he must be silent.

He struggled to keep calm. His body tensed as he considered his options. None of them were good. The outlaw's grip was firm. He imagined the sharp blade puncturing his skin and thought he could feel blood dripping down his neck.

# CHAPTER 18

WITHOUT RESTING AT SALT Fork, the drovers pushed hard for two days, moving toward Bluff Creek.

Bluff Creek was their last stop before leaving Indian Territory and entering Kansas. It was reassuring to know that soon, they would be back in the States.

As they approached their destination, dark clouds began to gather on the horizon. The horses were tired and progress slowed to a crawl.

Unease prickled at Seph. The sky turned an ominous shade of gray, and the wind picked up, whipping through the tall grass. He had learned to be wary when storms approached.

Electricity sizzled in the air. Thunder rumbled low in the distance, menacing and growling.

Torp rode over. In a high pitched voice, he said, "Storms like this look scary. You're sure they're gonna get you. But then, sometimes, they disappear in another direction." Seph could hear the fear in Torp's voice.

Seph offered, "Bluff Creek's not far ahead. We might make it before the storm hits." He knew it was wishful thinking.

Torp said, "We'd better get our rain gear out, just in case."

Seph agreed. "Reckon so. Good thinking."

The clouds rolled in like an angry sea.

Torp rode back to his position as Seph twisted in the saddle, untied his slicker, and tugged his arms through the sleeves.

Yet again, Seph longed for Sheriff as he muttered to Win, "This looks bad." Talking to Slaw's horse felt like talking to his fallen friend, and Seph found it comforting. "Real bad."

Seph was glad to see Torp donning his oilskin gear as he reached his position.

Dusty rode up next to Seph, adjusting his poncho. "I've seen storms like this before. They can turn deadly quick, son."

Thunder pounded in the distance. The cattle twitched and moaned. Win shifted nervously beneath him.

Seph nodded at Dusty. "Seen it coming. Hoped we'd reach Bluff Creek before it hit."

Lightning flashed, illuminating the dark clouds. The rumble of thunder grew louder, rolling across the plains like a drumbeat.

A chill crept down Seph's spine. It was getting closer. The storm was swelling fast. Its fury rattled his soul.

Before making his way over to Torp, Dusty said, "Keep your wits about you, kid."

At first, the fat raindrops splattered against Seph's hat. Half a minute later, the sky tore open, and a drenching downpour dumped buckets of water on drovers, horses, and beeves alike in a constant deluge. Steam rose from Win's overheated neck.

A lightning bolt struck nearby, its blinding flash followed immediately by a deafening clap of thunder. The ground shook with the force of it.

Win reared, pawed the air, and Seph quickly grabbed the saddle horn. He was glad when Win's front legs returned to earth. For a moment there, he was sure that he would slide from the saddle.

What had been an orderly procession became a confused tangle.

The cattle began to mill. Horns clattered as longhorns bumped into each other. Blue currents of electricity danced from the tips of one animal's horns to the next.

Seph gripped the reins tightly, trying to stay calm. The witch's fire created a frightening web, spidering its way across the manic herd.

Dusty rode by, shouting, "Keep them together!" His voice was barely audible over the roar of the storm.

Win sidestepped nervously.

The cattle's movements grew more frenzied.

Another bolt struck, barely missing Seph. The boom almost blew him from the saddle. The roar rang in his ears. His skin prickled, and after the brilliant flash of light, he worried that it had singed his skin and hair. It smelled like when they branded steers.

He figured the strike landed on the ground twenty feet away from him. He was shocked that it hadn't hit him instead, but there was no time to dwell on miracles. Because no sooner than the thought crossed his mind, the cattle broke. Their fear erupted into a full-blown stampede.

Seph's heart raced as he spurred his horse, trying to get out of the way. It was hard to know which direction to ride. There would be no turning the herd now. The best thing he could think to do was to surge along beside them.

The ground shook beneath him as thousands of hooves thundered across the plains.

He glanced around, trying to make sense of the scene that surrounded him.

He thought he could make out Dunk, urging the chuckwagon desperately out of the way. Bonita sat beside him, her arms wrapped around him. It looked like she was clinging to him to avoid getting bounced from the wagon.

Seph turned his head and saw Dusty riding hard, with a determined look on his face. He shouted commands, but Seph couldn't see who he was yelling at—maybe the beeves.

Minutes went by but they felt like hours.

Animals that had seemed too tired to walk now had plenty of energy.

Seph wondered how many miles they had run. It still felt like they were galloping in circles.

Seph saw Thumbs and Dredge on the outskirts. It was hard to make out expressions in the middle of a stampede, but it looked like they were enjoying themselves. Then he realized that they were firing their guns into the air, adding to the mayhem.

"Those rats," Seph muttered. They were trying to make the stampede worse. But why?

Then he caught a glimpse of an all too familiar figure. Swoop! And then a second. Chaw!

Suddenly, it all made sense. The outlaws were taking advantage of the storm. And Thumbs and Dredge were in cahoots with the outlaws.

But where was the third outlaw? And what about Stoke? It only made sense that Stoke was in on it too. What fools they had been.

Seph's thoughts couldn't keep up with the herd. As he galloped along, dodging steers, he saw his fellow cowboys, racing one way or another. He tried to keep track of them in his head.

He almost failed to dodge a steer that veered too close. Win leaped to the side just in time.

Seph saw Stoke struggling to control his bucking mount. The top hand was an expert rider, but Seph could see the panic in the man's eyes. That horse had picked a bad time to showcase its wily side.

Seph made a split-second decision. He spurred his horse and raced toward Stoke.

Stoke's frantic horse corkscrewed, pitching him to the ground. The self-proclaimed *Ignitor* slammed into the ground. Arms and legs twisted grotesquely as he rolled fast—too fast—across the prairie.

"Hyah," Seph urged Win forward, driving him faster.

It was dangerous to dismount in the midst of a stampede. But, Seph thought, *I have to do it. It's the only way.*

As Win closed in on Stoke's position, Seph saw several steers jump over the top hand's body. He also saw a huge beast's hooves hit Stoke's side, rolling his body into a prone position.

"Hold on!" Seph shouted.

He tugged his reins and Win skidded to a stop, inches away from Stoke.

Seph didn't dare let go of the reins. Hortense had taught him what could happen if he did. To free his hands, he held the reins between his teeth. It took all the strength he could muster to heft his groggy, barely-conscious fellow cowboy into his saddle, and then Seph sprang from the ground landing roughly behind Stoke. He wasn't sure if he was strong enough to keep Stoke upright, and the current of raging cattle hadn't slowed any.

He thought of finding a safe spot to drop Stoke. Maybe he could get away from the fray briefly, and then return to the herd. But which direction should he go to find such a spot?

The storm raged on. The stampede showed no signs of slowing down. It felt like it had lasted forever.

He could feel Win struggling to carry the weight of two riders. A strange sound, like a cough came from beneath him. He had to set Stoke down. He worried that Win would drop dead from the extreme exertion.

In the chaos, Seph saw Thumbs again. Thumbs lifted his pistol and stretched his arm forward.

Seph realized the man was aiming at somebody rather than shooting into the sky. He looked in the direction of his extended arm. A shot rang out, and a rider fell from his saddle.

Thumbs and Dredge galloped off to the northwest. Seph thought he could hear them laughing, even over the roar of the storm.

Seph's heart sank as he realized who Thumbs had shot.

It was Torp. Why would Thumbs shoot Torp?

Seph rushed to his partner's side, panic racing through him.

Torp lay on the ground, motionless.

Seph dismounted, leaving Stoke in the saddle, and knelt beside Torp. Seph's hands shook and he wondered what to do.

"Torp!" he called, his voice breaking.

The storm raged on around them, but all Seph could see was his friend's pale face. He couldn't tell if Torp was alive. The uncertainty tore at his heart.

Where did the bullet hit? Where was the wound? They had to save him.

Seph scooped Torp from the ground and started walking. He didn't bother to lead Win, but the dutiful horse followed nevertheless. He looked back and saw Stoke moaning, but he managed to remain upright in the saddle.

With a final sputter, the thunderstorm gave way to slow but steady rain.

Seph thought it would be hard to find the way back, but it wasn't. There was no mistaking the path left in the wake of thousands of thundering hooves.

He walked as fast as he could go, but guessed that he wasn't moving at a very quick pace. Every step felt like a gruesome nightmare. He couldn't count the number of grotesquely twisted carcasses of half-trampled longhorns. At one point, he stopped and drew a deep breath. He was winded. But when he looked down and saw that he was standing in a bloody puddle next to a massive steer with a crushed head, he picked up his pace.

He may have carried Torp for miles. It was hard to measure the passage of time. Relief washed over him when the chuckwagon came into view.

Dunk and Bonita were doing their best to enlarge a tiny fire. They had at least managed to unfurl the canvas awning beside the wagon.

Seph shouted. "Hello, the wagon!"

Dunk heard Seph's voice and met him. Win still followed, and Dunk looked up at Stoke.

Seph said, "Stoke's been trampled. Torp's been shot. Take care of Torp first." He passed the junior wrangler's body to Dunk, turned his body, and walked away.

Fury boiled in Seph's blood. He wanted to stay with Torp, just as he did when Slaw battled for survival, but he couldn't bring himself to go through that again.

He wanted to set out and find the gang of outlaws.

Losing the herd to a storm and a stampede was one thing. Letting the outlaws have the herd was another matter. He hated those thieving raiders. How many times had they robbed him and Ma when he was growing up? Maybe, he thought, he hated the double-crossing cowboys, Thumbs and Dredge, even more.

He stopped and pivoted. Looking at what was left of the Dagger D, Angry R outfit's first drive cooled his anger but steeled his resolve. *This must not stand.* He must do something.

Seph heard the mournful sound of a bellowing longhorn, but he didn't see many beeves. It would take forever to round up what was left of the herd.

He looked to the right. In the dim light, he saw Chops securing a picket line and tying lead ropes to it.

He looked to the left and saw Dusty walking toward him. Seph was not in the mood to listen to the boss or follow orders. Normally, he was inclined to take direction and defer to the men in charge. But nothing would stop him from doing what he knew he had to do now. Not even Dusty.

There was a reason he studied fistfighting, practiced shooting guns, and strengthened his grip. Turns out, it wasn't to take on Stoke. Now he knew what his gut was telling him all along. The time had come.

Dusty stood facing Seph. A few feet separated them. Seph looked down at the man and waited for him to speak.

Dusty didn't waste time on small talk. "Stoke's going to be fine. He's lucky. He'd be dead if you hadn't been there, and he knows it."

Seph nodded, acknowledging that he had heard Dusty.

"Torp's bad off. Could go either way. They're working on him now."

Seph fought to keep his emotions in check. He couldn't help but grimace.

Dusty said, "We'll pray for him."

Seph grunted. "Good."

The two men stood and looked at each other for a long fifteen seconds. Finally, Dusty broke the silence. "You're leaving, aren't you."

Seph nodded. "Yes, sir."

"But you ain't quitting?"

"No, sir."

Dusty frowned. "That's what I figured." He shifted his weight from one foot to the other. "Know what you're doing?"

"No, sir. Ain't got a clue. But I'll figure it out."

Dusty pursed his lips. Finally he said, "I'm worried about Squat. I'm afraid something has happened to him and the boys. Trinket and Yodel."

Seph said, "I'll find 'em, or I'll find out what became of 'em." He heard Ma's voice in his head.

*Don't be timid.*

"It ain't right. Horse thieving, cattle rustling, stealing from farmers, and shooting kids. I'm going to put an end to it."

*Be tenacious.*

Dusty had listened closely and nodded throughout. "I've been watching you, Seph. You might just be the best cowboy in this outfit. I admit I had my doubts at first. And along the way. But I'm glad we took your advice and hired you on."

Seph was surprised to hear Dusty utter such words. He said, "Thanks," but he wasn't in the mood to bask in a welcome compliment.

"I'll go with you," Dusty added, gruffly.

"No. You won't. I gotta do this on my own, boss. Besides, they need you."

The ramrod bit his lip. "Reckon they do." Dusty looked at his feet. "It's a fine mess we've gotten ourselves into."

Seph shook his head. "No, boss. We did good. We didn't do *this*, but I'm going after the ones that did."

Dusty looked back up and said, "Appreciate that. Needed to hear it too. Let's get you some provisions." Dusty gestured toward camp and added, "What do you need?"

Seph scratched his elbow and answered slowly. "Not much. I plan on traveling light. Uncle Yves, that's my rifle, Woodsy's Colts, ammunition, a canteen, and a couple of biscuits oughta do."

"You got it. And a horse." It wasn't a question, but a statement.

Seph repeated it back to him. "And a horse." Win was wore out and Sheriff was gone.

"Take your pick."

Seph sneered. "I'll take Hortense." They had a score to settle too.

Dusty's voice became uncharacteristically soft. "Whatever happens, we're indebted to you, Seph. Hurry back when it's over."

They walked back to the wagon, side by side.

Seph didn't make eye contact with the others. He couldn't bear to look at Torp. This wasn't a time for talking. Just doing. He methodically cleaned his rifle, loaded the Colts, and stepped toward the remuda.

Dusty met Seph at the remuda with fully-provisioned saddlebags and a canteen. Lullaby was two steps behind Dusty.

Seph didn't thank Dusty. He didn't mean to be rude but being polite wasn't on his mind either. His attention was on the trail, wherever it may lead. He was ready to go. He took the reins in hand and stepped into the darkness. He heard a voice behind him and stopped dead in his tracks.

Lullaby said, "I'll pray for you."

A second passed before Seph spoke without turning. "Pray for Torp."

He mounted the mustang and galloped into the night.

It was almost midnight before Seph's nerves settled, and he realized all at once that he was exhausted. He was certain that nightmares would ruin his sleep.

As it turned out, he was wrong. After ensuring Hortense was securely tied to the thick trunk of a tree, Seph stretched out on his back, gazed toward the heavens, and fell fast asleep.

He awoke at dawn and listened intently before opening his eyes. He had heard something. He was sure of it.

A sound reached his ears—one that didn't belong to Hortense. He opened his eyes and glanced at the staked mustang. Her ears turned, then tipped back. She had heard it too. More likely, she had heard the sound of approaching riders long before Seph had.

A quick glance confirmed that Uncle Yves stood nearby. Seph unsnapped the straps over Woodsy's Colts and waited. He could have tried to hide, but there wasn't time. He couldn't see them yet, but he could tell they were close. It sounded like three riders, but he guessed it was only two.

Hortense nickered softly and tossed her head. Her ears pricked forward, and Seph relaxed a bit, trusting her horse wisdom.

Seph had a hunch, and then the voices confirmed it. First he saw Yodel, then Trinket. He blinked quickly, scanning for a third rider. "Gosh, where's Squat?"

Yodel frowned while Trinket spoke, telling Seph what had happened and where to find the stolen horses. Seph told them about the storm, stampede, and what Thumbs had done to Torp.

Before leaving, Trinket warned him. "The bad guy, he said that they would kill Señor Squat if we did not vamoose. So, we vamoose."

As they rode away, Trinket turned and waved. *"Buena suerte."*

Seph waved back.

He saddled Hortense and muttered, "Hope that means *good luck*. We're going to need it."

Shortly after noon, Seph reached the spot where Trinket, Yodel, and Squat had spied the outlaw's camp. He had memorized their directions, but now the outlaws were on the opposite side of Bluff Creek, to the west of the Deatherage camp.

Seph squinted at the bedded-down herd, estimating the count. He figured the outlaws had rounded up about twenty-five hundred of the Deatherage three thousand. They hadn't stolen the entire herd. But they'd gotten most of it.

He had a history with these outlaws. For years they had tormented him and his family, descending on the family farm, stealing food and taking his savings. Every time he rebuilt, only for them to return and destroy it all again.

He was a child then. Now, he was a man. He would not tolerate allowing them to steal one miserable longhorn, let alone an entire herd. It didn't matter that the critters didn't belong to him. The fact they belonged to the Dagger D, Angry R was the same in his mind.

He'd had enough of thievery. And murder.

They killed Woodsy. Now Torp. Who knew how many others they had killed?

He didn't just want them stopped. He wanted to be the one to do it.

Lying on his stomach, he watched the movement of horses, cattle, and outlaws near the bend in the waterway. He plotted when and how to bring them down. Lost in thought, he didn't hear the man approach from behind.

Seph's body jerked, and he rolled to the side as a deep voice broke the silence.

"Is it naptime already?"

# CHAPTER 19

THE MAN QUICKLY SAID, "Woah! Hold your fire."

Never in his life had Seph been more surprised to see somebody than he was at that moment. "Stoke! What in the world are you doing here?"

After having rolled over quickly, he had managed to snap a Colt from the holster.

Stoke chuckled. "Put that thing away, man. Sheesh, first you go and save my life, next thing you know it, you want to shoot me. I seem to remember you begging me to be friends with you someday. What do you say we start now?" He dropped to the ground and sat cross-legged.

Seph sat up and thought about what to say. He wasn't at all used to conversing with the hot-headed top hand.

"I can be crass at times. Wild even. But I gotta say, I appreciate you helping me when I got throwed. I'm beholden to you, Seph."

Seph replied. "I'm glad you're alright. Yesterday, you looked like crap. What happened?"

Stoke laughed. "I keep telling you. You don't believe me. Maybe you don't understand. I'm like a locomotive. There ain't no stopping *me*. Sometimes I get derailed but I bounce back fast."

"But you got trampled."

Stoke nodded vigorously. "Sure did. You gotta see this." He moved to a kneeling position, pulled his shirt up, and pointed to a huge black and blue spot at the base of his ribcage. "Ever seen anything like that?"

"Don't it hurt?"

"Only if I think about it. And I ain't gonna think about it." He left his shirt untucked and returned to a cross-legged position. "After you left, I jumped into the river. Stayed in the water until my skin wrinkled and my teeth chattered. When I got out, I was good as new."

Seph thought about Torp. But he couldn't bear to ask the question or hear its answer. He had already assumed the worst.

Seph thought about the pain in his shoulder and realized that it was gone. He started to ask Stoke a question, but he wasn't quick enough.

Stoke said, "I gotta say, you impressed me. Didn't know you had it in you to be a hero." He was well on his way to answering the question Seph meant to ask. "I can't let you have all the fun. And glory. So here I am."

His head bobbled frivolously and he went on. "We should talk about what's next, but first, I also gotta say, that was quite a fight you put up. I didn't expect you to last more than a minute. There was a time or two I actually worried you might get the best a me. It ain't never happened before. This is the first time it *almost* happened. Next time, I might not be so lucky."

Seph didn't know what to make of Stoke. He'd always been wary of the unpredictable character. Sometimes he thought Stoke bordered on being evil. Other times, Stoke got so caught up in childish pranks it was hard to take him seriously. But there was no denying the man was powerfully strong and had a boundless energy propelling him constantly forward. Overnight, Stoke seemed to have become likable. Or at least, *almost* likable.

He had planned to do what needed doing by himself, regardless of the consequences. He had fully prepared himself for being injured, maimed, or killed. He never considered taking on a partner, but he had to admit the chances of success were better with Stoke's help than they would be if he sought vengeance on his own.

Seph smirked and nodded at Stoke. "I knew you would be hard to beat. I don't know why we didn't get along. But that's over now. Only, don't ever call me Nanny Joe Jo again. I won't tolerate it."

There was an unmistakable twinkle in Stoke's eye. He held his hands wide to his side, like he would if Seph were holding a gun on him, and laughed. "You got it. Never again. I swear."

Seph sighed and gazed back over the prairie. "So, what are we going to do about this mess?"

Stoke said, "I dunno. What's the options?"

Seph explained several possibilities. "It's dangerous, but I had half a mind to just walk in there, draw a bead on Swoop and say that if anybody moves, I'll blow his head off. It might just work. He'd sacrifice the others but never himself."

"What else you got?"

Seph grumbled. "It seems kind of cowardly, but we could snipe them from a distance, one at a time until Swoop is the only one left. It ain't as risky, but I'd kind of want them to know who's pulling the trigger. It might take some time, though, because we'd have to set ourselves up just right."

"Any more brilliant ideas?"

Seph rubbed his forehead then looked to the heavens. Then he glanced at Stoke. "I know this is going to sound kinda crazy. But hear me out. You know how they tried to get me to join up with them. I guess you witnessed that. I could wander in there and tell them I've changed my mind. They could use help driving the stolen cattle to market. And, they're lazy. So if they thought I'd do all of the work, they might jump at the chance to slack off some."

"Brilliant. Kind of risky though. Think they'll let you keep your guns?"

"I thought of that too. It occurred to me that I could leave the Colts up the trail and grab them on the way by. There'd only be six of us. I'm sure they'd have me ride drag. It would be tough to get them all. I'd need a fast horse. A horse like that crazy Hortense over there."

Seph paused and thought about Sheriff. He missed that horse as much as if he were a person. After reflecting on the stolen claybank, he continued. "Firing my guns might set off a stampede. Imagine hunting the enemy during a stampede. That's what they done to Torp." Seph bit his lip and tried to think about his chances of plugging five outlaws among twenty-five hundred mad beeves.

A jolt of exhilaration shot through Seph's gut. "Could be scary. I might get trampled. Who knows? It might just work."

Stoke jabbered, "Yeah, yeah. But what about me? You ain't said anything about me yet. All that stuff you said was just you alone."

With a sigh, Seph said, "Well, I know, Stoke, but you surprised me. I didn't have time to conjure up a plan for you yet."

Stoke seemed to be enjoying himself. "Okay, okay." He shifted his mouth from side to side. "If you barrel in—head on—I could storm in with you, or I could stake a position to the side."

Seph nodded and vocalized agreement. "Uh huh."

"And, if we snipe 'em, we could plan to take two at a time. Be harder for them to find both of us. It may be five against two, but if we drop two right off, the odds are much better."

Seph said, "Yup."

"And, if you pretend to join 'em, I could join 'em too. I still can't believe Thumbs and Dredge skunked me and joined them outlaws. We been riding together for years."

Seph said, "We'd have to be mighty convincing to pull it off."

Stoke raised his eyebrows. "That's for sure. I ain't saying I'm scared, but I'm not sure if I could play make-believe that good."

"Me either. How do you act cool and normal when you're all stirred up inside?"

Stoke laughed. "Cool? Normal? How would I know? I'm *always* all stirred up inside. How many times I gotta tell you that before you believe me?"

Seph didn't get a chance to answer.

The smirk dropped from Stoke's face and he looked at Seph as if he were first meeting him. "It's one thing to talk about what you're planning, Seph, but it's another thing to actually do it. It's easy to shoot at somebody when they're shooting at you. Pardon me for saying so, but you don't strike me as the vigilante type. When you're standing behind that gun, hunting them, you gonna be able to squeeze the trigger—knowing the guy on the other end of the bullet's gonna die? And that you killed him?"

Through pinched lips, Seph answered. "Before Woodsy, I wasn't certain. After Wobble, I was sure. When they shot Torp, I knew I had to hunt them down and kill them."

Dusty rubbed his lower back. It had bothered him for months, but something happened during the stampede. Now, it was almost impossible to bear. They had already planned to take the day off, but now it was a necessity.

He squinted across the camp as Dunk helped Bonita clean up after the mid-day meal.

Dusty's thoughts kept drifting back to Stoke. His top hand had disappeared overnight without a word. The day before, his cronies had disappeared. It's all the cowboys could talk about. The more he thought about it, the more sense it made. All morning, concern and speculation hung over the camp like a storm cloud. He wasn't the only one who thought Stoke had betrayed them.

"Reckon he quit?" Dunk asked, frowning as he secured a sack of cornmeal in a crate.

Dusty shook his head. "Hard to say. Maybe he's with the outlaws now. Looks like our bad luck's getting worse every day."

Before Dunk could respond, Bonita stomped through camp, her face flushed. "I don't understand why we're lazing about doing nothing!" she snapped. "We should be moving. Wills is out there, and my baby—we can't stop looking for them."

Dusty winced, more from the pain in his back than from her words. He suspected her family was already dead, but he kept that to himself. "Maybe we can push the herd tomorrow. The horses are spent, and my back ain't helping none. We need to graze the beeves, too. We'll move when we can."

Bonita huffed and marched off carrying an empty pail.

Dunk raised an eyebrow. "We really gotta wait till morning? We could get a couple of hours up the trail this afternoon.

Dusty sighed, leaning against a tree. "No, Dunk. We got good water and grass right here."

Swoop stood near the edge of camp. He looked to the south, then he looked to the east.

The gang gathered around him. Thumbs and Dredge stood to one side. Coyote and Chaw to the other. Nobody said anything about the baby cradled in Swoop's left hand. They had learned not to mention it.

The wind whipped through the camp, carrying the scent of rain and the distant rumble of thunder. In a voice devoid of emotion, Swoop said, "We don't need our captive anymore, Baby Doll."

Thumbs and Dredge exchanged glances. Dredge whispered, "Swoop's talking to the baby. Doesn't it seem strange to you, Thumbs?"

Swoop looked at Dredge and shushed him. He paced in front of Squat, securely tied to a mature cottonwood tree. The wind tugged at his coat and sent dry leaves swirling around their feet.

Squat squirmed. Sweat beaded on his brow. He cleared his throat and squeaked, "You don't have to do this."

Swoop's eyes narrowed as he looked at Squat. The baby in his arms cooed softly. "Oh, but I do," Swoop replied, his voice icy. "It'll send a message. Those schoolboys of yours will die of fright if they see it. Isn't that right, little one?" He gently rocked the baby as he spoke.

Coyote and Chaw moved closer, but Thumbs and Dredge stayed back. No one dared challenge Swoop's plan.

Swoop positioned his face inches from Squat. "Any last words, old man?" he asked.

Squat met his gaze with a fierce intensity. "You'll get what's coming to you," he spat, his voice stronger now.

Swoop smirked, unfazed by the trail boss's defiance. "Not likely."

He motioned for Coyote and Chaw, who approached with a length of rope. They tied a noose and slipped it around Squat's neck.

Squat struggled, but his bindings held firm.

Swoop stepped back. The wind howled through the trees. The branches creaked. Swoop croaked, "Have you ever been to a hanging, Baby Doll?"

Coyote untied Squat while Chaw tossed the rope over a branch that was just high enough to do the job.

Squat, having his legs and arms free and nothing to lose, fought back. He kicked Chaw in the behind, sending him sprawling and landed a solid punch on Coyote's jaw before Chaw tackled him.

Swoop scowled and shook his head. "Dunderheads." He looked at Dredge and commanded, "Tie his hands."

Dredge hustled to obey. Chaw had twisted Squat's arm roughly behind his back, but Squat's legs remained free.

Swoop chuckled. "He's a feisty one."

Coyote jumped in to help restrain the captive. Squat kicked him between the legs with all his might, and Coyote hobbled off, howling in pain.

Swoop barked, "Tie his legs, Thumbs."

As Thumbs tied Squat's ankles tightly together, he whispered, "Sorry, Boss."

Despite the bindings on his hands and legs, Squat fought, hopping, twisting, and thrashing.

Swoop set the baby on the ground. With a resolute jaw and a clenched fist, he marched over to the stubborn captive, swung his arm, and delivered a powerful blow beneath Squat's ribs.

Chaw drew the slipknot tightly beneath Squat's chin.

Swoop returned to pick up the baby as the four outlaws worked together to hoist Squat into the air. "Impressive, ain't it, Baby Doll? Gotta give it to that trail boss. He put up quite a fight."

Again, Thumbs whispered, "Sorry, Boss," as he stepped away. Dredge followed. Coyote hobbled away.

Swoop noticed Coyote's expression. "Feels like you got kicked by a mule, don't it?" His head bobbed when he laughed, but he held the baby still in his arms.

Squat gagged from the discomfort of the rope at his neck. Chaw shoved him high in the air. "Ready, Swoop?"

"Let him swing!"

Chaw let go of Squat as a gust of wind kicked up a cyclone of dust beneath the tree. Squat's body soared through the air, twisting violently.

Swoop said, "I think I heard his neck snap, Baby Doll."

Squat's body jerked and twitched.

The gang watched as the swinging corpse slowed to an eerie swaying motion. The cottonwood tree creaked but the gang stood silent. Finally, Swoop turned away. "Let's get moving, Baby Doll. We got a herd to sell." He turned back to the men and grunted. "Get along now."

Chaw jumped. He had an uncertain look on his face. "But what about the trail boss, Swoop?"

"Leave him be," Swoop said, a cruel smile playing on his lips. "Let him swing. Those kids will think twice about following us. But never mind them. They've probably already given up. Betcha they're halfway back to Texas by now."

Though it was well after noon, the outlaws hastily packed up camp, mounted their horses, and rode northward, leaving Squat's body swaying at the end of the rope.

The mules brayed in protest as Swoop shook the reins in his right hand. He spoke to the bundle resting quietly in the crook of his left arm, "Let's get these doggies to market, little lady."

Seph and Stoke had been watching the outlaw camp from a distance, planning their next move. They saw the outlaws leave but couldn't make out what had happened until they approached the now-abandoned site.

As they neared the camp, Seph felt a growing sense of dread. His gizzard gnawed within the pit of his stomach.

The wind still howled, carrying a scent that was hard to identify. They moved cautiously, their eyes scanning for any signs of danger.

Then they saw it.

Squat's body hung from a tree. There was a noose tightly gripping his neck, and his head tilted unnaturally. His face was pale and lifeless. The sight sent a shiver down Seph's spine. He dismounted slowly, his legs weak beneath him.

"Oh, God," Stoke whispered.

Seph handed the reins to Stoke. "Don't let go. She'll bolt if she gets the chance."

Stoke nodded. "Got it."

Seph approached the tree. He reached out a hand, but it shook so badly, he had to pull it back. The reality of the situation hit him like a physical blow. Just like when he found Woodsy's arm.

"They hanged him, Stoke." His voice was barely more than a whisper. "They hanged him, and then they just left him here."

Seph looked at Stoke.

The top hand's face looked ashen. His neck flexed as he swallowed hard, and then he tucked his chin tightly to his chest as if trying to avoid a noose himself. "I've seen everything, but I never expected to see this. We need to cut him down, Seph."

Seph took the reins back and secured Hortense to the hanging tree as Stoke dismounted.

Together, they worked in silence. They lowered Squat's body gently to the ground, laying him out with as much dignity as possible. Seph said, "His body ain't even cold yet."

Stoke replied, "This just happened. His arms and legs ain't set up yet."

Crisply, Seph said, "We have to make this right, Stoke."

There was a growl in Stoke's voice. "We will. They'll pay for this. You can count on it."

They stood there for a moment, the weight of their mission pressing down on them. But Seph felt a new strength rising within him. It was a powerful force. Whatever the cost, he would see justice done.

"Oh, they'll pay, Stoke, but first we gotta get Squat back to camp."

Seph and Stoke rode into the cow camp at sunrise.

Squat's lifeless body lay on a hastily constructed travois behind Stoke's horse. The makeshift sled dragged across the prairie. The sight of their fallen leader silenced the camp, and the cowboys stared at Stoke like he was a ghost. Did Seph capture him? Was he a prisoner?

Dusty was in the middle of issuing orders. His face twisted in a grimace. He shifted his weight constantly, his hand pressed to the small of his back. He winced with every movement. As Seph and Stoke approached, Dusty straightened with visible effort, his jaw clenched against the pain.

"Dusty," Seph called out as they drew nearer. "We found him in the outlaws camp. They left him. Must have wanted us to find him."

Stoke said, "We gotta go back and even the score."

Dusty's eyes hardened. He walked slowly to the travois, his steps halting and uneven. Each step seemed to jar his spine. The taciturn ramrod would normally go to great lengths to avoid letting anyone know that he was in pain, but now he was unable to disguise his discomfort.

Other cowboys gathered around, their faces reflecting a mixture of sorrow and anger.

Seph dismounted, his long legs propelling him quickly forward. He blurted, "We need to bury him." He paused, thinking of the lovely spot near Poesta Creek, back in Texas, where he buried Ma. "How about over there, near the riverbank?"

"No," Dusty snapped, his voice raw with emotion. He shifted his weight again, a low groan escaping his lips as he tried to find a more comfortable position. "Not here. I don't know where. Anyplace else, maybe. Anywhere but here."

The cowboys exchanged uneasy glances. Seph looked at Dusty, his heart heavy. "Where then?"

Dusty winced again, pressing harder against his lower back, his eyes briefly closing against a wave of pain. "North. Up the trail somewhere. Be ready in the morning. We leave at first light."

Conjure interrupted them and approached Seph. The wary cowboy was on edge. His eyes darted around nervously as if he were seeing ghosts. He glanced at Squat's dead body, blinked fast, and covered his face. He took a couple of side steps, putting more space between him and the dead man before speaking. "Seph! Come quick. Torp wants to see you."

Seph's heart skipped a beat. "What? He survived? He's alive?"

Conjure nodded, his fear evident. He tossed a worried glance over his shoulder. His teeth chattered and he stammered. "Y-y-yeah, he's alive. Dunk and the others are with him."

Seph felt a rush of relief mixed with anxiety. He followed Conjure, his mind racing with thoughts of Torp. The mournful sound of Yodel's harmonica drifted through camp. Seph paused and listened for a second, before continuing forward.

As they approached the backside of the chuckwagon, Seph's thoughts were a whirlwind. He remembered Torp's loyalty and bravery. The kid had always been like a younger brother to him. He had already started grieving. It was shocking to learn that Torp had survived the gunshot.

Seph hurried forward.

Dunk, Bonita, and Lullaby shuffled back and away from where Torp lay on the ground.

The haunting sound of Yodel's harmonica grew lower and slower.

Seph knelt beside Torp, his heart in his throat. Over his shoulder, he begged, "Is he going to make it, Dunk?"

# CHAPTER 20

SEPH KNELT BESIDE TORP. The young cowboy's pale face twisted in pain.

Dunk, Bonita, and Lullaby stood nearby, but they stepped away so that Seph and Torp could talk.

The wind carried an eerie tune from Yodel's harmonica.

Torp's eyes fluttered open, and a weak smile tugged at his bluish lips. "I knew you would come," he whispered in a faint voice.

Seph swallowed hard and his throat felt tight. "Of course, Torp. I'm here."

Torp's eyes filled with tears. "Why did Thumbs shoot me, Seph? I just can't figure that out."

Seph shook his head, struggling to find words. "I don't know, Torp. I don't understand it either. But I aim to find out. I can promise you that."

Torp coughed, wincing in pain. The wound had festered and he clutched his side where the bullet had struck. "I don't want to die, Seph." His lower lip jutted forward as he looked into Seph's eyes before glancing away. "I want to keep being your partner. I don't care if we have to ride drag forever.

I don't mind the dust. I already swallowed half of Texas. I just want to keep on cowboying."

Seph felt a tear slip down his cheek and he turned his head away slightly. "I want that too."

Torp's eyes searched Seph's face. "Do you remember what Slaw said before he died? About taking him along with you where you go?"

Seph touched his tongue to his lips and said, "I'll never forget it."

Torp's eyes grew wide. "Do you believe a soul can live more than one life?"

Seph said, "Gosh, I never heard of such a thing." His heart ached, his head hurt, and he had trouble following Torp's logic.

Torp blurted, "Seph... if you ever have a kid, could you name him after me? Just so... just so folks remember I was here."

Seph's heart broke at the request. He gripped Torp's hand tightly. "I promise, Torp. Somehow, I'll make sure your name lives on."

Torp's eyes welled up with tears but he fought off the urge to sob. "Thank you, Seph." He took several ragged breaths. "You made me feel like I belonged. Like I had a family. Like I was a man and not a kid."

Seph felt a torrent of emotion rise in his throat. His voice broke as he said, "You're a cowboy, Torp. You're one of us. You're my partner. Always and forever."

Torp's breathing grew more labored. He struggled to amplify a whisper. "I'm going to wherever Slaw went," he murmured. He turned his head and his eyes glanced about. "I think I hear Ma calling me. They shouldn't have left me so soon. I never wanted to be no kind of orphan."

Seph's heart ached as he listened to Torp's words.

Torp's grip on Seph's hand tightened briefly. "Promise me, Seph. Promise me you'll keep on cowboying. Don't stop because of me."

Seph nodded. He couldn't prevent tears from cascading down his face now, but he wiped at them with his sleeve. "I promise, Torp. I'll keep going."

Torp's grip weakened, his eyes closing. "I'll be watching over you, Seph. Don't stop gazing at them stars at night."

Seph tipped his head forward, overcome with grief.

A comforting hand gripped Seph's bad shoulder. Seph turned his head and looked at the hand but wasn't a bit surprised by Lullaby's presence.

Lullaby's voice was a comfort in that moment. The man's soothing voice implored, "Let's pray, Seph."

Seph nodded. He tipped his head forward, gently resting his forehead on Torp's chest. He closed his eyes as Lullaby began.

"Lord, please welcome our brother Torp into your loving arms. Give him peace and rest after his struggles. Comfort those of us left behind and guide us through our grief. Amen."

Seph didn't want to say it, but he whispered "Amen," feeling the weight of his loss but also a newfound sense of belonging. He had found his place among these cowboys. It was true for Torp, just as it was for Seph. This was his family now.

And though Torp was gone, his memory would ride with Seph up every trail and back.

Seph stood beside the river. The strengthening sun reflected on the surface of the water. It was as if the gentle flowing sound was a gift from the heavens, meant to provide comfort. But Seph wasn't in the mood to be comforted.

He took a deep breath and began digging, the shovel cutting into soft earth.

As if speaking to the galaxy, Seph murmured, his voice thick with emotion. "This is the perfect place for a lonely orphan boy's wild cowboy spirit."

As he worked, Seph felt a surge of power flow through him. Each punch of the shovel seemed weightless, and time blurred as he dug deeper and deeper. Sweat soaked his shirt. Dirt flew over his shoulder in a frenzy of motion. He didn't acknowledge the soreness in his shoulder, the ache in his muscles, or the sting of sweat in his eyes.

When Seph finally stopped, the grave was deep and ready. He stood back, taking a moment to catch his breath and say a silent prayer for Torp. Then, with a heavy heart, he made his way back to camp.

Stoke had tried to sleep but hadn't succeeded. To Seph he said, "It's done already?" His surprise was evident in his voice. "You sure it's deep enough?"

Seph nodded. "Yeah. It's done. It's deep enough. I'm sure."

Still shaking his head in disbelief, Stoke said, "Man, I thought that was going to take a couple of hours."

Seph shrugged but didn't offer an explanation. He couldn't explain what happened if he tried, but this wasn't the first time he couldn't explain such a phenomenon. Sometimes it seemed to him, daunting physical tasks almost did themselves when he set out to accomplish something.

Stoke stepped closer, jabbing Seph's arm with his elbow. "You did right by him, Seph. Torp would be proud." Stoke coughed uncomfortably. "I'm downright sorry I called him a baby. I never shoulda done that."

"Thanks, Stoke. He was just a kid but he did a man's work. Every day."

Stoke added, "And loyal as a hound."

Seph repeated what Stoke said. "Yes. Loyal as a hound. Well, I reckon it's time to ride."

Lullaby appeared beside them, concern etched on his face. "Wouldn't you like to be there when we bury Torp?"

Seph shook his head. His voice was steady despite his swirling emotions. "No. We said our goodbyes. I got something I gotta do." He thought about Dusty's back and then he thought about Dunk. The men needed them. Bonita needed them. They couldn't be spared.

It was up to him to save the herd. Him and Stoke.

Now that they knew where the outlaws were, it didn't take long to find the herd. It would be impossible to disguise the trail left by that many beeves. They caught up with them at dusk, but kept a safe distance.

After not sleeping the night before, they were exhausted. They didn't bother taking turns standing watch. Instead, they slept through the night.

Seph figured they were about fifteen miles northwest of the cow camp. The herd had moved, but not far. It must have been difficult keeping that many critters together with so few cowboys.

They peeked from the cover of a copse of trees near a small creek, just east of the outlaws' position a little after dawn. They watched as the outlaws prepared to move. Seph pondered the situation and quietly thought about what to do. Meanwhile, Stoke described everything he saw. Stoke reminded Seph of Slaw—always chattering.

To quiet Stoke, Seph tossed a gentle punch into his shoulder. He looked at the top hand. From their first meeting, they hadn't seen eye to eye. Now they were partners. And this was a life or death matter. Seph felt his brow tighten. He had foretold that they would one day be friends, but he would never have predicted a situation like this.

The muscles in Seph's abdomen tightened as they often did when his grinding gut took charge. His head tilted closer to his unlikely partner, and he said, "Here's the plan, Stoke. If you're still willing, ride in there and tell them you want in. Give them the dickens for cutting you out and leaving you behind. Ham it up good."

Stoke nodded, and a thin smile curled at the corner of his mouth. "What are you going to do?"

"I'll follow along and pick them off—one at a time," Seph replied, lifting his rifle. "It's time to put Uncle Yves to work. I think this is why he came along." The weight of the weapon felt both reassuring and heavy.

Stoke's smile widened. "Be careful where you point that thing. You sure you know what you're doing? I wouldn't want you to make a mistake and accidentally shoot me! Wouldn't be fair to the ladies I ain't had yet."

Seph blinked and his mouth twitched. "Don't worry, Stoke. I've been practicing. I won't miss. Uncle Yves won't allow it."

The two men shared a moment of silence before Stoke mounted his horse. Seph watched as Stoke took a deep breath and straightened his shoulders.

Seph said, "Do whatever they tell you to do, Stoke. Meanwhile, I'll even the odds. If something happens to me, you'll have to figure out a new plan on your own."

Stoke said, "Count on it, kid. Let's get to rescuing them beeves." With a wink, he added, "And when we get to Abilene, I'll buy you a beer." With a chuckle and a cluck, Stoke was off, trotting slowly toward the rustled steers.

Seph climbed into a tall tree, keeping a keen eye on the enemy. The camp was bustling with activity as the outlaws readied themselves for the day.

Swoop sat on the wagon bench, waiting. Seph could see the man scanning the eastern horizon. Occasionally he glanced in other directions. Sometimes he glanced at his left arm. Seph wondered if his arm was injured, in a sling—or maybe the man was holding something. Seph tried to think of what he might be carrying but couldn't think of anything.

He watched as Stoke rode into camp. Seph's heart pounded. It was as if he were the one riding in to double cross the enemy. He shimmied a couple of inches away from the tree truck as if to get a closer look ahead.

Stoke's horse maintained a steady trot, and the top hand's posture looked confident. If the cowboy was nervous or worried, it didn't show. Stoke removed his hat and shouted, but Seph couldn't hear what he said. They were too far away. Stoke waved his arms, hollered again, and kicked his horse up to a lope.

Swoop turned and reached for his sidearm.

Seph imagined Stoke shouting, "Hold your fire." The seasoned cowboy continued forward and stopped in front of the pirated prairie schooner.

After a brief conversation, Swoop holstered his gun and Stoke rode toward the herd.

It still felt strange to Seph, working with Stoke. He thought about the evening he met the man who called himself The Ignitor. He thought about the grown man's idiotic pranks. And he thought about that fight they had. Seph scratched his chin and sighed.

As he dropped from branch to branch and returned to the ground, Seph wondered if he had made a good decision. What was to stop Stoke from switching sides? Despite their history, Seph's instincts told him that he could trust Stoke.

Seph knew it wasn't rational to trust a man like Stoke, but that's the thing about trusting your gut. Sometimes it don't seem rational.

Seph shook his head and spat as he untied the horse from a small tree. "Fine. I'll be wary, but you'll see, Hortense. Stoke won't let us down." He led the horse slowly off to the west before turning north.

Dunk stood at the edge of camp. He watched the narrow column of cows and cowboys, pushing northward. It was a sorry sight to see the small fraction of a herd moving north.

He could hear the lowing of the cattle and the shouts of the cowboys as they pushed the beeves. The sight was both familiar and strange, as what was left of the Deatherage drive began the next leg of its march toward Abilene.

Torp lay under a makeshift shelter. His breath came in shallow gasps. Dunk watched Bonita kneel beside him, her face etched with worry and exhaustion. She was desperate to find her missing husband, Wills, the lost wagon, and most importantly, her baby girl. The uncertainty and fear in her eyes tugged at Dunk's heart.

Dunk was torn. Bonita was desperate to move, but he worried that her chances of finding her family were slim. And it was a miracle that Torp was still alive, clinging to life by a narrow thread. Traveling might be the end of him. Leaving was up to Dusty, not him. All he could do was try to make the youngster comfortable.

He turned away from the scene and busied himself, cleaning up after feeding the cowboys breakfast. After each motion, he glanced at the woman. He stowed the iron tripod in the chuckwagon and watched Bonita for a minute. Then he put away the coffee pot and looked at her again.

She started to turn to face him and a startling realization clobbered him. Dunk's hand covered his mouth and he turned away from her. He hadn't just looked at her to make sure she was safe. He didn't just glance her way to take note of where she was. He had looked at her with longing in his heart. Dunk swallowed hard.

He crossed his arms, tucked his hands into his armpits, and shivered. How did it happen? Why hadn't he realized sooner? He wasn't some wet-behind-the-ears cowpoke, fresh off the farm. After twenty-seven years on this earth, he was amazed by the suddenness of the situation. He had fallen in love with Bonita.

Saying it in his mind made him want to slap his own face. How could he be in love with *her*? He barely knew her, and she was a married woman, for all he knew. For all she knew. The thought of her being a widow, or the possibility that her husband was still out there, searching for his family, only made his feelings more complicated.

He'd seen his fair share of impossible situations and hardships. As a kid, he'd traveled the Oregon Trail. As a young man, he fought in the war. But this—falling in love with a woman whose future was so uncertain—was a new kind of challenge. He glanced back at Bonita, who was now tending to Torp with a tenderness that only deepened his feelings for her and made his heart ache with longing.

He shook his head, trying to clear his thoughts. Why now? Why had he gone and fallen in love in the middle of all of this turmoil? He signed on with the Deatherage brothers for an easy ride.

The timing couldn't be worse. Dunk felt a mixture of frustration and helplessness as he struggled to make sense of everything.

As he pondered, Dusty approached, sitting rigid on his horse with Squat's body dragging behind on the travois. Dunk noticed Dusty's grimace as he shifted in the saddle. The ramrod was clearly in pain.

"Dusty," Dunk called out, "What are you gonna do with your brother? It's too hot to leave the dead unburied this time of year." He thought of the grave that Seph had dug for Torp but didn't mention it.

Dusty turned his head, looked at the travois behind him, and winced.

Dunk wondered if Dusty had forgotten that his brother's body was dragging behind his horse.

Drawing a deep breath, Dusty crisply said, "Squat wouldn't want to be buried in Indian country. We've got to get him to the Kansas line at least."

Dunk sighed, feeling the weight of another impossible situation. "But Dusty, we entered Kansas when we crossed Bluff Creek."

Dusty shook his head stubbornly. "It ain't Kansas to me until we cross the Arkansas River."

"But that's five days to the north," Dunk argued, frustration edging into his voice. "Besides, I'm telling you, we're already in Kansas."

"I know how many days off it is. And I don't care if it is Kansas or it ain't. I ain't planting him here and that's that."

They stood in tense silence for a moment. Finally, Dusty relented a bit. "I'll keep him away from the woman. And the chuckwagon," he said, his voice softening slightly. "Never mind about Squat. He's my problem. Not yours."

Dunk watched as Dusty rode away, the wooden feet of the travois scratching lines in the dirt. Dunk felt a pang of guilt for his outburst. Had it hit Dusty that he was now ramrod *and* trail boss? Instead of being partners, he was now the sole proprietor and owner of the Dagger D, Angry R brand. All of the responsibility for its accursed first drive rode squarely on his shoulders.

Returning to kick sand over the remains of the cookfire, Dunk tried to refocus on his duties, but his thoughts kept drifting back to Bonita. He glanced over at her again. He saw a mix of hope and despair on her face, and his heart melted.

*What am I going to do?* Dunk wondered. He cast one final glance at Bonita, then turned his attention to stowing the last of their provisions.

It wasn't right to move the wounded boy. Dunk frowned. *The kid don't have a chance anyway.*

# CHAPTER 21

SEPH LAY PRONE, HIDDEN in the tall grass, baking in the late afternoon sun.

The outlaws struggled to move the large herd. Being under-manned made the task difficult. The cattle bellowed and milled about. The cowboys shouted and waved their hats to keep them moving.

Seph's position on a ridge gave him a clear view of the scene below, allowing him to carefully select his target. He estimated the distance and was sure that he was well within Uncle Yves' range.

From his vantage point, Seph could see Stoke moving among the outlaws, blending in as if he belonged. Despite their history, Seph trusted Stoke to play his part.

Seph's mission was clear: take out one of the traitors and sow discord among the outlaws. The plan was simple but dangerous: one shot, one victim, then disappear back onto the south Kansas prairie.

He tightened his grip on the heirloom rifle. Uncle Yves was one of the last possessions remaining from his previous life. If what Charlie told him in Fort Worth was true, carrying that firearm amounted to carrying his family's legacy along with him on the trail.

Scanning the outlaws, his focus sharpened as he located Thumbs. The man was busily driving critters forward, shouting at the herd.

Seph's blood boiled as he thought about Torp. Thumbs was the one who shot him.

His thoughts drifted momentarily to the past. Swoop, Coyote, and Chaw had been a blight on his family's farm for years, stealing and causing havoc. But today, Seph's focus was on avenging Torp. Thumbs and Dredge must pay for their betrayal.

As Seph watched, he saw Skillet pushing ahead of the herd as he had since they left the ranch on the banks of the San Antonio River. He thought of the gash the bull's horn sliced into his leg, and yet it wasn't the bull's fault.

It irritated him to think of Skillet working for the outlaws. A pang of longing swept through him—a longing to return things back to the way they should be.

In the distance, he saw Sheriff and it rankled. Sheriff was more than just a horse to Seph. They hadn't been together long, but the horse he had traded for the family farm meant more to him than anything else. He blinked and thought of the empty cigar box, also gone, but that was just cardboard. Sheriff was a man's possession. His horse was a living thing, composed of flesh and blood. The picture of the girl on the cigar box belonged in the imagination of a farm boy, not a cattleman. Seeing Sheriff with the outlaws filled Seph with a fierce determination.

"We must get the herd back," Seph muttered to himself, his voice a low growl. "For Dusty. For all of the cowboys."

He took a deep breath, steadying himself. He spoke to the rifle as if it were a man, not a gun. "It's time to go to work, Uncle Yves," he said.

He looked down the barrel at the man on the wagon. "That's Swoop." Seph's lip curled. "Not yet."

Seph moved the rifle and aimed at another rider. "That's Coyote."

Next, he pointed the gun at Chaw.

"There he is." Seph grunted. He lined up his shot, calculating the distance and accounting for the slight breeze. Thumbs shouted at the cattle, urging them forward. Seph imagined he could hear his harsh voice.

If only the man would stand still.

Seph's heart pounded, but his hands remained steady. He thought of his mother's words, telling him to be tenacious.

He did not feel tentative today. He was deliberate but did not hesitate. One could be careful *and* tenacious. It was better than making hasty mistakes.

He squeezed the trigger, and the rifle bucked against his shoulder. The crack of the shot echoed across the prairie.

Thumbs' head snapped back, and his body slumped in the saddle before sliding to the ground. For a moment, everything was still. Seph knew that it was time to move, but instead, he watched for a moment as Dredge rode toward his partner, leaving his position along the column of cows.

Seph's breath caught in his throat. He felt a surge of elation as he confirmed that his shot had found its mark.

He was sure that Thumbs was dead. Justice had been served. There was no room for guilt or sorrow. This was the way of the west—the harsh reality of life on the frontier.

Dredge began shouting and galloped away from his fallen friend, pointing in Seph's direction.

Seph remained calm, his eyes fixed on the drive below. He knew he had to move quickly. He had other targets to take down, but he couldn't afford to stay in one place for too long.

He slid back into the underbrush. As he crawled back to retrieve Hortense, he couldn't shake the image of Thumb's slumping body.

This was the first man he had killed. If only it could be the last. But there were others that needed killing fast. While he knew it was necessary, the weight of the act settled heavily on his shoulders. *Thou shalt not kill.* There was no ambiguity in those four words, but there was no time for reflection.

He had to stay focused.

The plan called for one outlaw at a time. Now Stoke would have to work even harder to push the beeves. Seph would save Dredge for another day. Seph retreated, blending into the rolling prairie. He moved like one of the natural inhabitants, as silent and elusive as a pronghorn or a rattlesnake.

He vanished into the grassland, his thoughts already focused on his next move. Now he was a hunter. A bringer of justice in a lawless land. And as he disappeared into the vast expanse, he was determined to see the outlaws face the reckoning they deserved.

Seph watched the sky as the sun set. After dark, he stretched out on his back and gazed at the stars—the same stars he gazed at as a kid, but everything was different now. He was no longer a helpless victim. He was glad that he had sent Thumbs to his maker.

There was much more to be done, but it would keep.

Darkness descended on the cow camp. Lullaby stood near the campfire, his hat in hand, head bowed in silent prayer, surrounded by the crew.

It had been a long and grueling day, and the weight of their losses hung heavy in the air. As he finished his prayer, he looked up at the men gathered around him. Then he was ready to speak.

"Alright, boss," Lullaby began, his deep voice steady and calm. "Me and the boys have talked and we all agree. We need to talk about getting our herd back."

Dusty shifted uncomfortably, grimacing as he tried to find a position that didn't aggravate his back. "We ain't got enough men for that," he grumbled. "And I can't lead an attack now. Besides, Stoke and Seph are out there."

Dunk, who had been tending to Torp, looked up from his ministrations. He said, "I should join 'em. But I can't leave Torp." His voice was heavy with worry. "He's barely hanging on, and Bonita—They need me."

Lullaby nodded. "I know. It's a tough situation," he said. "But we can't just let them outlaws get away with the herd. We didn't drive them all this way to lose 'em now."

Dusty shook his head. "Nobody wants the herd back more than me, but we just can't risk it. Better to stick with what we got left. I can pay everybody if we can get them to Abilene."

Lullaby nodded as Dusty spoke, then said, "Yes, boss. But what if Stoke and Seph need our help? We should be there too."

Yodel stepped forward. "Lullaby's right," he said. Lullaby was surprised by his brother's words. He didn't usually speak unless spoken to.

Chops rubbed his chin thoughtfully. "We could try a nighttime raid," he suggested. "Catch them off guard while they're sleeping."

Weakly, Dusty said, "No."

Trinket shook his head. "That's risky," he said. "They're likely to have guards posted. We'd need to be real careful."

Blaze clenched his fists. "I say we hit 'em hard and fast. Show 'em we mean business."

Again, Dusty said, "No."

Conjure and Hork exchanged a glance.

"We're with Blaze," Chops said.

Yodel nodded in agreement. "It's now or never."

Lullaby raised a hand to quiet them. "Alright, boys," he said. "But we need to be smart about this. We can't afford to lose any more men. Let's bow our heads and pray for guidance."

Blaze groaned but tipped his head forward and closed his eyes. The men fell silent as Lullaby spoke. "Lord, we ask for Your guidance. Show us the way, and give us strength. Watch over Torp, Bonita, and her family, we beseech Thee. Keep us safe and help us reclaim our critters. Thy will be done, oh Lord. Amen."

Dusty's face contorted with pain. "You're talking crazy," he said. "Running off half-cocked. You'll get yourselves killed."

Lullaby walked over to Dusty, placing a reassuring hand on his shoulder. "We'll be careful, boss," he said. "But we can't just sit here and do nothing. We owe it to ourselves, to Torp, to Squat, and to Woodsy to try. If it be God's will, we will succeed."

Dusty looked up at Lullaby, his eyes filled with frustration and worry. "You don't understand," he said. "I can barely move. I can't lead you into battle."

Lullaby nodded in agreement. "We'll figure something out," he said.

Yodel stepped forward again. "We can scout their camp," he suggested. "Find out their weaknesses and plan our attack."

Lullaby smiled at his brother. "That's a good idea," he said. "We can do this if we work together. We can't leave Stoke and Seph out there."

Dusty shook his head stubbornly. "No," he said firmly. "It's too dangerous. I don't want anybody else getting killed." His tone was firm. "I forbid it—and that's final."

The camp fell silent. Lullaby looked around at the determined faces of his fellow cowboys, knowing they wouldn't back down easily. But for now, Dusty's word was law.

"Alright," Lullaby said softly. "You're the boss, Dusty."

The grumbling cowboys made their way to their bedrolls. Lullaby and Yodel had night watch.

After an hour of singing to the beeves and thinking, Lullaby spoke to his brother. He said, "There's a time to obey and a time to do what needs doing. What time do you think it is?"

Yodel grunted. "It's time to do something. I don't care what the boss says."

Lullaby frowned. "Everybody feels that way, don't they?"

Yodel cussed and then added, "You better believe it. Even Conjure and Hork."

Lullaby said, "Let's give it another day. Then we'll see."

As Lullaby made his rounds, singing to the fraction of the herd that remained, a sense of resolve settled over him. If Seph and Stoke didn't return tomorrow, there would be no stopping the gang of cowboys.

Swoop was in a foul mood, his dark eyes scanning the horizon as if seeking answers in the distant hills.

Stoke crouched beside the fire fixing coffee and waiting for it to heat.

"It's time we abandon the wagon," Swoop announced abruptly. He handed Lily to Coyote, who looked up in surprise.

"You take care of Baby Doll," Swoop growled, his voice low and menacing. "Anything happens to her, I'll kill you myself."

Swoop turned to the rest of the gang. "We're heading northwest instead of northeast," he announced. "Instead of Abilene, we'll drive these beeves to Denver town."

Stoke stepped forward, his brow furrowed in protest. "But that's over 500 miles away. We don't have a big enough crew to get *there*."

Swoop's eyes narrowed, and he rubbed his whiskered cheeks thoughtfully. "I think I know where we can hire up some cowboys." A slow smile spread across his face. He turned to face Stoke, his gaze piercing. "Will they ride for us if we double their pay?"

The camp fell silent. The outlaws exchanged uncertain glances. Stoke hesitated. The question hung in the air. The promise of double pay could be a temptation, but Stoke knew the Deatherage outfit would never go for it.

Swoop's eyes bore into Stoke, waiting for an answer.

Stoke shrugged as Swoop looked eastward. "It just might work. They'd be fools not to jump at the chance to make that much money."

Swoop barked an order and Chaw jumped to fetch him a horse.

Stoke shook his head and crossed his eyes when Chaw saddled Sheriff.

Late in the afternoon, exactly a day after he plugged Thumbs, Seph perched high in the branches of a sturdy bur oak. Uncle Yves rested securely in his hands. From his vantage point, Seph had a clear view of the herd below.

His gut churned. The memory of Torp's brutal end was fresh in his mind, fueling the fire that burned in his chest. Seph knew what he had to do. There was no hesitation. There was no doubt. This was justice and he was eager to deliver it.

As Seph watched Dredge, he wondered if the man grieved the loss of his partner. No matter, they'd be reunited soon.

Seph's jaw tightened. He saw Thumbs shoot Torp, but didn't know if Dredge was also a murderer. But, what difference did it make? Even if he wasn't a killer, he was still a cattle rustler. They didn't just betray the bosses but the entire outfit.

*This is for Torp. For Squat. For the Deatherage Longhorn Cattle Ranch,* Seph thought, his grip tightening on Uncle Yves.

Seph's breathing slowed as he focused. He adjusted the rifle, and whispered to his long departed great uncle. Then, the world seemed to fade away, leaving only him and his target.

Dredge continued to ride toward him. Every step his horse took brought him closer to the patient sniper.

When he was certain, Seph's finger tightened on the trigger. This was what he had trained for, what he had steeled himself to do.

Seph exhaled slowly, a calm washing over him as he squeezed the trigger. He welcomed the shock of the rifle against his shoulder. The crack of the shot whizzed through the still, afternoon air.

Dredge jerked in the saddle, his body slumping forward before thumping to the ground in a lifeless heap.

A rush of elation surged through Seph as he watched for a reaction below. As spread out as the herd was, Seph was uncertain whether anybody knew that Dredge was down. It was tempting to snipe another outlaw, but he and Stoke had agreed on a slow and measured plan. Besides, none of them were close enough.

In his gut, Seph felt a sense of righteousness. The weight of his actions settled over him. Often, justice was swift and brutal, but it could also be measured and deliberate.

Seph remained in the tree for a few moments longer. They might find his position in the tree, but it would take a while. He scanned the terrain, looking into the hazy horizon and considered where to go to set up his next shot. It was important not to be predictable.

Seph climbed from the tree and weaved through the tall prairie grasses. He felt like a predator, but remembered all too well what it felt like to be a victim. Later, there would be time to plan his next move. For now, he needed to disappear—to become one with the landscape.

As he slipped away, the weight of Uncle Yves still comforting in his hand, Seph's thoughts turned to the future. He had made his mark, but there was still work to be done. The fight for justice was far from over.

The traitors were gone and Torp's killer was dead, but whoever hacked off Woodsy's limbs lived on.

He had killed two men in two days. It was a sobering thought, but his mission was unfinished. It was time to make the men who terrorized his family pay.

As dusk approached, Seph found a secluded spot on the edge of a small grove beside a trickle of a creek. His position was hidden from view by thick foliage. He settled in for the night, enjoying the cool earth beneath him after a hot day. The stars began to emerge, twinkling in the heavens.

The night sky was Seph's favorite sight. He marveled at the beauty of the shimmering stars. The dazzling spectacle seemed haphazard to him.

Is that where God lives? Seph wondered, his mind reaching out into the infinite distance. He felt a sense of peace wash over him. The heavens seemed so serene, and far removed from the struggles of the earth.

He settled deeper into his hiding place, feeling a sense of contentment. Such places were hard to find on the open plains, but he had managed to secure a spot that felt safe and sheltered. His eyelids grew heavy. His mind drifted between the celestial wonders and the day's events.

Suddenly, Seph's tranquility was shattered by the rough jab of metal against his ribs. He jolted awake, his hand instinctively reaching for Uncle Yves, but a harsh voice stopped him cold.

"Don't even think about it," came the snarling command. Seph looked up to see the business end of a rifle pressed against him, held by none other than Swoop.

"Well, well, well. It's *you*. You're the one that's been causing all this trouble. Didn't know you had it in you, hayseed." Swoop sneered, his eyes gleaming with malicious delight. "But look at you now. Hiding out like a scared rabbit."

Swoops words stung. It was that same old feeling, all over again. The one he resolved never to feel again. How had Swoop found him? He had been so careful, so sure of his hiding spot.

"Did you really think you could pick us off, one by one?" Swoop continued, his voice dripping with contempt. "You might have taken down Thumbs and Dredge, but you won't get the rest of us."

Swoop's face twisted into a cruel smile as he leaned in closer. "You know, Seph, you remind me a lot of someone I used to know. A long time ago."

Seph stared at him, confusion mingling with fear. What was Swoop talking about?

"But never mind about that." Swoop laughed, a harsh, grating sound that sent chills down Seph's spine. His expression turned serious. His eyes narrowed as he studied Seph. "What should I do with you now?" he mused, his voice low and menacing.

Swoop jabbed his rifle forcefully into Seph's ribs. "I tell you what we're gonna do. You're going to work for us. This time, I'm not asking you, I'm telling you. Like it or not, you're joining up with us."

# CHAPTER 22

SEPH FELT A SURGE of defiance well up within him. His anger gave him strength.

Conflicting thoughts swirled through his mind. Could he roll away and escape Swoop? Then what? He looked beyond Swoop and the rifle pressing into his ribs.

Seph gasped at the sight of Sheriff. He couldn't blame the horse, but knowing the outlaw rode Sheriff felt like salt in a wound. Did the outlaw know that the horse belonged to him?

"Get up," Swoop ordered.

Seph didn't speak. When he reached his feet, he spat in disgust. The wad hit the ground near Swoop's feet.

Swoop's face darkened with rage. He twisted his body and slapped Seph hard across the face.

The force of the blow snapped Seph's head to the side. Then he slowly turned his head back to face the outlaw.

"Mind your place, hayseed," Swoop growled, his eyes cold and unforgiving.

Seph's eyes blazed with fury as he stood firm. His voice was steady despite the sting. "Hang you, Swoop. I won't, I tell you." With a sneer, he repeated, "I won't."

Swoop's lips curled. "Your job is to keep me fed. Always has been. Always will be. Don't you ever forget that." Swoop's gun still pointed at Seph's chest. "You done good bringing me these beeves all the way from Texas. It's time you finished the job." He disarmed Seph, taking Uncle Yves and stripping him of Woodsy's Colts.

Seph felt a pang of loss as the weapons were taken, but his resolve did not waver.

"Get on your horse," Swoop commanded, shoving Seph toward Hortense.

Seph saddled and climbed on, praying that she would buck, but she did not.

His mind raced. What could he do? He sat in the saddle, unarmed. It irked him something fierce knowing Swoop rode Sheriff.

It was hard to be optimistic when a murdering outlaw sat behind him with a gun pointed at his back. He was disappointed in himself. How could he allow himself to be found and captured?

As they rode, Seph fumed. His thoughts were consumed with plans to get the best of Swoop. He knew he had to be careful, but he was determined not to be a victim. Somehow, he would find a way to turn the tables, to bring justice to those who had wronged him, Ma, and his friends.

The ride was silent. Seph's mind worked furiously, plotting one bad move after another. In the absence of a good plan, he decided to wait for an opportunity. The fight was not over yet. He was determined to be ready for whatever came next.

As Seph rode ahead of Swoop, he looked for a chance to escape and thought about vengeance.

A series of wild shrieks pierced the air, echoing across the plains. The shrill whoops sounded like Indians.

Seph turned and saw a sight that swelled his heart. Lullaby and a gang of cowboys charged toward them, like warriors on a battlefield.

His eyes widened. The cowboys rode hard, their horses kicking up clouds of dust as they galloped in a tight formation. It was as if they'd done so many times before.

Without a second thought, Seph dug his spurs into Hortense's belly. Just as Blaze taught him to do, he dropped alongside the mustang. His body hung precariously close to the ground as the horse galloped forward. He tried to concentrate on the challenging maneuver, but couldn't help thinking of the outlaw. He imagined a look of shock and horror on Swoop's face.

One hand clung to the saddle horn. A leg draped over the horse's rump. The wind whipped past his face, and the horse's hooves thundered beneath his head.

The ground was a blur beneath him. A surge of excitement shot through him, fueling his wild ride.

He heard the bark of gunfire. It was rapidly followed by more, and he counted the shots. His move had made him a harder, almost impossible target. With a powerful heave, he swung back up into the saddle. The motion was seamless and fluid. With his strong legs, he guided Hortense into a wide circle. Seph and Hortense barreled toward Swoop from behind.

Swoop aimed his rifle at the oncoming cowboys. Before he could fire a shot, Seph urged Hortense forward, his focus razor-sharp on Swoop. He dug both heels into Hortense at once, and with a burst of speed, he closed the distance. The roar of the charging cowboys filled his ears.

At the last possible moment, Seph leaped from Hortense. His body slammed into Swoop with all the force he could muster. They tumbled from Swoop's saddle, hitting the ground in a tangled heap. The impact knocked the wind from Seph's lungs, but he didn't hesitate. His younger, more agile frame gave him an advantage over the heavier man.

After wrestling for a couple of minutes, they made their way back to their feet. Swoop spat, "You should know better, but you never were very smart."

Swoop fought fiercely, his fists swinging widely. He landed a solid punch to Seph's ribs, and Seph gasped in pain. Seph's vision blurred momentarily, and he felt the ground shift beneath him as Swoop rolled him over, pressing his weight down upon him.

"You ain't got it in you, hayseed." Swoop snarled. His face twisted with rage. "You never did."

Seph gritted his teeth, refusing to give in. He glanced around and caught sight of his friends, closing in around them. They looked amazed and concerned. Did they think that Swoop would win?

Lullaby shouted encouragement and Yodel was beside him, eyes wide with worry. The others formed a circle around them, shouting, but Seph couldn't hear them.

It didn't matter what they said—Seph drew strength from their presence. These were his friends. His brothers. They believed in him, and he wouldn't let them down. With a burst of energy, Seph twisted his body, using Swoop's momentum against him. He managed to break free and roll away, scrambling back to his feet.

Swoop lunged at him again, but Seph was ready. He dodged the attack and tackled Swoop, bringing him to the ground once more. They grappled, their bodies locked in a fierce struggle. Seph's muscles burned, his breath came in ragged gasps, but he held on, refusing to give up.

The older man tried to leverage his weight again, but Seph shifted his position, using his agility to his advantage.

He pinned Swoop's arm behind his back, forcing him down with a brutal twist. Then he cranked harder. Swoop howled in pain, but Seph didn't relent. He pressed his knee into the man's back. Swoop's face twisted in pain and rage, his struggles growing weaker as Seph's grip tightened.

The gathered cowboys howled in delight. Their triumphant cheers echoed across the plains. Lullaby dismounted and ran over, his eyes gleaming. "We got him, boys!" he shouted.

Seph's breath came in ragged gasps, his body trembling with exertion. But he didn't let go. "You're done," Seph hissed, his voice low and fierce. "You hear me, Swoop? You're finished."

Swoop groaned, his body going limp.

Seph's eyes burned. He understood that he was victorious, but it took a moment for it to completely sink in. He looked down at the outlaw boss, the man who had terrorized his family for ages. The weight of their history lifted from his shoulders.

Lullaby tugged the collar at the back of Seph's neck. "You did it, Seph," he said, his voice filled with admiration. "You got him. You can let up now."

Seph nodded, his eyes never leaving Swoop's face. "Yeah," he said softly. "*We* got him. I sure am glad you fellows came along when you did. I don't know what I'd do without you all."

He looked from one man to the other. He didn't need to say another word to let them know how he felt. It was clear that they understood. And they reveled in the part they played, capturing Swoop. But they weren't finished yet.

They remained a short distance from the outlaw's night camp, and darkness had settled in. Swoop, despite his defeat, mustered the strength to speak. His voice was raspy and weak, but the malice in his words was unmistakable. "You think this is over, hayseed?" he wheezed, a twisted grin on his face.

Chops shouted out, "They'll hang you." He shoved Swoop hard.

The outlaw stepped fast and stumbled, but did not fall.

Seph leaned in close. He could hear the chill in his own voice. "Stoke double-crossed you, Swoop," he said, enjoying the flicker of surprise that crossed Swoop's face.

Swoop laughed weakly. The raspy sound sent chills down Seph's spine. Swoop said, "You're still a dimwit, trusting the wrong people. Remember, it's the snakes closest to you that bite the hardest."

He turned to the Deatherage cowboys and said, "Listen up, men. Here's the deal. If you help me drive these critters to Denver town, I'll triple your pay. How about that? You'll be rich. What do ya say?"

Chops answered instantly. "No dice."

Lullaby crossed his arms. "I'd rather make an honest dollar than have three of yours."

The rest of the gang howled agreement.

Hork said, "You're gonna regret tangling with the Dagger D, Angry R brand, mister."

Seph said. "Nice try, weasel." He hadn't planned to tack on an insult. As soon as he said it, he couldn't explain why he'd singled out the weasel. If he could do it over, he'd call the outlaw a buzzard instead.

With that, Swoop fell silent. His breath came in shallow gasps. The cowboys kept a close watch on him as they moved toward the camp.

As they approached, the sounds of a struggle reached their ears. It grew louder the closer they got.

Seph tensed as he entered the camp and saw Stoke locked in a fierce knife fight with Chaw. The outlaw, notorious for his skill with blades, muttered to his knife, "*Rodaja de Muerte*, tonight you will taste blood once again."

In that instant, Seph knew. It was Chaw who dismembered Woodsy. It was unsettling to hear the outlaw speak to his knife as if it were his partner, but then Seph realized that he was no different. He spoke to his rifle just as Chaw spoke to his knife. As he watched Stoke and Chaw circling, he had a strange feeling of holding a detached limb. He winced as he imagined *Rodaja de Muerte* slicing off Woodsy's arms and legs.

His eyes widened in horror as he took in the scene. Coyote's lifeless body lay sprawled on the ground, blood pooling beneath him.

A crying baby's howls pierced the night. Seph didn't see any women. What was a baby doing in an outlaw's camp?

The sound of the cattle nearby added to the pandemonium. Their restless movements threatened another stampede.

The camp was a tornado of confusion. The cowboys, including Seph, were momentarily stunned by the wild and violent scene before them.

Conjure shivered and stepped closer to Seph. "Hope there ain't no ghosts around here," he whispered to Seph.

"Don't worry, Conjure. Ain't no such thing as ghosts." Seph realized that Conjure was using him as a shield, trying to hide behind him so that the spirits wouldn't see him.

Seph's focus snapped back to the fight between Stoke and Chaw. Stoke, though outmatched in skill, fought with a desperate ferocity. Seph knew he had to intervene before it was too late. As he stepped forward, a movement caught his eye.

Stoke managed to land a blow, but Chaw retaliated with a vicious slash across Stoke's arm. Stoke howled, clutching his injured arm. Blood seeped between his fingers. The wound was deep. If it didn't hurt now, it would later, and for a long time to come.

Seph lunged at Chaw, tackling him to the ground. The two rolled in the dirt, grappling for control. Chaw's knife flashed dangerously close to Seph's face, but Seph pinned Chaw's arm, forcing the blade away. With a final, powerful push, Seph slammed Chaw's hand into the ground. The knife flew from his grasp.

The cowboys surrounded them. Their cheers mingled with the bellowing of the beeves and the baby's wails. Seph looked up as Lullaby and the others secured Chaw, tying his hands behind his back.

Lullaby raised his voice. "I'm gonna head out and quiet the herd."

Yodel nodded. "I'll join you."

Chops said, "I gotta check on the horses. I ain't seen them since the outlaws took the remuda."

Seph turned to face the remaining men. He pointed at the bloodied outlaw. "Chaw must be the one who killed Woodsy and hacked off his limbs," he said, his voice hard.

Hork's eyes burned with fury. "Let's string him up," he growled, and nobody argued the point. Trinket and Blaze stepped forward, ready to help.

Seph crossed his arms and watched as they fashioned a noose and dropped it over Chaw's head. The outlaw's whining protests fell on deaf ears.

Chaw begged, "It ain't my fault. Swoop made me do it."

"This is what the outlaws deserve," Seph said coldly. "It's just what they did to Squat. We must avenge the murder of our trail boss."

"No," Chaw begged. "I'm just a soldier, taking orders, doing what I'm told. You can't hang me for that."

Hork said, "What would you say to Woodsy's mother? Huh? Ain't nothing you could say to her. But I wouldn't have any trouble telling *your* mama that we hung *you*. She'd probably understand. She'd probably thank us if she heard what you done."

"No." Chap protested. "Mama loves me. She can't live without me."

Hork had heard enough. Those were to be Chaw's last words. Hork lifted Chaw in the air, and Blaze pulled the rope tight as the rest of the cowboys watched the outlaw swing like a pendulum.

Finally, Blaze said, "He's dead."

Hork pumped his fists in the air and cheered. The rest of the gang joined in. It was as if they were celebrating the Fourth of July rather than witnessing a hanging.

Blaze let go of the rope, all at once, and Chaw landed with a thud on the ground.

The cowboys grew silent and stared. It was as if they half expected the outlaw to jump to his feet, but Blaze was right. He was dead.

As they stood silently, each man lost in his thoughts, Seph wondered what was going through their minds. As for himself, Seph was pleased. Chaw got what he deserved.

Again, the baby began to howl. Conjure stepped toward her, gently picked up the bundle, and soothed her cries as best he could. Humming as he walked, Conjure stepped over to Seph and placed the baby in his arms. "This must be Bonita's baby, Lily."

Seph looked down at the tiny, frightened face, and felt a rush of protectiveness. He held her close, vowing silently to keep her safe. He couldn't remember having ever held a baby before. He was the youngest of seven children—there were none after him.

As he held the infant, Seph suddenly realized that Swoop was nowhere to be seen. Panic surged through him as he turned and scanned the darkness. "Where's Swoop?" he shouted. His voice boomed. Baby Lily howled and Seph stopped hollering.

The cowboys exchanged confused glances, realizing that their captive had disappeared. "He was right here," Conjure whispered loudly, looking around frantically.

Hork cursed under his breath. "He must've slipped away in the melee."

Seph's spirit plummeted as the reality hit him. Swoop had escaped. To make matters worse, Sheriff was gone. The outlaw boss got away and took his beloved horse with him.

Turning back toward the camp, his eyes took in the scene before him. His mind scurried as he tried to process everything.

Stoke was injured. Coyote was dead. Chaw's body swung at the end of a rope. Swoop had vanished into the darkness and Sheriff was gone.

Seph said, "We'd better hunker down for the night, men. Come morning, we've got a herd to push."

Hork said, "You don't suppose Swoop will come back and kill us in our sleep?"

Seph frowned. "It's possible." His gut told him that Swoop was already miles away. He hated knowing that the outlaw was out there somewhere. One day, he was certain, their paths would cross again. He didn't figure that day would come soon, but to be safe, he said, "I'll stay awake half the night while you sleep."

Conjure said, "I don't know if I *can* sleep. I might never sleep again."

Softly, Seph said, "Try."

Trinket announced he would take the second watch and Seph agreed to wake him after a couple of hours."

Before long, Conjure was snoring softly. The rest of the men seemed to have fallen asleep as well. The baby was another matter. She seemed content to be carried, but every time Seph looked at Lily's face, she giggled back at him.

He didn't have any experience with babies, but he had cared for Ma before she died. And he had tended farm animals. But babies weren't like barnyard critters, were they?

Seph quietly moved about camp, organizing provisions one-handed, and looking for something that might fit between the baby's lips. He finally settled on his specialty, lukewarm corn mush and was surprised to find that the baby liked it.

It was well past midnight, more likely one or two in the morning when Seph shook Trinket's foot. As the young cowboy sat up to take watch, Seph stretched out on the ground and tucked the bundle gently between his left arm and chest.

What a day! So much had happened since he last slept. He tried to calculate how many days remained before they'd deliver the herd to the stockyards in Abilene. He was glad that they had reclaimed what was rightfully theirs and started figuring estimates in his head, but was asleep before reaching any conclusions.

# CHAPTER 23

THE MOOD IN THE outlaw's camp was jubilant. Seph wondered if Hork would ever stop pumping his fists in the air.

It seemed everyone wanted to slap him on the back and congratulate him on rescuing the herd. But he wished that they would stop. He hadn't done it alone, after all.

It was time to point the herd toward Abilene.

Blaze approached Seph as he saddled up. His serious expression worried Seph, who turned away from his task. "Hey, Seph," Blaze began, his voice low. "Last night I forgot to mention—Torp ain't dead. He's still alive. Maybe he'll make it, maybe he won't, but he's fighting on. Thought you should know."

Seph blinked in astonishment. It was impossible to believe. "Torp! Alive?" A smile broke across his face. "That's the best news I've heard in days."

Blaze nodded urgently. "Yep. He's a tough one, that kid. Don't count him out just yet."

Laughter rang out as the men gathered their gear. Conjure slapped Blaze on the shoulder. "We'll be in Abilene 'fore you know it! Ain't that somethin'?"

Blaze grinned, his eyes twinkling. "Heck, I might buy myself a new hat when we get there." He stopped himself abruptly. "Oh, wait! I'm saving to buy a horse."

Seph nodded. He remembered Blaze's affection for the horse he called Noomoo, newly rescued and freshly saddled.

Yodel jested, "Y'all better save some coin for the saloons," he teased, sparking a round of hearty laughter from the group. "Been on the trail so long, I reckon I forgot how to be a sinner."

Lullaby overlooked his brother's words and changed the subject. "We did it, boys. We got our herd back. Wait'll Dusty sees *us*!"

Hork looked exhausted and Chops seemed exhilarated. Together, they finished packing up.

"This is what it's all about," Chops said, his voice filled with satisfaction. "All this hard work is finally payin' off."

Stoke, his arm bandaged from the knife fight, swung himself into the saddle. It must have hurt, but he would never let it show. "Ain't no way a little scratch is keeping me from *this* ride," he declared.

Seph, carrying baby Lily in a makeshift sling, did his best to shield her from the early morning sun. He held his hat so that it cast a shade over her. Tiny hands clutched at his shirt and tickled him. "Don't you worry," he murmured softly. "We'll get you back to your mama. You'll see."

Trinket double-checked the supplies strapped to his horse. "We're about seven miles from the regular trail," he calculated. "Maybe eight. Shouldn't take us long to get back on track."

The restless herd moved northeasterly. Bringing up the rear, Seph rode drag. He felt as if Slaw was riding on one shoulder and Torp was riding on the other.

The rhythmic clatter of hooves against the earth was comforting after all they had been through. He had grown to love the sounds of lowing cattle and the easy pace of the slow moving herd. Riding in the worst position didn't faze him. He was glad to do it. Today, he wouldn't have it any other way.

He thought about his companions and felt a swell of pride. Conjure, Trinket, Blaze, Yodel, Lullaby, Chops, Hork, Stoke, and himself—somehow, they forged a brotherhood along the trail. They had faced adversity, battled outlaws, and reclaimed the Deatherage herd. Maybe they didn't deserve the brand, Dagger D, Angry R at first, but there was no denying it suited them now.

The journey to Abilene wasn't over, but with his friends by his side, he had no doubts that they would make it. It was what they were meant to do. It's as if the long column of critters stretching as far as his eye could see were the reason he had been placed on this earth.

Lily cooed and flapped her arms like a baby bird. Seph spoke to the infant, "Maybe someday I'll become a father and have a little girl just like you."

Dunk was making coffee when he saw the brindled steer—Skillet! Then he saw Stoke. "Dusty!" He shouted as he ran. "Look, Dusty! You'll never believe it."

The trail boss groaned. He had been resting in the shade, leaning against a wagon wheel. "What's that, Dunk?" He dragged himself up and shielded the sun with his hand. "Well, I'll be... those jaspers did it! You're right. I don't believe it."

Bonita exclaimed, "Ooh, ooh. They must be hungry." She raced to the wagon and filled a basket with biscuits.

Stoke slowed his horse briefly as he passed Dunk. "We got a surprise for you," he whispered. "Seph's got a baby with him. We think it's Lily."

Dunk leaned forward to make sure he was hearing correctly. "Bonita's Lily? How can that be?"

Stoke shrugged and laughed. "Who else could it be? How many infant runaways do you suppose there are traipsing about on the prairie?"

Dunk couldn't contain his excitement. He wanted to tell Bonita right away. He watched her dash about and decided to wait.

The parade of longhorns passed to the left of the smaller herd. The drovers lucky enough to ride on the right side of the herd were treated to the boss's praise and Bonita's cooking.

Dunk hastened to help Dusty saddle up and checked the travois that carried Squat's remains. Then he packed up camp. Torp begged to ride along with the herd, but Dunk insisted that he ride in the chuckwagon. Torp was feeling better, but his chest was bandaged like a mummy. Seeing the herd restored his spirits, but he still had a lot of healing yet to do.

Before setting the wagon back on the trail, Dunk spoke to the team of mules. He had a way with animals. It's as if they heard him and did as he asked, but mules required more persuasion than most beasts. Dunk didn't want them to move fast. He wanted them to go slow. That would be better for Torp, and it might allow Seph to pass the wagon. He could hardly wait to see the look on Bonita's face when she discovered that her baby was alive.

Bonita sat beside Dunk on the chuckwagon's bench and chattered happily. It's as if she had briefly forgotten about her troubles and losses. There was a sparkle in her eye and Dunk wished he could put his arm around her.

The five hundred critters from the cow camp merged seamlessly into the procession. Dunk smiled as he watched the beeves find their proper places in line. It was as if they had remembered where they belonged.

It felt good to be on the move again, albeit at a snail's pace.

As the afternoon went on, the tail end of the herd grew nearer but never caught up to the chuckwagon.

Seph saw Dunk in the distance, picketing the mules, and abandoned his position at drag. The last of the beeves would have to make their way to the bedding ground without him. He rode toward the chuckwagon and thought of the reunions to come.

He couldn't remember a time when he had felt better than this. He smiled so hard, his face hurt. He could only imagine the joy this cooing bundle would bring Bonita. And, as if that was not enough, Seph caught a glimpse of his partner, looking as alive as ever, peeking over the edge of the chuckwagon.

Dunk pointed toward him and called to Bonita.

Her eyes widened in disbelief. She took a few steps and then stopped, covering her mouth before she began screaming. It was a joyful sound, not frightening.

Seph carefully dismounted, making sure not to upset the precious bundle he carried.

Bonita ran forward, bouncing. "Lily?" she whispered, "My baby!" Tears welled up in her eyes.

Seph's long legs swiftly carried the baby to her mother. "I believe this little angel belongs to you," he said gently, handing Lily to Bonita.

Her hands trembled as she took the baby, her tears flowing unchecked. "Oh, Lily," she sobbed, hugging her child close. "My sweet, sweet girl. I thought I'd lost you."

Dunk made a strange sound. Seph looked at the cook. Was he choking? Dunk wiped his eyes with the back of his hand.

The moment unfolded slowly, as though time had paused to let it linger. It seemed like one of those moments that was worth remembering.

Slowly, the crew gathered round and watched. Nobody said a word until Stoke strolled up and said, "What's for supper? I'm famished."

Dunk didn't answer. It was as if he hadn't heard him. Seph shook his head slowly. How could Dunk not hear Stoke? The man was hard to ignore.

Dunk looked back and forth between Bonita and Lily. Seph thought, *Something is different.*

What had changed? Seph's skin prickled and he felt a spark in his gizzard. It was just a hunch. It hadn't occurred to him before.

Was Dunk smitten?

The camp was quiet. The last of the cattle had settled down for the night. The fire crackled as Dusty stood up, eager to address the crew. He cleared his throat and the cowboys looked up.

Dusty took a deep breath, looking each of them in the eye. "Evening, men. I got a few things to say to you all. Tonight, I'm a proud man." His voice wavered slightly. "We've been through a knothole—together—but we've come out stronger. I can't think of a better time or place to bury my brother than right here."

He paused, looking down at the ground as he gathered his thoughts. "Squat would be proud of you too," he said, his voice thick with emotion. "Every last one of you." Dusty sniffled and his nose twitched. Even in the low light, it was plain to see. "I swear, I don't know what I'd do without you." He went on to say, "You should be proud. This work will create the strongest generation of men that ever lived or ever will."

Dusty's eyes found Seph, and he smiled warmly. "Seph, I'm glad you and Stoke are pals now. It means a lot to me—to see you two getting along."

Seph nodded and removed his hat.

Dusty cleared his throat again and looked at Lullaby. "Would you say a short prayer? Make sure it's short, though. These tired cowboys need a good night's sleep."

Lullaby lifted his head and steadied his gaze. "I'll keep it short, boss," he promised. He stood and removed his hat, bowing his head. The cowboys followed suit.

"Lord, we thank you for guiding us up these trails and bringing us together. We ask for your blessings as we lay Squat to rest. Watch over us and keep us safe. And, if it ain't too much to ask, could you lift the pain from the boss's back? Amen."

"Amen!" The cowboys cheered.

Dusty flashed half a grin. "Thank you, Lullaby. I think my back is feeling better already. And thank you, men. Now, somebody start digging."

As the cow hands began to settle down for the night, Seph spread his bedroll near the wagon. He couldn't see Torp but it was good to hear his voice.

Seph stretched out on his back and looked up at the stars. "I'm mighty glad you're doing so good, Torp."

Torp answered, "Well, you didn't think I'd let you have *all* the fun around here, did you?"

Seph chuckled. "We've had ourselves a big old time, ain't we?"

"Sure enough, Seph."

Seph thought that he heard a whimper and realized that it had been a while since he'd heard Torp do that.

"Remember when I was dying?"

"Yeah."

"And I asked you if you'd name a kid after me someday?"

"Uh huh."

"Well, forget it, Seph. Since I lived, you ain't gotta do that after all. Heck, who knows, maybe I'll have a kid of my own someday. Can you imagine that?"

The thought amused Seph. "That'd be something to see. A little Torp junior running around!"

Torp laughed.

From a nearby bedroll, somebody shushed them.

Torp whispered, "Well, stranger things have happened, Seph."

Seph nodded, feeling a deep sense of camaraderie with his partner. "That's true, Torp. We got many miles to ride together. I sure am glad to know you plan to survive. Hopefully, it will be a few years before you settle down and father a herd of Torplets."

In a thin voice, Torp said, "Do you remember the other things I said when I was dying?"

"I reckon I do, Torp."

"Well, I meant 'em. I'm glad I said them things."

"Me too, Torp. Me too."

"Did you and Stoke really become friends?"

"It's hard to believe, ain't it. It's like he changed overnight."

Torp said, "I'm glad, Seph. It's a miracle, ain't it. Maybe it's because you saved his life."

"I reckon so."

Seph was quiet for a couple of minutes. As he gazed into the heavens, a fluttering sound reached his ears. The long day must have tired the kid.

He was tired too, but he lay awake thinking about everything they had been through, the bonds they had forged, and the miles that still lay ahead. And this was just their first drive.

With a contented sigh, he closed his eyes. His fellow cowboys felt like family. He no longer felt like an outsider. "This is where I belong," he whispered to the heavens.

His eyes blinked open and he realized, *I never felt like this before.*

Wills Tanner stumbled through the darkness, his legs barely able to support his weight. He couldn't have known that his wife and daughter were a long day's march to the south any more than they could know where he was.

His lips were cracked and parched, his skin raw and blistered. He couldn't remember what had happened to his hat.

The ache in his stomach had long passed hunger. Now it was a gnawing, empty void. Each step was a monumental effort. His body screamed for respite, but he pressed on. How long had it been since he'd seen them? Had his wife and baby girl survived?

The outlaws' laughter echoed in his mind. They had stolen his gun, the only means he had to protect himself and find food. They had beaten him mercilessly, their fists and boots leaving him bloodied and broken. And then they had left him on the open prairie, laughing at him as they rode away. That was days ago, maybe a week even, perhaps longer.

Wills had tried to find game, but the land had been unyielding. With no weapon and no strength left to chase even the smallest of animals, he was reduced to scavenging. Whenever he could find and catch them, he ate live grasshoppers. The prairie offered little mercy, and Wills found himself growing ever weaker.

He had to find Bonita and Lily. The guilt of leaving them unprotected gnawed at him. He had only meant to be away for a couple of hours.

It was well past dark when Wills collapsed, his body unable to go any further. He clawed at the dirt, dragging himself forward inch by inch. His body was battered, but he refused to give up. He couldn't. Not when his family needed him.

The air cooled at dusk. The oppressive heat of the day was replaced by a biting chill and Wills shivered uncontrollably. His thin shirt offered little protection against the night air. His mind drifted in and out of consciousness. The line between reality and delirium blurred as exhaustion took its toll.

He didn't know how long he crawled or how many times he collapsed, only to force himself back up. Time had lost all meaning. If only he could find water, he might have a chance.

Wills felt his strength ebbing away. Darkness dimmed his eyesight. But then, he heard it, the faint, unmistakable sound of water. Flowing water. Hope surged within him—a desperate, fragile faith pushed him forward.

The sound of the river grew louder. The promise of salvation was just within reach. Somehow, he was still alive, fighting for every breath.

He smelled it—and then he saw it—a glimmer of water under the moon-light. With a triumphant surge, Wills dragged himself to the river's edge. He plunged his hands into the cool water, bringing it to his cracked lips. The relief was immediate. Cool water soothed his parched throat and renewed his strength.

The weight of his ordeal washed over him. He had made it. Somehow, against all odds, he had reached the river. As he lay there, his body trembling, he thought of Bonita and Lily. He had to find them, and had to bring them to safety. If only they had stayed in Ohio. It was his fault. He remembered that he was to blame, but he couldn't remember why they had left.

With a sharp, chalky stone, Wills scratched a message on a boulder near the river. Then he said a prayer and closed his eyes. The Arkansas River flowed gently beside him.

He thought, *Even in the darkest of times, hope can still be found.*

With his family on his mind, he succumbed to sleep, but the malnourished pioneer did not awaken in the morning.

After yet another hot summer day on the trail, the push was on. Everyone yearned to reach the Arkansas River.

Bonita spent the day fawning over Lily. She hardly set the child down. The infant seemed content, cooing and gurgling in her arms, her tiny hands grasping at her mother's hair and clothes.

Bonita, Lily, and Dunk were the first to reach the Arkansas River. The air was cooler near the water, and she looked eagerly into the distance. "What's that?" she asked, squinting. There was a boulder beside the river, and an odd shape beside it.

"I'm not sure," Dunk replied. "Stay here with Lily. I'll go take a look."

Despite Dunk's warning, Bonita held Lily tight and followed Dunk, peeking around him. As they drew closer, the shape became clearer. There was a man, lying motionless on the ground.

"Merciful heavens, Dunk! It's Wills!" Bonita cried, her voice breaking. She rushed forward, her feet barely touching the ground.

Dunk hesitated before following her.

Wills lay still, his face sunburned and gaunt, his clothes torn and dirty. Bonita dropped to her knees beside him, her hands shaking as she gently touched his face. "Wills, please wake up. Please," she whispered, tears flooding her cheeks.

Dunk knelt beside her. "Let me check him," he said gently. He placed his fingers on Wills' neck, searching for a pulse. "He's alive," Dunk proclaimed. "We need to get water into him. He's parched and weak."

As they worked to revive Wills, Bonita looked at the nearby boulder. Wills had scratched their names on its surface. Wills, Bonita, and Lily. 1868. Her breath caught in her throat, and she looked back at Wills.

"He never gave up on us," she whispered. "He kept fighting to get back to us."

Dunk nodded, his face serious. "We need to get him fed. I'll make some broth."

As the herd caught up, the cowboys pushed across the river and set up camp.

Dunk and Bonita worked tirelessly to get water into Wills, using a damp cloth to moisten his lips and coax small sips of water into his mouth and down his throat.

Wills' breathing grew steadier, but he remained unconscious.

When the chuckwagon reached the other side of the river, Dunk set off to make a broth.

He couldn't deny the affection he had developed for Bonita, but seeing Wills fighting for his life stirred a mix of guilt and determination in him.

As the sun set and the camp settled in for the night, Dunk sought out Lullaby. The young cowboy was like an old preacher. He found the singing cowboy near the river and joined him.

Lullaby said, "You got a troubled mind, don't ya?"

Dunk sighed, running a shaky hand through his hair. "You know it. I'm mighty weak, Lullaby. I've grown fond of Bonita. Too fond. And now, seeing her husband like this—I'm forcing myself to pray for her man."

Lullaby placed a comforting hand on Dunk's forearm. "You've been a big help to Bonita and Lily when they needed you most. You're doing the right thing, praying for Wills. It ain't always easy doin' what's right, but it's what makes us who we are."

"Thanks, Lullaby. It's not easy, being a sinner."

Lullaby smiled gently. "We're all sinners, Dunk. Every last one of us. Get some rest. You'll need your strength. I'll pray for you. We'll both pray for Wills. Just do the best you can."

Dunk stood. He'd spent much of the journey guiding these young men but had overlooked the impact that the tenderfoots had on him.

The big war had taken its toll on him. He had tried to ignore it. He had thought he was there to help turn overgrown kids, like Seph, Lullaby, and Torp, into men. As he walked back to the chuckwagon, he felt as if the tables had turned. He felt like his old self again. Like the young man he was before the war. But that didn't help ease his heartache.

He glanced at Bonita, who sat beside Wills, holding his hand and whispering words of encouragement. Dunk knew that he would help them, no matter what happened.

Why did he have to go and let himself fall for the woman? He closed his eyes and prayed.

# CHAPTER 24

AFTER A MUCH NEEDED day off, they left the Arkansas for the Smoky Hill River. On the first day Torp remained in the chuckwagon. Many of the provisions had been removed and packed on horses to make room for him. To accommodate Wills, more provisions were offloaded. There was precious little space in a wagon that was never meant to carry people.

Torp couldn't help constantly bumping into Wills. His chest was still bandaged and Bonita fretted about what would happen if Torp overexerted himself. Torp spent most of the day kneeling and watching the herd. Dunk told him to take it easy and reassured him that he'd be back on horseback soon enough.

Seph noticed that Dunk had gone out of his way to befriend Wills. He admired Dunk for being kind to the man who seemed to be on the mend. By the second day, Wills was able to sit up.

On the third day, Torp insisted on riding. He declared, "I can't stand sitting around any longer."

Dunk relented, but only after Torp promised to take it easy. Dunk insisted that Chops pick him a horse with an easy gate.

When Torp rode back into place, he told Seph that it felt good to be home. He winced frequently and Seph knew that his recovery was incomplete.

On the sixth day, Wills was strong enough to walk beside Dunk. The two men laughed and shared stories. Bonita sat on the wagon seat, watching them. She spent her days tending to Lily and helping Dunk with the chores as if she had been hired to do them.

The seventh day brought cooler weather and a welcome respite from the relentless sun. The Smoky Hill River was just a day away. The end of their arduous journey was in sight. On one hand, Seph was glad to reach the end of the trail. On the other, despite the challenges, he felt a little blue.

On the morning of the eighth day, Dusty rode off alone. The cowboys watched him go, and Seph figured that he rode off to find a buyer for the herd.

That evening, Dusty returned, a rare smile on his face. The man of few words seemed as if he couldn't wait to talk to his crew. "Gather 'round, men. I've got some good news," Dusty shouted. "I found a buyer for the herd. Got $35 a head. All you fellas gotta do is bring 'em on home. These critters should be in the stockyard by early afternoon—tomorrow."

A cheer went up from the group.

Seph did some figuring. 3,000 head times 35 dollars came to $105,000. He estimated the total payroll for the year at $6,000. That left a profit of $99,000—enough to buy something like 600 horses. The trail boss was a rich man.

Dusty held up his arms to quiet the crowd. "Tomorrow is payday. You fellas have worked hard. You deserve every cent that's coming to you. And a couple a days off." He shook his head and frowned. "But you are a sorry looking lot."

The men laughed.

The ramrod made a show of disgust, pinching his nose and twisting his face like he just chugged vinegar. "So, I got a surprise for you. Every man gets a new hat, a fresh pair of boots, a crisp shirt, and store-bought trousers. Call it a bonus."

Dusty rubbed his face as if wondering whether to say more, then did. "Squat had it in mind and was planning on surprising you with the news himself. Think of him when you gawk at yourselves in the mirror."

Dusty was startled when the cowboys crowded in and hoisted him in the air. "Put me down," he shouted, but nobody listened. Their cheers were almost loud enough to stampede the herd again.

Seph wished that Slaw could have experienced the glory of reaching the end of the trail. It was hard to think of anything more satisfying.

Torp tapped Seph on the shoulder. He held up his hands and counted off the rivers, one by one: "Guadalupe, Colorado, Brazos, Trinity, Red, Washita, Canadian, North Fork, Cimarron, Salt Fork, Bluff Creek, Arkansas, and Smoky Hill. We made it Seph. Thirteen rivers. Can you believe it?"

Seph answered proudly. "We did. I'm proud of you, Torp."

As they settled around the campfire, Stoke shouted, "We're almost to Abilene, boys. First round's on me! I'm gonna show you jaspers how a man paints a town."

Trinket's eyes lit up. "I can not wait to hit the saloons," he said, a wide grin spreading across his face. "And my first time with a señorita!"

Conjure kept glancing at Lullaby.

Seph thought about the night Conjure and Hork tried to quit. Maybe Conjure was pining for the girl he left behind. Did he still plan to ride home and steal Mary away?

Lullaby frowned. "You boys ought to think twice about visiting them saloons. They ain't nothin' but trouble. Drinking, gambling, women—none of it is good for you."

Yodel rolled his eyes. "Ease up, Granny. We done earned this. Let us have our fun."

Dunk piped in. "Lullaby's got a point," he said. "A little bit of whiskey goes a long way. Look out for each other in town." Dunk gripped Lullaby's arm protectively and looked from face to face. "I ain't your mama, and Lullaby's not your granny." Dunk looked directly at Torp as he finished speaking. "But if you'd rather stay in camp with us, there ain't no shame in it."

Torp violently shook his head. "I ain't staying back in camp."

Seph thought of Torp's bullet wound. The kid still had some healing to do.

Stoke paced around the campfire. "We worked hard. A man deserves to blow off steam at the end of the trail. That's what cowboys do. It's time to go hog-wild."

Seph's stomach lurched. He wasn't just a man. He was a cowboy and this was his first drive.

He had felt torn. Lullaby's prayers and talk of God's mercy had gotten under his skin. Ma had taught him about sin, and Lullaby reminded him of the words in the good book. And yet, thoughts of what might happen on the other side of those swinging saloon doors made his gizzard pulse with excitement.

As Wills and Bonita stepped away from the campfire, Stoke let out a ferocious yell. At first it sounded like the scream of a cougar. A series of yips followed. A shivering sensation corkscrewed down Seph's spine.

Stoke's head was still tipped back as he said, "Don't forget. I'm the top hand around here. That means I get first dibs. Remember what I told you. I am The Ignitor. I got a fire in me. Ain't nothing gonna stop this locomotive. Them calico queens ain't never gonna forget doing a bit of business with me."

Seph wasn't certain that he wanted to go hog-wild, as Stoke put it. But it was hard to deny how often he thought about the ladies. One lady in particular. He tried to reconcile the wanton images Stoke described with the tenderness Wills showed Bonita. A man should treasure a woman, not pay to be with them. He sat quietly between Torp and Chops and was glad that they were quiet too.

It was unsettling—thinking about painted ladies, calico queens, or other words he preferred not to think of. He thought of the picture of the beautiful, cigar box woman. It was a childish notion and he hated to admit that he missed the carton, even if he only had to admit it to himself. His cheeks felt hot, and he was glad that his discomfort and embarrassment were disguised by darkness around the campfire.

Stoke wasn't the only one with a fire blazing in his furnace. Seph longed for the mysterious woman of his dreams.

Seph wandered down to the banks of the Smoky Hill River and looked at the waterway. Gazing at the final milestone on the way to Abilene failed to turn his thoughts away from romance.

For the millionth time, he thought, *If only she were real.*

As the cowboys approached the outskirts of Abilene at midday, the stock-yards bustled with activity. The herd moved steadily, guided by the experienced cowboys, who shouted and whistled, urging the beeves forward.

Seph rode at the back, ensuring that no stragglers fell behind. The closer they got, the louder the sounds became. The lowing of cattle mixed with the shouts of stockmen and the clatter of wooden gates being opened and closed.

"There it is, boys," Dusty called out. "Let's get these critters into the chutes."

The cowboys spurred their horses, closing in around the herd and nudging them toward the pens. They obediently funneled into the narrow passage-ways.

Seph watched as the last of the cattle were enclosed. It was satisfying to know their mission was complete. The herd was safe and they had made it.

Dusty dismounted and approached the stockyard foreman, a rough look-ing, middle-aged man with a tally book in his hand and a no-nonsense look on his face. After a brief exchange, the man nodded and handed Dusty a sack that looked heavy.

Just before he turned away, Dusty pointed at the farthest pen. "Check the bill of sale, friend. Cut out the brindled bull. Skillet ain't a part of the deal. We're gonna need him back on the ranch."

Seph's heart swelled with pride. The sturdy lead bull would be spared. What a triumph. It was a miracle, and he felt like celebrating.

Dusty turned to the group, holding the sack of cash. "We did it, boys! We just got paid!" he shouted, his face breaking into a broad smile.

Cheers erupted from the cowboys as they lined up, single file.

The cowboys mounted up.

Dusty gave a nod, and the drovers spurred their horses to a gallop.

Stoke hollered in a booming voice. "Let's whoop it up, boys!"

The rest of the outfit joined in. It was tough to separate the chorus of yells from the sound of thundering hooves.

Seph and Stoke rode side by side. They fired their guns into the air and added their laughter to the ruckus.

It was a short ride from the stockyards to the center of Abilene.

"Time to frolic!" Blaze shouted, veering off with Conjure and Hork.

The other cowboys followed, splitting into pairs or small groups.

Seph reined up beside a barber shop. "First stop," he said, grinning at Stoke. "I could use a trim." He'd never had a real haircut.

Stoke nodded and lifted his lip into a sneer. "Good thinking. You sure ain't presentable looking like you do."

As they approached the barber shop, they wondered if it was open. It looked like it had been built, but not yet occupied. Abilene had sprung up almost overnight.

A red, white, and blue pole jutted out at an upward angle from the wall. The door swung open with the jingle of a bell as Seph and Stoke stepped inside.

The fragrant interior of the barber shop clobbered Seph's senses. It smelled like wood smoke and pepper. There was also a vibrant, citrus scent. Seph found the strong smells pleasant enough. But there was something about the place that made him feel crowded in.

In addition to the barber and his customer, three fidgety men waited in chairs along a wall. A freckle faced boy darted through the front door and disappeared into the back room.

The barber, who looked to be a couple of years shy of thirty, turned to greet Seph and Stoke. "Lorcan Muldoon, at your service. If you be friends, then you can be calling me Can-Doon. Make yourself right at home."

Seph and Stoke gave their names and declined a seat, preferring to stand and wait.

Crudely painted signs hung on the walls:


*No Bloodletting,*
*No Dentistry,*
*Dirty Baths 25 Cents,*
*Fresh Baths 50 Cents,*
*Don't Spit on the Floor,*
*No Refunds, and*
*Don't Shoot the Barber.*


Above a plush, red upholstered chair, a sign read: "Private. Reserved Seating." Seph figured that some, but not all, of the signs were serious.

The boy darted back into the room. "I got two baths ready."

Can-Doon looked away from his customer and said, "Good work, lad." To the three men, he asked, "One of you men mind waiting a few more minutes?"

As the boy led two customers into the back room, Can-Doon turned to Seph and Stoke and said, "That's me boy, Maximilian. A grand name, don't you think? A good boy, he is. My Maxie-Doon."

The man in the barber's chair said, "That boy will make an excellent cowboy someday."

Can-Doon stepped over toward the corner to jettison a stream of tobacco juice into an ornate spittoon. It featured a castle, complete with a moat. Curiosity got the better of Seph, and he stepped forward for a closer look.

"Aye, admiring the dragon? Some people do not believe in them, sad to say."

The barber passed a steel blade across a horsehair strop and said, "This here gentleman is Mr. Joseph McCoy. He thinks that every boy should become a cowboy. But maybe my Maxie-Doon wants to stay in town, like his Papa."

While the powerful cattleman waited in the chair, Can-Doon took a shaving mug from the shelf. Adding a quick pour of hot water from the top of a small wood stove, he made quick work of lathering soap with a boar bristle brush. "Mr. McCoy built this town."

It seemed to be just the introduction Mr. McCoy was waiting for. He added, "And Mr. Muldoon followed me into town. The truth is, I made it worth his while. I couldn't do without his service." He looked up as if he were offering a prayer and added, "This town's gonna rule the prairie for hundreds of years." With a grand gesture of his arms, he continued. "Mark my words, lads. Abilene will be the heart of the cattle industry, bringing prosperity and growth beyond what we can possibly imagine."

Seph and Stoke stood by the wall, hats in hand, waiting patiently for their turn and trying to imagine the thriving future Mr. McCoy had planned for Abilene.

The barber's young son darted back into the front room. Speaking to the third cowboy, he said. "Gimme just a couple more minutes, sir."

Maxie-Doon reminded Seph of himself, though he had labored on a farm rather than in town. He tripped over his too-long trousers and kept shoving his sleeves up, only to have them fall back down. As he dashed by, Maxie-Doon flashed a toothy grin at Seph and Stoke, eager to help his father.

Joseph McCoy also turned his attention to the barber's son. "You've got a fine lad there, Can-Doon, but you might want to get him a new set of duds. Those trousers trip him up."

The barber laughed. "Aye, Mr. McCoy, I've been meanin' to get him somethin' that fits him proper. It's just been busy times. If only we hadn't lost his dear mother. But consider it done."

Maxie-Doon shrugged, unfazed by the attention. "I'm alright, Papa. Can I fetch anything for you, Mr. McCoy?"

"No, lad. Thank you just the same," McCoy replied with a wink.

When Mr. McCoy's shave and haircut were finished, the barber massaged the cattleman's neck and shoulders. Mr. McCoy let out a contented sigh, enjoying the treatment while Stoke squirmed, anxious to get on with the day.

The barber filled the shop with a song while he worked.

Joseph McCoy turned to Seph and Stoke. "Can-Doon ain't the best barber in the world, but his singing does wonders for the soul." He retired to the reserved seating. As he made himself comfortable, he confided, "This is my hideaway. A business man needs a place where he can go to escape for a while."

Seph wondered what a business man was and what they did. He'd never met one before. Seph watched for a moment as the man lit a cigar and picked up a newspaper.

Stoke rolled his eyes and slapped his hat against his legs as the singing barber swept away Mr. McCoy's hair. He told Can-Doon not to bother with housework on his account.

When Seph looked back at the man, he realized Mr. McCoy was watching him over the top of his newspaper. He inquired, "What outfit do you fellas ride for? That one that just rolled in today, I'm guessing."

Can-Doon motioned to a hat tree and Stoke made use of it before sitting in the barber's chair.

Seph added his hat to the tree as he answered, "Deatherage, sir," meeting the man's gaze with a steady look as the cattleman set the paper on his lap.

McCoy chuckled, smoke curling from his lip. "Ain't heard of it," he said.

Seph grinned. "You will, sir. Just you see!" He glanced at Stoke to see if his friend had anything to add, but Stoke seemed preoccupied, his gaze focused on his image in the barber's mirror.

Mr. McCoy asked, "What's your trail boss's name?"

Seph thought for a moment. Should he tell the man their business? The frown on his face must have given his thoughts away.

"Pardon me, son. I don't mean to pry. I did purchase your herd, but my clerk took care of the transaction, you see?"

Should he tell Mr. McCoy about Squat and Dusty? He figured that it would be better to provide Dusty's formal name. "It's Glenn Deatherage, sir."

The barber sang quietly and snipped vigorously, working on Stoke's dark hair.

McCoy asked, "You aim to come back again next year, don't you?"

Seph shrugged. "I reckon so." Where else would they go? Seph wondered whether there were other options. There was so much he still didn't know about driving cattle. "I guess that's up to Mr. Deatherage."

Mr. McCoy asked many questions about the drive and listened patiently. Finally, Mr. McCoy said, "You and me have a lot in common. I bet one day, I'll be buying a big herd from *you*. We're both named Joseph, and we're both cattlemen, to the bone."

Seph smiled but didn't say anything in reply.

When Mr. McCoy lifted the newspaper back in front of him, Seph glanced at the headline on the front page. It read: "ANOTHER EXPRESS ROB-BERY."

When Can-Doon was done with Stoke's haircut, he brushed Stoke's hair back and applied a waxy, apple-scented pomade, smoothing it neat. Stoke wrinkled his nose, allowing the treatment, but seemed eager to get it over with. When Can-Doon slapped lilac water on his face, Stoke sneered.

Seph caught Stoke's eye and pointed at the sign that warned, "Don't Shoot the Barber."

Just as Seph was about to take his turn, the door swung open. A man stormed in demanding immediate service.

Can-Doon held up a hand. "You'll have to wait your turn, sir. These boys been waiting a long time. Why don't you set a spell and relax?"

The man scowled, stomped, and left the shop without another word.

Finally, it was Seph's turn. It felt strange having a stranger touch his head. Before he was a cowboy, when his hair grew too long, he'd snip off the excess himself.

When Can-Doon was done, Seph declined the pomade, preferring a simple cut and shave. He had a hard time sitting still when Can-Doon held the sharp, steel blade to his throat, and he was glad the Irishman had a steady hand. The smooth soap felt good on his face and it was good to have his scraggly whiskers scraped away.

When the barber asked him what he thought, Seph looked at the mirror. The man he saw looked unfamiliar to him. There was no denying that the last few months had changed him.

As Seph stepped away from the barber's chair, Stoke asked Can-Doon about the ladies in town.

Mr. McCoy chuckled, but didn't lower his newspaper.

Can-Doon looked toward the back room before answering. "There's a couple of places you could go."

From behind his paper, Mr. McCoy said, "Don't ask me, boys. I'm a happily married man with a sweet baby girl."

Maxie-Doon shuffled in and guided Stoke and Seph out back. Steam rose from the wooden tubs in the humid room. It smelled like vinegar which Maxie-Doon must have used liberally when cleaning the place. Seph tried to ignore the foul smell and sank into the hot water, sighing in relief.

"Feels like heaven," he murmured.

Stoke laughed, splashing water at him. "Ain't nothin' like a good soak after weeks on the trail. While I'm at it, I'm fixing to wash that flowery perfume offa my face."

Clean and refreshed, they proceeded to the general store. Seph browsed the shelves, picking out a new hat, boots, and a set of clothes. The clerk helped him find the perfect fit.

"Now you're looking sharp," Stoke said.

Their next stop was a small restaurant. The smell of food wafted through the air, making Seph's stomach rumble. They sat at a wooden table, scanned the menu, and Seph set his new hat on the wooden bench beside him.

Bonita, Wills, Dusty, and Dunk dined together two tables away. Seph nodded in their direction.

When the waitress asked him what had caught his eye, Seph looked perplexed. "Roast pheasant with chestnut stuffing?" Seph asked, raising an eyebrow.

She chirped, "Trust me, honey. You'll love it."

Seph nodded. "I'll have that. And some of that turtle soup too."

The meal was a feast. The pheasant was tender, the nutty-flavored stuffing was filling, and the spicy soup made his tongue tingle. Seph savored each bite. It was the fanciest food he'd ever eaten.

As the afternoon turned to evening, Seph and Stoke wandered the streets. The town was alive with the sounds of celebration. They passed other cowboys, some dancing to the music of a fiddle, others laughing and sharing stories over drinks.

Seph took it all in—the sights, the sounds, the smells. Abilene was a place of life and energy. He thought about the drab grays and dull browns of farming in Texas. Abilene was new and vibrant.

Seph smiled. They cleaned up good. He thought of Hork and had to admit—it was nice eating something other than beans.

Stoke clapped him on the back. "Now it is time to frolic!"

# CHAPTER 25

THE SUN WAS SETTING as Wills, Bonita, Dunk, and Lullaby prepared to leave Abilene. Dunk's saddle horn was weighed down with sacks of dirty clothes, old boots, and weathered hats.

Lullaby's face showed his disappointment. His eyes lingered on the bustling town as they mounted their horses. Dusty patted him on the back, but said nothing.

"We'll see you cowpunchers tomorrow," Dunk said, trying to lighten the mood. "Time to get these nice folks back to the safety of camp."

As the sun disappeared over the horizon, the sounds of the town seemed to grow louder. Fiddles and the plunking keys of pianos filled the air, blending with laughter and shouted conversations, boasts and brags. The Alamo Saloon, Drovers Cottage, Drovers Oasis, and The Bull's Head Saloon were alive with boisterous activity.

Seph noticed Dusty sitting in a rocking chair in front of the general store, smoking a cigar. It was as if the boss had decided to oversee their visit to town. From there, he could step in, if things got out of hand. Maybe he intended to let the cowboys enjoy their frolicking without interference.

The Deatherage crew wandered through the streets, lured by the festive atmosphere from one establishment to another, many establishments under the cover of tents rather than buildings. They drifted in and out of all of them, taking in the sights and sounds.

The Alamo Saloon was packed. Cowboys crowded the bar, exchanging stories. The Drover's Cottage offered a more subdued setting, with men playing cards and talking quietly. The Bull's Head Saloon was raucous, with a brawl nearly breaking out as they passed through.

But it was The Agitator that held their attention the longest. The saloon was lively, with singing and dancing girls entertaining the crowd.

Stoke led Seph to the bar, grinning as he ordered two beers. "Time to get you started," he said, handing Seph a mug. "Here's to the end of a long drive."

Seph took the mug, hesitating for a moment before taking a sip. The taste was bitter and unfamiliar. He rolled the fizzy liquid around in his mouth, trying to decide if he liked the grainy taste. It had a bit of a skunky smell to it. He thought back to his first taste of coffee and decided that it would be easier to get used to drinking beer. Not one to complain, he said, "Not bad."

Stoke laughed. "You'll get used to it."

The gang continued their exploration, moving from saloon to saloon. At The Alamo Saloon, Seph tried whiskey for the first time. The amber liquid burned as it went down, leaving a warm sensation in his stomach. He caught his breath and blinked back tears. "That's... strong," he managed.

Stoke gently punched his shoulder. "That also takes some getting used to, but it'll warm you right up."

As the night progressed, they ended up at The Fancy Frolic, a brothel also known for its bawdy shows. The atmosphere was electric. Singing and dancing girls captivated the audience.

Seph was shocked by the songs they sang. The naughty girls on stage were fascinating, but made him uncomfortable. Around him, the cowboys laughed and cheered. Seph couldn't help noticing the difference between the performers here and at the Agitator. The Fancy Frolic ladies' costumes were far more revealing.

He watched a scantily clad woman play the fiddle. She smiled at him as she slid the bow across the strings. She picked up the pace, and he felt like his heartbeat quickened along with her tune. It was hard not to get caught up in the excitement.

In the middle of a number, one of the performers stepped from the small stage, bent at the waist and planted a smooch on Torp's face. He stood, dazed for a moment, with a goofy smile on his face. Seph was afraid he'd fall to the floor, but instead Torp bolted for the door.

Seph followed, peering over the top of the batwing doors.

Dusty rose from the comfort of his rocking chair and stepped slowly toward the young cowboy. Seph could just make out what he said. "I think you've had too much to drink, son. Best call it a night." Dunk pointed the way back to camp.

Torp nodded sheepishly and headed toward camp, leaving the raucous sounds of The Fancy Frolic behind.

Seph had worried about Torp and was glad to see him go. He had hoped that he wouldn't have to end the evening early to look after him.

The thought of fleeing crossed Seph's mind. He'd already seen things he'd never expected to see. Maybe other people were used to what happened in saloons, but he was not. He turned back from the swinging doors and looked back into The Fancy Frolic.

Stoke called him over. "Here, have another beer," he said, though Seph only took a small sip this time. He remembered Dunk's and Lullaby's advice and resolved to restrain himself. How much was too much? After drinking a beer, he didn't feel differently, but the burning shot of whiskey made him feel a little light headed.

Seph's second beer touched his lips, but he only drank a little. Stoke nudged him and said, "See that?" He pointed to a sign over the doorway in back that read, "Jolie's Girls." Stoke flashed his eyebrows. "What do you suppose we'll find back there?" He laughed as his friends squirmed.

It was clear that the cowboy knew exactly what to expect from Jolie's girls. Seph gulped hard, leaving his mostly-full beer on the table as he followed Stoke. He was pretty sure that he understood the promise of the pink, painted letters on the placard too. Trinket, Chops, and Hork followed so closely behind Seph that they almost tripped over each other.

When they stepped through the doorway, they encountered an extravagantly dressed lady and seven scantily-clad girls behind her. The woman greeted them with a forced smile and a husky voice. "Howdy, fellas."

Her words were full of cheer, but she seemed nonchalant. "I'm Jolie, and these are my girls. For a dollar, you can spend an hour with a pretty girl. For five, you can spend the night." She looked at Stoke and added, "You look like a big spender. For ten dollars, you can take two of my girls upstairs."

Seph barely heard what Jolie said. One of the girls had caught his eye. She tipped her head down, innocently, but maintained eye contact. She had dark hair and a pretty face. Seph told himself that this girl was not the girl of his dreams. She looked something like the picture of the girl in the cigar box, but not exactly like her.

His gizzard felt ablaze. Things were moving too fast for his taste. He barely heard Stoke say that he wasn't a big spender and only needed an hour. That is, he only needed an hour at a time.

As Stoke escorted a blond-haired, busty girl quickly up the stairs, Jolie turned her attention to Seph. "Well, cowboy. Ain't you a good looking young fella. What's it gonna be?"

Seph felt a jab in his back and turned to look at Trinket. "Let's go, Seph. You're holding us up. C'mon, man."

Seph tripped over his tongue and tried to speak politely. "I'd like to... meet the lady in the green dress, ma'am."

Jolie shook her head and handed Seph a key.

There was a strange look in Jolie's eyes as she looked at Seph's face. It was a look that stuck in his mind despite his state of distraction. He was sure that he had never seen her before, but he wondered about her for a moment before she vanished from his thoughts.

The pretty girl in the green dress stepped toward him and his heart thundered. The reality of what was about to happen seemed impossible.

Jolie said, "What's your name, cowboy?"

He turned his head, surprised to see that Jolie was still there. "Seph," he answered.

"This is Hazel." She said, matter-of-factly. "You got room number seven, cowboy. Lucky number seven—at the end of the hall."

The tip of Seph's new boot caught the lip on the bottom step and he stumbled. It sounded like there was a bucking horse in room number one.

Seph wiped beads of sweat from his brow on the sleeve of his new shirt. The long trip up the stairs and down the hall felt like half the distance from San Antonio to Abilene. He was sweaty, blushing, and nervous.

The door closed behind them, sealing him into the small room with Hazel. There was no going back now.

He felt awkward. His stomach tumbled and Seph feared that he might hork. And yet, he also felt a burst of excitement, like when Hortense commenced to bucking. Only different.

Seph thought back to Stoke's fireside tales. At the time, he had barely believed the ridiculous things the man said. He pushed those thoughts from his mind and told himself the truth. He was a man. Here was a woman. They both had hopes and dreams. Maybe she was as uncomfortable as he was. Maybe she was as excited as he was. Whatever the circumstances that brought them together, he would forget about everything beyond the door to room number seven. He would let his instincts guide him.

His fingers trembled as he placed his hand beneath her chin, lifting her head, and she gazed up at him. Seph saw her lips part, and the tip of her tongue briefly moistened them. She spoke sweetly. "I was hoping you'd pick me." She sighed and said, "I wanted you right off."

Seph didn't know what to say, but he had to say something. "You're the prettiest girl I ever seen," he blurted out. He hadn't seen that many girls, truth be told, but decided not to tell her that. "I ain't never done nothing like this before." As he said that, he wondered whether he should have kept that to himself.

"Oh," Hazel said. She sounded disappointed. "I'm new at this too." She bit her lip and Seph couldn't help but wonder whether she was telling the truth. Hazel said, "Let's pretend we just got married. We just said our vows, and you're the first one to kiss me."

His heart beat faster than he could ever remember it beating. "I'd like that." Seph said, his fingers still touching her chin.

He arched his back and gently touched his lips to hers. Then he pulled his head back and looked at her face, close up. He shuddered as she slowly unbuttoned his new shirt and he thought he would leap from his body when she unfastened the top button of his trousers. He was caught between the feelings of wishing she would move more slowly and desperation to smother her with affection. It was as if he had waited his whole life for this moment and this woman.

She tugged the shirttails from his britches, ran her dainty hands up his chest, and pushed the crisp shirt and suspenders from his shoulders.

He kissed her again, not as gently, and was surprised when her tongue fluttered at his lips. A half second later, his trousers fell to his feet.

Seph felt overcome. Anything might happen now, and he didn't care. He looked into the depths of Hazel's eyes and said, "That was a beautiful wedding, Mrs. Vermillion."

She ran her hand down his back and didn't stop there. "Yes, it sure was, Mr. Vermillion." She pinched his backside and said, "Can you spend the night? Or are you just here for an hour?"

Seph stretched his neck and swallowed hard. "I got all night." His head swam.

"Then let's take it slow, Mr. Vermillion." She placed her hands on his chest and gently pushed him backwards until he was forced to sit on her bed. She backed away slowly and slid the window open. A light breeze stirred the drapes. Moonlight beamed through the window. He felt her eyes looking at him. He felt self conscious and exposed.

Hazel stood by the window, caressing herself and undressing slowly. She had been quick to unbutton his shirt. His trousers had hit the floor before he knew what was happening. But she removed her emerald dress so slowly that he felt like it might never come off.

It didn't feel right to watch her, but he couldn't stop. Then it hit him. Hazel knew what she was doing. She knew that she was driving him crazy. He wasn't spying on her and she didn't mind. This was part of it. This was part of their night together. He placed his hands back on the mattress behind him and tried to ignore feeling like a frayed rope that might snap at any moment.

When her dress finally slipped to the floor, Seph's mouth opened widely. It was as if he had forgotten to breathe. She twisted and turned, showing him what she looked like from one angle and then another. Then she turned around, wiggled her behind, and giggled over her shoulder.

He didn't know what would happen next. He'd never grow tired of looking at her and yet he was desperate to touch her. There was a big smile on her face and a hunger in her eyes. Seph never thought that being with a woman would be like this.

When she came to him, he stopped thinking all together. Now and again, she guided his hands, here or there, repositioned his body, one way or another, and sometimes she slowed things down. Other times, she sped things up.

Seph felt like a wild beast and yet, as he moved, he felt protective. He had heard that women were delicate, but Hazel seemed anything but fragile.

When they had finished coupling, Seph didn't think that anything could top what they had experienced together.

An hour later, he learned otherwise. After their second coupling, Hazel fell asleep beside him.

He listened to her as she snored softly. The moonlight that earlier reached a few feet beyond the window now flooded the room. If he lived to be a hundred years old, he was sure that he would never forget this night.

It felt wrong to look at her while she slept, but he couldn't stop. He let her sleep until he couldn't restrain himself any longer. He had to have her again, or he had to leave. The poor thing was tired. She must need her sleep. The moonlight faded and Seph could tell that it would soon be dawn. He should probably go. Perhaps he had overstayed his allotted time. He hated to go without speaking to this woman that he would never forget.

The bed creaked as he swung his legs to the floor. He tiptoed toward the doorway, carefully trying to avoid obstacles, but hoping to find his heap of clothes near the foot of her bed.

A soft voice melted his heart. "Mr. Vermillion. Where do you think you're going? Come on back to bed and hold me."

Their third coupling started slowly. They moved together like a gentle breeze that slowly built into a feverish tempest. Seph felt like a bomb went off when it ended.

Before Seph's wits returned to him, there was a heavy banging on the door. A woman's deep voice shouted, "Time's up, stallion. Finish up and get on outta here. My fillies need their beauty rest."

Sadly, Hazel said, "I wish it didn't have to end."

Seph quickly answered. "Me too."

"If only it were true, Mr. Vermillion. I swear, I never experienced a night like last night. All men care about is themselves, but you're different." Hazel whimpered. "Oh, Seph. You're the best lover a woman ever knew. Why don't you take me away from here? I'd go anywhere with you."

The door to room number seven flung open. Jolie swirled in, scooped up Seph's clothes, and shoved them into his chest. "Let's go, cowboy. This love story is over. It's time for the cowboy to ride away. That means you."

Seph hesitated and Jolie barked. "Now."

Hazel groaned in protest.

It was unnerving, climbing into his clothes while the madam sneered at him. It didn't seem right, but he did as he was told and hurried up.

Jolie stood with her hand on the doorknob.

Before leaving, Seph turned toward Hazel and said, "Good night, darling." He didn't like the feeling of walking away from her. All he could think of, as he was leaving, was that he couldn't wait to see her again.

Jolie muttered, "Oh, ain't that sweet. *Darling!* Save that sugar for your coffee, cowboy. Get a move on, honey."

At the bottom of the stairs, the madam said, "You sir, are the last cowboy to leave." She laughed and shook her head. "You just missed your friend." She sighed and rolled her eyes. "Last night, he set a record. That Stoke fella visited four of my girls."

Jolie placed a hand on her hip, turned her head, and looked into Seph's face. "What did you say your name was, again?"

"Seph, ma'am. Seph Vermillion."

"Joseph! Joseph Vermillion?"

"Yes, ma'am."

"From Poesta Creek?"

"That's right."

With a flourish and roll of her eyes, Jolie said, "Well, ain't that something. I do declare! I thought I recognized you." Jolie leaned forward and roughly pinched Seph's cheek. "I ain't seen you since you were a little boy."

"Ma'am?"

"You're just as cute now as you were when I last saw you. Maybe you were five years old when I left home. I hope you enjoyed this *family reunion* as much as I did." She blew a raspberry and Seph felt the splatter. He hadn't been in any hurry to leave, but now he couldn't wait to get away from The Fancy Frolic.

Jolie held out her hand. "That'll be five dollars, stallion."

She laughed as he fumbled in his pocket and produced the fee.

The early morning streets of Abilene were practically abandoned.

Seph looked at Slaw's horse standing at the hitching post. He ran his hand along Win's neck and looked up at the window above. His heart skipped a beat when he saw Hazel standing in the window looking back at him. She wasn't wearing anything, and the thin curtains shrouded her like a woman in a dream.

Seph waved his hat, climbed into the saddle, and rode in the opposite direction.

# CHAPTER 26

THE SHORT DISTANCE FROM Abilene to camp felt like miles.

Seph was exhausted from a long night with no sleep, and yet, it was the best night of his life. His heart soared. Crazy thoughts tumbled in his head. But he knew it would take a big pot of strong coffee or a long nap to make it through the day.

He replayed the strange conversation he had with Jolie. He was so distracted by thoughts of his night with Hazel that he didn't fully appreciate what the madam had said.

She hadn't seen him since he was five years old. She knew that he came from Poesta Creek. Was he to believe that his sister was a madam at the end of the trail?

Ma had told him to find his siblings. Their names were listed in the family *Bible*, but he didn't need to confirm them. They were committed to memory: Alexander, Genevieve, Gabriel, Scott, Jolene, Mitchell, and Joseph. There was no Jolie on the list.

He thought maybe painted ladies didn't use their real names. It dawned on him that Jolie was close to Jolene. That must be it. He checked his tired memory and did the math. Jolene would be thirty-one years old.

But what about Hazel? He wondered if that was her real name and frowned. It didn't matter what her name was. That's not what he had fallen in love with.

So this is what love felt like. After all of those years of imagining the woman of his dreams, he thought he would know how it felt when that dream came true. Sometimes he had wondered if it would live up to his expectations. As he recalled last night, he was amazed by the fact that reality far exceeded his youthful fantasies.

Soon, the Deatherage outfit would pull out of Abilene and return to the ranch in Texas. Tonight, another man would visit Hazel in room number seven—or, worse... many men would.

Hazel told him that he was different from other men. She said he was the best lover a woman ever knew and she begged him to take her away from The Fancy Frolic. She even said that she'd go anywhere with him.

He tried to imagine what life was like for a woman like Hazel. It was impossible to comprehend. Whatever he thought it was like, it was probably worse—way worse. He reckoned that it was a good thing that the fates had brought them together last night. How could he leave Hazel to a fate she despised?

Seph smelled the coffee before he crested the hill and rode into camp. That smell reminded him of what it was like to be a cowboy. How could he think of riding away? For the first time in his life, he felt like he belonged somewhere. And now, after one blissful night, he was ready to leave the life he loved for the woman he loved.

Hazel's words floated in his head. "I'd go anywhere with you." He couldn't very well bring her on a cattle drive, could he?

Bonita seemed to thrive on the trail, but that was temporary. Seph thought about the bunkhouse at the ranch and snorted. That surely wouldn't do.

Seph dismounted near the chuckwagon and looked around for Chops. The wrangler was one of the men who had celebrated too much. Seph would have to take care of Win himself. But that could wait. He tied Win's reins to a sapling and stepped toward the campfire.

Dunk poured coffee for Seph and asked if he wanted some biscuits and beans.

Seph took the cup and nodded. "Thanks, Dunk. I'm famished."

Dunk scooped a large portion onto a tin plate, raised his eyebrows, and asked, "How was your night?"

Seph almost choked on his coffee. He looked at Dunk and quickly looked away. When he looked back at the man, there was a quizzical look on his face. "Tell ya later," Seph mumbled.

"Very well," Dunk nodded. "You don't look like you got whiskey fever, so you're doing better than most of the crew."

Seph looked around and frowned at the site of sprawled out cowboys, snoring off the effects of a wild night in Abilene. He glanced at the camp-fire, and saw Bonita, Wills, and Lily. Torp looked to be in poor shape.

Trinket looked happy, almost too happy, and Seph remembered Trinket nudging him at The Fancy Frolic.

The rest of the crew was still sacked out. He spotted Stoke. The top hand slept soundly. The others looked like they were having fits of nightmares, but Stoke looked like he was having a peaceful dream. Then he recalled the madam telling him that Stoke visited four of her girls last night. "That dog!" Seph muttered to himself, shaking his head. It didn't seem right, but who was he to judge?

He scarfed his beans like he hadn't eaten in days. It crossed his mind to wonder if Hazel was as hungry this morning as he was. It made him happy to think of her, but at the same time it didn't seem right to think about such doings while eating breakfast.

When he passed his plate back to Dunk, the cook said, "I figured you'd be one of the first ones back to camp, not the last one."

Seph smiled and shrugged. He couldn't help himself. He took a big sip of coffee and made his way over to Trinket and Torp.

Torp clutched his head and groaned. "What a night, eh Seph? My head feels like it's been trampled by stampeding cattle. But I don't care. Did you see that dancing girl? Did you see her pucker up and lay one on me? I swear. Heck, where you been all night?"

Seph answered, "Never mind that." He turned to Trinket who beamed knowingly back at him. Seph said, "Looks like you had a good night."

"Si, Señor. It was the best, I can assure you." He guffawed and declared, "I had room number six."

Seph closed his eyes. "Oh, no." He thought for a moment and asked, "How long?"

Trinket laughed and slapped his knee. "Just for one hour, but that was plenty of time for me."

Seph raised an eyebrow and said, "Do you remember it?"

"Yes. I will never forget it."

Torp butted in and whispered. "So you did it? Both of you. You visited those painted ladies? Oh man, I shoulda stuck around." He clutched his head.

Seph said, "You remember the smooch, but do you remember walking back to camp?"

Torp strained himself but couldn't say.

Trinket said, "Maybe next time do not drink so fast."

Seph thought about telling Torp he should wait a few years before drinking and visiting the back room at The Fancy Frolic, but he knew his partner was sensitive about his age.

Dunk kneeled beside Torp and said, "You don't look too good, kid. How about you drink some water. Have some beans. Then drink a pot of coffee. You'll feel better soon."

"Thanks, Dunk. Don't worry about me. Whiskey fever ain't near as bad as getting shot."

Dunk chuckled. "I reckon you got a point."

Seph excused himself. "I'm plain wore out. Maybe I can catch a nap while all these other cowpokes are still sacked out." He made his way to his bedroll. He wouldn't have thought it was possible that he could fall asleep with so much on his mind, but he fell asleep almost instantly.

It was well after noon when Seph woke up, sweating. He wasn't accustomed to sleeping while the sun shone.

He rubbed his eyes and thought of Hazel. Maybe she was used to sleeping during the day. Seph frowned when he thought about the reason why.

Riding back to town to rescue Hazel would be easy. Telling his friends that he was leaving would be hard.

He took a walk down to the river and was glad to find Lullaby sitting beside the water.

"Are you doing alright, Seph?" his friend asked.

"Yeah. No. I don't know." Seph explained the situation and the impossible decision he had made. He loved riding for the Deatherage outfit, but he loved Hazel more. It wasn't possible to have them both. He understood and accepted that fact. "It ain't right," Seph confessed, "but maybe it don't matter how love begins."

Lullaby agreed. "I expect you're right about that, Seph. If you're sure it's love and if she is also sure."

"Thanks, man." It was good to know that Lullaby approved. Most men wouldn't consider marrying a soiled dove.

Seph hesitated, then added, "That's the thing about being a sinner. Sometimes you have to force yourself to regret it. I ain't proud to say that I don't regret it."

The man's response surprised Seph. "Jesus died for our sins. Every one of us is a sinner. I think it is more about repenting and trying not to sin again. Giving and receiving forgiveness. You see?"

Seph shook Lullaby's hand and said, "I'm going to miss you. You sure got a way with words."

Lullaby sat back down as Seph was leaving. He said, "I'll pray for you and your bride."

Seph stopped, didn't turn back around, but thanked Lullaby.

As he walked toward camp, Seph was amazed by how fast things had changed. Words like wife and bride were sobering. The truth was, he couldn't stop thinking about Hazel and he couldn't wait to get back to her. The night in room number seven at The Fancy Frolic had changed something inside him, maybe many things.

But finding a gang of fellows and riding for the Deatherage Longhorn Cattle Ranch had also changed him. He had never felt a part of anything before. Now he was making plans to leave his brothers of the trail for the sweet young woman from the bordello. Mrs. Vermillion—that would take some getting used to.

Seph glanced around the camp. Everyone looked strange in their fancy new clothes. The worn and dusty gear they usually wore seemed more fitting. Camp didn't feel like the same place.

He wondered how he would support a wife. He had already realized that he couldn't keep Hazel in a bunkhouse. Maybe he could work at the stockyards. What difference did it make where he worked as long as they were together? What else mattered?

The crew was shocked when Seph packed up his saddle bags and prepared to leave. Dunk said, "Let's go for a walk."

Seph was grateful for the man who had taught him so much. If it weren't for Dunk, Seph didn't know if he could have accomplished half of what he had. He was going to miss the man who felt like an older brother. "Sure thing," Seph answered.

Dunk said, "I'm surprised to see you go, Seph. Can you tell me what happened?"

Seph explained. He went into more detail than he shared with the others. "I've got to go back. I want to get Hazel out of there fast as I can. Don't know how I'll support her, but I can't leave her there."

Dunk said, "I see," and "I understand."

That's what Seph liked most about Dunk. The fact that he was so understanding.

"Seph," Dunk added, "I've also got news. I'm planning to escort Wills, Bonita, and Lily back to Dayton. Why don't you and Hazel come along with us? Who knows, we might all settle down there."

Seph made a face. "Dayton? I don't belong in ." He shook his head. "That's east of the Mississippi, ain't it?"

Dunk smiled. "I think so."

Seph frowned. "Gosh. I don't know about that, Dunk. Let me see. I'm making decisions kind of fast right now." He had decided to rescue Hazel. Someday he had to visit Slaw's family back at Poesta Creek, and he still yearned to go north. Heading east would never have occurred to him. "I don't know what we'll do, Dunk."

Dunk said, "Well, I am ready for my next adventure. I guess I'm just a drifter. Have been since the war. Maybe I'll always be that way." The older man offered his hand. "Whatever you decide, I wish you the best, Seph. I sure hope our trails cross again. I'm proud to call you friend."

Hard as it was to say goodbye to Dunk, it was much harder to say goodbye to Torp. The young cowboy had been through so much, and yet he kept on going. *Someday, that kid will be a top hand.* When Seph promised to write and visit, he meant it. But who knew what the future would bring?

Before riding out, Seph looked around for Stoke. Blaze told him that Stoke went back to town. Seph didn't want to ride off without saying goodbye to the man who had become an unexpected friend.

As he mounted Win and prepared to ride back to Abilene, Seph felt a mixture of excitement and fear. He didn't know what the future held, but he was ready to face whatever the fates had in mind.

Hazel was worth fighting for. His heart leapt like a pronghorn blazing across the prairie. Seph spurred Win and galloped into Abilene. As he draped the reins over the hitching post, it occurred to him that the town looked a lot different late in the afternoon than it had at dawn. It almost looked like Texas. But this was a time for action, not reflection.

He sprang onto the boardwalk and stepped into The Fancy Frolic. He made his way directly to the back room, looking for Jolie, and found her in the same spot as last night.

The madam looked up at him. "Oh, Seph. What brings you back?" She frowned. "You shouldn't have come."

He was undeterred. "I wanted to talk to you about Ma and Pa," Seph began. He told her about Ma being sick and then dying. He told her about meeting Charlie Coppedge in Fort Worth. She didn't seem surprised or get emotional.

Jolie offered Seph coffee, but he declined. "Very well," she said. "I could use a strong cup of coffee. Don't go running off. I'll be right back."

When Jolie disappeared through the doorway to the kitchen, Seph bounded up the stairs, his heart pounding. He reached Hazel's door, turned the knob slowly, and eased it open, forgetting to knock. Inside, he saw Stoke with Hazel. Seph heard her begging Stoke to take her away, saying almost the same things that she had said to him.

Seph's heart plummeted. What a fool he had been.

He turned to leave and ran into Jolie at the bottom of the stairs.

"I told you to stay put," she chastised. "What happened?"

Seph looked at Jolie. He closed his hands into tight fists. He wanted to cry but forced himself not to. "I was going to take Hazel away with me. She begged me to do it." He pointed up the stairway. "When I went up there, I heard her telling Stoke the same things she said to me."

Jolie sighed. "I'm sorry, kid."

Seph was unsure whether she was truly sorry.

She took three small sips of coffee and added, "Ain't that a heartbreak." Rolling her eyes, Jolie continued, "Hazel says the same thing to every cowboy that passes through here."

Seph scowled. "That's why you ran me out of here so fast this morning, ain't it?"

She took another sip of coffee and shook her head. "That's how it is around here, little brother. If you ever visit a fancy house again, remember—this ain't where you come for hope, love, and dreams. That ain't what we do here. Your buddy should of told you that."

"Maybe he did." Seph tipped his head and offered his hand. He looked up the stairway, then back at Jolie who briefly took his hand. He said, "I'll see you again next year," leaving his sentence unfinished. Then he weakly concluded, "Sis."

With a quick pivot, Seph bolted from The Fancy Frolic. He climbed into the saddle, rode down the street, and stopped in the shade of a tall building. *Now what?* he thought.

The minutes dragged on. Each one felt like an eternity. He had no idea how long he would have to wait, but fortunately, it wasn't long. Stoke stepped out of The Fancy Frolic half an hour later.

Seph's mind raced. He was angry and frustrated. He wanted to pound his fists into Stoke, to vent his rage and ease his heartbreak.

But reason got the better of him. They weren't adversaries anymore. It wasn't Stoke's fault that Seph had fallen in love with a fancy lady after one night alone with her.

Stoke was just doing what Stoke does. He probably didn't even know about Seph and Hazel.

As Stoke approached, Seph took a deep breath and steadied himself.

Stoke looked up, surprised to see Seph waiting. "What are you doing here?" he asked. "Something wrong?"

"I need to talk to you," Seph said. Despite the turmoil in the pit of his stomach, his voice was steady. "I need you to tell Dusty and Dunk to save me a place on next year's drive."

Stoke frowned. "You're leaving?"

With a nod, Seph said, "I'm a loner. Maybe I don't belong on a ranch. Maybe I was meant to be by myself."

Stoke guffawed. "I've heard you say lots of stupid things, but that's the dumbest yet. I ain't never met somebody more destined to ride for the brand. Smarten up, kid. You were never meant to spend all of your time by yourself. A crowded old cattle ranch is just the place for you. Ain't you learned nothing this year?"

Seph frowned. As it spread across his face, it turned into a smile. Before he could stop himself, he was laughing. But then he contained himself. "Yeah. I reckon you're right. All that may be true, but still, I need some time on my own." He told Stoke a short version of what had happened with Hazel, and concluded, "I'll meet y'all back at the ranch."

Stoke shook his head. "You sure you want to ride that dangerous trail alone?"

Seph inhaled deeply, looking down the dusty street. He thought about Wobble, and how he had worried when he rode off alone. But that didn't seem the same to him. "I don't know if I want to or not, but it's what I aim to do."

Stoke didn't seem to know what to do or say to that. Finally, he replied, "Well, take care of yourself, Seph. Don't get scalped out there. We'll see you back in San Antonio then."

Seph nodded. He'd miss his fellow cowboys, and yet he knew that he needed to get away on his own for a while. "Thanks, Stoke. Look after them boys for me."

He watched as Stoke barreled into the nearest saloon. Seph turned Win around and rode down the middle of the street, headed south. The town of Abilene faded into the background, but Seph focused on the path ahead.

As he rode away from the wild cow town and its memories, Seph felt a new sense of resolve. Stoke was right. The Deatherage Longhorn Cattle Ranch *was* where he belonged.

He still wanted to see towering peaks. Someday, he'd like to meet the woman of his dreams.

Maybe Hazel said the same things to every cowboy, but he couldn't deny the way she had made him feel. She wasn't a fantasy. Hazel was a real woman. He sniffled and blinked away watery eyes.

Seph thought of the man whose horse he rode as he watched the sunset from the saddle. Slaw knew that they needed to become cowboys, even if Seph had not known.

What did that flyer say? "Ride the trail to Abilene. Depart as cowboys, return as cattlemen." There was no denying he had changed.

Seph Vermillion was a cattleman now. Maybe he always would be.

Slaw's last request came to mind, as it often did at dusk. "Live large. Take me with you. When you see a brilliant sunset, think of me so I can see it too."

Seph felt a trickle of goosebumps circle his shoulders. He ran a hand along Win's smooth neck. To Slaw's horse, Seph said, "Let's ride, pal."

What's next? Seph Vermillion and the Deatherage boys are on an all out race to the end of the trail when the boss bets the herd. Snap up your copy of Dead Heat to find out who survives the deadly race to Abilene.

In case you missed the series' prequel novella, you can still claim your free copy of *Farewell to Poesta Creek*.

A Tip of the Hat

Thank you for signing on with the Dagger D, Angry R, and for reading *First Drive*. You've spent months in the saddle, eaten way too much trail dust, and galloped into town with the herd. It's been a pleasure having you along.

If you enjoyed the ride, I'd be most obliged if you could share your thoughts with a review. Even a few quick words or brief thoughts can make a big difference, and help folks discover my fiction.

It's an honor and a privilege to write for you. Your emails are welcome in my inbox and you can reach me at dave@itsoag.com

I look forward to many more journeys together... if the good Lord's willing and the horse don't buck.

With gratitude,

David Fitz-Gerald

If you haven't read the series, Ghosts Along the Oregon Trail, why not start today?

Embark on a harrowing trek across the rugged American frontier in 1850. Your wagon awaits, and the windswept wilderness calls. This epic adventure will test the mettle of even the bravest souls.

Delve into an unforgettable saga of empowerment, sacrifice, and the haunting echoes of a harrowing journey. Immerse yourself in an expedition where every decision carries the weight of life, death, and shattered dreams.

Ghosts Along the Oregon Trail was written as if it were a single volume rather than a series of five novels. It has been divided into five books which split the Oregon Trail into segments, or legs, of the journey. Readers will enjoy this series most when read in order, beginning with *A Grave Every Mile*. Hop aboard!

# About the Author

David Fitz-Gerald writes westerns and historical fiction. He is the author of more than a dozen books, including the series, Ghosts Along the Oregon Trail set in 1850. He's a multiple Laramie Award, first place, best in category winner; a Blue Ribbon Chanticleerian; a member of Western Writers of America; and a member of the Historical Novel Society.

Alpine landscapes and flashy horses always catch Dave's eye and turn his head. He is also an Adirondack 46-er, which means that he has hiked to the summit of the range's highest peaks. As a mountaineer, he's happiest at an elevation of over four thousand feet above sea level.

Dave is a lifelong fan of western fiction, landscapes, movies, and music. It should be no surprise that Dave delights in placing memorable characters on treacherous trails, mountain tops, and on the backs of wild horses.

www.ingramcontent.com/pod-product-compliance
Lightning Source LLC
Chambersburg PA
CBHW060413030726
47495CB00003B/559